She was only aware of Armand's lips upon hers

His breath was sweet and his lips hot; and for an instant she felt a fire that she instinctively knew could consume them both.

Almost without thinking, she slapped his face.

"How dare you!" she said harshly. "You had no right."

"I had no right, true," he said, "but you wanted it, also. Even if you deny it, your body told me differently."

Rebecca felt a hot wash of anger. How could she deny that she had kissed him with the same passion with which he had kissed her? And then she felt her wits and her control return.

"You may as well know that I care for someone else, so I would appreciate it if you would bear that in mind in the future."

"Jacques?" His smile was a bitter grimace. "Of course you mean Jacques. You are in love with my charming brother. You think that he is more of a gentleman than I and that because he speaks well and is kind, he will make a good husband. Well you are mistaken." Armand laughed roughly. "But have it your way, Rebecca. I will make no further demands upon you. I wish you joy of one another."

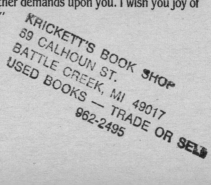

Patricia Matthews

Enchanted

W🌐RLDWIDE

TORONTO · NEW YORK · LONDON · PARIS
AMSTERDAM · STOCKHOLM · HAMBURG
ATHENS · MILAN · TOKYO · SYDNEY

This book is dedicated to my perspicacious
and supportive editor, Kate Duffy,
and to my publisher, Worldwide Library,
with appreciation for their many kindnesses.

Chapter One

Summer, 1817

THE MAN WAS MIDDLE-AGED and foppish, not at all the sort that Rebecca Trenton would usually have encouraged. However, he apparently knew a great deal about local history and gossip and was obviously eager to share this knowledge with two attractive young women.

Ignoring her cousin Margaret Downing's look of prim disapproval, Rebecca smiled sweetly at Joshua Sterling as they all three leaned over the rail of the small coastal packet that was making its way slowly along the summer-humid coast of South Carolina.

"Why, I think that is absolutely fascinating," Rebecca said in a gushing tone, knowing that Sterling was far too fatuous and obtuse to detect her insincerity, and also she was fully aware that it would annoy Margaret.

Sterling beamed under what he took to be Rebecca's approval. "Well, I must say that it is a real pleasure to find two young Englishwomen so interested in our local history. Most young women today seem to care nothing about the past."

Rebecca gave him another flashing smile. "Oh, we're interested. Particularly concerning Pirate's Bank. Edouard Molyneux is only a distant cousin. We know very little about him or his home, and I really think that it is very important to learn as much as you can about every place you visit. Don't you, sir?''

Sterling gave her a broad smile, showing large, rather yellow teeth. He looks very much like an aging horse, thought Rebecca, and forced herself to suppress a smile. It would never do to have him realize that she was making sport of him; at least not until he had told them all he knew about Pirate's Bank and the fascinating and evidently rather outré Molyneux family.

''Now, you were saying that Pirate's Bank was actually a stopping place for pirates in the old days?''

Sterling nodded. ''Yes, indeed. There seems to be no doubt about it. Local legend has it that there is even treasure buried there, although I must admit that no one has ever found any.''

''And the Molyneuxs, when did they come to the island?''

''I'm not certain of the exact date, but it was about fifty years ago that Jean Molyneux had the Folly built for his bride, Mignon.''

''You said, the 'Folly'? Is that what he named his home? That strikes me as rather strange.''

Sterling laughed and extracted a large lace-trimmed linen handkerchief from his pocket to mop his brow. He considered it his great good fortune to have met up with such charming traveling companions, even though they *were* British.

The shorter girl, Miss Rebecca, was a real beauty; young, but nicely filled out in all the right places, and those dark blue eyes were extraordinarily striking, combined with that pale skin and silver-blond hair. He had never seen a woman so fair-complected and, he was willing to wager, neither had most Southerners. She would soon attract male notice, that was certain, and he would be able to state that he had been the first to meet her. The second girl, Miss Margaret, was worth a look or two, also, particularly if you caught a glimpse of her on her own. However, her soft brown hair, hazel eyes and even features seemed rather plain and ordinary next to the luminous, moon-pale beauty of her cousin.

"Sir, you were going to tell us the reason why Cousin Edouard's home was called Molyneux's Folly."

Sterling, belatedly realizing that his thoughts had caused his conversation to lapse, grew a bit flustered. There was no doubt of it. This woman, Rebecca Trenton, was unsettling.

"Yes, indeed. My humble apologies, ma'am. I was just trying to recall all the details. Of course, it wasn't your cousin's father who gave such a name to his home, but some of his friends and the locals hereabouts. Molyneux's own name for the place was, and is, quite lovely: Maison de Rêverie, House of Dreams. However, the design of the place was very radical, you know, for the times. It is still considered unusual by a great many people."

"Maison de Rêverie. What a beautiful name! Doesn't it sound beautiful, Margaret?"

Rebecca gave Margaret a none too gentle nudge on the arm; and her stern look told the other girl that she had better come forth with a contribution to the conversation or risk her cousin's ire.

Margaret sighed heavily. It seemed that she was always giving in to Rebecca in one way or another and had been for as long as she could remember. She admired her cousin for her beauty and her ability to shape life to her own satisfaction; yet she often wished that Rebecca was a bit less domineering and sharp-tongued and a little more tolerant of other people's wishes. What Mr. Sterling had to say was all very interesting, true; and at another time, Margaret knew she would have enjoyed hearing about it. But at the moment she was weary unto death after the uncomfortable and tedious trip from India, and the three days spent resting in Charleston had hardly been enough to restore her strength or her spirits.

And now here they were, again on a boat, heading toward an island they had never seen, relatives they had never met and who knew what kind of life? From all that Margaret had read about the United States, she had drawn the conclusion that this part of the country might not even be civilized. How *could* Rebecca be so cheerful? And where did she get her energy and strength?

Oh, well. It would be easier to concede to Rebecca's wishes than to have to tolerate her displeasure.

Margaret said, "Why, yes, it does sound lovely, Mr. Sterling. Is the island itself beautiful? Many of the islands we have been passing appear to be heavily wooded."

Sterling smiled and nodded, inordinately pleased to have both women hanging on his words.

"Why, yes, it is, although I understand that it is nothing now compared to what it was in the old days. Edouard keeps the house up very well, and the immediate grounds, but I'm afraid that he has let the remainder of the island revert more or less to its natural state."

Margaret, intrigued in spite of herself, leaned forward. "What do you mean, sir? Was it not always in a 'natural state'?"

Sterling chuckled. "Oh, my, no! Of course, I never saw it in the old days, being not quite *that* old, but I have heard the stories, and there are also some paintings and sketches made by the painter Polydoro, who was very famous and a close friend of the Molyneuxs.

"In those days, the entire island was landscaped, covered with winding pathways, small temples, hidden gardens and rare plants and trees. Jean Molyneux called it his enchanted kingdom, and, from what I hear, it was just that. I have been told that he ruled his little island like a true king, surrounded by a court of friends and acquaintances, most of them quite famous in their own right. Yes, the famous and the near famous mingled there with the merely notorious. It has been said . . ." He shot Rebecca a sly glance. "But perhaps I shouldn't tell you this. After all, you might be offended, two well-bred young ladies like yourselves."

Rebecca, knowing that he was aching to impart some tidbit of information that was slightly scandalous, urged him on with a smile and a flirtatious glance. "Oh, you wicked thing! Of course, you must go on. You cannot just tease us like this."

Sterling took advantage of the opportunity to lean closer to Rebecca and to steal a not too subtle look down at the rounded swell of her décolletage. Sterling had a strong interest in feminine fashion, and he knew that she was very fashionably, and flatteringly, attired.

Her dress of fine cambric, which closely followed the lines of her body, was topped by a low-cut pelisse of blue-shot sarsnet, trimmed with blue satin riband, beneath which peeped blue Morocco slippers the color of the trim. Rebecca carried a reticule, fashioned in the same shade of blue satin; and the ensemble was topped by a smart Oatlands hat, which matched the pelisse and showed off her lovely face and pale curls as a good frame enhanced a painting. And the child had a really marvelous bosom!

At that moment the boat heeled, and Sterling reached out to steady her, but Rebecca quickly shrugged his hand away. To cover his embarrassment, Sterling quickly began to talk again. "Too bad. It looks like we're going to have a bit of weather, a summer storm. But it should hold off until you two are ashore. I doubt that I shall be as fortunate. Now, where was I?"

"You were about to tell us a marvelous bit of scandal, I believe, concerning Jean Molyneux's 'court.'" Rebecca's eyes were cool, and Sterling, anxious to get back into her good graces, hurried on.

"Yes, indeed. Well, as you may realize by now, Jean Molyneux was a man ahead of his time. He was quite artistic himself, a very good painter and sculptor. He designed Maison de Rêverie, you know. And the majority of his friends were drawn from the artistic world—painters, writers, actors, singers, and those who appreciate the arts. Molyneux would invite them all to his island, where he and his wife would give lavish and, if the stories are to be believed, somewhat shocking parties."

"And what was he like personally? Do you know?"

"A man of great charm, I am told; a handsome man, and clever. I have also heard that he was a man of quick and violent temper, but that his fits of anger did not last long and that he enjoyed 'odd' entertainments."

Rebecca saw Margaret drawing back, and with a wicked glint in her eyes, she said, "Odd in what way, Mr. Sterling?"

"This is all rumor, of course, old stories. However, where there's smoke, eh? At any rate, some say that Edouard and Mignon held strange rites and played at odd sorts of games on the island, pastimes in which they even allowed their children to participate. Of course, there was the usual, ordinary type of debauchery, as well—heavy drinking, a great deal of slipping back and forth between bedrooms at night..."

Margaret gave a horrified gasp, and Sterling pretended remorse. "Oh, my dear young lady, I *am* sorry. I quite forgot myself. Please forgive me."

Margaret turned her face away, but Rebecca, fully aware that the aging roué knew quite well what he had been doing, only nodded composedly. "So they were very sophisticated people, Jean Molyneux and his wife? And rather strange, it would seem. I gather they are both dead now?"

Sterling nodded and worried that he had perhaps gone too far and lost the sympathy of his audience, hurried to reply. "Yes, indeed. Dead these many years, but even the manner of their deaths was unusual. Mignon Molyneux was found in the tower room, laid out all in white, with her hands folded upon her breast. It is said that the doctors were unable to uncover the reason for her death. And Jean..." Here Sterling lowered his voice and affected a look that he hoped was mysterious. "Jean was found hanging by the neck in the trophy room.

"It was his son, your Cousin Edouard, who found them. He was just a child at the time. You can imagine the shock!"

Margaret's slender, sensitive face had gone pale. "I think I shall go and see to our things, Rebecca, if you don't mind. Perhaps you should come, also. We will be docking soon, will we not?"

Rebecca smiled indulgently and patted her cousin's shoulder. "Why, of course, dear. You *do* look a bit peaked." She had gotten what she wanted out of Sterling and was anxious to be rid of him. She turned to him. "Margaret is not a good sailor, you know, and I have been thoughtless. But our little talk has been *so* interesting. I thank you so much for your kindness, sir, in sharing all this with us. Now I feel that we know so much more about Pirate's Bank and the Molyneux history."

Despite the tilting deck, Sterling bowed low. "It was my pleasure, my dear. I hope that you will allow me to call upon you during your stay. As I told you, my home is in Beaufort, on Port Royal Island, which is only a short way coastward from Pirate's Bank. In fact, I should be only too happy to have you call upon me. Beaufort is really the only town close by, and everyone comes there to the shops."

Although she could envision no circumstances in which she would call upon this man, Rebecca bowed her head graciously. "Of course, sir. Both Margaret and I would be delighted. And now we must see to our things. Oh! Is that Pirate's Bank we're approaching?"

As if they were all puppets, directed by the same hand, their heads turned to face the bow, in front of which a low, lush mound of greenery seemed to float.

Sterling leaned forward to peer through the darkening air at the island they were approaching. "Why, yes. Yes, indeed! That is Pirate's Bank. The company of you two young ladies has been so charming that the trip seems to have taken no time at all."

Rebecca, in her first uncalculated move of the afternoon, gripped her cousin's arm in her excitement. "There it is, Margaret," she said softly. "Pirate's Bank! What do you suppose it is *really* going to be like?"

On the wooden dock of Pirate's Bank, Armand Molyneux stood with legs braced and wide apart, hands clasped behind his back, his dark, strong-featured face set in a scowl that made him look older than his twenty-four years. Heavy shouldered and sturdy legged, Armand had, since his teens, appeared a man and not a boy. Squatting near him were two black men, one little more than a lad, the other of middle age.

As Armand stared at the packet that was approaching, his dark eyes were bleak and hard. He had a great deal of work to do, and he had no taste or talent for the task which his father had assigned to him. Surely someone else could have met these two distant female cousins who were about to descend upon them, bag and baggage, for God only knew how long a stay. Now the whole afternoon would be wasted. He would have to escort the two young women and their luggage up to the house, and by the time he could decently escape, the working day would be over—wasted, not only for him, but for the two men he had taken away from their regular duties to handle the luggage. Armand knew very little of women, but he knew enough to be sure that the new arrivals would be accompanied by a quantity of luggage.

If only Jacques were home—this was certainly far more in his older brother's field—but Jacques was in Savannah, with their father, Edouard, handling some business affairs. Jacques would have known just what to say to two young women. He would have been polite and charming, and most of all, he would have thoroughly enjoyed the task. Edouard, also, could have handled the meeting with ease. It was only he, Armand, who lacked the proper social graces, just as he lacked so much else that his father wished him to have.

A light wind had come up, and the sea was growing a bit choppy. Pirate's Bank was only a few miles from the South Carolina coast and was not the most seaward of the cluster of islands of which it was a part; but still, the waters that surrounded it could become dangerously rough in foul weather, and it looked as if a storm was brewing.

The small coastal packet appeared to be having a rough time of it, heading almost directly into the wind, as it neared the dock. Armand's full lips crimped in a slight smile. If his two cousins were not good sailors, they were going to disembark feeling not at all well. He had no idea at all why this thought should bring him satisfaction, but it did. Perhaps it was because arriving wet and seasick would put them at somewhat of a disadvantage, and this would somehow make *him* feel less awkward. Not exactly an admirable emotion to have toward one's own relatives, no matter how distant, yet he could at least be honest with himself about it.

Feeling a bit less gloomy, he motioned to the two squatting men, and together they walked to the edge of the dock, taking up a position where they could take the lines when the boat came close enough to dock.

Armand's first sight of his cousins was somewhat obscured by the confusion of docking. He had only a blurred impression of colorful clothing, pale faces and girlish voices.

The slight roughness of the sea made disembarking difficult, and the young women's narrow skirts and delicate slippers made it even more awkward. Armand reached out and grasped the first one—she seemed to be frozen on the gangway—under the arms, hoisting her onto the dock, where she teetered, her eyes going wide with surprise and fear. She was dressed in something pink. Pretty, Armand supposed.

As he turned back to the gangway to help the other one, he saw that she had managed to make it on her own. As she stepped onto the dock, he stopped as if poleaxed. He had never seen *any* woman who looked like this one. Fair to the point of seeming not quite a human woman, she appeared to glow in the humid, storm-grayed air, almost as if she were some kind of lamp, illuminated from within. Her image seemed to burn into his eyes. He knew that he was staring but could not seem to stop. She was easily the most striking woman he had ever seen.

And then he noticed that her deep blue eyes were studying him with some amusement, and he came to himself, feeling both foolish and angry that he had allowed himself to be caught so unaware.

The men began bringing up the luggage—great piles of it—and Armand was grateful to be able to switch his attention away from the women for a moment.

When he finally turned back to them, he did so with formal politeness but little real courtesy.

Stiffly, he made a little bow. "I am Armand Molyneux, at your service. I have come down to see you up to the house. Welcome to Pirate's Bank, and to Maison de Rêverie."

The taller girl, the one he had lifted up onto the dock, gave a slight nod. Her face was very pale, and she swayed a bit as their eyes met. "I am your cousin, Margaret," she said with a pronounced British accent. "I'm not feeling very well. I would appreciate..."

Armand bowed again. "Of course. You are weary. I have brought the chaise, as you can see. It will take only a few minutes to drive up to the house. The men will bring your luggage along in the wagon. If you will follow me, please."

Turning, he led the way toward the small chaise, which was parked next to a large, wooden wagon on the lane that ran down to the dock.

Rebecca, despite her fatigue and the moist, heavy stickiness of the air, felt wound tight with excitement. Mr. Sterling had been right about one thing—the island, at least what she could see of it from the dock, *was* lovely, even through the dimness of the storm. A narrow white sand beach, undulant with dunes anchored by graceful sea oats, edged a wood. Lush with tall trees, plants and vines, the wood gave off the humid, flowery odors of a giant hothouse.

"It does look to be enchanted, doesn't it?" she whispered to Margaret.

The little chaise parked in the road at the edge of the dock was beautifully made, and the horse that stood restlessly between the traces, a strongly built bay with beautiful lines, looked to be of excellent stock. It was clear that Cousin Edouard knew, and used, the best.

As for the young man who had come to meet them, her Cousin Armand—well, he had a great deal to learn about manners, yet he was a handsome creature all the same, in a wild, rugged sort of way. He was wearing fitted pantaloons of drab cloth and top boots, which showed off his strong legs to advantage. His blue coat was well cut, showing heavy shoulders, and his white waistcoat accented his dark, rather shaggy good looks, although his black hair, which he wore natural, could certainly have used a good trim. Rebecca wondered briefly if all the family were as good-looking and hoped that they were not as ill-tempered.

Taking Margaret's arm, she noticed with some shame how tired and worn her cousin looked. Margaret's normally rosy face was pale as milk, and her eyes were ringed with dark shadows. Rebecca realized that she should not have insisted that Margaret stand at the rail of the packet with her; she should have found a seat for the other girl and let her rest, but her own energy and spirits had been running high. She knew that Margaret did not have the physical stamina that she did, and yet she always seemed to conveniently forget this fact when there was something that she wanted to do. She really must try to be less selfish.

Now, she tenderly patted her cousin's arm. "Come along, Margaret. We must get you up to the house, where you can have a lie-down."

Margaret looked at her cousin in gratitude. Despite Rebecca's willful ways, she could be surprisingly thoughtful and kind at unexpected times, and the very unexpectedness of her kindnesses made them all the more appreciated.

Armand, his face turned half aside, helped her and Rebecca into the chaise, seated himself and clucked to the horses. In a moment they were moving down the well-cared-for road that led away from the dock, under tall green trees, past charming rustic fences and banks of vivid flowers.

It was all very beautiful, of course, but something about the lushness of the growth—the ripeness of it— made Margaret uncomfortable. The air, heavy with the threat of the impending storm, felt like a hot, damp blanket draped across her shoulders. Not for the first time since this trip had begun, Margaret wondered at the wisdom and the reason for their journey and wished herself back with her parents, in Poonah. Although she rarely spoke of it—it was a dubious talent that both embarrassed and frightened her—Margaret had, since childhood, been plagued with strange visions of the future. This, in itself, would have been bad enough, but she had found, through experience, that these premonitions very often came to pass. She had felt, or had, just such a premonition before this trip, but in the face of the urgings of her own family and Rebecca and *her* family, she had been powerless to voice her fears. After all, what could she have said?

Now, as the small chaise bounced briskly down the narrow country lane, Margaret looked over Rebecca's glowing face and wished fervently that she might share her cousin's positive and fearless outlook. Rebecca was always eager for whatever came next in her life.

After all, Margaret thought, her apprehensions didn't *always* come true. Perhaps this time, her fears for the future were simply due to the fact that she was, for the first time in her life, leaving her parents and the country in which she had spent most of her twenty-one years.

Feeling disoriented and confused, she gripped Rebecca's hand tightly and endeavored to draw from the touch some of her cousin's strength, as they moved toward Maison de Rêverie and the relatives whom Mr. Sterling had made sound so frightening.

Chapter Two

THE SEAT OF THE CHAISE was barely wide enough to accommodate the three of them, and Rebecca was acutely conscious of the fact that her thigh was touching that of her newly met cousin, Armand. She imagined that she could feel the heat of his body through the thin stuff of her clothing, and she found the idea very stimulating. She felt her heartbeat accelerate. Of course, Armand was a bit of a boor; still, he was very handsome, and there was a brooding vitality about him that projected a certain power.

She smiled softly to herself, wondering how this contact was affecting him. Although she was a virgin, Rebecca felt that she knew a considerable amount about the male species and their urges.

It seemed to her that she had been born knowing how to manipulate boys and men, and since early childhood, her beauty had drawn them to her. When she began to mature into womanhood, she had started to take note of the effect she had upon them.

In a way, it was quite comical. They would go all red in the face, and they would stammer; and she had noticed other changes, as well. It was really pitifully easy to get a man, any man, upset simply by standing close to him or by leaning over so that he might see her décolletage; in fact, so easy as to be a bit boring.

However, usually her own feelings were completely under control. She found it quite interesting that now, seated so close to her handsome cousin, she felt a strange excitement in her own body.

To distract herself, Rebecca leaned forward, peering out of the vehicle at the lush greenery that pressed up against the neat split-rail fence that lined the dirt road, seeking a glimpse of the old temples and gazebos that Sterling had told them still dotted the island. She was also very anxious to see the house, wondering precisely what Sterling had meant when he had called its design "radical."

And then, abruptly, the chaise swept around a curve in the road onto an elegant, circular drive of crushed white rock. The drive framed a formal garden, in the center of which stood a small golden-yellow pavilion of unusual design, with curving eaves that ended in strangely designed ornamentations.

Margaret emitted a sound of surprise at the sight of the pavilion, but it was the house itself, Maison de Rêverie, that caused Rebecca to sit forward excitedly on the edge of her seat.

It was an enormous building, and even the gray of the gloomy afternoon could not dim the glow of the pale gold plaster with which it was finished. Rebecca had never been to China; however, she had seen pictures of the temples of China, and that was what this huge structure looked like. No wonder the local populace had been, and apparently still was, startled by its appearance. The older houses she had seen during their brief stay in Charleston had been built in the Georgian style. The newer houses, which she had much admired, were—she had been told—designed in the Federal style, which, as far as she was concerned, much resembled so-called Regency architecture. However, none of them bore any resemblance whatsoever to this oddly beautiful building, with its strange, sweeping roof lines and intricately carved eaves. The house was fronted by a long, shaded porch—the top of which was a continuation of the sweeping roof—supported by tall pillars, which had been painted with some sort of shiny lacquer in a shade of gold deeper than that of the house itself.

The front of the building was centered by a pair of magnificent double doors, which appeared to be faced with brass, beaten into a convoluted design that Rebecca couldn't make out at their present distance.

The size of the house was magnified by two trellised walkways, held up by columns similar to those which fronted the house. These two promenades extended from both sides of the house in a curve that matched that of the drive and were covered with grape and flowering vines. Exotic statues in the Oriental manner were positioned beside the columns and among the gardens and the greenery that surrounded the house. The whole effect was amazing and dazzling; no wonder its builder had called it a "house of dreams."

On the top of the row of steps that led up to the entrance of the house from the drive stood a tall, dark-haired woman wearing a modish dress in French stripes. And beside her stood a slender man attired in the garb of a well-to-do East Indian. A small black boy came trotting around the house as the chaise approached the steps.

"Well, for heaven's sake!" Margaret exclaimed.

Rebecca shared her cousin's astonishment. It was certainly unexpected to find an East Indian in this part of the world, and she had to wonder what he was doing in this out-of-the-way place and why he was waiting with this woman, whom Rebecca surmised must be Felicity, Cousin Edouard's wife and the mother of Armand and Jacques.

The bay had now come to a stamping halt in front of the steps, and Armand handed the reins down to the grinning black boy, who apparently relished his job of driving the vehicle to the stables.

Armand got down from the chaise and, without a word, went around to the other side, where he helped first Margaret, and then Rebecca, down from the seat.

As Rebecca rested her weight on Armand's proffered arm, she gave him a quick glance. If he appeared at all friendly, she was prepared to offer him a token smile. But his dark eyes were fixed straight ahead, and she felt an unaccustomed sting at the implied rebuff. What a boor he was! She certainly would not even *consider* a friendly overture again!

Taking Margaret's hand, she commencéd to climb the broad steps that led to the porch. She looked upward with considerable curiosity at the two people waiting at the top, as Armand came along behind them.

The woman was still quite attractive, despite the fact that she must be old—at least forty-five—and she had a calm, gentle face, with kind hazel eyes.

The man, seen closer up, had light brown, tight-skinned features, with a hawk nose and deep-set black eyes. His lips were thin, unsmiling, and his face showed no expression whatsoever. Again Rebecca wondered at his presence here. He wore the clothing of a high-caste Hindu, and yet he had no caste mark upon his forehead.

As they stepped up onto the porch, Rebecca released Margaret's hand and stepped forward. "Cousin Felicity?"

The older woman's smile widened, and she grasped Rebecca's shoulders, then kissed her on both cheeks.

"You must be Rebecca! Of course, you are. Your mother wrote me that you were the fair one."

She released Rebecca and turned to Margaret, who held herself rather stiffly as Felicity embraced her. "And you would be Margaret. I am delighted to have you both here. Welcome to Maison de Rêverie, and to Pirate's Bank. I hope Armand welcomed you properly."

Rebecca, avoiding looking at Armand, gave a cool nod.

Margaret, very conscious of the inscrutable gaze of the Indian, suffered Felicity's greeting and smiled palely. She did not know why the Indian's presence disconcerted her, since she had lived in India most of her life. Perhaps it was because he seemed so out of place here in this far-off spot.

"We are pleased to be here, Cousin Felicity," she heard Rebecca say. "It is so kind of you and Cousin Edouard to have us."

Knowing that she had to say something, Margaret found herself murmuring an echo, "Yes, so kind of you to have us."

She saw that Felicity, who had a handsome, motherly looking face, was staring at her with some concern. "Oh, you do look tired, my dear. I'm sure that it has been a long and arduous journey, and I am certain that the first thing you will want to do is to bathe and rest for a bit. I have had Dhupta here, who is our factotum, instruct the upstairs maids to prepare your rooms, and you will find there all that you need. Of course, I'm absolutely dying to hear all of the news from your families and the details of your journey. But I shall try and restrain my curiosity until you have rested.

"I will escort you to your rooms now, and you won't need to make an appearance until dinner, which will be served at eight. By that time, Mr. Molyneux and Jacques should have returned from Savannah. My husband asked me to tell you he was terribly sorry that he couldn't be here to greet you upon your arrival. Something came up after we received word that you would be arriving on this week's packet. He begs your forgiveness, but his business was pressing." She clapped her hands together. "Oh, I can't begin to tell you how pleasant it will be to have two young women in the house!"

Margaret mustered another smile. Felicity seemed very kind, but she was also a bit of a chatterbox, and Margaret knew that later she would remember very little of what had been said. She was simply too fatigued.

Positioning herself between the two young women, Felicity took an arm of each, as Dhupta, his face still inscrutable, opened the huge double doors—which bore the design of two elegant but fierce-looking dragons—so that they might proceed, three abreast, into the cool interior of the great house.

As weary as she was, Margaret scarcely noticed the interior of the large, high-ceilinged entryway, as Felicity herded her and Rebecca toward the wide staircase that rose to a landing, where it then divided into two sweeping curves that made their way up to the next floor.

The newel posts were ornately carved, as were the banisters. As she mounted the stairs the carved wood felt warm and almost alive under her hand, and Margaret experienced a vague distaste and apprehension at the fact that she couldn't tell just what sort of depictions were passing beneath her fingertips.

Above the landing hung a huge chandelier, of a type unknown to her. It looked foreign and odd, and she seemed to feel the weight of it over her head like a threatening presence.

As they passed beneath the huge chandelier, they came face-to-face with two large oil portraits in heavy, carved gilt frames, hanging on the wall of the landing.

Margaret had no desire to peruse them at this time, but she was halted by Rebecca's hand upon her arm.

"What arresting portraits," Rebecca said, holding Margaret firmly in place. "The style of the painting is quite unusual. Who are the subjects?"

"Jean and Mignon Molyneux," said Felicity. "The portraits were painted by their friend, Polydoro, just six months before their deaths. The portraits are considered to be some of his best work."

Margaret, forced to give the paintings her attention, looked upward into a pair of dark painted eyes that held her gaze despite herself. Jean Molyneux's was not a kind face. The cheekbones were strong, almost Slavic, and the deep-set eyes seemed to mirror both arrogance and amusement. The mouth, full lipped and well defined, was, Margaret thought, far too sensual for a man. An elaborate white wig framed his dark-skinned features and seemed to accentuate them, as did the rich red velvet cloak that he was wearing.

Turning her glance to the portrait of the wife, she found it equally upsetting. Mignon Molyneux was dressed in a cape similar to her husband's, the full hood pushed back to form a background for her long, slender white throat and narrow, pale face.

Her eyes too were dark, but much larger than her husband's, and there was something mirrored in them that spoke to Margaret of dark things. The woman's hair was auburn and piled high upon her head in an elaborate confection of curls and twists. Her nose was long and aristocratic and her lips thin, red, and somehow avid.

Neither portrait portrayed a person whom Margaret would have been desirous of meeting, and she urged Rebecca on, by pulling her arm away and moving toward the stairs.

And then they were on the upper floor, and Felicity was showing her into a sunny room containing a large, four-poster bed.

On a low chest was a large pitcher and washbowl, with clean white linens stacked beside it, and on a lovely Sheraton table by the window was a tray containing another pitcher, a glass, a bowl of fruit, cheese and crackers, and sweet biscuits.

Turning to Felicity, Margaret gave her a wide, tremulous smile, whispered, "Thank you," and, hoping she was not showing indecent haste, firmly closed the door.

THE SKY HAD BEGUN TO CLEAR a bit, and a shaft of late-afternoon sunlight, as if directed by the hand of God, struck straight into Rebecca's bedroom window and spread over her like a transparent blanket.

Gazing down the length of her body, stretched out on the chaise longue in her undergarments, Rebecca admired herself. The effect was really quite nice.

Reaching out for another of the delicious peaches that Felicity had so generously provided, she bit into the sweet, golden meat, savoring the taste of it. She was hungry for fruit, for there had been little available aboard ship, and she realized that she was making a pig of herself.

She knew she should be resting. Her body *was* tired, but her mind seemed to be as busy as a hive full of bees, and she simply couldn't sleep. At any rate, Margaret was no doubt already sleeping soundly enough for both of them.

Poor dear! Rebecca smiled to herself. Margaret had looked so dreadfully pale. Rebecca hoped that she would be feeling better at dinner, for it would lessen her own pleasure if her dear friend and cousin was unable to participate in the dinner conversation with enjoyment. Also, it might put a damper on the whole evening, and Rebecca wanted to fully enjoy her first evening in this odd but elegant house.

She hadn't yet seen much of the interior, yet she liked what she had seen thus far. This room, for instance, was perfectly delightful; large, sunny, high ceilinged. The furniture was Chippendale, with a touch of chinoiserie. The tops of the chairs were pagoda shaped, and the splendid Chippendale four-poster bed looked like a small pagoda itself, with a canopy that seemed almost a copy of the swooping Chinese roof of the house.

The main portion of the polished wooden floor was covered by a thickly woven Oriental rug. The colors had faded slightly, yet the softening of the color only added to its beauty. It glowed warmly in the shaft of sunlight that spilled over Rebecca, and she found herself regarding it as if it somehow had entranced her, seeing in it strange shapes and forms, such as one saw in clouds.

Drowsily she wondered how her mother and father were faring at home; and for a brief moment she experienced a pang of homesickness for the big, airy white house in Poonah, which was shared by her family and Margaret's. Rebecca knew that she should make an effort and write to her parents tomorrow. Letters took such an awfully long time to reach India, and they surely must be wondering how she was getting on.

Of course, Margaret, always the conscientious one, had written to her parents during their three days in Charleston; and Aunt Mary would share the letter's contents with her sister Amanda, Rebecca's mother. So it would be *almost* as if Rebecca herself had written. Still, she must get a letter off herself. She had promised, and it had been generous of her parents to send her on this long and expensive trip.

The trip had been planned as a coming-of-age gift to her and Margaret, so that they might broaden their experience; for they had been living in India since their eighth year, with only occasional trips back to England.

The original plan this time had been for them to travel to London, and then to visit France, in the company of their great-aunt, Lavinia. However, just before their plans were set, Lavinia very unexpectedly died, and there were, unfortunately, no other relatives in England who could put them up or chaperone them. Both the Trentons and the Downings were, it seemed, poor breeders. Rebecca was an only child, and Margaret's only sibling, an elder brother, had died of a fever in India when he was fourteen.

Rebecca had attempted to persuade her mother and aunt to accompany them, but neither woman wanted to be separated from her husband for such an extended length of time. Rebecca, who had a keen interest in politics and world affairs, was aware that there had been much talk of unrest among the Indians in their area, and knowing her mother, she suspected that this was one reason that she did not want to leave her husband's side.

Amanda Trenton was made of stern stuff—the sort of woman who stood by her man no matter what life might bring. Rebecca admired this quality in her mother, yet, at the same time, she wondered how a woman could feel this way. How must it feel to love a man so much that you would stay with him even if it placed your own life in danger? Certainly Rebecca had yet to meet a man who could make her feel this way.

At any rate, with Great-Aunt Lavinia's death, the trip to London had seemed impossible. At this point, both young women had almost resigned themselves to the fact that they would not be able to travel this year. Then a letter had arrived from Rebecca's mother's cousin, Edouard Molyneux, in the state of South Carolina, in the Colonies.

Of course, they weren't really the Colonies any longer, not since the Revolutionary War. They now called themselves the United States of America; but it was of no consequence what they called themselves. What mattered was that Cousin Edouard, with whom Rebecca's father had kept up a desultory correspondence over the years, had, in this latest letter, put forth the suggestion that Rebecca's father, if he ever had the time and the leave, bring his family to visit their American relatives in the new country.

And so it was that other letters were exchanged, and it was finally agreed that Rebecca and Margaret would get their trip after all, although to an unusual destination, and a bit later than they had planned—for by then it was so late in the year that it was necessary to wait until the following spring to begin their journey.

By the time their sailing date had arrived, Rebecca had been just as pleased that they would not be going to England, for she was curious to see these new United States.

Also, the news from England seemed to be unusually depressing. What Rebecca's father referred to as the "industrial depression" seemed to be dragging on, and early in the year riots had broken out in London on the opening of Parliament. While driving to the House of Lords, the Prince Regent, now grown thoroughly unpopular because of the scandals concerning his wife, had been hooted by a crowd in St. James's Park. The police had claimed that an air gun had been discharged at the prince, and they had retaliated with an attack on the crowd. A number of persons had been injured.

Shortly thereafter, news had reached India about what the London newspapers referred to as the "Great Green Bag Inquiry," when Lord Sidmouth placed before Parliament a green bag filled with reports concerning seditions. This led to hangings and further riots, until it appeared that London was no longer safe for decent people.

Of course, Rebecca realized, this new country had its danger, too. She had read of the red Indians who roamed vast areas of unsettled land, but Cousin Edouard's letters had assured her parents that life on his island, Pirate's Bank, offered all the amenities, without any danger, and that Savannah, Georgia, where Edouard had a winter home, had many lovely homes and public buildings and offered an active social life.

Well, he certainly had not lied about Pirate's Bank. So far, it seemed that every comfort was available, and there was a feeling of excitement, of exciting things about to happen, that had possessed her since she had first set foot upon the dock. She just knew that something wonderful was going to happen to her this summer. She was as sure of it as she was of her own name. . . .

Startled into wakefulness, it took Rebecca a moment to realize that she had fallen asleep. The swatch of sunlight was gone, and the sky had grown darker outside her window.

There came a repetition of the sounds that had awakened her—the stamping of horses' hooves, the jingling of harness and the voices of men talking.

Getting up from the chaise longue, Rebecca crossed to the other window, which faced out to the front of the house and the circular drive and garden.

Down below, she saw the chaise in which Armand had delivered her and Margaret to the house. Two men were alighting from it.

For a moment she wondered who they were, and then she remembered. Felicity had mentioned that Edouard and the other son, Jacques, had been away to Savannah and would be returning in time for dinner.

Wide awake now, Rebecca pulled the curtain forward to shield her state of undress and peeked around the edge.

The two men appeared to be of an almost equal height and build, and both had strong, deep voices. From her vantage point, it was not easy to see their faces, but then one of them, striding up the front steps, removed his hat, and she saw a thick, wavy head of auburn hair, tied back with a black riband. Surely this must be Jacques, for Cousin Edouard would be much older.

As the man reached the top of the steps, he paused and threw his head back.

Rebecca's first instinct was to draw away, but she made herself remain stationary as the man glanced upward, seeming to look directly at the window where she stood.

Even in the fading light, it was apparent that he was extremely well favored and that he was obviously much more of a gentleman than his brother Armand.

Well dressed and immaculately groomed, he moved with a masculine, assured grace that impressed her. If this *was* Jacques, she thought, things were going to be even more interesting here than she had anticipated. She must really begin to prepare for this evening.

Thoughtfully, she tugged the tapestried bellpull to summon one of the upstairs maids to unpack her clothing and freshen one of her nicest gowns for her first dinner at Maison de Rêverie and her first meeting with the entire Molyneux family.

Chapter Three

THE DINING TABLE was very long, and much to her annoyance, Rebecca had been seated next to Armand, while opposite her, Margaret was situated next to Jacques, who had proved, upon closer inspection, to be even more attractive than he had seemed from Rebecca's bedroom window earlier.

Edouard and Felicity both seemed very far away at the table's respective ends.

Edouard smiled down the table at her. "And so your trip was comparatively comfortable, Cousin Rebecca, if one may use that word at all in describing a long sea voyage."

Rebecca smiled brightly. "Well, I cannot say that it was exactly enjoyable, yet we managed to bear up. Fortunately, we ran into only brief periods of bad weather. I believe that I found the lack of fresh food the most annoying thing. That, and the absence of the amenities that one is accustomed to on land."

Edouard—whom she had not really gotten a very good look at from her window—was almost as attractive as his elder son. Both men were tall and slender, with narrow, aristocratic faces. Both had the same hazel-green eyes, high cheekbones and full-lipped mouths that hinted at sensitivity. The only real difference was that Edouard's hair was attractively streaked with gray, and he had a few lines etched around his eyes and mouth, but this in no way made him less handsome.

However, it was Jacques who fascinated Rebecca, and she was quite piqued that she had not been seated next to him.

He was being very polite to Margaret, talking to her, and now and then giving her his rather melancholy smile. Armand, on the other hand, sat in his chair rather stiffly, as if he was a stranger at his own table. His table manners, Rebecca noticed with some surprise, were quite good, but he ate quickly, as if in a rush to get through the meal. As far as conversation was concerned, she might as well have been sitting next to one of the statues in the garden.

Still, she could gaze across the table at Jacques, and more importantly, he could look at her, which he did with some frequency.

At that moment, the factotum, Dhupta, appeared in the doorway with a huge silver tureen on a serving cart. Approaching the women first, he began to ladle into the flat soup bowls a rather thick soup. It had a mouth-watering aroma.

Looking down into her bowl, Rebecca could see bits of shrimp, chicken, ham, corn, tomatoes and an unidentifiable sliced green vegetable, in the hearty stock. When she tasted the soup, she found the flavor robust, but not any more so than some of the Indian dishes she had partaken of at home.

The table had been beautifully set and arranged. In the center was a lovely epergne filled with fresh flowers, and at each end of the table, a heavy silver candelabra.

The china had a delicate blue willow, and the flatware was of good, heavy silver; the knife and fork matching, the spoon of a different, more delicate design. Again, as she had when she had seen the chaise and horse at the dock, Rebecca reflected on the fact that Edouard Molyneux spared no expense in making himself and his family comfortable.

"Do you like music, Rebecca?" Jacques was speaking to her across the expanse of white linen that covered the table.

"Oh, yes," she replied, lowering her lashes, and then raising them, giving him what her mother often teasingly referred to as "the look." She went on, "I play the piano, although not too well, and I sing a little, although my voice is not strong."

"I am sure that you are just being modest. After dinner we usually spend an hour or so in the music room, and if you will allow me, I shall play for you so that you might sing for us. Father and I are getting rather tired of our own performances, and I am sure that Mother would be very pleased to hear a fresh, female voice."

Rebecca smiled, hard put to conceal her pleasure. It was obvious that both Jacques and his father were men of culture. It was also true that Jacques was right—she had been purposefully modest in describing her own talents. Actually, she played the piano passably well, and her voice was sweet, true and strong.

She said, "I should enjoy that very much."

Jacques turned to Margaret. "And are you musical as well? If so, perhaps you would honor us with a duet."

Margaret was looking much rested after her long nap; looking, in fact, unusually pretty in a peach gown, with her hair pulled back in soft curls.

She blushed slightly at Jacques's question. "Oh, I play a bit of piano, but I have no voice."

Embarrassed by Jacques's interest, Margaret glanced down the table at their hostess. "And you, Cousin Felicity? Do you sing?"

The older woman smiled and shook her head. Although she had been very talkative when the girls arrived, she now seemed to be quite restrained.

"Heavens, no, my dear," she said. "I am afraid that I am unmusical in the extreme. As Edouard will tell you, I have no ear at all. Still, I do love to listen. I make a good audience."

Rebecca glanced at Armand. "And you, Armand? Are you like your brother and father? Or do you take after your mother?"

Armand's face seemed to tighten, and his cheeks showed the flush of blood rising to the surface.

He turned to face her, and his eyes glittered in the candlelight. His expression was so grim that Rebecca felt nonplussed. What on earth was wrong with the man? It seemed an innocent enough question to her!

"I'm afraid that I take after no one, Cousin Rebecca," he said in a sarcastic tone. "The family has often discussed that deplorable fact. I have often wondered if I was not perhaps left upon the doorstep by a band of goblins."

Edouard set down his glass of wine with a thump, and his pleasant laugh rolled over them.

Smiling broadly, Jacques leaned across the table. "Armand is something of a joker, Rebecca. Actually, my brother plays several instruments and has a fine baritone voice. Of course, I must confess that his taste in music runs a bit contrary to my own."

Surprised, Rebecca looked at Armand again. She would never have suspected him of being interested in any of the arts. There was more of the peasant about him than the gentleman. Despite the fine suit and gleaming linen he was now wearing, his hair looked tousled; but it was his attitude, in particular, that denied his background. He had none of his father's, or his brother's, charm or sophistication. He really did, it appeared to Rebecca, seem like a changeling in this otherwise charming family.

After dinner was finished—the sweet had been a delicious trifle—and after the men had retired for their brandy and cigars and the ladies for their demitasse and sherry, the family gathered in the music room.

ALTHOUGH MARGARET HAD BEEN in grand music rooms in London, none she had ever seen had held as many instruments as did this one.

The room itself was quite large and, like the parts of the house she had seen so far, contained touches of chinoiserie in its decor. There were two beautiful pianos, both inlaid with precious woods and mother-of-pearl, placed near each other on one side of the room. Near the window was a large gilded harp, and in a tall cabinet she could see a large collection of flutes and recorders. A violin case lay upon a small table, and several other tables held a variety of odd-looking stringed instruments that she could not identify.

She had consumed only one small glass of sherry, yet she felt somewhat giddy and quite happy. Although she always felt awkward conversing with members of the opposite sex, she had much enjoyed the company of Jacques Molyneux at the dinner table. He had been so polite and charming that he had almost put her at ease. Truthfully, she had been very surprised to find a gentleman of such refinement and sensitivity in this out-of-the-way spot, and in such a new, raw country. Jacques and his father were certainly the equals of any English gentlemen she had met in London or India. However, the younger brother, Armand, remained an enigma, and a rather unsettling one.

Margaret looked at the two brothers now, as they ranged side by side near the fireplace. Outside of a certain similarity in the set of their eyes, they looked nothing alike, and their temperaments were certainly not the same. They were both handsome, that could not be denied. In fact, she thought, in some ways, Armand might be considered the better looking, but the surliness of his nature and the obvious muscularity of his body structure gave him an aura that she found rather threatening. Jacques was much more the type of man she admired.

Jacques glanced her way now, and she found herself flushing. Of course, his attention didn't really mean anything. He had been attentive to her at the table, but that was probably because he had been seated next to her, and good manners decreed that he should be polite. If events followed their natural course, Margaret knew he would soon fall madly in love with Rebecca, as all men did.

Rebecca's attraction for the male sex had always been a given in their relationship. Ever since Margaret could remember, first boys, and then men, had flocked around Rebecca, eager for a glance or a kind word.

Margaret considered herself a sensible girl; and although she knew that she was pretty enough in her own way, she was also well aware that she paled in comparison to the extraordinary good looks of her cousin. Still, she didn't resent Rebecca's beauty or her popularity. Not much given to introspection, she had never really wondered why.

She was extremely fond of Rebecca, whom she thought of as more sister than cousin. The two girls had been born only a month apart and had seldom been out of one another's company since that time. Although as different in their ways as Jacques and Armand, they had formed a close bond over the years.

Margaret had long since realized that it was she who made the most adjustments in the relationship and that she at times gave more, but it was in her temperament to do so. Also, she knew that she did not possess the passion, fire and drive of her cousin. She was just as glad that this was the case. If one thought in theatrical terms, one might say that Margaret had been born to play a supporting role, while Rebecca had been born to be a star. That was the way it was, and it would do little good to fret about it. At any rate, it had been nice to have Jacques behave as if she was Rebecca's equal in attractiveness and desirability, and she was quite looking forward to having a very pleasant time this summer.

Felicity had moved over to her, and Margaret turned to ask: "What are those odd stringed instruments on the tables? I have never seen anything quite like them."

Felicity nodded with a musing smile. "Yes, they are rather odd, aren't they? They belonged to my husband's father, Jean Molyneux. I understand that he brought them over from China after a visit there. They say that his wife Mignon could play them, but none of us has any idea how to go about it. However, they *are* attractive, don't you think? Oh, look, I believe that Rebecca and Jacques are about to entertain us."

Margaret had often heard Rebecca sing, always finding her voice pleasing. Jacques, she was happy to learn, played the piano well, and was a good accompanist—which she knew was not always the same thing.

The selections received appreciative applause, and then Edouard turned to Armand. "Armand, your brother and our charming guest have been kind enough to play and sing for us. I think it would now be appropriate to hear from you."

Armand gave his father a scathing look that caused Margaret to wonder again at his uncivility. That was certainly no way for a son to react to his father's suggestion, especially a perfectly normal one.

"I would prefer not to, Father," Armand said. "You know how much I dislike performing in company."

Edouard said firmly, "Nonsense, my boy. This is not company. This is family. Come now. Let us have your contribution to the evening's entertainment."

Lips tight, Armand stalked—there was no other word for it—over to the larger piano, as Jacques got up to give him his seat. It seemed to Margaret that Jacques's smile was meant to placate his brother, but it had no noticeable effect on Armand's scowl.

Throwing back his coattails, Armand sat down and, for a moment, stared morosely at the keyboard. Then, with a movement so violent and sudden that it startled, he began to play.

After listening for a few chords, Margaret looked over to where Rebecca had taken a seat, so that she might exchange glances with her. What on earth was he playing? It was certainly nothing that she recognized.

Rebecca gazed back with an amused smile and raised her eyebrows as the music crashed through the room, all thunderous chords and wild passion.

Stealing a glance at Edouard and Felicity, Margaret saw pained looks upon their faces. They appeared as unfamiliar as she and Rebecca with this strange, wild music their son was playing.

Margaret grew more and more uncomfortable as the music continued. She really did not care for violent displays of feeling; and during Armand's performance, it seemed to her that she was seeing something private and full of dark violence that she had no wish to witness. She heaved a heartfelt sigh of relief when he finished.

REBECCA WAS NOT CERTAIN what had awakened her; she only knew that she had suddenly been roused from a deep sleep and that she had felt for a moment the disorientation that was often felt upon waking in a strange place.

At last finally realizing where she was, she lay with her heart thumping wildly, eyes straining in the darkness, watching and listening for whatever had startled her awake. The bedroom windows were open, and she could see the ghostly paleness of a curtain moving in a slight breeze.

Rebecca was not by nature a timid girl, and yet at this moment she experienced the cold touch of fear. She had the distinct and eerie impression that she was not alone, that someone, or something, was in the room with her. It was ridiculous, of course. Who would come into her room in the dead of night? She must have been having a bad dream.

And then she saw it—a dark shadow against the lighter darkness of the window—and she gave a muffled cry.

Then the shadow was gone, and there was a sound, like the sliding of wood against wood.

Hands trembling badly, she fumbled for a box of lucifers on the nightstand and, managing to strike one, she lit the candle in its holder.

The small flame spurted to golden life and wavered as she raised the candle holder so that it might better illuminate the room. She was quite alone. *Could* it have been a dream?

And then from somewhere below, there came another sound—music, very soft, barely heard; the sound of an unidentifiable stringed instrument playing an odd sort of melody that had something in it that reminded her of the music of India.

"AND THAT IS ONE of the old pavilions. There are still three or four left. In my grandfather's day, I understand there were at least a dozen."

"It's beautiful," Rebecca said. She held onto Jacques's arm as he guided her off the main path, into the side path that led to the delicate latticed building he had indicated. The pavilion nestled in a very small clearing amidst a tangle of flowers and vines gone wild.

"We do try to keep them painted and in good repair." Jacques deposited Rebecca at the base of the pavilion and then turned back to extend his hand to Margaret.

"Father has never tried to keep the whole island landscaped, as his father did," Jacques continued. "However, we do try to keep the paths clear for walking and riding, and to keep the remaining statues and gazebos preserved for the future."

"I think that's admirable," Rebecca said, fanning herself gently. The day had dawned clear and hot, and it was quite humid in the small clearing. She could feel the thin stuff of her dress clinging to her back, and perspiration was collecting between her breasts.

She and Margaret had slept late, had a good breakfast, and now, in the late morning, they had gone walking with Jacques, so that he might show them something of the grounds and the old paths and gardens.

Watching Jacques as he led Margaret to stand beside her, Rebecca experienced a sudden realization. He was treating Margaret with the same consideration and interest that he showed to her, Rebecca, and this was unusual enough to bring it to her attention and to pique her interest.

"Is it clean enough so that we might sit inside?" she asked with a provocative glance over the top of her slowly moving fan.

"If it isn't, I shall clean off a seat for you," he said with his gentle smile, which, for some reason, always managed to look a trifle melancholy.

Taking a large linen handkerchief from his pocket, he climbed the three steps to the platform of the gazebo and began dusting the wooden seats.

After they were all seated in the shade of the pavilion's curved roof, where it was at least a bit cooler, Rebecca gazed at Jacques directly—an act which usually set a young man to stammering and flushing. Jacques, however, only gazed calmly back at her.

"In your father's letters, he mentioned that you only recently returned home, that you had been away serving as an officer in the American Army. He wrote that you had fought at the Battle of New Orleans. It is very fortunate that you survived that experience without injury."

His face had gone quite still. He looked off before nodding slightly. "Yes, that is correct. I served under General Andrew Jackson."

Margaret dug a sharp elbow into Rebecca's ribs, and Rebecca said hurriedly, "I didn't mean to remind you of anything unpleasant, Jacques. If I did, please forgive me. I just wanted to say that I hope you don't hold the fact of our being English against us. In India we received accounts of the war from the London papers, although they reached us very late, and I was quite upset at the time, thinking that our American cousin and our British soldiers were fighting one another."

Jacques raised one eyebrow in a quizzical expression that Rebecca was learning was common with him. "I find it astonishing, Rebecca, that you know so much of what has been going on here. And of course I don't hold against you the fact that you are English, no more than you hold it against me that I am an American. At least, I hope that is the way of it."

His glance went to Margaret. Rebecca found it irritating that he appeared determined to devote equal time to both of them.

"And you, Margaret, do you take an interest in politics and wars?"

Margaret flushed. "No, I'm afraid not. I must confess to a horror of violence and a dislike of politics. There are enough problems in India, which I cannot avoid hearing about constantly, and I blame most of them on politics. I don't even *want* to know what is going on in the rest of the world."

He nodded seriously. "Well, perhaps you are wise."

His words were almost drowned out by the drumming sound of a horse's hooves on the pathway, and Rebecca looked up to see a large black horse pounding along the main path. A rider was bent over the pommel of the saddle.

"Well, for heaven's sake!" she exclaimed as the horse and rider thundered on out of sight. "Who on earth was that?"

Jacques was smiling. "I believe it was Armand. He is the only one on the island who rides like that."

"But what if we had been on the path?" Rebecca asked. "Would he have ridden right over us?"

"Oh, I don't believe he would go quite that far." Jacques laughed lightly. "Although he might have given us quite a start."

The faces of both women registered disapproval, and Jacques hastened to add, "You mustn't judge Armand too harshly. He uses riding as some men use drink, to ease his angers, to release his tensions."

"Well," Rebecca said, furiously fanning herself, "I imagine, then, that he must do a great deal of riding, for since we have been here, I have only seen him in a bad humor."

"Rebecca!" Margaret said. "It is most impolite of you to say such a thing!"

Rebecca shrugged. "That may well be, but it's true, nonetheless."

Jacques gestured with one hand. "His anger is not directed at you, Rebecca. Or at you, Margaret. I can assure you of that. It is simply that he doesn't wish to be here, on Pirate's Bank, and Father has insisted that he remain, for at least a few days. Armand doesn't like the island; he never has. He would much rather be at Les Chênes."

Rebecca stopped her fanning. "Les Chênes? The Oaks? What is that?"

"One of our two plantations. We grow cotton there and some indigo. We have another larger plantation nearby, where we grow rice. Armand supervises Les Chênes, and I have recently taken over from my father the task of running Middlemarsh, our rice property."

"Do you usually stay there, then, at Middlemarsh?" Rebecca asked. She awaited his answer with some apprehension. Life on the island would not be nearly so interesting if Jacques was not here.

He shook his head. "No, we have no manor house there at present. It is near enough so that we can visit it frequently from either the island or from our home in Savannah. Of course, we do have cabins for the workers and the overseer and barns for storage."

Two plantations, a house in Savannah and Maison de Rêverie, she thought, the Molyneuxs *are* quite wealthy. She asked, "And at Les Chênes?"

"Yes, there is a home there, but it is nothing like Maison de Rêverie, I'm afraid. It is very simple and quite small, yet it seems to fit Armand's needs. He certainly seems to prefer it to the island."

Rebecca shook her head. "Well, I simply can't understand why he doesn't care for Pirate's Bank. I think it is lovely here. Don't you, Margaret?"

Margaret nodded. "It is indeed lovely, but perhaps Armand has reasons of his own for wishing to stay at The Oaks."

"Yes," Jacques said musingly. "I suppose he does, but I must confess to you that I have never known what they were. Armand is not one to confide his secret thoughts to anyone, not even members of his own family."

When they returned to the house, they found tea awaiting them in the small parlor, which was on the shady side of the house.

Edouard and Felicity were already seated on a beautiful, blue silk-covered sofa, but Armand had not yet put in an appearance. Rebecca found herself hoping that he would remain absent. It would no doubt be much more pleasant without him.

As she took a cup of aromatic tea from Felicity, Rebecca noticed that the older woman was not looking at all well. She was quite pale and her eyes looked red, as if she had been weeping. She had very little to say.

Edouard, on the other hand, seemed to be in an ebullient mood. His narrow face was high with color, and his eyes were bright as he arose to help each young woman to her seat.

Rebecca noticed that the pressure of his hand upon her arm was perhaps more intimate than necessary, but she did not really mind.

"Well, did you young ladies have a nice stroll?" he asked suavely. "Did Jacques look after you properly?"

Margaret blushed furiously, and Rebecca idly wondered why.

"Why, yes, Cousin Edouard," Margaret said in a low voice. "We enjoyed the grounds very much."

"And Jacques looked after us like the perfect gentleman that he is," Rebecca said with a flashing smile.

"Well, I should hope so. I have tried to raise him to appreciate beauty, as I do, and beauty always deserves the gentlest of care."

He gave a slight bow of his head, and Rebecca nodded to acknowledge the graceful compliment, thinking that Edouard was as charming as his son. It always buoyed her spirits to be in the company of attractive men.

"It is too bad that I haven't had the same success with his brother," Edouard continued, setting down his cup and reaching for a delicious-looking pink-frosted cake.

"But how can you be blamed, Father?" said Armand's mocking voice from the doorway. "After all, you didn't have the same good material to work with, did you?"

Margaret stared intently down into her tea cup. She hated unpleasantness so, and she expected that Edouard would be chagrined to learn that his younger son had overheard his remark; but when she stole a quick glance at Edouard, his features were bland.

"Ah, Armand. So you have deigned to join us. Do take a seat, my boy, and stop glowering at us. Our guests will think that you have no manners at all."

Rebecca looked up at Armand with some curiosity. He was a boor, no question about that, yet it seemed to her that Edouard was unnecessarily harsh in speaking to him. There was a tone there, a way of speaking, that bordered on contempt. Evidently,

Edouard was not very fond of his younger son. Most interesting!

She glanced over at Margaret but found the other girl's gaze lowered. Rebecca knew how much Margaret detested scenes. Perhaps it was time to introduce another subject into the conversation.

She said quickly, "Felicity, last night in the music room, I overheard you telling Margaret that no one in the family knew how to play those odd Chinese instruments. Am I remembering correctly?"

Felicity looked a little flustered. She turned in her seat to face Rebecca; but as she did so, a slight grimace crossed her face, as if she were in pain. The only other person who appeared to notice was Armand, whose expression darkened even further as he chose a chair near the tea table.

"Why, yes, my dear. I believe that is what I said. It is certainly true, at any rate."

"Then that is very odd. Late last night I awoke, and heard faintly but quite clearly, the sound of a stringed instrument playing. It was no instrument that I am familiar with, and the melody being played was very unusual."

Felicity's face went paler still, and an expression crossed her face that could only be interpreted as fear.

Feeling a bit nonplussed—she had only meant to change the subject—Rebecca glanced quickly around at the others. Margaret and Jacques were staring at her in surprise, and Armand with what seemed to be smoldering anger. The only one completely unmoved by her announcement appeared to be Edouard, who was choosing another cake for his plate.

"Oh, but you must be mistaken, my dear," Felicity said very quietly. "Those instruments have not been touched in a great many years. They must be dreadfully out of tune. And no member of the household would have been up and about at such a late hour. You were dreaming, perhaps?"

Rebecca experienced a touch of irritation. She was quite certain that she had not been dreaming. What would they say if she told them the rest of it—that she was sure someone had been in her room?

"Old houses, you know," said Edouard, arranging the cake just so upon his plate. "They settle, you see. And the wind also makes odd noises. You'll soon get used to it, I'm sure. And now . . ." He paused dramatically. "I have some news for all of you. I have been waiting until we were all present," he said with a reproving glance at Armand. "Next weekend, we shall have a party, in honor of our lovely young guests!"

He turned to his wife. "It's been too long since we've hosted a gala, don't you think so, my dear?"

Felicity nodded quickly. There was a note of anxiety in her voice as she said, "Oh, yes, Edouard. That will be lovely."

Armand was scowling blackly. "And I suppose you will want me to stay for it?"

"I most certainly do want you to stay. Your overseer can certainly handle matters at Les Chênes."

Armand subsided with a curt nod, and for a moment his glance crossed Rebecca's and she felt herself recoil under the intensity of his look. What an odd man he was!

For that matter, she thought, what an odd family altogether. Edouard and Felicity were not at all like her own or Margaret's rather staid parents. There was something here, an undercurrent between these people; something dark and hidden yet full of odd tension, as of barely suppressed violence. Strangely enough, she found it not entirely unattractive.

Chapter Four

REBECCA PULLED UP her peignoir so that she might expose her bare legs to the breeze coming in through the window of the upstairs sitting room which she and Margaret had been told they might share. In India, she had been familiar with heat and humidity; however, she had never grown entirely used to either condition.

She had just finished writing a short letter to her parents, and Margaret was now sitting at the writing desk, busy with her own letter.

This evening, after dinner, there had been no musical hour, as Edouard had told them that he had some business to conduct in Beaufort and Felicity had pleaded a headache.

Instead, Rebecca and Margaret had retired to this attractive sitting room, situated between their two bedrooms, and Margaret had insisted that they use this opportunity to write to their respective parents.

The chair upon which Rebecca sat was placed just next to one of the windows, and she gazed pensively out onto the moonlit garden at the side of the house. It would be nice to be strolling there, in the moonlight, and yet it was nice in here as well, relaxed and comfortable, gazing out. Rebecca had always had a special affinity for the night and the moon, particularly the full moon.

Since early childhood she had believed that there was a certain magic in the night that was not present in the harsh glare of day. At night everything was beautiful, softened by the darkness, frosted by moonlight—which showed only the barest shape of things. When she was small her father had called her his "Moon Princess" because she was so pale and golden; and, all evidence to the contrary—she was much stronger physically than Margaret, for instance—she had always rather enjoyed the idea that she was a creature too delicate for the harsh rigors of the day.

Smiling at her fancies, she glanced over at Margaret, who was still earnestly at work on her letter. "Meggie, what do you think of our American cousins now that we have gotten to know them a bit?"

Margaret put down her pen with a sigh. "Rebecca, I *must* finish this letter. You heard Cousin Edouard say that the packet was coming tomorrow. I can't finish it if you keep talking to me. And please don't call me Meggie. You know how much I hate that name."

"I know. That's why I used it, knowing that it would catch your attention," Rebecca said unrepentantly. "But now, since I've so rudely interrupted you, what *do* you think of them?"

Margaret sat looking down at the letter in front of her, half of her mind still on what she had been writing. "Oh, I think they are very nice. At least, they have been extraordinarily kind to us, and they seem to be very well-bred, not at all what most people back home think Americans are like."

"Hmm. And attractive, too. Don't you think they are an attractive family, particularly the men?"

Color rose in Margaret's face. "Why, yes. I suppose so, although Armand always seems to be in a foul temper. It is difficult to find a man attractive when he is so brusque."

Rebecca stretched against the back of her chair. "Yes, that's true enough. Still, he is a handsome brute, you must admit. It's indeed a pity that he hasn't a more agreeable nature. Of course, Jacques is just as handsome, and his temperament is agreeable, certainly. Don't you find it so?"

Margaret flushed again. She knew that Rebecca was deliberately baiting her, but, as usual, she didn't know quite what to do about it, except to do what she almost always did—pretend that she did not know Rebecca's purpose.

"Yes, Rebecca," she said quietly. "I agree that Cousin Jacques's temperament is very pleasant."

"And have you also noticed that Edouard is something of a ladies' man?"

Margaret looked up with a frown, wondering if this was another of Rebecca's little gambits, but her cousin's face was quite serious and thoughtful. "Rebecca, how can you say that! You really are awful. After he's been so kind to us. He *is* a married man, you know, and he must be at least fifty!"

Rebecca shook her head in amusement. "Oh, Meg! You really are so naive! We have spent our whole lives in the same places and under the same circumstances, and yet I often think you go through life with blinders on. If I were to tell you of all the married men— some of them older men, friends of our fathers—who have flirted with me, and even, on some occasions, attempted to go further...then you would really have occasion to be shocked!"

Margaret, her cheeks now flaming red, resolutely picked up her pen and turned to her letter. "And you really are mean sometimes, Rebecca. You know I hate that sort of talk, and besides, I don't believe a word of it. You are just feeling bored and want to enliven things by teasing me."

Rebecca, recognizing Margaret's genuine distress, sighed. She and Margaret could talk about so many things, and yet there were some things that Margaret simply would not discuss. It was as if anything regarding men and women and their relationships was frightening or shocking to her, which was utterly ridiculous, as these relationships did in fact exist and were obviously an important part of life, a part of life that Rebecca, personally, found irresistibly interesting. It would be so much nicer if she could discuss such matters with Margaret, but she supposed she might as well cease any efforts in that direction.

Rebecca was roused from her thoughts by a knock on the door, and Margaret put down her pen and got up from the desk.

"Now who do you suppose that can be?" She darted a quick glance at Rebecca, and her cheeks pinked again. "Rebecca! Please! Do pull your skirts down. I certainly cannot answer the door with you sitting there like that!"

With a shrug, Rebecca pulled her peignoir down decorously, so that only her bare feet showed.

The knock came again, louder this time.

"Rebecca, your feet. Do put them down or cover them. Please!"

Rebecca drew her feet up so that they were hidden under her skirts. "There, Margaret dear. Am I decent enough for you now?"

Margaret, still flushed, flounced away to open the door.

In the doorway, carrying a large silver tray, upon which could be seen a tall painted china pot, two delicate cups and saucers, and a plate of biscuits and cakes, stood the factotum, Dhupta.

"Oh," Margaret said.

Dhupta, his thin, dark face showing no expression whatsoever, gave a slight nod of his head. "The mistress thought that you might care for some refreshments before retiring. May I?"

"Oh, yes, of course." Margaret stepped back.

Dhupta came on into the room. He placed the tray upon the small round table that stood in the center of the room.

Rebecca studied him with undisguised interest. He spoke English quite well, with no trace of an accent, and his manners could not be faulted. Why, then, did she get the feeling that he disliked both her and Margaret?

"Shall I pour, young misses?"

"No, thank you, Dhupta," Margaret responded. "That is not necessary. Thank you very much."

The Indian bowed and backed out of the room, and Margaret closed the door after him.

"I don't know why," said Rebecca, rising and heading toward the table, "but that man disturbs me."

Margaret glared at her in exasperation. "Rebecca, you seem determined to be difficult tonight. As far as I can see, he appears to be the perfect servant. He is quiet, obedient and very efficient. And Felicity seems to depend on him a good deal."

"Mmm. Yes, perhaps too perfect." She poured out two cups of the creamy chocolate and chose a crisp sugared biscuit for herself. "As I said, I don't know *why* he makes me uncomfortable. Nonetheless, I would be willing to wager that there *is* something odd about him. For one thing, haven't you noticed his clothing?"

"What's wrong with his clothing?" Margaret reached for her cup of chocolate. "He dresses very well, if that's what you mean, but I would suppose that is the wish of the Molyneuxs."

Rebecca sighed heavily. "Margaret, he dresses in the style of a wealthy Brahman. Did you ever see any servant at home dressed in such a fashion? And he wears no caste mark. Also, he seemed to be a well-educated man. I cannot help but wonder how he came to be here and how he happens to be working as a servant. As for the feeling I get from him, well, I think that he dislikes us—you and me, that is—quite intensely."

"But he hasn't done the slightest thing or said the least thing out of the way. And besides, Rebecca, why *should* he dislike us?"

"Because we are English. Many Indians dislike *all* the British; you very well know that. Why do you think our fathers are always rushing off to quell some disturbance or another? It is not because the Indians are satisfied with their lot, you can be sure."

Margaret blinked. "I know they are always complaining about one thing or another, and I also know that there are some troublemakers among them, but I think you exaggerate, Rebecca. After all, they need us. We have done a great deal for India and her people."

Rebecca sat back and took a sip of the chocolate. "All I am saying, Margaret, is that all Indians do not love the British and that some of them are our enemies. Who is to say that this Dhupta is not one of those who hate us?''

''Well, I don't care to discuss it. As you very well know, I detest political discussions, particularly before bedtime.''

''I'm not sure this is a political discussion,'' Rebecca said with a small laugh. ''At any rate, I shall talk of something else. I didn't have time to tell you today, we've been so busy. Did you hear anything last night, after you went to bed? It was around midnight or perhaps one o'clock.''

Margaret stared at her askance. ''*What* was about midnight or one o'clock?''

Rebecca sighed. ''The sounds I heard. Did you hear anything?''

Margaret, still dubious, shook her head vigorously. ''Not a thing. Despite my nap, I was quite fatigued. I went right off to sleep after I finished making my toilet. What sounds, Rebecca? The music that you mentioned to Felicity at tea this afternoon?''

''That was only part of it.'' Rebecca put her cup and saucer down and leaned forward. ''Before that, I heard someone in my room. I'm sure of it. I couldn't see anything—it was too dark—but I'm sure I heard someone.''

Margaret's face had grown pale. ''Rebecca, are you teasing me again? If you are, it is very cruel of you.''

Rebecca said impatiently, ''No, Margaret. I swear I'm not. It was after I heard someone in my room that I heard the music. It sounded to me as if someone was playing one of those odd Chinese instruments.''

''But Felicity said that no one knows how to play them.''

Rebecca nodded quickly. "I know what she said. That's what I find curious. The whole incident strikes me as very strange, and I think it would be a good idea if we both kept our doors locked from now on. Now..." She sat back, picking up her chocolate. "I've said all I have to say. You may go ahead and finish your letter."

FOR TWO DAYS both the large carriage and the chaise had been going to and from the dock, picking up arriving guests for the gala. Many of them had been delivered by Edouard's beautiful sloop, the *Harbinger*. Others arrived in their own boats.

Looking out of her window, Rebecca watched as a fashionably dressed trio—two women and one man—walked among the sweet-smelling roses that surrounded the pavilion in front of the house.

Oh, it was going to be a wonderful gala, Rebecca just knew that it was. Edouard had spared no expense; the finest food and drink had been ordered, and Rebecca had been in the kitchen building behind the main house and had seen the dishes that were being prepared. It was certain that no one would go hungry and that almost any taste would be satisfied.

Felicity had had the house staff busy all week readying the house and the guest rooms—a veritable flurry of cleaning and polishing. Intricate arrangements of flowers beautified and scented all the rooms.

As for the guests themselves, Rebecca had already met a number of those who had arrived early, and in general, they seemed an interesting group. Ranging widely in ages, interests and occupations, they seemed to have two things in common—they were either clever or attractive and sometimes both. Rebecca hugged herself, feeling excitement rise in her like a thousand tiny bubbles. She was very glad that she and Margaret had made this trip. The past few days had been very pleasant, and she was certain that the weeks to come would be equally enjoyable—and a good deal of this anticipation had to do with Jacques.

He had been so kind, so attentive. He had taken them for walks and drives over the entire island, from the beautiful inland groves and meadows, to the peaceful marshes and lovely beaches, as well as to the family burial plot—a peaceful, green white-walled area surrounded with graceful weeping willows, which hung over the elegant marble mausoleum where Jean and Mignon Molyneux were interred.

Jacques often took the young women riding—there was an excellent stable—and sailing on both the *Harbinger* and on a smaller pleasure boat, the *Felicity.*

On Sunday he had escorted them and his mother to the nearest town, Beaufort, on the island of Port Royal, so that they might attend church. Beaufort was a charming place, with some lovely homes and several quite nice shops. Rebecca had wondered why Edouard did not accompany them and had been told that Edouard never attended church, for he was an atheist, a bit of information that surprised her.

Rebecca had never met a man who intrigued her so or who stirred in her romantic feelings as Jacques did. Accustomed to being in charge of any situation where boys and men were concerned, it was surprisingly pleasant to relinquish this control, or perhaps it would be more honest to say, "to have it taken away." With Jacques she never knew quite how he was going to react, because she was unable to manipulate him.

She had spent a good deal of time thinking about this, about why he seemed to be immune to her manipulations, but she had come to no firm conclusion, except that it was not because he did not find her desirable. She felt certain that he was strongly drawn to her, yet he seemed to be fighting the attraction. Rebecca was practiced at reading responses, both male and female, and time and time again, she had seen Jacques turn toward her. She had seen him hold back from touching her, except when necessary; had turned unexpectedly and caught the hungry look in his eyes. No, it wasn't for lack of desire for her, but then what was it? He was not betrothed; she had ascertained that during their first few days on the island, by dint of a little discreet questioning. He would make an ideal husband—handsome, charming, accomplished and sensitive. He might even make a good husband for *her*. She was startled by this sudden thought. Yet it was getting close to the time she should be thinking of marriage. Her own mother had been married when she was a year younger than Rebecca was now.

It was too bad that Armand was so bloody difficult, Rebecca thought, for wouldn't it have been a lark to have Margaret marry one brother and she the other? Then they would never have to be separated. But of course that was out of the question. Armand, who had been absent most of the week tending to his duties at Les Chênes, frightened Margaret, and he seemed to be equally ill at ease with both young women.

For the moment Rebecca toyed with the idea of being married to Armand herself, as if it was really a possibility, and of Margaret marrying Jacques. But this venture into fantasy left her with an odd feeling that she did not wish to investigate further, for something in the very thought both thrilled and repelled her.

Frowning, she turned away from the window. Why on earth should she even flirt with such an outlandish idea? She had best finish dressing and go downstairs. The festivities would be starting soon.

ARMAND STOOD IN THE DOORWAY of the ballroom, looking at the colorful assemblage inside with a jaundiced eye. He found no pleasure at the sight.

As usual, his father had spent a great deal of money to entertain his guests. There was a string quartet, imported from Savannah for the occasion, and the large, gracious ballroom was decorated with flowers and swags of ribands. The new rose-colored-glass hanging lamps that his father had had installed along the walls earlier in the year gave off a rosy glow that flattered the complexion and created a festive mood.

Yes, it all looked very attractive, and everyone seemed to be having a grand time, except for himself. Why did he let it matter so much? If his father spent more money than he should on frivolities, well, it was his father's business, his father's money. Still, it galled Armand, all of this money spent entertaining his parents' shallow friends, while his father refused to spend a cent on improvements for Les Chênes.

Of course, having the English cousins here was the excuse for this extravagance, but if they had *not* been here, Edouard Molyneux would have found some other excuse. It must be something in the blood, something that his father had inherited from *his* father, Jean Molyneux. Even Jacques had a touch of it. How had he, Armand, escaped? Why was he the only Molyneux who seemed to think of practical things?

Well, he was here, unwillingly perhaps, but he might as well try to make the best of it—to please Felicity, if nothing else.

Looking around the room for her, he saw Felicity standing near the punch table that was situated off to one side, at the end of the room where the musicians were seated. She was talking to a rather portly gentleman who had his back to Armand.

As he made his way through the crowd toward her, Armand's attention was snagged by the figure of Rebecca moving gracefully through the movements of the dance on his brother's arm.

Scowling, he slowed to a stop, watching them intently, torn by the uncomfortable mix of emotions that the damned girl always invoked in him. She was so uncommonly beautiful! Every time he saw her, it struck him anew, like a blow to the midsection. Why did she have to look like that? Any man who saw her would want her, on the basis of her appearance alone. No matter, he told himself, that she was spoiled, arrogant and an Englishwoman to boot. Being near her still fired an ache in him that drove deep into his body. Observing her and his brother, he had to wonder if Jacques experienced the same ache, the same surge of wanting. Jacques and he had never been close—they were too dissimilar—but for a moment he felt an unaccustomed pity for his brother.

As the dancers turned Armand saw his father and one of the women guests dancing near Jacques and Rebecca, and the look upon his father's face as he stared at Rebecca caused Armand's scowl to darken. Edouard's lecherous ways always embarrassed Armand, and not only for Felicity's sake. There was something foolish about an aging man panting after

young women like a superannuated satyr. His anger
spiraled as he thought of Edouard making an advance to Rebecca, but surely even Edouard would have
the good sense to refrain from forcing his attentions
upon the daughter of his own cousin!

He watched as Rebecca tilted her face up, like a
flower toward the sun, and gave Jacques a practiced
look that bespoke a veiled invitation.

So she was interested in Jacques. For a moment he
felt a savage gladness and then a feeling of deep
shame. It was an unworthy thought. Although she had
made it clear that she thought little of him, Armand,
he should not wish misery upon her. To be fair, he
knew that he had been responsible for her dislike by
being as ill-mannered and surly as possible to both
young women since their arrival on Pirate's Bank.

He had been in a black mood that first day; and although he now regretted his initial rude behavior, he
seemed unable to change it. He bore no ill will against
the quiet one, Margaret, but something in Rebecca's
personality challenged him, perhaps her obvious intelligence and teasing manner, which he found con-
descending.

However, he should not be standing here ogling her
like some raw bumpkin. He must greet Felicity and
attempt to make the best of the evening. At the very
worst, he should get a good meal out of it.

As he approached Felicity, Armand thought that
despite the fashionable gown, elaborate hairstyle and
a careful application of rouge and pearl powder, her
face looked drawn.

Again he felt a blaze of anger at his father. Did the
man never bother to think that the frequent galas he
so enjoyed giving took a great deal of work and prep-

aration? Didn't he realize that even with all the servants to help, his wife always worked herself to the
point of exhaustion to prepare for such an event?
Edouard, of course, never raised a hand! Armand
scowled to himself. A bad choice of phrase, that.

Then he was at her side, and she broke off her conversation to smile at him. Her smile was too bright,
and her eyes had a glitter—the rum punch, Armand
was sure.

She took his arm and squeezed affectionately. "Armand, you know Mr. Sterling, don't you?"

Armand gave a short bow. Joshua Sterling was an
individual of middle years who was noted for being
one of the greatest gossips in Beaufort County. Armand found the man vapid and affected, but he forced
himself to be polite for Felicity's sake.

"To be sure. How have you been keeping, Mr.
Sterling?"

Sterling smiled and nodded rapidly. "Admirably,
sir. Admirably, yes, indeed. I was just telling your
charming mother that I had the pleasure of traveling
home from Charleston on the packet that brought
your two lovely cousins to the island. Delightful girls,
yes, indeed!"

The man's gaze had turned to follow Rebecca, and
he smirked as she bowed to Jacques at the end of the
dance. As she did so, the bodice of her dress—which
was cut far too low, in Armand's judgment—exposed
the top portion of the pale, almost luminescent
mounds of her breasts.

Armand felt a powerful desire to smash his fist into
Sterling's smug, pink, well-powdered face. Another
aging satyr; but, of course, the fault was not his alone.
There she stood, exposing herself in that, he sup-

posed, fashionable dress, the thin white material of which clung to the lines of her figure and exposed her delicate ankles and narrow feet in the flat white satin slippers. It was no wonder that men stared at her.

Jacques and Rebecca were now coming toward them, and Armand saw that Sterling was straightening his cravat. Armand knew, of a certainty, that the man was going to request the next dance with Rebecca, and the thought of her on the arm of that pompous ass was suddenly more than he could bear.

When Rebecca and Jacques were still a few feet away, he moved quickly toward them and bowed low to Rebecca, who stopped and gazed at him with an unfathomable look.

"Cousin, I believe that the next dance is mine," Armand said as he nodded a greeting to his brother.

Jacques smiled and relinquished Rebecca's arm, his glance going to his mother and Joshua Sterling. "I certainly hope it is," he said in an amused tone. "For if it is not, I can see that Joshua Sterling there has it in mind to request the next dance, Rebecca. Although Sterling fancies himself an excellent dancer, many young women have complained to me that he danced more upon their feet than his."

Involuntarily Armand drew back against the sudden brightness of Rebecca's smile.

She said, "Why, of course this is your dance, Armand, and I think the music is about to begin."

Chapter Five

AS THE MUSIC BEGAN and they took their places on the floor, Armand felt the touch of Rebecca's gloved hand upon his arm and fancied that he could feel the heat of her hand through his clothing.

Acutely conscious of her presence, he suddenly felt a desire to show her that he was something other than the clod that he had made himself out to be. Although he did not dance very often, he had an aptitude for the pastime, and when he made the effort, he could be an excellent dancer.

It pleased him that Rebecca took on an expression of mild surprise as they went though the figures of the dance. When the pattern brought them close to one another, Armand initiated a conversation.

"Have you been enjoying your visit to Pirate's Bank, Rebecca?"

"Why, yes, very much indeed. Everyone has been most kind, and the island is very beautiful."

At the next near approach, she said, "We have not seen much of you, Armand."

"I know. It is necessary that I spend a good deal of my time at Les Chênes, supervising the cotton crop. It will soon be time to pick."

His words were polite, yet Armand's thoughts were angry, for he could not help thinking that it was the cotton crop that would be paying for this extravagant evening. He was also thinking that it was ridiculous that social conversation between men and women had to be so artificial, as well as superficial. Of course, what he really wanted to do was not to talk at all, but to take Rebecca by the arm and lead her outside into the warm, perfumed darkness, crush her in his arms and bruise her lips with his until he had shattered her maddening veneer of composure and self-satisfaction, until she collapsed in his arms, weak with a desire to equal his!

Rebecca, watching Armand's dark, brooding face, was somewhat bemused. She had agreed to dance with him on a whim—there had been something so hot and dangerous behind his handsome face when he had claimed her for the dance that it had stirred in her a dark and rather frightening response. And, of course, it pleased her to have him ask.

That inner heat was still present, burning behind his eyes, and she recognized it well. With some pleasure she realized that his pose of disinterest was just that— a pose. He was human, after all, and just as susceptible to female charms as any other man.

Should she be nice to him or now that she sensed her power over him, be cruel? But he *was* being well-mannered and gentlemanly this evening, so she decided that she would be kind. As they turned in the dance, she smiled at him over her shoulder.

TURNING AWAY from Joshua Sterling after thanking him for the dance, Margaret found Jacques smiling down at her.

"My dance, I believe, Margaret?"

Already flushed from exertion, Margaret felt her cheeks flame. Wordlessly she held out her arm.

As Jacques swept her away he nodded in the direction of Sterling. "I'll wager you didn't really mean that. You couldn't have much enjoyed dancing with him."

Margaret had to smile. She found it so easy to talk with Jacques, despite the usual difficulty she had in making conversation with other men. "He did trod on my toes a time or two," she said lightly. How was it that Jacques could make her feel so poised and charming?

Once she had gotten over her initial nervousness at meeting so many strangers, Margaret had begun to enjoy the evening. There had been a surfeit of dancing partners; and although Rebecca was, as usual, the primary center of attention, the guests also seemed interested in her, and she had received a good deal of attention on her own.

This was her second dance with Jacques, and since it was a galop there was little opportunity to exchange pleasantries, but she didn't mind too much. She did not even mind that, while they danced, his gaze often sought out Rebecca, who was dancing with Armand. Margaret could not help noticing how handsome Rebecca and Armand looked together—he so dark and masculine, she so fair and feminine. The contrast was striking. It made Margaret uncomfortable in some way she did not understand; and so she tore her glance away from them, thinking that a man like Jacques was so much safer, so much more comfortable, than a man like Armand.

It was Jacques, she was beginning to realize, that Rebecca was going to marry. She felt a deep certainty concerning this and was already quite resigned to it. Jacques was the most perfect of men, Rebecca the most perfect of women, so it was only natural that they should be attracted to one another. Margaret's own feelings toward this kind, charming man, she carefully avoided thinking about. She did not find it odd that, although she often knew what was going to happen to other people, she rarely thought about or pictured her own future. She never mentioned this fact to her friends or family, not even to Rebecca, for most young women she knew talked incessantly about men and about the kind of man they wished to marry. They would think her very odd indeed if she admitted that she seldom thought about men, as men, or about marriage.

ALTHOUGH THE PARTY went on until quite late, Margaret excused herself early and retired to her room.

She had enjoyed herself very much, but after a certain amount of time spent in the company of a large number of people, she always reached a point where she had experienced enough stimulation and wished to be by herself.

The sounds of music and laughter followed her down the hallway, and she was humming lightly to herself when a shadowy form appeared abruptly in her path.

Startled, she gave a slight gasp, but then she saw that the figure was that of Dhupta. He stood aside with a slight bow to let her pass, but his smooth features looked forbidding in the dim light, and Margaret could not help thinking of Rebecca's appraisal of the man.

Feeling slightly uneasy, she hurried on to her room, not looking back, although she had the feeling that he had turned and was watching her.

Once in her room, her good spirits revived. She felt pleasantly weary and looked forward to slipping into her soft bed. Margaret had always enjoyed sleeping, finding slumber both an escape and a refreshment. As she eased between the crisp sheets, relishing the smell of the fresh linen, she thought of Jacques and the delight she had experienced dancing with him. Easily she drifted into sleep, never noticing when the music finally stopped, the voices stilled and darkness settled over the big house.

IT WAS A LOVELY DREAM. She and Jacques were in one of the hidden pavilions, deep in the woods. Everything around them was green and softly lit, as if by hidden lanterns. From somewhere out of sight came the sound of music—string music, played in an Oriental scale—and she and Jacques were dancing to the music. It did not seem strange to be doing so, nor did it seem strange that the pavilion was, somehow, as large inside as a small ballroom.

As they danced Jacques reached out toward her and touched her arm. This, too, seemed natural to Margaret, and quite pleasant. Then he touched her face, drawing his finger down one cheekbone and under her chin, and that *did* seem odd. And then his hand was upon her breast, and she felt shock and a kind of sick horror as the scene began to fade. She woke with a muted cry dying in her throat, certain that the intruding touch had not been a part of the dream, but frightening reality.

Panting, her heart thudding, Margaret lay staring into a darkness that seemed stifling. She could see and hear nothing except the pounding of her own blood in her ears. However, her skin prickled with the feeling that she was not alone.

Terrified now, she thought about what Rebecca had told her concerning her own, similar experience, and Margaret tried to remember whether or not she had locked her door. She was certain that she had.

And then she heard the music, the same music that she had heard in the dream. It was quite faint, but the fact that it was there at all added to her terror. Rebecca's story had not, then, been a fabrication. The implications were horrifying. Someone in this house walked during the night. This person had been into Rebecca's room and now hers, while they slept, and that someone had just taken ... liberties with her person. She hugged herself, shivering.

Despite her overpowering fear, her face burned in the darkness. I must go to Rebecca, she thought. But she was afraid to light the candle, afraid of what she might see.

Finally, after what seemed an endless time during which the sound of the music faded and during which she heard no more unusual sounds in her room, Margaret reached for the candle holder. With trembling fingers she managed to light the wick. Not even stopping for her peignoir or her slippers, she ran to the door to the sitting room, through it and then to Rebecca's bedroom. In another moment she was at Rebecca's bed, shaking her violently.

Rebecca awoke reluctantly and stared at Margaret with sleep-fogged eyes.

"Margaret! What on earth? And do stop shaking me!"

Margaret, weak with relief now that Rebecca was awake, let go of the other young woman's shoulders and let her breath out with an explosive sound.

"Oh, Rebecca! I'm sorry that I didn't believe you before. I thought you were teasing me again, but I heard it, too."

Rebecca, frowning in puzzlement, sat up and placed her pillow behind her back. "Margaret, do you know how late it is? And what in heaven's name are you going on about?"

Margaret took a deep breath in order to calm herself. "Remember, you told me about hearing someone in your room and then hearing the sound of music? Well, the same thing just happened to me."

Rebecca was fully awake now. "There was someone in your room?"

Margaret nodded. "Yes, yes. And..and whoever it was *touched* me. I felt someone touch my arm and then my face..." Even to Rebecca, as close as they were, she could not bring herself to mention the touch upon her breast.

"I was so frightened. When I managed to gather my courage, I lit my candle and came here to see if you were all right. Oh, Rebecca, who do you suppose it was? And why would anyone do such a thing?"

Seeing the barely controlled fear on Margaret's face, Rebecca reached out and took her hand. "I really can't imagine," she said slowly. "It certainly is very strange, I agree. Did you remember to bolt your door before going to bed?"

Margaret bobbed her head. "The door to the hall, but the door to the sitting room was unlocked, as was yours."

Rebecca released Margaret's hand and leaned forward. "But the *outside* door to the sitting room was locked. I know, because I drew the bolt myself."

Margaret sucked in her breath sharply. "Then how did someone get in?"

"Perhaps there is a secret panel. I understand that many old houses have them, and it's the only logical explanation, unless our visitor is a ghost."

Margaret clapped a hand to her mouth. "Oh! Don't say such a thing! You don't suppose it could be...?"

"Of course not. Don't be absurd, Margaret," Rebecca said crossly.

Margaret shuddered. "Knowing that someone, a stranger, was there in my room, looking at me while I slept...touching me... Rebecca, what are we going to do? Should we tell Felicity or perhaps Edouard? After all, it *is* their house."

"No, I don't think that we should say anything," Rebecca said thoughtfully. "At least not just yet. Let's wait for a bit."

"But why wait? I mean, the person could come back. How will we ever be able to sleep, knowing that at any time some stranger can come into our rooms?"

"That's just it, don't you see? It might not *be* a stranger."

"Do you mean that it might be one of the family? Surely not!"

"Oh, Margaret, don't be such a ninny. If there is a secret passageway, who else but the family would know about it? Also, there aren't that many people on the island. You can't imagine that it's one of the slaves, can you? Why, they wouldn't dare do such a thing, even if they knew of such a passageway, which isn't very likely."

"It's still possible," Margaret said stubbornly.
"And then there is Dhupta. He isn't a member of the
family, and you said yourself that there was something odd about him." She remembered then. "You
know, I saw him tonight as I was going to my room.
He was coming down the corridor, and he looked at
me most boldly as I passed. Do you suppose that it
could be Dhupta? Perhaps you are right about what
you said, about him hating us. What if he means to
kill us in our beds?"

Rebecca slid down until her head rested on the pillow. "Well, he didn't, did he? Don't be so melodra-
matic, Margaret. Whoever was in our rooms didn't
hurt us or even try to hurt us, now did they?"

Margaret was silent, thinking again of the touch
upon her breasts. "Well, I don't like it one bit," she
finally said. "What are we going to do? We have to do
something."

Rebecca yawned widely. "I think right now we
should get some sleep. You can stay in here with me if
you like, and we'll leave the candle burning. In the
morning we'll look through both bedrooms and the
sitting room for a hidden panel. If we find it, perhaps
we can find some way to seal or block it off. After
that, we will wait to see what happens and act accordingly."

Margaret, feeling somewhat reassured by the prospect of taking some kind of action, slid into bed beside her cousin. Comforted by the light of the candle
and Rebecca's presence, she was soon asleep.

It was Rebecca who lay awake for a time, her
thoughts whirling, seeing in her mind's eye the faces
of the Molyneuxs and Dhupta and wondering which
of them was doing this strange thing, and why.

"LISTEN, I THINK this might be it!" Rebecca, her face pink from exertion, rapped smartly on the section of paneling on the right side of the fireplace in the sitting room and was rewarded by a hollow sound. "Can you hear the difference?" Moving to the right, she rapped upon the adjoining panel.

Margaret nodded excitedly. "Oh, yes! It sounds very different. Much more solid." She came over to Rebecca, who was now sliding her hands over the carving that bordered the first panel. She asked, "But how does it open?"

"There is usually a hidden spring to press, and it is usually concealed by some ornamentation," Rebecca said absently. "Do you remember the time we visited the Arlingtons at their country home when we were children? They had such a hidden passageway, and young Will Arlington showed it to me. It ran from one of the small salons, through the house and underground to the stables. Will told me that it had been built so that the original owners could escape the house if an enemy approached. The spring that opened the door was hidden in the center of one of the carvings bordering the panel. Will knew a good deal about such things, and he also told me that many old houses had such passageways all through them."

She stood back, looking along the panels. "There doesn't appear to be anything in the borders here. Let's try the fireplace. Will told me that sometimes the spring is hidden behind a brick that is movable."

Together they poked and pulled at the ornamental stonework around the fireplace. All of a sudden, as Margaret's fingers pressed into the base of a graceful stone leaf, she let out a cry. Her fingers had seemed to melt into the stone, and as they did so, there was a slight movement on her right.

"That's it, that's it!" Rebecca shouted. "You've found it!"

Margaret stepped back in alarm as the entire panel to the right of the fireplace slid back, almost noiselessly, to expose a rectangle of darkness.

Rebecca leaned over to peer inside. "I can't see a thing—it's as dark as a cave—but I can feel air moving. I wonder where it goes?" She wrinkled her nose. "Phew, it certainly has an aroma!"

Margaret took her arm, as if to hold her back. "I don't care where it goes. What worries me is that it is here in our sitting room. You said if we found it, we would block it, but how will we manage to do that?"

Rebecca gazed thoughtfully at the opening. "Well, since it *is* in our sitting room, there is really no problem. We will just lock our doors to this room, as well as our doors into the hallway."

"But that means we won't have access to one another's rooms. What if one of us should need the other during the night?"

"Whichever one needs the other will simply have to unbolt her door and go and rap on the door of the other. I must confess that I feel much better now that I know where our mysterious night visitor has been getting in."

Margaret turned away abruptly. "I am not certain that I do... Oh, perhaps a bit, but the very *idea* that someone is doing this is quite upsetting."

"I know," Rebecca said with a sigh. "I feel that way, too. Perhaps if we explored the passageway..."

"No!" Margaret said violently. "You mustn't even think of it. It would be the utmost folly. Who knows what's down there? We will do as you said, keep our doors locked. Perhaps nothing more will happen.''

Rebecca touched her palm to the same pattern Margaret had pressed, and the door slid smoothly shut. "Very well, but I shall do one other thing. I'm going to talk to Felicity. Not to tell her what we found, but just to ask her, casually, you know, if the house has any passageways. That way we can at least learn if she knows about it."

"Why not ask Jacques? We will be riding with him again this afternoon."

Rebecca stared at her in exasperation. "It could be Jacques."

Margaret's hand went to her throat. "Oh, it couldn't be Jacques!"

"But we have no idea, have we? And until we do I think it is safer to ask Felicity. She is, after all, a woman."

Chapter Six

IT WAS LATE AFTERNOON of a warm, lazy day, and Rebecca, Margaret, Jacques and Armand had just finished a game of whist in the small salon.

Since that first party, Armand had been spending more time at Maison de Rêverie, and Rebecca suspected that she was the reason for the frequency of his visits. Also, his manners had definitely improved. It flattered her that she had had such an effect on him and pleased her, as well, for it really made things much more pleasant, to have two escorts when she and Margaret went walking or riding. As often as was decently possible, she managed to arrange it so that Jacques was paired with her, and Armand with Margaret, much to Margaret's displeasure.

Although she thought often of both men, Rebecca thought of them in different ways. Thinking about Armand was darkly exciting, in an almost frightening way, but she was quite certain now that she was in love with Jacques and that she wanted to marry him. After all, she would have to marry someone, and she really had no liking for any of the young army officers she had encountered in India. Army men—her father and uncle being the exceptions to the rule—were a stiff and rather pompous lot. The only problem seemed to be in getting Jacques to propose, and she found it puzzling that he had not already done so.

Although she usually didn't have to make any effort to attract a man, Rebecca found herself having to use all her wiles and charm to win Jacques. He responded by being in her company as often as possible, and with admiring glances, but he still had not said one word to declare himself, and the date was fast approaching when she and Margaret must return to India. Perhaps if she had an opportunity to be alone with Jacques, he would speak what she knew must be in his heart. She was determined that he should do so; she did not wish to leave this lovely island and this seemingly charmed life.

During the three months that she had spent here, she had grown more and more enchanted with the island and the Molyneuxs' gracious and easy way of life. Edouard had given two more parties, and everyone had spared no effort to see that the two young Englishwomen enjoyed themselves. There had been no reappearance of their mysterious night visitor, and Felicity, when Rebecca questioned her, had denied knowledge of any passageway. The whole affair had almost faded from Rebecca's thoughts.

As they had become better acquainted with the Molyneux family, Rebecca discovered a number of things. One was that she had been quite accurate when she had told Margaret that she suspected Edouard of being a womanizer. So far he had done nothing really overt, but the unnecessary touches, the way he held her when they danced, the look in his eye, caused her to be very careful never to be left alone with him. Despite the fact that she considered herself fairly sophisticated and tolerant of male foibles, Rebecca thought that since he was her father's cousin, a married man and older than her father, it was bad form for him to make advances toward her, no matter how subtle. Still, he was very good to both her and Margaret and had entertained them royally. She bore him no ill will, for she thought that she understood and thus could cope with him.

On the other hand, Felicity, whom Rebecca thought would be easy to understand, had proven to be a bit of a mystery. Rebecca felt that she had a talent for understanding people and their motives, and it always intrigued her, and piqued her a bit as well, whenever she had difficulty fixing a person in her mind.

In Felicity's case, it was a matter of inconsistency. When she was alone with Rebecca and Margaret, she was a great talker, animated and charming, with a sly sense of humor. However, when Edouard was present, she was like another person—subdued, and very obviously, to Rebecca, apprehensive.

Also, although Felicity was certainly not a delicate woman and usually seemed the very picture of health, she seemed to suffer from some sort of recurring ailment. Some days she would not come out of her room for the entire day, and when she did finally emerge, she would walk stiffly, as if in pain, and her face would be pale.

But she never spoke of her condition, and Rebecca didn't think it would be diplomatic to introduce the subject. Still, it did make her curious.

Now, Armand placed his cards upon the table and glanced at Jacques. "I must return to Les Chênes in the morning. What do you say to bringing Rebecca and Margaret to the mainland and riding with me? We could take along a hamper and have a picnic. After we have shown them the place, you can escort them home. That is, if the ladies are at all interested."

"A capital idea!" Jacques glanced at Rebecca and Margaret in turn. "What do you say? There isn't a great deal to see there, except the cotton and indigo fields, but there is a fine stream and a rather lovely meadow nearby. It might make a nice day's diversion for you."

Margaret said at once, "I think it sounds delightful! Don't you, Rebecca?"

Rebecca pretended to consider the proposal. She wanted to go, naturally. She was interested in seeing the plantation, and she was curious to see the place where Armand spent so much of his time. Still, she did not want to appear too eager.

"Why, I suppose it might be pleasant," she said in a bored voice. "If you all wish to go, I suppose I shall go with you."

THE MEADOW, as Jacques had promised, was lovely, an expanse of green, brightened by scattered wildflowers. A clean, narrow stream ran the length of it, bordered here and there by the huge, spreading oaks that had given the plantation its name. The four young people and their mounts paused for a moment upon a slight rise at the edge of the meadow.

Jacques gestured with his riding crop. "See that hill opposite us? That is where the old plantation house was located. They say that it was quite handsome in its day."

Rebecca gazed curiously at the low mound of the hill. Only a low pile of rubble remained to show where the building had once been. "It must have had a beautiful view," she said. "What happened to it—the house, I mean?"

"It was burned," said Armand, and his voice had a strange, harsh timbre that caused Rebecca to look at him curiously. "It was burned to the ground on the same night that Jean Molyneux and his wife died."

Margaret gasped in shock. "How terrible! Was anyone hurt in the fire?"

Armand didn't remove his gaze from the ruins of the old building. "Yes, a man and his wife, and two house slaves."

Rebecca, watching him closely as he spoke, had a strange feeling that Armand knew a great deal more about what had transpired those long years ago than he was telling them, and he had an emotional involvement in this past tragedy. She could not imagine what it could be, but it intrigued her.

When the silence grew too lengthy, she finally asked, "What was the family's name?"

Armand did not answer.

"Huntoon," Jacques finally said. "Richard and Elizabeth Huntoon. There was a child, a daughter, Elissa, but fortunately her nursemaid woke up in time and took the child from the house before the fire spread to her room."

"What happened to the child?" Margaret asked.

"She had no known relatives, so she and her nursemaid, a black woman named Bess, were taken in at Maison de Rêverie, and she was raised as a sister to our father, being near his age."

Rebecca frowned. "But who looked after them? They were both orphans."

"My grandmother's sister and her husband came to the island and took charge of things until my father was old enough to assume his inheritance." Jacques broke off with a rueful smile. "But we had best turn our thoughts to less gloomy matters. After all, we brought you here to show you the plantation and the beauties of the spot, and here we have been talking of death and destruction.''

Armand did not seem to hear his brother, but Rebecca could see his lips tighten at the implied rebuke.

All of a sudden he spurred his horse into a trot toward a huge oak tree on the bank of the stream, and the other horses moved to follow. However, there was still something that Rebecca wished to know, and she reined her horse over close to Jacques's mount.

''Jacques, just one more question, if you please. What happened to her in the end? To the girl, Elissa? Did she marry and leave?''

He shook his head. ''That is another sad thing, Rebecca, and we have talked enough today of sad things. Come, we'll settle ourselves in the shade of that tree and wreak havoc upon the hamper of food that Mother packed for us.''

He spurred his horse into a brisk trot, and Rebecca, far from satisfied, was forced to follow suit. She was not resigned to his answer and was determined to find out the answer to her question at the first opportunity.

In the deep shade of the oak, with an excellent feast spread out before them upon a linen cloth, talk turned to happier matters.

After a few glasses of good wine, even Armand seemed to shake off his usual dour mood, and soon the four of them were laughing and conversing easily.

When the food was finished they visited the small white wooden house where Armand lived when he was at the plantation. It was very modest, with only a few rooms, but Rebecca was a little surprised to see that it was very neat, clean and quite comfortable looking.

There were several fine pieces of furniture in the parlor, which evidently also functioned as a library, for the walls were lined with shelves, all filled with books. There was also what looked to be a very good piano, and several excellent paintings hung upon the walls. She inspected the paintings but found that she was unfamiliar with the names of the artists, except for that of Charles Stuart, whom she knew to be an American artist of some reputation. The house was not quite what she had expected, and she wondered who kept the place so immaculate.

Adopting a light tone, she said, "It seems very cozy here, Armand. You must have a good house staff to do for you."

Armand shrugged. "Only one person," he said. "It is a small house, after all."

Stepping to the fireplace mantel, he picked up a small, ornately etched silver bell and rang it. The sound was sweet and clear.

After a moment a tall, light-skinned black woman appeared in the doorway. Her high cheekbones and narrow lips seemed to belie the amber-brown of her skin, and her dark hair, which was only moderately curly, was uncovered and drawn back into a knot at the back of her head.

Rebecca tried to conceal her start of surprise, for the woman was very striking.

"This is Lutie. Housekeeper, maid and cook." Armand seemed to be enjoying the effect the woman was having upon the two young women, for he smiled faintly.

Rebecca frowned slightly. The woman, although probably a good ten years older than Armand, was entirely *too* good-looking to be living alone with an unmarried man. Rebecca could not help but wonder if housework was *all* the woman did for him. Feeling more than a little put out, she nodded coolly to the woman and then turned away abruptly, feeling that she had seen quite enough of her.

After leaving the house, they inspected the outbuildings of the plantation and the cotton field. The long rows of stalky plants, with their bursting pods startlingly white against the brown stalks, gave the impression of abundance and order.

Slaves, both male and female, long cotton sacks looped over their shoulders, were in the field picking the crop. Their movements looked graceful and practiced and made rather a pretty picture. Rebecca commented to that effect.

"It may look like a pretty picture to you, but it's damn hard work," Armand said sourly. "Those cotton bolls are rough and sharp, the workers' hands become badly cut. It's also backbreaking labor, stooping like that all day."

Rebecca, who had been feeling quite mellow after the fine meal and the wine, gave him a sharp, annoyed look. Why did he always feel it necessary to make everything seem so unpleasant? It was as if he could not stand to see anyone, particularly himself, happy for more than a few moments.

Turning her back on him, she smiled over at Jacques. "You know, I think I'd like to ride to the top of the hill where the old house stood and inspect the ruins. Would anyone care to accompany me?"

"I think I'd rather return to the stream and rest for a bit," Margaret said. "It's quite a long trip back, and a brief nap under that old oak would refresh us before starting out."

Jacques smiled impartially at both women. "She's right, Rebecca. We really should be starting back before long, and a brief rest sounds good to me, too. We were up so early this morning. Besides, there's really nothing to see."

Rebecca, who had naturally assumed that Jacques would immediately fall in with her suggestion, felt her cheeks flush. She said sharply, "Well, I don't feel the need for a nap. In fact, I feel quite energetic. I'll just ride on by myself, then, if you don't mind. I'll meet you all back at the stream."

Jacques raised his eyebrows. "But you should not go alone..."

"I will be happy to go with you, Rebecca," Armand said, his voice colored with what sounded to Rebecca like amusement. "I wouldn't want it to be said that we did not treat you gallantly, and it would be most *un*gallant of us to let you go wandering off by yourself. Jacques, you and Margaret go on ahead. We will join you in about half an hour. That will give us time to ride back to the boat before dark."

Furious, Rebecca quirted her horse. There was nothing that made her angrier than to outsmart herself. She didn't often do it, but she had certainly done it this time. Her plan for this day had been to arrange it so that she might have some time alone with Jacques. Now she was going to be alone with Armand!

In her anger, she applied the quirt again, this time harder than she had intended. With a startled snort, her mount bolted. She shouted in fear, then gave up trying to rein the animal in. She tightened her leg around the front of the sidesaddle and hung on with both hands.

Why was it that women had to ride sidesaddle? At least if she was astraddle the horse, she could grip with both her legs and her thighs.

Hearing the pound of hoofbeats behind her, she risked a terrified glance over her shoulder. Armand was coming after her, leaning low over his mount's mane, urging him on.

Rebecca clung to her horse with all her strength. Then out of the corner of one eye, she saw Armand's horse drawing even with her on the right.

"Hold on!" he shouted.

Then he was alongside her. Leaning far over to his left, he looped one arm around her body. "All right, Rebecca, let go now. I have you."

She had to force herself to let go, and then, with a rib-bruising jerk, she was swept off the racing horse by Armand's powerful arm. She hung suspended for a heart-stopping moment in space, with the ground racing past, until Armand could rein his horse to a halt. Lowering Rebecca to the ground, he eased himself out of the saddle. Weak with relief, Rebecca leaned against him, and he put his arm around her. He smelled of male sweat, and his body felt as strong and secure as a rock. They stood for a moment without speaking.

"That was a very foolish thing to do, Rebecca," he said in a harsh voice.

"I know. I'm sorry. I didn't mean to..." her voice faltered. Why was she apologizing to this man? And why hadn't Jacques rescued her?

She looked up and met Armand's glance. He was still holding her against him, and she was acutely aware of their closeness. His dark eyes blazed down at her, not in anger but in naked desire. His face was very close, and she could feel his breath hot on her cheek.

Then she was pulling away from him, stepping back, tugging and smoothing at her disarranged clothing. Without once looking at him, she said in a low voice, "Thank you, Armand."

"You could have been badly hurt, you know," he said gruffly.

To save a response, she turned to look behind her. She saw Jacques galloping his horse toward them. He was a little late, she thought angrily. At that moment she did not want to see him, to talk to him. She waved her arms, calling out, "It's all right, Jacques. I'm fine."

He reined his horse in, staring at her for a moment, then turned and rode to the spot where Margaret was waiting.

Rebecca glanced around and saw the horse she had been riding, grazing contentedly, fifty yards away. She also saw that the runaway animal had headed straight for the knoll in his flight.

"Well, at least he bolted in the right direction," she said with a shaky laugh. "Shall we go on?" She finally looked at Armand.

His face was without expression, the fire in his eyes banked now. "I suppose we might as well."

He extended his arm. Rebecca took it, and they started walking toward the mound.

The view from the top of the hill was indeed grand, but Rebecca only gave it a part of her attention. They picked their way among the fallen and charred stones of the ruined mansion, and Rebecca pretended a great interest in these items so that she would not have to meet Armand's gaze.

The remains of a huge chimney stood above the ruins like a lonely sentinel, and suddenly Rebecca was swept by a feeling of melancholy, a feeling usually foreign to her nature. Despite the beauty of the view, there was something very sad about this spot, she thought. Perhaps it was the spirits of those who had died so horribly here. Or perhaps it was simply a reminder that no matter how grand the building, it could be easily destroyed; no matter how lofty your plans, they, too, could be destroyed, cruelly and unexpectedly. Property, people—everything that man did or built—could be brought down in a moment, by an act of either man or nature.

She faced about, looking in the direction of the stream, where she could just make out the tiny forms of Jacques and Margaret reclining in the shade of the oak. Restlessly she picked her way to the other side of the ruins.

"Rebecca?"

She felt Armand's touch on her elbow and, turning, found herself face-to-face with him.

At such close quarters she could not avoid his eyes, and when she looked up she found them fixed upon her with a burning intensity. His breath was coming quickly, and she knew, before he pulled her toward him, what was about to happen, and yet she did not demur, did not pull back.

As he brought her rather roughly against him, one part of her mind took note of the fact that his horse stood between them and the slope of the hill so that their actions would not be visible from the stream below.

And then she was only aware of Armand's lips upon hers and his arms hard around her. She could smell the wool of his coat and the faint scent of pomade. His breath was sweet and his lips hot; and for an instant, she felt a pleasant fire that started low in her abdomen, a fire that she instinctively knew could consume them both.

It took great effort of will, but she pushed him away in a great confusion of feeling, part of which was fear and part anger at herself, as well as him. Almost without thinking, she slapped his face.

For an instant they stood toe to toe, like adversaries, as her handprint flamed red upon his now-white face. Rebecca could feel her heart pounding fiercely, and her breathing was uneven.

"How dare you!" she said harshly. "You had no right!"

Armand started to raise his hand, and she drew back at the violence in his eyes. Slowly he dropped his hand, and the fire in his eyes dulled. He nodded stiffly.

"I had no right, true," he said, "but you wanted it, also. Even if you deny it, your body told me differently."

Rebecca felt a hot wash of anger at his arrogance but was for once at a loss for words. How could she deny that she had not stopped him immediately, but had kissed him back with the same passion with which he had kissed her? And then she felt her wits and her control return.

"The body does not always speak for the mind or for the heart," she said crisply. "You may as well know that I care for someone else, so I would appreciate it if you would bear that in mind in the future."

"Jacques?" His smile was a bitter grimace. "Of course you mean Jacques. You are in love with my charming brother. You think that he is more of a gentleman than I, and that because he speaks well and is kind, he will make a good husband."

Rebecca's cheeks flamed. "What I think and feel is my business alone," she said coldly.

"Well, you are mistaken about Jacques." Armand laughed roughly. "But have it your way, Rebecca. I will make no further demands upon you. You are an arrogant and bossy woman, but then it is true that Jacques takes a saddle better than I do. I wish you joy of one another!" He turned on his heel and strode toward where her horse grazed. She stared after him in outrage.

In a moment he led her horse through the rubble to her. In a distant voice he said, "If you will permit me to put hands upon you one last time, ma'am, I will help you mount, and then you may ride back to your prospective lover."

Her face set against him, Rebecca accepted his help in mounting, knowing that she could not manage alone; but as soon as she was firmly in the saddle, she turned her horse and headed for the stream and Jacques without a backward look.

Armand, his face fixed in a black scowl, watched Rebecca as she rode down the slope and across the meadow. He felt at once hot with anger and cold with loss. By God, he was not wrong! He knew in his heart that he was right. When he had taken her into his arms, she had not repulsed him; and when he had

kissed her, he had felt her body burn with the same fire
that blazed in his.

Why were women so perverse? She wanted him, as
he wanted her; and yet she felt called upon to deny it—
to him and to herself. She thought that she loved
Jacques. What a tragic farce! If he could only tell her
about Jacques, but of course he could not. Even
though Jacques and he had little in common, they
were still brothers; and he had sworn an oath of silence. Besides, even if he was free to tell her, Rebecca
would not believe him, perverse creature that she was.

And of course Jacques would never go so far as to
marry her, not under the circumstances. Although,
like Edouard, he had many frivolous habits and lacked
a certain strength of character, he certainly would not
do something as cruel and unfair as that. No, Rebecca would find that she was wasting her time attempting to lure Jacques into marriage, and she would
return to India and be lost to them both.

Damn all women! He swore to himself that here-
after he would remain at Les Chênes until it was time
for them to leave for India. What was the point of
putting himself through the torture of seeing Rebecca
and not being able to touch her, of watching her flirt
outrageously with Jacques, or of watching Edouard
fawning over her like an overage lap dog?

Mounting up, Armand turned his horse toward the
small house that he called home. It might be small and
plain, but it was peaceful and it was his, at least for the
moment.

It had been his intention to ride as far as the boat
landing with them, but he was just as glad to be rid of
Rebecca Trenton.

ON THEIR WAY BACK to Pirate's Bank, Rebecca was unusually quiet. For some reason that scene on the hill with Armand kept playing itself over and over in her mind, and she found it extremely disturbing. She had the fancy that she could still feel his arms around her, still feel the scorch of his lips upon hers.

She was very annoyed that in this instance she had seemed to have no control over a man; this had never happened to her before. Somehow the situation had slipped out of her grasp. Why had she not pushed him away the very instant she knew what was going to happen? Even worse, why had she responded to his kiss? She had not wanted to.

And she had failed in her plan to get Jacques alone. All in all, despite the pleasant ride and the picnic under the oaks, it had been a very unsettling day.

As far as Margaret was concerned, it had been a nearly perfect day. The weather had been very nice, the ride to Les Chênes pleasant and the picnic delightful. It had been one of the best days she had experienced since coming here. Even the fact that Rebecca had fallen into one of her moods on the trip home had not taken the edge off Margaret's enjoyment of the outing. After all, she had long since grown accustomed to Rebecca's moods, and it was futile to worry about them, for they came and went in a cycle so mysterious as to be incomprehensible.

However, just as they were riding into Beaufort, she experienced one of her uncomfortable premonitions, and as the boat neared Pirate's Bank, it became stronger. Something was wrong. The feeling made her uneasy, but as was her wont, she did not speak of it. It was bad enough that she had these feelings, for it made her seem strange even to herself. She could not bear it if others thought her strange, too.

It was quite late when they finally returned to Maison de Rêverie, and as they approached the house in the dusk, Margaret could see that Felicity was waiting for them on the veranda.

"I had begun to think that you were lost," Felicity said. "Did you have a nice time?"

"Oh, yes," Margaret said, although her sense of unease was stronger. "It was a delightful day."

Rebecca, still brooding, said nothing.

"I expect you are all starving," Felicity said. "I had Cook prepare a cold supper for you, since I didn't know just when you would be returning. I also have some news for you. The packet came today, and there are letters for both of you from your parents."

She hesitated, then continued slowly, "Your parents wrote to Edouard also, and it seems as though there has been a change of plans concerning your return home. But then I had better let you read your own letters before we discuss it further."

Margaret said fearfully, "There is nothing wrong, is there? Our families are well?"

Felicity waved her hand. "Oh, it's nothing like that, my dear. Your families are fine. But do come in and read your letters, and you will see for yourself."

WITH A SIGH, Margaret dropped the letter she had been reading into her lap. "Mother says that we had best postpone our return to India. She says that the Pindarees are growing restless, and that Father is convinced there will be trouble soon."

Rebecca, who was still reading her letter, paused to look up. "Yes, and my father says that they are also worried about Baji Rao, who is growing impatient for our forces to withdraw from his dominions. Father has attempted to make his letter casual, but I sense that he is worried."

"Who is this Baji Rao?" asked Felicity.

"He is a powerful Indian ruler, the peshwa of the Mahrattas," Rebecca said. "There has been trouble with him in the past."

Margaret felt tears sting her eyes. This was undoubtedly the bad tidings that her premonition had been warning her of, and she was suddenly very fearful for her family. "Oh, Rebecca! Do you think they will be all right?"

Rebecca moved over to the divan where Margaret was sitting and put her arm around her cousin's shoulders. "Of course, dear. Both our fathers have fought many battles and have always come out unhurt. Besides, we aren't even certain that there will *be* an uprising. So far, there is only the threat of one. Everything could be quiet by now. These threats have been made before, and nothing came of them."

Margaret said dolefully, "Or they could be in the midst of a terrible battle! Oh, I wish it didn't take so long for letters to reach us. These letters were posted months ago. Anything could have happened by now."

"There, child, don't fret so," Felicity said soothingly. "I'm sure that everything is fine and that your parents are safe. The letter they sent to Edouard requested that he keep you with us until we get further news from them. We are really quite pleased not to be losing you so soon. You are welcome to stay as long as you wish. You cannot imagine how pleasant it has been for me, having you here. It can be quite lonely for a woman on the island, you know."

For a moment Felicity's face assumed a drawn look, and Margaret reached out impulsively and took her hand. "Cousin Felicity, we have enjoyed being here with you. All of you have been so kind, so thoughtful." She waved the letter. "If only I could know how it is with my parents..."

The older woman patted her hand. "I understand, my dear, I really do. But we shall just have to be patient, and you will have to stay with us, at least until spring." She brightened. "We will be moving to Savannah for the winter months, and you will find that things are much livelier there."

Rebecca stared down at her letter thoughtfully. She was, of course, worried about the news and the safety of her parents, and yet she felt a secret delight. Now she would have more time to be with Jacques. Surely, by spring, he would speak what she felt certain was in his heart.

Chapter Seven

REBECCA, MARGARET and Jacques stood in the bow of the *Harbinger* as she made her slow way up the Savannah River toward the town. Despite the time of year, it was a beautiful day, pleasantly warm, but with a brisk breeze that lessened somewhat as they sailed farther inland.

Rebecca glanced up to where the sails billowed against the deep blue of the sky and sighed. Standing as close to Jacques as was decently possible, she gazed up into his face. "How far up the river must we travel?"

Jacques smiled down at her. "Fifteen miles or so. It seems longer since we must go slowly, not only because of the other boats but also because the river is full of sandbars that shift position from month to month. But it won't be too long now. Look, there are the outer wharves. Soon you will be able to see the town."

Pointing with one hand, Jacques placed his other hand on Rebecca's arm, and she felt a surge of warmth at his touch. Although she had been standing ever since they entered the mouth of the river, she felt wonderful; her excitement kept away any possible trace of fatigue.

It was a lovely day, and she was heading toward a new and possibly exciting town, in the company of the man she loved and her dearest friend. The only thing that might shadow such a day was the thought of her parents and what was taking place in India. However, there was nothing she could do about that at the moment, and she had great faith in her father's capabilities. If the uprising had occurred, or was going to occur, she was confident that he would come out of it unscathed.

Margaret, standing next to Rebecca, was thinking very different thoughts. She was not immune to the day or to the excitement of the trip, but since receiving her own letter, thoughts of her parents had been uppermost in her mind, and she was unable to shake the fear that something dreadful was going to befall them.

Now Rebecca clutched at her arm. "Oh, look, Margaret! There's Savannah. Can you see it, just up ahead?"

Margaret, whose eyes were not as good as Rebecca's peered ahead, shading her eyes with her hand, and saw without enthusiasm a high, sandy bluff, beneath which stretched a busy waterfront crowded with boats of every description, large and small. There was even one of the new steam-powered boats of which she had heard, docked at one wharf. It was an odd-looking vessel, with huge wooden wheels mounted one on each side.

She saw a jumble of wharves covered with piles of goods—bags, crates, barrels and bales. A motley, rough-looking crew of half-clad men, both black and white, swarmed over the wharves like beetles. Dozens of heavy carts and wagons moved to and fro. The noise was horrendous, a mingling of shouts, curses, raucous song and the neighing and stamping of the cart horses.

Atop the steep bluff, Margaret could see warehouses and other buildings, and the green of trees.

There seemed to be a great deal of refuse, an offense to her delicate stomach. She clamped a handkerchief to her nostrils.

Jacques looked down at her in apology. "It is a bit fragrant, isn't it? But then all waterfronts are, aren't they? When we get up above Factor's Row, you'll soon see that it is a lovely town."

Margaret looked at him doubtfully, and Jacques laughed heartily. "Truly. Savannah is very charming once you get beyond the waterfront area."

"My son speaks the truth, ladies," said Edouard, who, at that moment, strolled up beside them, with Felicity on his arm.

Rebecca noticed that Felicity looked uncommonly well today and that there appeared to be no evidence of the apprehension that she so often showed in the presence of her husband.

Edouard maneuvered himself into a position so that he was standing very close to Rebecca, and she could smell the scent of the hair pomade he wore, as well as the odor of tobacco and rum. He seemed to be in a very fine mood.

"You know, my dears, Savannah is a very unusual city; unusual in the type of people that settled it and in the way it was originally laid out."

Rebecca smiled up at the man who she sincerely hoped would be her future father-in-law. "You make it sound very interesting."

"It is. You see, Savannah began as a noble and philanthropic experiment. James Oglethorpe and the

Trustees envisioned it as a Utopia, a refuge for those who suffered from religious persecution and those who had been impoverished by debt. It was to function as an example of the mercantilist theory of national wealth, by producing raw products for England."

"No doubt a noble plan," Margaret said, looking confused.

"Yes, it was that," Jacques said, "even though in practice it did not work out entirely as Oglethorpe intended. The silk industry, in which the Trustees placed such high hopes, never really flourished, although at one point, I understand, the queen of England did have a gown made of Georgia silk. But many of the rare plants sent here did not survive, and then the original rules began to fall by the wayside. Papists and Jews were allowed to settle here, the proscription against rum was abandoned and the people were allowed to bring in slaves. After that Savannah became more like cities in the other colonies. Still, it is now a flourishing city of some consequence."

"Are most of the inhabitants of English descent?" Margaret asked, lowering her handkerchief for a moment.

"A great many of the inhabitants are of English origin," Edouard answered. "But many settlers have come from many other countries. We have Salzburgers, Moravians, Scottish Highlanders, Swiss, Welsh, Jews and, of course, Frenchmen. You know, the most stringent sifting process of would-be colonists ever made for an American colony was conducted here in Georgia. Only people of reputable family and high moral character were accepted as settlers.

"Another point you might find of interest is that the city itself did not just grow, as most cities do, in a haphazard fashion. It was laid out atop Yamacraw Bluff by James Oglethorpe in the plan that it retains to this very day, an orderly design with a series of squares dispersed throughout the township, so that there would be places for public meetings and market days. Nowadays these squares serve mainly as ornamental parks."

"Yamacraw! What an odd word," Rebecca exclaimed.

Edouard grinned. "It's an Indian name, my dear. There are many Indians still in the area. When Oglethorpe arrived, what is now the town was the site of an encampment of Yamacraw Indians, an outlawed tribe of the Creeks, with their old chief, Tomo-Chi-Chi, as their leader."

Rebecca raised her gaze to the sandy bluffs. So here, in this new country, she thought, it was much the same as with England. Still, she did not voice her thoughts. She said merely, "Are there any Indians here now?"

"Oh, you will see one now and again."

"Do they look like our East Indians?" Margaret asked. "I should imagine not, for I have heard them called 'Red Indians.' Are they really red?"

Edouard laughed. "They don't resemble Dhupta, if that is what you mean. They are of a different race, and their skin has a reddish cast instead of brown or black. But you will probably see for yourself while in Savannah."

THE EVENING WAS GROWING DARK, and Armand, in the large chair by the window of the house at Les

Chênes, sat staring out at the fading light, with a
frown upon his face. His mood was melancholy.

Almost silently, Lutie approached him, carrying a
tray with a large glass on it, and he was startled at the
sound of her voice.

"Here, I have brought you something cold to drink.
Perhaps it will improve your mood."

He turned to scowl at her but then accepted the glass
from her without comment. The odor of strong rum
arose from it.

Putting the tray down on a nearby table, Lutie sank
down upon a hassock near Armand's chair and put
her hand upon his arm. "I'm sorry," she said gently
in her deep, rich voice.

He glanced at her. "What on earth should you be
sorry for?"

Lutie's smile was pale in the dimness. "I am always
sorry when you feel this way. So sad, so bitter. It is the
young Englishwoman, isn't it? She is very beautiful."

Armand drained half of the contents of the glass in
one long swallow. "That would be no concern of
yours, even if you were right." He made a scornful
sound. "What would I do with a spoiled young Englishwoman who probably doesn't even know how to
run a household?"

Lutie's smile widened. "Oh, I can think of several
things, young master. Several things."

Despite himself, Armand gave a wry smile. "Lutie,
you are the only person I would allow to say things like
that to me. Why aren't I angry at you for your imper-
tinence? I should be, you know."

"Because I am your second mother, and you know
that I have only your welfare in mind," she said softly.

"Is it the girl, or are you thinking of your father again?"

"Both, I suppose." Armand drained the glass and handed it to her. "You know that if Edouard would give me a free hand here, I could make twice as much from the land. I would put in more cotton. That's where the money is going to be. And I would also rotate the crops so that the soil would not be depleted. However, no matter what I suggest, he always refuses. Father has no business sense at all. All he knows how to do is spend money. And Jacques is almost as bad. Ever since my brother returned from the war... But it does little good to go on about it."

"What you say is true," Lutie said with a nod. "I have watched. I have seen that it is so. Still, you do not approach your father in the right way. You storm at him like a young bull, and that only sets his mind against you."

Armand's laughter was a bitter bark. "He's already set against me. He was set against me long before this."

Lutie sighed heavily. "I should not have told you. I can see now that it was wrong, but at the time I thought that it would help you to know the truth, that you would feel less bitter if you understood what had happened in the past. But it has not. I think that it has only given you that much more to brood upon."

Armand reached out to touch the woman's hand. "No! No, Lutie. You did the right thing. It has been easier for me, knowing the truth. Truly, it has. You and your mother were both true friends to me—perhaps the only real friends I have ever had—and I will be eternally grateful to you both. Your mother is dead, so I will never be able to repay her, but someday I hope to be able to repay *you*. I would give you your freedom if the lot of freed slaves was not so precarious here or if I had sufficient funds to send you elsewhere."

"Maybe someday, yes." Her smile was faintly sad. "Someday when you no longer need me, when you have someone like that pretty, little English girl to look after you."

Armand shook his head. "I'm afraid that particular young Englishwoman is out of the question, Lutie. She has her sights set upon someone else and has no interest whatsoever in me."

"Ah, well!" Lutie clapped her hands and got to her feet. "I will prepare your supper, then, and I will make it a good one, for a full belly helps to balance an empty heart."

She left the room on silent feet, leaving Armand to stare again into the growing darkness, vividly remembering the feeling of Rebecca's mouth and the softness of her body.

"FELICITY SAYS that it will be a grand party," Rebecca said, examining her newly coiffed hair in the glass at her dressing table in the large bedroom that she and Margaret were sharing in the Savannah house. "Most of the important people in Savannah will be here, and I overheard Edouard telling Jacques that he had a tremendous surprise for him, a very special guest. I wonder who it can be?"

Preoccupied with dressing, Margaret made no reply.

Pensive, Rebecca let her thoughts drift back over the past few weeks. The weeks that they had been in Savannah had been, as far as Rebecca was concerned, a delightful experience. The lovely Federal house was smaller than Maison de Rêverie, but the same care had been taken with its construction and the furnishings. It was situated on a large lot facing Reynolds Square and was surrounded by a well-landscaped garden containing fine examples of native and rare plants.

The town itself, as Jacques had assured them, was quite attractive. The main thoroughfare, Bull Street, offered a wide, sand-covered lane from the river on the north to the edge of town on the south.

Bull Street was strung with a necklace of squares, which were shaded by Pride of China trees and fenced about with chain links supported by white cedar posts. Small well-tended pathways bisected the squares and made them pleasant for walking. Other squares ornamented other streets and gave the town a green and spacious feeling.

There were many lovely residences and public buildings. Right on Reynolds Square, there was a graceful building that had been built in 1789 for Mr. James Habersham, Jr., who Rebecca understood was one of the town worthies, and was now the home of the first bank in Georgia, the Planters Bank. Rebecca thought it a shame that it was not still a residence, for its exterior was a lovely deep shade of pink, caused, Edouard had told them, by the seeping of color from the red bricks, of which it was constructed, through the white plaster that had originally covered it.

The house that Rebecca thought the most admirable was still under construction—a large, elegant Regency home, which would, when completed, cover the depth of an entire block. The house had been designed by the distinguished architect, William Jay, and promised to be the most splendid home in all of Savannah. It was plain to see that the city was still growing, for there was much such building going on.

Now Rebecca turned away from her mirror. "Margaret, do you like my hair this way?"

Margaret studied her carefully. "I think so. Although it *is* very sophisticated, you must admit."

Rebecca turned to smile at her own image. "Good! I want to look absolutely smashing. Felicity says that everyone of importance in Savannah will be here tonight, and I do not wish to be overshadowed by the local belles."

"As if you could! You know that you are always the prettiest girl at any affair." Margaret said this with no envy and with considerable pleasure. Personally, she had no desire to be the belle of the ball, yet it was nice to be related to someone who drew admiring and envious glances. The glow that reflected from Rebecca shone on Margaret with just the proper amount of light; any more would only serve to embarrass her.

Margaret, too, had found the weeks in Savannah extremely pleasant. She enjoyed sharing a room with Rebecca. In fact, she preferred it to having a room to herself, and in her quiet way, she even relished the attention they had received since arriving.

Savannah was a small enough town so that everyone knew everyone else, and the arrival of newcomers always caused a flurry of excitement, particularly when these visitors were two attractive young women. Margaret and Rebecca had been invited to teas, galas, card parties, church socials and every other kind of social event the town had to offer. There had hardly been a moment to themselves, and tonight the Molyneuxs were honoring their social debts by hosting an extravagant party in their own home.

Yes, it had been a gala season, and even Margaret, who did not consider herself especially skilled at reading the nuances of social relationships, could not help noticing that everyone in the household seemed to be in a more cheerful mood. Even the mysterious Dhupta seemed less sinister here.

As if reading her thoughts, Rebecca said, "Margaret, have you noticed how differently Felicity acts here? I don't believe that she has taken to her room once since we arrived, and she seems much stronger and more lively. Have you noticed?"

Margaret nodded. "It is strange, but I was thinking something of the same thing. I was also thinking how much better I sleep here." She flushed briefly, and Rebecca, who missed little, took note of it.

She said, "You aren't still thinking of our night prowler, are you? Why, it's been months since we discovered the secret passageway, and I never heard anything unusual after that. Did you?"

Margaret looked uncomfortable. "Well, I never really heard anyone in my room, but I was always afraid that I would. But I'm sure that I heard that strange music again, once or twice. At any rate, I never really slept well after that, not until we came here to Savannah."

"This house is hardly the type for hidden passageways, I suppose. Still, it does seem strange to me that everyone acts rather differently here."

"Do you suppose it is because Armand is not here?" Margaret frowned in thought. "He does seem to annoy his father so, and his presence is disruptive."

Rebecca turned away, afraid that her face would reveal what she was thinking. Despite their hectic schedule since arriving in Savannah and her preoccupation with Jacques, her thoughts returned to Armand and that afternoon on the hill with more frequency than she liked to admit to herself. She could not put out of her mind the memory of his body against hers or the feelings that encounter had engendered within her, and this fact annoyed her. Why should she keep thinking of that boor Armand, when she was—she was certain—within reach of her goal?

Jacques had been more attentive than ever since their arrival in Savannah. Rebecca believed that it was at least partially due to the fact that here, he had been forced to compete with other admirers. She smiled to herself. There was nothing like the admiration of others to kindle a flame in a man. Men were such competitive creatures. They always wanted something the more if someone else coveted it; and she was certainly coveted.

Also, there was an additional factor acting in her favor. Just before they had departed form Pirate's Bank, she had happened to be passing the parlor when Edouard and Jacques were having a discussion, and what she heard had caused her to stop and press herself against the wall near the door, so that she could eavesdrop.

"Really, son," Edouard was saying, "don't you think that it is time you thought seriously of marriage? You are almost thirty, you know, and it is time you were producing an heir. I won't live forever, and it would delight me to the very soul to have a grandson before I'm too damned old to enjoy him."

Jacques's voice sounded subdued when he answered. "I suppose you are right, sir. I'm afraid that

I have not really given it much thought. The war, you know..."

"Nonsense, my boy! The war is over, and you're home now. There is no reason that I can see not to get on with your life. It's not as if there are no likely candidates. Savannah is full of suitable young ladies. Not only that, but you have two beauties right here under your own roof." Edouard laughed slyly. "I have eyes in my head, you know," he continued. "I've seen the way you look at your Cousin Rebecca, and I've seen the way she looks at you. You could do no better in the matter of beauty, and you could do far worse as far as her family and fortune are concerned. Her father is quite well off, and I am sure he would give her a handsome dowry. And it's not as if she is your first cousin. Actually, either she or Margaret would make you an excellent wife."

Rebecca felt her face burn, but it was more a matter of pleasure than embarrassment. She was an intelligent woman of her day and knew quite well that practical matters such as one's background and fortune, were important considerations in marriage. Edouard was only being sensible, and he was right; her father would settle a good sum on her husband when she married, and he would no doubt consider a closer relationship with his American cousin's family quite desirable. She held her breath, listening intently for Jacques's response to his father.

When he finally spoke, Jacques's voice was low. "You are right, Father. I don't deny that I am quite taken with Rebecca or that I find her company most agreeable. What man could say the opposite? However, I am not certain that I am ready for marriage just yet."

Rebecca heard a slapping sound and was sure that Edouard had clapped his son on the arm or the shoulder. "Then you should *be* certain, my son. It is time to seriously consider getting wed."

At that moment Rebecca heard footsteps coming down the hall. Facing around, she saw one of the housemaids approaching. Rebecca hurried off in the other direction.

Edouard was right, she thought. Jacques must be made to decide that he was ready for marriage. And she would help him decide! At the party tonight, all of the most eligible bachelors in town would be present, and she intended to flirt outrageously with all of them. If that didn't prompt Jacques to propose, then she determined to bring up the subject herself. Of course, it was not really proper for a woman to initiate such a subject, but because of her beauty and daring, Rebecca had always been able to get away with things that other women could not. She would manage to do it in a subtle manner, so that she did not appear *too* forward. Yes, tonight just might be the night that Jacques would propose!

Turning to Margaret, she studied her thoughtfully. Margaret had an uncanny ability to foretell the future. In fact, her ability in that respect was sometimes almost frightening. Rebecca wondered what feelings her cousin might have in that direction.

"Margaret," she said, "you know that I want to marry Jacques, don't you?"

Margaret looked up without surprise. "Of course. I suppose I've known it from the first."

Rebecca pulled her chair over close to Margaret's. "Well, what do you think about it? How do you feel about it? Do you think I will? Will we be married?"

Margaret looked away, staring at her own reflection in the mirror on her vanity table. "What do you mean? How could I know the answer to that?"

Rebecca smiled and wagged her finger. "Now, Meggie, you *know* that you have premonitions about the future and that they often prove to be right. Just tell me what you think about Jacques and me. I promise that I won't be upset if it isn't what I want to hear."

Margaret slammed down her hairbrush, suddenly annoyed. "Well, I don't care if you are upset! And don't call me Meggie. You know very well that I don't like to talk about this kind of thing. It makes me very uncomfortable."

And indeed it did, for she still had the strong feeling that things were not going at all well in India; and if it was true—if her premonitions came to pass—then it did not bear thinking about.

Rebecca was somewhat taken aback at the usually even-tempered Margaret showing irritation. She adopted a wheedling tone. "Please, Margaret. Don't be a stick."

Margaret knew that Rebecca would keep at her until she gave her an answer. "Very well, then," she said, sighing. "I do think that you will marry him. As I said, I have thought so all along, but..."

Rebecca let out a squeal of delight. "Oh, Margaret! How grand!"

"But I see something else," Margaret went on, "and you should know that, as well. I feel that it will turn out badly. I have no idea why."

Rebecca's smile died. "What an awful thing to say! How could it turn out badly? Jacques is the kindest and gentlest of men . . .'' She paused. "Why, I think you are jealous!''

"You know that is not true, and you know that I love you as a sister, despite the fact that you can be very trying at times,'' Margaret said severely. "You asked me for the truth, and I have told it to you as I see it.''

Rebecca could not remain cross. Margaret's verification of her own feelings made her too happy, and then, of course, *all* of Margaret's premonitions did not prove out. If she was correct about the first half of this one—that Rebecca and Jacques *would* marry—the second half of her prediction was really not worth being concerned about.

Chapter Eight

BY THE TIME Rebecca and Margaret came downstairs, many of the guests had already arrived, and the house hummed with the sound of their voices. Above the chatter could be heard the strains of music from the direction of the main parlor and large sitting room. Since there was no ballroom in the Savannah house, the rugs had been taken up and the furniture moved out of the way for dancing.

"They all look so splendid," Margaret whispered from behind her gloved hand to Rebecca, as they stood on the grand stairway gazing down at the guests arriving in the main foyer.

"They do, indeed," Rebecca said, giving her cousin's hand a squeeze. "But not any more so than we!"

Indeed, both girls looked lovely.

Margaret wore a new gown of lilac satin cloth, trimmed about the bosom and waist with a rich white silk trimming, called frost work, which was in turn set with small white pearls. Her soft brown hair, arranged in curls, with the addition of false French curls parted up on the forehead, was topped by a small evening cap of frost work, also ornamented with pearls. She looked, Rebecca thought, very à la mode, and she felt very proud of her cousin.

Rebecca herself had chosen a gown of Nicolas blue silk, trimmed with a border of stamped leaves in silver satin. Her thick, elaborately curled pale hair, which had no need of false curls to look its best, was bound by a fillet of the same silver leaves as the trim of her gown, interwound with a wide riband of Nicolas blue satin. She knew that she looked as well as, or better than, she ever had, and she was almost giddy with happiness and anticipation of the evening ahead.

As the two young women came down the stairway, Edouard advanced to meet them. His handsome face was flushed with wine and pleasure, and his eyes glittered. "Well, our two lovely doves! Don't you both look beautiful! You must come and meet our guests. It is going to be a very successful evening, my word on that."

As was his wont, in taking Rebecca's arm, Edouard managed to press his own arm against the underside of her breasts. Although she disliked his sly liberties, Rebecca did not pull away. After all, he was going to be her father-in-law, and there was really no harm in him. If his furtive touches and squeezings gave him a little pleasure, she would put up with it, at least until she and Jacques were man and wife.

So, she looked up into his face and smiled sweetly. "And just who is this mystery guest you have been talking about? Is it someone important?"

Edouard threw back his head and laughed. "You might say that, my child! Yes, he is very important."

"Ah, so it is a man, then!"

Edouard steered the two women toward the main parlor. "That is very true, and quite a man, at that Yes, tonight you two young ladies will meet a real man of the Americas, and I will wager that you will not soon forget him or this night."

Rebecca was to remember his words later, for the night proved them true, in more than one way.

She had just finished a dance with a rather pompous young man, who had spent most of the dance talking about himself, and had joined Margaret, who had been dancing with Edouard, when there was a general rise in the level of conversation, a rise that swept like a wave of sound from outside the main parlor, through the doorway and across the room to where the two young women stood against a far wall, carrying with it bits and pieces of conversation:

"Someone says that Jackson is here."

"Oh, I don't believe it!"

"General Jackson? Here?"

"Andrew Jackson and his Rachel are here. Someone saw them in the foyer."

"How does he look?"

"How does *she* look?"

"What is she wearing?"

"Have you ever seen her?"

"Of course, you know what they say about *her*."

"You had best not let General Jackson hear you say that!"

"Ooh, of course not! I wouldn't dare. I have heard he's fought many a duel over her."

"Old Hickory is here? In Savannah? You mean *here*? How did that come about?"

Rebecca and Margaret exchanged puzzled glances, and Rebecca put her hand upon Margaret's shoulder, to support herself while she stood upon her toes. Everyone seemed to have their eyes fixed upon the wide double doorway that led into the foyer. Then, suddenly, all conversation stopped for an instant, and there was an almost reverent hush.

Edouard's voice boomed out into the momentary silence. "Ladies and gentlemen, may I present General and Mrs. Andrew Jackson!"

In a flurry of frustration and despite Margaret's scandalized whisper, Rebecca used the other girl's shoulder to help herself mount to the seat of a low chair positioned against the wall.

From this elevated spot she was able to see the wide doorway and, framed in it, Edouard and a distinguished middle-aged couple.

The man was tall and thin, with a long, fair, thoughtful-looking face, interestingly seamed with a faint scar that lost itself in a great shock of ruddy hair sprinkled with gray, that rose above his forehead like a rooster's comb. There was much strength and character in that weathered face, Rebecca thought. This was indeed a man to command attention.

The woman with him was of middle height and full-figured, with olive skin, thick dark hair and lustrous large, dark eyes. Despite the fact that she was not a young woman, there was something about her that was very attractive. Rebecca recognized it at once, although she could not really put a name to it. Her first thought was that when Rachel Jackson was young, she must have been very beautiful and must have had many suitors. There was something about her full, well-molded lips that still spoke of passion.

At that moment General Jackson saw Rebecca standing upon the chair, gaping at him. Clearly amused, he gave her a charming and roguish grin.

Others, seeing the direction of his glance, began to turn, and Rebecca, suddenly flustered, quickly jumped down from the chair.

"Rebecca!" Margaret whispered, looking at her crossly. "Honestly! Why can't you mind your manners?"

Unfazed, Rebecca waved the complaint aside. "Well, at any rate, I got to see them. He is very impressive. There is something compelling about him. I do hope Edouard introduces us."

The musicians had begun to play again but few people were dancing. Most of them were congregated around the new arrivals.

"Come," Rebecca said, grasping Margaret's hand tightly. "Let's see if we cannot get closer."

With Margaret unwilling in tow, Rebecca began to work her way through the crowd toward the parlor door. As they made their slow progress she listened to the comments being voiced around her. Again she heard several references to Rachel Jackson, references that implied there had been some scandal involving the general's wife.

Stopping by the side of a young woman she and Margaret had come to know slightly, she paused. "Oh, Mary," she said gaily. "Isn't it exciting to have General Jackson as a guest?"

Mary Williams, a young woman full of her own importance, smiled back as if it hurt her to make the effort. She was thinking, Rebecca was sure, of the fact that this event constituted a social coup for the Molyneux family that would not be bested this social season. "Yes, a most exciting surprise."

"Mary," Rebecca said, "since we are not native to your country, there are a great many things we do not know."

Mary smiled patronizingly, but this time more sincerely. "Of course, dear Rebecca. That is quite understandable. So, if you have any questions, I shall be happy to do my best to answer them.''

''Well, there *is* one thing I have been wondering about. I have heard several people make references to something—something a bit out of the way in Mrs. Jackson's past. I wonder if you know what they are referring to?''

Mary's plump face turned pink, and Margaret whispered, ''Rebecca!''

Rebecca ignored the whisper and continued to smile sweetly at Mary.

''Well, yes, there is something, although I don't know if I should tell you. They say that General Jackson has killed men in duels for mentioning it.''

''Yes, I overheard that. It must be something really scandalous, then. But if you are afraid to speak of it, I will understand...'' Rebecca allowed her voice to show her disappointment.

Mary flushed again and glanced around furtively. ''Well, I don't suppose it will do any real harm. After all, everyone has known about it for years. They say— or, at least, some people do—that General Jackson's marriage to Mrs. Jackson was not quite... well, not quite right!''

Rebecca assumed a baffled look. ''Not quite right? In what way?''

Mary cast another quick look around and leaned close so that she might whisper in Rebecca's ear. ''Rachel Jackson was married before, and they say— *some* people say, that is—that Mrs. Jackson was not properly divorced from Captain Robards when she first married the general. There was a great to-do about it, and it is still considered something of a scandal.''

Rebecca's smile widened, and Margaret, who had heard the whole exchange, gave a sharp gasp. Rebecca promptly dug an elbow into the other girl's ribs.

"Well, that *is* quite scandalous, if true. I can see why the general might become incensed by such gossip about his wife. Tell me something else, Mary. Why is the general called Old Hickory?"

"My father told me that the general received that name from the soldiers in the field during the War in 1812. A soldier supposedly said admiringly that General Jackson was as 'tough as hickory wood.' Anyway, the name stuck and they added 'old' to it as a sign of affection. They say that the men under the general's command love and respect him."

At that moment Rebecca was interrupted by Jacques, who had apparently been looking for them. His face bore an expression of unease, which Rebecca thought odd under the circumstances. Surely he would be happy to see his old, beloved commander!

"Rebecca, Margaret," he said. "There you are. I've been looking everywhere for you. Father wishes to present you to General Jackson and his wife."

Rebecca smiled up at him. "Well, what do you think of your father's surprise? I imagine that you never could have guessed it would be General Jackson!"

Jacques smiled somewhat wanly. "You're right, I had no idea that the general would be here tonight. Father surprised everyone."

"Mary tells me that his men love him. Are you pleased to see him again?"

Jacques nodded, but it struck Rebecca that there was something uneasy about his expression. Still, his voice was hearty as he answered. "Yes, of course. I like and admire the general very much. He is a brilliant military commander, and I am most pleased that he has honored us with this visit. I don't know how Father discovered that he was going to be in Savannah, but then Father has many important connections. Ah, here they are now.''

Seen at close quarters, Rebecca noticed that the general's piercing eyes were of an intense blue and that his face was slightly pockmarked. There was a sense of power about him that impressed her greatly.

Edouard gathered one girl on each arm and herded them before the general and his wife.

''Mrs. Jackson, General Jackson, I should like to present two young relatives, first cousins once removed, who are visiting with us. Rebecca Trenton and Margaret Downing.''

Both women curtsied.

''Well, you are to be congratulated on the fairness of your family, Edouard,'' Jackson said. Rebecca was surprised to learn that he spoke with a trace of a North Irish brogue.

Rachel Jackson nodded pleasantly, and Rebecca studied her face surreptitiously. She found the gossip about this woman quite fascinating. After all, she, too, knew what it was like to have men constantly falling in love with her, and she did not consider it something that she should feel guilty about. Of course, to marry one man while still married to another, that *was* rather shocking, particularly when the present husband was an important American general. In India, such a scandal concerning a British officer would damage, if not destroy his career, but apparently the gossip had little effect on this imposing man, as far as his career was concerned.

Jackson had turned to Jacques, and Rebecca thought that she saw genuine affection in his eyes as he spoke to the younger man. "Jacques, my boy, it is good to see you again. You are looking well."

He then turned to Edouard. "Edouard, you have a fine son here. I don't know how much he has told you about his experiences in the war, but he was a brave and valiant soldier, a credit to his country and his family. I was proud to have him as an officer in my command."

Jacques's face had turned a dull red. "Yes, well, I appreciate your saying that, General, but I only did my duty and should not be commended for that."

Jackson put his hands behind his back, a posture that made his thin, wiry body appear even taller. "Nonsense, my boy! A man should feel no embarrassment at accepting honest praise. Your son, Edouard, was a good officer, well respected and liked by his men. You know, my mother always used to say, 'Make friends by being honest, keep them by being steadfast,' and that is what Jacques was. Honest, steadfast and brave."

He nodded his head gravely. "So don't be embarrassed, Jacques. I speak only the truth. You know, if this business in Florida grows worse, I may need you again. You have heard, I assume, of the trouble building in Florida?"

Edouard spoke up. "Yes, we had some news of that just this week." He glanced at Margaret and Rebecca. "But perhaps you two ladies might wish to return to the dancing. We don't wish to bore you, or frighten you, with tales of wars, or rumors of wars."

"Thank you," said Margaret, bobbing a curtsey and turning away.

Rebecca stood fast. "If it pleases you, sir, I should like to stay. I am much interested in history and political affairs, and few people are granted an opportunity to hear the news from such an illustrious source."

General Jackson laughed heartily and took his wife's arm. "You see here, dear Rachel, a young woman who bears your own stamp. You should find her congenial."

Rachel Jackson smiled, and her rather heavy face became animated. "By that, I presume you mean that she is a young woman of spirit and intelligence?"

Jackson gave her a slight bow. "Of course, my dear, like your charming self." And to Rebecca he said, "Of course you may remain, lass. I will speak of nothing that will not soon become common knowledge."

Edouard said, "The information I received says that the renegades on Amelia Island are attempting to organize a revolution, with the aim of adding Florida to the South American Republics. Is that correct?"

"I am afraid that is basically correct, Sir. Fort Negro and Fernandina should have been cleared out long ago, in my opinion. The town is nothing but a haven for criminals of the worst sort, and they have grown so strong that the Spaniards themselves cannot handle them. I know for a fact that there are many hundreds of thousands of dollars of smuggled goods there. It is an explosive situation, and I do not believe that it will improve so long as the Spanish hold Florida."

"And the Seminoles?"

Jackson rocked on the balls of his feet. "Unfortunately, there is trouble brewing from that area as well. The Seminole Indians are refusing to vacate the lands that were included in the Creek cession. Something is most certainly going to have to be done."

At that moment several other men approached the group, and Rebecca thought it best that she leave. In the excitement of the arrival of the Jacksons, she had almost forgotten her foremost plan for the evening—to get Jacques alone and in the proper frame of mind to propose. She did hope that the stir caused by the appearance of General and Mrs. Jackson would not interfere with her being alone with Jacques.

Stepping to his side, she put her hand upon his arm. "Jacques," she said in a low voice, "would you escort me into the other room?"

Jacques smiled down at her. He appeared to welcome the chance to escape. Briefly she wondered why he should feel the need, but it was not of paramount importance at the moment.

"I should be delighted, Rebecca." Jacques turned to Jackson and his wife. "If you will excuse us, General?"

General Jackson made a slight bow. "But of course. Delighted to have met you, Miss Trenton."

"The honor was mine, General and Mrs. Jackson."

Rebecca made a graceful bow and then retreated on Jacques's arm.

Chapter Nine

As THE EVENING PROGRESSED, Rebecca found Jacques very willing to spend most of it at her side, despite the presence of General Jackson. She felt immensely flattered and pleased. The evening was going according to plan.

Since the arrival of the Jacksons had, to some extent, disrupted the ordinary course of the evening, Rebecca was able to have several more dances with Jacques than her dance card called for. At the end of a particularly energetic mazurka, she began to fan herself furiously, until Jacques caught her meaning and asked her if she would care to step out onto the porch for a breath of air, a suggestion she graciously accepted.

In spite of the lateness of the year, the weather was still pleasant.

"My," said Rebecca as they stepped out onto the empty porch, "I cannot seem to get over how nice the weather remains. It is almost as warm as India."

Jacques, leading her over to the rail so that they might look out onto the square, had a bemused expression upon his face, which she could discern quite clearly in the light from the ornamental lantern that had been suspended from a hook near the top of the porch steps. A faint sheen of perspiration covered his forehead. Removing a large linen handkerchief from his pocket, he wiped his brow. "This autumn has been warmer than usual. It can sometimes be quite cool by this time of the year."

A silence fell, and Rebecca leaned toward him, knowing that her glowing face would look attractive in the light of the lantern.

"Oh, Jacques," she said breathlessly, widening her eyes. "I have been having such a lovely time these past few months, and most of it has been because of you. Do you know that?"

Jacques tried for his usual melancholy smile, but it somehow slipped, becoming an expression of intense longing and sadness, an expression that pulled at Rebecca's emotions like a hand upon a harp string. Why should he be sad? Why didn't he just kiss her? She was practically begging him to do so.

Glancing quickly around, she saw that the porch was empty except for the two of them. She moved closer still to him, rose upon her toes and touched her lips to his.

With a groan that seemed to come from the very depths of his being, Jacques reached for her, gathering her into his arms, and returned her butterfly kiss with a fierce pressure.

Rebecca was so pleasantly startled by the success of her maneuver that she scarcely noticed if the kiss was pleasurable or not. She did notice that his lips were rough, and that his mouth tasted faintly of liquor.

She had no time for further thought, for at that moment, Edouard's voice boomed out behind them. "Well, what is this I see? Capital!"

Jacques pulled back from Rebecca hastily, leaving her standing a bit shaken, but triumphant.

Edouard was clapping his son upon the back, his expression a mixture of paternal pleasure and envy. "I take it that this means you have proposed!"

Even in her state of excitement Rebecca noted that his words were more statement than question, and she thanked the turn of fate that decreed that Edouard should come out onto the porch at that exact moment. One kiss, of course, did not necessarily signify an engagement. However, under the circumstances, since she was a guest in Edouard's house and a young woman of good family and reputation, a kiss, publicly witnessed, could certainly be considered compromising. Unless Jacques was a cad—and she knew that he was not—their marriage would now be assured.

REBECCA, IN A PLEASANT DAZE from the mingled effects of the wine and the excitement of the wedding, lay upon the large, canopied bed in the master bedroom of the Savannah house, awaiting Jacques.

She was dressed in a night robe of silk so fine that its pale yellow cloth shimmered over her skin with the transparency of sunlight.

She felt giddy, disoriented, but outrageously happy; for this was her wedding night, and in a few moments, when Jacques came to her, she would leave the ranks of girlhood forever, to join her mother, her Cousin Felicity and other women in that mysterious sisterhood of those who had experienced an intimate relationship with a man.

Madame Molyneux! How lovely, how grand, it sounded. Soon, she would be in his arms, with no restraints upon him as to what he might do to her.

She raised her head and experienced a wave of dizziness. Perhaps she should not have drunk so much wine, for she was unaccustomed to it, but in her nervousness and high excitement she had taken several glasses.

Carefully she lay down, looking up at the rose satin canopy above the bed. It had been a lovely wedding. Everyone of importance in Savannah had been there, and it was agreed by all that it was the affair of the season.

The only dark cloud had been the fact that Rebecca's parents had not been able to attend the ceremony and that Armand had. Rebecca had wondered if he would attend the nuptials, half hoping that he would not, for she still had not forgotten that afternoon on the hill, and it seemed to her that he would cast a pall of gloom over the festivities. However, he had ridden in from Les Chênes for the occasion, looking as dark, brooding and gloomy as ever. But the odd thing was, he had been quite nice. Very quiet and polite, treating her almost as if she were ill, an oddity that she did not have time to concern herself with.

The latest letter from her parents had contained bad news. There had indeed been an uprising; in fact, two. The Pindarees had sent out plundering bands from Malwa, and to suppress them, Lord Hastings had been forced to muster an army of one hundred twenty thousand men, the largest force yet used in India. Shortly thereafter, the Mahrattas, led by Baji Rao, burned the British Resident's house in Poonah, including his expensive, Sanskrit library; and then had attacked the military post in Khirki with twenty-six thousand men. Although the Mahrattas had been repulsed, Rebecca's father had written that he feared there was more violence yet to come and that he was much relieved that both she and Margaret were in a safe place.

Of course she and Jacques could have waited to be wed. In fact, Jacques had even suggested that it might be best to delay the wedding. Rebecca would not have it. Who knew how long it would be before the troubles were over in India? And even after it *was* over, there would have to be the exchange of letters and the trip itself. It might take two years or more, and now that Jacques had proposed, Rebecca knew that she could not possibly wait that long. Jacques was so gentlemanly that he would hardly kiss her, stating that he must control himself until they were man and wife; and her body actually ached with a need that heretofore she had never felt so fiercely, and which, she instinctively knew, was the desire to fulfill her function as a woman.

Happily, Edouard also saw no need to wait. In fact, he had seemed as anxious for the wedding to take place as Rebecca. And so it was arranged, with word sent to her parents. And her plan had become fact this first day of the new year.

Now the wedding was over, and the rest of the family had repaired to Pirate's Bank, so that the bridal couple could have the Savannah house for their own for a time, before they too returned to the island.

Raising her head, gingerly this time, Rebecca looked toward the closed door to the sitting room, to which Jacques had gone while she made herself ready for him. Surely it was time now for him to come to her. Her body felt soft and warm, and yeasty as rising dough, and she wanted him beside her very badly.

Propping herself up on one elbow, she called his name, and when there was no answer, she called again, much louder this time. "Jacques? I'm ready for you!"

At the second call, the door slowly opened and she saw him framed in the soft light from the other room. He was attired in a handsome dressing gown of brocaded satin, of a marvelous deep shade of red. He looked incredibly handsome, and he belonged to her from this day forward.

Smiling, she held out her arms to him and he walked slowly, almost haltingly, toward her.

Her happiness just had to spill out in words. "Oh, Jacques, darling! I am so happy! It was such a lovely wedding, wasn't it? Such a lovely day all around, one that I will remember for the rest of my life."

He smiled down at her, and she felt herself rising toward the glowing love in his eyes. "Jacques, do kiss me. Please!"

She felt the bed sag beneath his weight, and then his upper body was bending over hers. Eagerly she lifted her lips to his and gloried in the feeling of her body throbbing as his hand pressed against the filmy fabric of her gown where it covered her breast. At his touch, her nipple seemed to come alive, like a small flower opening. Awash with languorous heat, she instinctively opened her lips, also, so that he might taste the inside of her mouth, as a bee tastes a flower.

For a few blissful moments, his lips and tongue possessed her mouth and his hands made themselves familiar with her body, causing her to burn as if she was racked by a raging fever. Then his mouth left hers, and his head dropped to her shoulder.

She felt him shudder violently and heard a strange sound issuing from his mouth so close to her ear.

It took Rebecca a moment to realize that he was crying! Shocked into a frightening sobriety, she clasped her arms tightly around him. "Jacques! What is it? What's wrong?"

"The wrong is mine. Forgive me, Rebecca!" He was sobbing openly now. "Will you ever be able to forgive me?"

"Forgive you for what?"

And then he tore himself from her arms, and in a moment she heard the door to the sitting room slam, the sound shockingly loud in the nighttime stillness.

At a loss to understand, Rebecca sat up, trembling as if from a chill. What had happened? Had she done something she should not? Nothing in her experience or expectations had prepared her for this.

"Jacques?" she called softly. "Jacques?"

There was no answer. What should she do now, wait for him to return? Follow him into the sitting room?

Not able to bear the indecision, she unsteadily rose from the bed and tentatively approached the door. She stood with her hand on the coldness of the doorknob, her heart pounding erratically. She placed her ear to the door but could near nothing from the other side.

Taking a deep breath, she willed herself to open the door. Jacques was sitting in a chair by the table where a lone candle burned, casting its flickering light upon the despairing lines of his slumped figure. He was bent forward, face supported by his hands.

Uncertainly she crossed over to him and kneeled at his feet. She longed to touch him, but did not dare.

"Jacques?" she whispered. "Darling, please tell me what is wrong. If it's something I have done, I want to know. Please talk to me."

Slowly, painfully, he raised his head and stared at her. She was profoundly shocked by the expression in his eyes. She watched him swallow, as if there was a bitter medicine in his throat.

"I'm sorry," he said finally. "I'm handling this badly, I know, as I have everything else. I am only hurting you the more, and after what I have done to you, that is inexcusable!"

Rebecca felt the visceral clutch of cold fear. What on earth was he talking about? Why was he acting like this? Despite herself, she began to weep, slow, silent tears that burned, blurring his image.

Jacques gave a muted cry as her tears started and reached out tenderly to brush them away. "Please don't cry. I'll try to explain." He took both her hands in his. "I must tell you straight out. It is the only way. Rebecca, I have done you a heinous wrong by marrying you."

He paused, struggling for words, and Rebecca, anxious and afraid, filled the silence with words of her own: "But you love me! I know you do. You have told me so, not only with words, but by your actions . . . !"

He squeezed her hands tightly, but she welcomed the discomfort, for it helped to ease her emotional pain.

"Rebecca, my love is the one thing you must never doubt. I do love you, and that is part of the reason why I find myself in this position. If I did not love you so well, I would not have been tempted to indulge my own weakness. I would have had the strength to let you go."

"Jacques, you are not making sense. Tell me what you're talking about. I shall go mad if you don't!"

"Yes. Yes, I am trying." His grip upon her hands was acutely painful now, but she did not attempt to pull away. "Rebecca...I said that I should not have married you, that I have wronged you in doing so, and that is also the truth. I..." The rest of it came out in a rush. "I can never be a proper husband to you!"

Rebecca felt her mouth fall open. The words meant nothing to her. "What do you mean?" she cried. "Why?"

She could see that he was weeping now, and the sight of this only added another measure of unreality to the nightmare scene.

"I was wounded at the Battle of New Orleans. Wounded so that I cannot ever be with a woman again. Do you understand me now?"

Rebecca felt herself begin to tremble. "But that cannot be! Your parents told me that you had returned from the battle unscathed. In fact, everyone made much of the fact that you had emerged without harm."

Jacques tried to smile. "That is what they believed to be true. I remained in New Orleans for almost a year after the war was over, until I was healed as much as I ever would be. For a time I considered never returning home, but I had no place else to go. Since no one knew, I let them go on thinking that I was unhurt.

"Mine is not the kind of wound that a man wishes to discuss. How do you think people would treat me if they knew that I had been unmanned? My father urged our marriage, and I weakened and consented. He has no idea of my situation, and so he is not to blame. Only I was at fault for letting my own selfishness and weakness lead me into taking the easiest way, when I knew that I could never be a real husband to you."

At last he released her hands, and Rebecca let them fall lifelessly into her lap. Tenderly, he cupped her face in his hands. "I love you so, my dear. I could see that you cared for me, and Father was insisting that it was time I married. He wanted a grandson. Dear God!" His bitter laughter wrenched at Rebecca's heart. "And when we came here to Savannah, and I saw the way other men looked at you, it drove me mad with jealousy. I could not bear the thought of you belonging to anyone else. And so now I have condemned you to a marriage that can never be consummated." His voice thickened. "That is the reason I must ask your forgiveness."

Rebecca could only stare at him silently, too numb to think clearly.

Sighing, Jacques released her face and leaned back in his chair, his body suddenly going limp, as if his spate of words had drained him.

Rebecca finally found her voice. "Jacques... Tell me about how it happened. Perhaps then I can understand what you are saying. It... it seems so unreal!"

"You're sure you want to know?"

She nodded mutely.

He sighed again. "All right, I'll tell you, although God knows how it will be of any comfort to you."

JACQUES HAD NEVER BEEN a violent person. Even as a lad, he had avoided as much as possible the brawls so common to rambunctious youths. He was not a coward. It was just that he had no taste for violence of any sort.

Yet when rumors of war with Great Britain spread throughout the country in 1812, Jacques began to feel his patriotic blood quicken. Edouard Molyneux had known Andrew Jackson for a number of years and was one of the first to receive a copy of Jackson's stirring "Volunteer to Arms:"

Citizens! Your government has yielded to the impulse of the nation. War is on the point of breaking out between the United States and Great Britain! and the martial hosts are summoned to the Tented Fields! A simple invitation is given for fifty thousand volunteers. Shall we, who have clamored for war, now skulk into a corner? Are we titled slaves of George III? the military conscripts of Napoleon? or the frozen peasants of the Russian czar? No—we are the freeborn sons of the only republick now existing in the world.

Are we going to fight to satisfy the revenge or ambition of a corrupt ministry? to place another diadem on the head of an apostate republican general? No...we are going to fight for the reestablishment of our national character...for the protection of our maritime citizens...to vindicate our right to free trade.

The period of youth is the season for martial exploits. How pleasing the prospect to promenade into a distant country and witness the grand evolutions of an army of fifty thousand men. To view the stupendous works of nature, carrying the republican standard to the heights of Abraham....

Andrew Jackson
Major General!

When Jacques read the document, his patriotism was affirmed. Edouard himself had his estates to manage, so as the elder son, it was left to Jacques to uphold the family honor. When war was finally declared and Jacques made known his intention of fighting, Edouard wrote to General Jackson informing him of his son's wishes. By return post, Jackson offered Jacques the commission of major under his command. The usual method of selecting field officers for the militia was by election by the men, but General Jackson had different ideas; he insisted that they be appointed by the commander, proclaiming, "We want men capable of command—who will fight and reduce their soldiers to strict obedience."

Jacques joined General Jackson's infantry at a place called Fort Deposit on the Tennessee River, in October, 1813. Jackson's first engagement was to be with the Creek Indians, who had been rebellious for some time. When the war with Great Britain erupted, the Creeks seized the opportunity to join with the British. In August of that year, the Creeks had massacred 240 people at Fort Mims in the Mississippi Territory. Jackson's orders were to defeat the Creeks.

Jacques was dismayed when he saw General Jackson. The general had been sorely wounded in a duel in Tennessee only months before and had nearly died. He had taken pistol balls in his left arm and shoulder, and the surgeon had wanted to amputate. Barely conscious, the general had said firmly, "I will keep my arm."

Jacques was shocked at the general's pallid, haggard appearance. He had his wounded arm in a sling and could barely sit on his horse, and yet Jacques had learned that he had just marched his men thirty-two miles in nine hours.

And he still retained the fire and spirit that Jacques so well remembered from a visit Jackson had made to Maison de Rêverie. He clapped Jacques on the shoulder with his good arm. "By God, Molyneux, it's grand to see you! There won't be much time to train you; we march on the Red Sticks within sixty days or less. If we don't starve first. There is an enemy I dread much more than I do the hostile Creek, that meager monster, Famine. But I am determined to push forward if I have to live on acorns! I would rather die than retreat."

In the days to come Jacques was to see the truth of this. Food and other necessary supplies were hard to come by. Once Jacques overheard a soldier tell the general that he was hungry. "By the eternal, fellow, so am I," the general exclaimed. "I will share my last pouch of acorns with you."

In the next two months Jacques absorbed what he could about soldiering, which was not a great deal; but Jackson solved the problem by making Jacques one of his personal aides. Since the general drove himself to the point of exhaustion, making do with little sleep, so did Jacques.

Most of those sixty days were spent on the Coosa River, where the soldiers were put to work cutting trees to build a stockade that would be named Fort Strother.

Then word reached them that over two hundred Indians were gathered in the village of Tallahatchie, thirteen miles away. General Jackson, not yet completely healed and fearing that his condition might hamper his troops, dispatched one of his most trusted officers, Brigadier-General Coffee, with a thousand men, to engage the Red Sticks.

Thus it was that Jacques was engaged in his first battle on the morning of November 3, 1813. "You are to be my eyes and ears, Jacques," General Jackson told him. "Go along with Coffee and report back to me."

Since the American forces were far superior, the Indians were overwhelmed. As one of the men, Davy Crockett, later reported, "We shot them down like dogs."

Jacques was in the thick of it, caught up in the excitement of battle, firing his pistol repeatedly. In the dust and smoke it was difficult to be sure, but Jacques was almost certain that he accounted for several of the enemy. Later he was sickened by the carnage and went behind a tree out of sight of the men and vomited until his belly was sore.

All the Indian warriors were killed, and eighty-four women and children were taken prisoner and herded back to Fort Strother. Of the Americans, five were killed, forty-one wounded. As General Jackson wrote in his report, "We have retaliated for Fort Mims."

When the prisoners were brought back to Fort Strother, Jacques saw a side to General Jackson that, considering the general's fierceness in battle, both touched and surprised him.

Among the prisoners was a three-year-old Indian boy. The Creek women would not take care of him, and his own parents were dead. Some of Jackson's officers said, "Kill him!"

With his one good hand, Andrew Jackson dissolved some brown sugar in water and teased the boy into drinking. Then he sent the boy to Huntsville to be looked after and cared for at his own expense.

Then Jackson turned to Jacques and his other aides and said briskly, "Well, gentlemen, we have begun! While still abed at the Hermitage, on learning that I was to take command, I made plans. We will go on the offensive, moving south and west, destroying all the Red Stick bands, then push on to Mobile, thus opening a highway from Tennessee to the Gulf. And then the crowning stroke! We shall invade Florida, seize Pensacola and once and for all eliminate the influence of Spain, the despicable if silent supporter of Britain and the Creeks!"

It was a grandiose plan, and it took far longer than Jackson had anticipated. Jacques rode by the general's side, fighting with him when they engaged the enemy, despairing with him when they had to go hungry during the all too frequent times when food was hard to come by.

Finally, on August 9, 1814, almost a year since the first Indian engagement, a peace treaty was signed with the Creeks, who were forced to surrender twenty-three million acres, which would eventually become a large part of two new states, Alabama and Georgia.

The victory was not without its costs, however. Food was always in short supply, and although Jackson's arm had healed, he was constantly plagued by fever and malnutrition. In addition, the impetuous Jackson was always at loggerheads with his superiors and the government in Washington. To make matters worse, the men in his militia had signed up for a year, which was now up, and disgruntled with poor food and weaponry, they were leaving in droves. Jackson had to scour the country for new volunteers, but since he was now a popular military hero, because of his victories, new recruits flocked to him.

Jacques's year was also up, but he elected to stay on. He was sick of war, but he was fascinated by Andrew Jackson, sensing that he was close to a man who would go down in history as one of the country's heroes.

And now Jackson came to realize his dream of twenty years—the capture of Pensacola. Spain had now allied itself openly with Great Britain, and British troops were quartered there. Rumors were rampant that the British intended a full assault either on Mobile or New Orleans.

General Jackson made his move on Pensacola, and he moved alone, on his own initiative. Washington had fallen to the British, and during the British occupation of the capital, Jackson was, in effect, without a government to report to.

On November second, General Jackson marched for Florida with three thousand men, reaching Pensacola on the sixth. There were seven British men-of-war in the bay.

As a gesture, the general sent one of his officers under a flag of truce to demand that the three forts in the area—Barrancas, St. Rose and St. Michael—surrender to the Americans "until Spain could prove its neutrality." But the flag was fired upon, and the message was never delivered.

Jackson's troops stormed the town the next morning. After brief but fierce fighting, Pensacola and Fort St. Michael belonged to Jackson. But the Spanish showed such bad faith and wasted so much time surrendering their forts that Jackson had to delay his attack on Fort Barrancas—fourteen miles away and manned by British forces—until the following morning.

At three the next morning, Jacques, who had not slept since the attack began, was with Jackson as he briefed his officers for the attack on Fort Barrancas, when the ground shook with a mighty explosion. Word soon came that the British had blown up Fort Barrancas and fled on board their ships.

A thwarted Jackson, realizing that it had all been for naught and fearing that the British were on their way to attack Mobile, immediately marched his men toward Mobile.

But the target of the British was New Orleans, not Mobile. The British had decided to forgo the tactically superior route through Mobile and land directly on the Louisiana coast. The British armada sailing for New Orleans consisted of ten thousand seamen, fifteen hundred marines and ninety-six hundred soldiers. Even the officers' wives were along, with their prettiest frocks, preparing for a lengthy stay in New Orleans. Meanwhile, General Jackson, unaware of the size or location of the British forces, was also on his way to New Orleans.

Thus it was that on the evening of January seventh, Jacques was in Jackson's headquarters near the Rodriquez Canal, where their main line of defense had been set up, on the eve of what was to be the crucial engagement of the Battle of New Orleans.

Jackson, ill from dysentery during most of his time in the city, had moved like a man possessed. He had scoured the streets of New Orleans for soldiers, recruiting Negroes and the pirates of Jean Lafitte. These, along with many expert long riflemen from Tennessee and Kentucky, waited behind the entrenchments along the canal, a total of four thousand five hundred men, all told. That evening Jackson had received word that the commanding general of the British, Sir Edward Pakenham, was attacking early in the morning across the cane fields with seventy-five hundred veteran soldiers.

The first real engagement had taken place just before Christmas when Jackson's forces had repelled the British, and there had been other skirmishes since, but Jacques, along with Jackson, sensed that this was to be the crucial battle.

Jackson had ordered half of his men at the rampart to remain at their posts while the other half slept. The general and his aides, including Jacques, retired before midnight. The aides slept on the floor, with only their pistols placed aside and their sword belts unbuckled.

Shortly after one in the morning, they were awakened by a courier reporting strong enemy attachments crossing the river.

Jackson addressed his aides. "Gentlemen, we have slept long enough."

They went out into the creeping cold of the night for a last inspection of the lines. Jacques remained close to the general's side. As they passed from company to company, Jacques was amazed at how many of the soldiers Jackson knew by name.

At one battery they came upon a group of Lafitte's pirates crouched around a mound of red embers dripping coffee in the old Creole way.

"That smells like better coffee than we get," Jackson remarked to Dominique You, who was in command. "Smuggle it?"

"Maybe so, General," Dominique You said. He filled a cup and passed it to the general.

At six o'clock a milky light filtered through the fog, which would soon be lifting. Pickets reported that the British were forming in columns not a half mile away. Jackson stood on the parapet with Jacques and two other aides, sweeping the area with his telescope. Then, from the field in front, a rocket rose with a shrill sigh, bursting into a blue and silver shower.

"That is their signal for advance, I believe," Jackson said. Turning to Jacques, he added in a low voice, "I feel like my whole life has been a preface for this moment."

As Jacques stood on the parapet alongside the general, a breeze suddenly came up, dispersing the fog, disclosing the British advance. Jacques would never forget the sight that met his eyes. The British were immediately in front, about 650 yards away. The night's heavy frost had colored the cane stubble silver. Across this silver carpet moved a mass of red tunics, broken by white cross belts and a veritable hedge of bayonets.

The American rifles were not effective beyond four hundred yards, so they waited patiently. General Jackson passed the order down the line "for each man to pick out his target and aim above the cross plates."

The order came: "Fire!"

Orange flames burst in a sheet from the parapet. The first rank stepped back to reload, and a second took its place. Again came the order to fire, and the third rank moved up.

The advancing ranks thinned as men fell; the ground was red with blood and British redcoats. Still, they came on, disorganized and stumbling over their own dead. Jacques saw officers on horseback riding among the foot soldiers, urging the men on. Another volley of musket fire struck them, and Jacques saw horses rear and officers tumble off. After the battle he was to learn that the British commander, General Pakenham, was among the officers killed.

It appeared that the British had been repulsed. They were caught up in panic and confusion. Then Jacques saw several officers running up behind a group of soldiers, beating at them with the flat of their swords, driving them forward. One officer ran before them, straight at the canal, waving his sword. About a hundred British soldiers followed him, and about half that many made it to the canal. Not far from where Jacques stood, about twenty men crossed the canal and charged up the bank of the American breastworks.

Caught up in the heat of battle, Jacques drew his sword and joined the melee. It was all close work now, sword against bayonet, with a few pistols firing. Jacques engaged a redcoat, thrust and counterthrust, sword clanging against bayonet steel.

Feeling possessed of superhuman strength, Jacques drove hard and felt a surge of triumph when the soldier tumbled down the bank. Transfixed, staring down the bank, Jacques dimly heard a shout of warning, and he whirled—just in time to take a bayonet thrust in the groin. Pain blazed through him, hot as fire, and he felt the warmth of blood flood his loins. He fell headlong into unconsciousness.

When he awoke he was in a medical tent. Raising his head, his gaze blurred, he was surprised to see that he was almost alone in the tent. Only one other cot was occupied.

"Awake, are we?" A bearded man wearing a surgeon's smock smeared with blood was approaching where Jacques lay.

Jacques felt numb all over and a little giddy, and he assumed, correctly, that he was dosed rather heavily with laudanum.

"The battle, is it over?" he asked in a weak voice.

"It is over, Major."

"Did we win?"

The doctor smiled for the first time. "Oh, yes, we won. The British are defeated, and the war is all but over."

"But I don't understand..." Jacques gestured around. "Where are the wounded?"

"As General Jackson was heard to comment after the battle, 'The unerring hand of providence shielded my men.' We only lost seven men, and six were wounded." The doctor's face fell grave. "Of which you are one, unfortunately."

"How badly, Doctor?" Jacques whispered.

"Sorely, I am afraid, sir." The doctor's glance slid away. "Without going into details, the bayonet thrust has made a eunuch of you, Major. Terribly unfortunate in a man so young, but you will never have relations with a woman again."

AFTER JACQUES FINISHED telling his story, they each sat silently, staring at one another for a long moment, until Rebecca became conscious of the fact that her position on the floor had long since numbed her legs, and she stirred.

"Did General Jackson know the extent of your wound?"

"No." He leaned toward her. "Rebecca, I believe that I know how much I have hurt you, but I have been doing a great deal of thinking, and I believe that it is possible for us to have a life together, a kind of happiness. I believe that you enjoy my company, and I certainly enjoy yours. I promise never to treat you badly, and I will give you anything that is in my power *to* give. We can still have a good life, and the rest of the world need never know our secret." He paused briefly. "Only one other person knows of my... condition."

"The doctor who treated you?" Rebecca managed to say.

Jacques shook his head. "No, he died before I left New Orleans, of the fever. The person I meant is Armand."

Rebecca let out a gasp and rose to her feet, propelled by a feeling of scalding shame. Armand! To have him know that she would be a wife in name only! How he must be laughing at her situation!

"You said that you didn't even tell your parents!" she cried wildly. "Why did you tell Armand, of all people?"

Jacques raised his hands as if to defend himself. "It was unintentional, I assure you. When I first returned home, Armand and I got drunk one night. I was feeling sorry for myself, and I felt I had to tell someone. However, you needn't fear. The secret is safe with him. I know that you dislike him, but Armand is an honorable man, a man of his word, and he *is* my brother. He swore that he would never tell anyone, and I believe him."

Rebecca stood staring down at her husband, and her body began to tremble uncontrollably as the full meaning of all that he had told her became finally clear to her. As it did, she felt a terrible anger and pain twisted, knifelike, deep within her. This man, Jacques, her husband, had just destroyed all of her hopes and dreams, and for a moment she hated him with all the passion she was capable of.

Chapter Ten

AT NO TIME did Armand feel like laughing at Rebecca or her situation. Not only was it tragic for her, but when the news of the upcoming wedding reached him, he realized that it was tragic for him, as well.

All along, he had been denying the truth, telling himself over and over that it was just an infatuation, that he would eventually get over her.

Now he knew better. He loved Rebecca with his heart and soul. His situation would have been bad enough if she had returned to India, but now she was going to be Jacques's wife—lost to him but ever present. He would have to see her, face her, each time he returned to Pirate's Bank.

No, he didn't feel like laughing at her; he felt a deep sorrow for her, and he was furious with his brother. How could Jacques have married her? Did he think that because his own life was ruined, he had the right to ruin someone else's? Although Armand knew his brother to be weak in some ways, he had never believed him capable of a deliberate act of cruelty. He considered the act of marrying Rebecca exactly that.

Armand debated with himself long and hard about attending the wedding. The reason he finally decided to go surprised him somewhat. It did not bother him that either Jacques or Edouard might be offended, but the thought that Rebecca might be offended did concern him. And there was also Felicity—she would wonder as to his absence and be hurt.

Seeing Rebecca so radiantly happy struck him like a blow. Fully aware of what a brutal awakening was in store for her, he drank steadily throughout the ceremony and made his escape as soon as possible. He slipped away when the line formed to kiss the bride. He could not bear the thought of kissing her; it would be, truly, a Judas kiss.

Instead he mounted his horse and rode hard for Les Chênes; and then, changing his mind, headed first for Beaufort. The combined effects of the liquor he had consumed and the final, ultimate loss of Rebecca had him in a savage mood by the time he reined his horse in before a waterfront tavern in Beaufort. It had been a long ride, and it was well after dark.

Not being a social person, Armand was not a frequenter of taverns, but he occasionally stopped in at the Boar's Head for a mug or two on his way to and from Pirate's Bank, and he was known to Annie Condon, the buxom barmaid.

He took a table in the dim rear of the tavern, and Annie came swinging down to him. She was a merry wench, and rumor had it that she was free with her favors.

She stopped before his table, hands on hips, her warm blue eyes regarding him saucily. "Well, Master Molyneux, 'tis a rare evening that we see you!"

"Just fetch me a mug of rum," he said in a growling voice.

"A mug, is it?" she said with raised eyebrows. "What would be the celebration?"

"It isn't every day that a man's brother gets wed," he replied with a harsh laugh.

"Master Jacques? I've heard nothing of that."

"Why should you have?" Armand glowered at her. "Just fetch me the rum."

"Don't get in a boil, love." Annie beat a hasty retreat toward the bar.

For the first time Armand looked around the dim tavern. This late, it was practically empty, with only three other men scattered about the room. Armand was relieved. He certainly was in no mood for social chatter.

Annie came back with his rum on a tray. As he paid her she lingered for a moment.

Glancing up, he said, "What is it, Annie?"

"I was just wondering…" She gestured. "'Tis a nasty night out, cold as a witch's tit. It's a nice night for—" She broke off, with a gamin grin.

"Nice night for what?" he demanded impatiently.

"A nice night for company, was my thought."

"Oh, it was, was it? I came in here for a drink, not for company. If I want anything more, I'll let you know."

"Well, la-dee-da!" Hand on one hip, Annie flounced away.

Armand watched the seductive sway of her buttocks for a moment, then picked up the mug and drank the fiery rum. He sat, brooding, his thoughts inevitably circling back to the wedding and to Rebecca.

How beautiful she had looked, how happy! He would have given anything to have had her look at him the way she had looked at Jacques! If he could only be in his brother's place! A vision of himself and Rebecca together seared his brain and fired his loins, and he groaned aloud.

Were she and Jacques alone now? Had she already learned that she was going to be a wife in name only? Would she remember what he, Armand, had told her that day at Les Chênes? If she did, she might guess that he knew of Jacques's plight. At least she would know that he had tried to warn her, if obliquely.

Why had he handled things with her so badly? From their first meeting, he had done nothing but antagonize her. If he had been kinder, more gentle, then perhaps... No! It was not entirely his fault. She had been arrogant and haughty, obviously accustomed to having men do her bidding....

His musings were interrupted by the sound of loud voices at the front of the tavern. He glanced up curiously and saw Annie in the grip of a burly man at a table. The man had the girl by the arm, and he was trying to pull her down into his lap.

Armand vaguely recognized the man—a fisherman by the name of Brock. He was a brutish lout and intoxicated almost every time Armand had seen him. He was quite obviously drunk now.

Armand watched for a moment, slightly amused, as Annie struggled with him. Usually, these barmaids could protect themselves; otherwise, they did not last long in a tavern such as this.

Annie spat angry words at the big man, and he roared with laughter, then exerted more pressure on her arm. Desperately Annie swung at him, her open palm smacking his bearded face.

Brock bellowed with anger and twisted her arm cruelly, finally bringing her down into his lap.

Armand was on his feet without thinking, his anger and frustration boiling up in him like steam about to explode. He moved across the room in lunging strides.

Looming over the table, he said in a grating voice, "Let her go, you great lout!"

Brock blinked up at him blearily. "Go 'way, fellow. Mind your own damned affairs."

"I'll tell you once more . . . let her go."

"Blast you, no! The money I've spent in here this night entitles me to some pleasuring."

Without another word, Armand clamped his hand around the man's thick wrist and squeezed powerfully. Brock bellowed in pain but loosened his grip enough for Annie to escape. She scooted out of the way.

Brock glared up out of reddening eyes. "You got no right to stick your snout in! For that I'm going to break your head!"

He put both hands on the table and started to rise. Armand scooped up the heavy ale mug on the table, raised it in both hands and brought it smashing down on Brock's head as he was halfway to his feet. The mug shattered, ale splashed across the table and Brock slowly collapsed, splintering the chair as he went down.

Armand stood over him for a moment, but the man was unconscious. A smear of blood showed through his thick matted hair. Armand bent, seized a booted leg in each hand and dragged the man to the front door. He heaved Brock out into the street and dusted his hands together with a sense of savage satisfaction. It had been an oafish thing to do, but it had succeeded in venting his anger.

As he turned Annie looked at him with appreciative eyes. "Thankee, sir. No telling what Brock would have done. He's a mean one!"

Armand smiled down at her. "Not so mean at the moment, I wager. Not likely he'll bother you again tonight, Annie."

He returned to his table to finish his rum. He had just drained the mug and was ready for another, when Annie approached his table.

"We be closing now, Master Molyneux. No one left to drink but you."

Looking around, Armand saw this was true. He got to his feet. "I've had enough anyway. It's time I was getting back to Les Chênes."

"'Tis a long ride, and the hour is late." She looked at him boldly. "I have rooms above the tavern. You may stay if it suits you."

He hesitated, looking at her intently. She was at least clean, passably handsome and certainly willing. Visions of Rebecca entered his mind, and he felt a leap of arousal. Why not? Nobody else seemed to want him, and this would certainly be preferable to going home to a cold, lonely bed.

He dipped his head. "Your invitation is accepted, Annie."

A few minutes later he was following Annie's swaying buttocks up the rickety stairs running up the side of the building. The night was chill, with an icy wind off the bay. Armand shivered and bumped into her as she fumbled to get the door open. The interior of the small room was filled with a mingling of cooking odors, not all of them pleasant.

He waited while she went inside to light a candle, illuminating a poor room with a neatly made bed, clothes hanging on hooks on the walls. Aside from the bed, there was no furniture, not even a chair.

She faced around, smiling. "I know you are used to better, but at least I try to keep it clean."

"It will suffice," he mumbled.

She stepped closer, close enough so that he could feel the heat of her. She insinuated her hands inside his shirt, running her fingers along his rib cage. "I have often admired you, such a handsome gentleman!"

"Not many people think so," he muttered.

He cupped her face and drew her mouth to his. To his dim surprise, her mouth tasted sweet. He could feel the fullness of her breasts against him, and his arousal was complete.

In a moment they were on the bed, her skirts pushed up around her waist. She helped him unbuckle his trousers, then guided his readiness into her.

Armand was surprised again, this time at the fierceness of her response. He knew that it was not in the least feigned, and this helped to fuel his own passion.

Driving into her, again and again, he felt as if he was acting out the anger and pain he could not express in words. Each pounding entry was like a blow, but she did not complain. On the contrary, she gave every evidence of enjoying it, lifting her lower body to meet his thrusts, until at last she cried out and clung to him, legs wrapped about his waist. As Armand's own passion reached a shuddering peak he shouted aloud.

A short time later, as they lay together side by side, Annie said softly, "A bit ago, you cried out a woman's name."

He tensed. "I did?"

"Yes. It sounded like Rebecca."

FOR REBECCA, the return to Pirate's Bank was very difficult. Although she could dissemble when necessary, she was not a person who was good at hiding her true feelings for any length of time, and it seemed that her situation was going to demand that she continue to live a falsehood, to permanently act out a role that she found distasteful in the extreme. Edouard and Felicity would expect her to return to them happy and fulfilled, a contented bride.

And then there was Margaret. Although Margaret was not particularly sensitive to other people's feelings, she and Rebecca had always been so close that Margaret was sure to sense something odd if Rebecca showed her true feelings of unhappiness and depression.

The weeks she and Jacques had spent in Savannah had been, for Rebecca, like a period of convalescence after a violent illness. Since people did not expect newlyweds to do much visiting or entertaining, they had, blessedly, been left alone. Rebecca had used the time to gather her inner resources, and to come to grips with the painful truth about her marriage. Now, she felt in control, although a deep hurt and anger still simmered just beneath the surface.

Her anger was intensified by Jacques's apparent adjustment to the situation. After his painful confession he seemed much happier, as if, in telling her, he had exorcised whatever demons had been tormenting him. He was, as always, attentive, kind and entertaining. What bothered Rebecca the most was that his actions and manner seemed to assume that they were a completely normal couple, and he appeared to expect her to accept this and act accordingly. Rebecca found his seemingly easy acceptance of an almost intolerable situation very hard to bear.

Although it was still early in the new year, and a pearly fog obscured the tops of the trees and trailed ghostlike along the ground, the island still looked beautiful. Despite her constant inner depression, Rebecca felt a surge of gladness as she drank in the beauty of the landscape. It was nice to be back. This would be her home henceforth.

And she had missed Margaret. It was really a pity that she would be unable to speak freely to Margaret concerning Jacques. It would have been a relief to be able to talk about it, but of course that was impossible.

At Maison de Rêverie, the family welcomed them with open arms and a sly jape or two from Edouard on the state of the newly married. He also expressed surprise that they had returned to the island so early. "I thought you would have stayed at least until Easter," he said with a smirk. "That is the usual custom. I certainly would have, were I in Jacques's place."

Rebecca, feeling much put upon, told them the story that they had concocted—she was lonely in town, being a stranger, and she had missed them all too much to be comfortable away from them. She gave her reasons very charmingly, and they seemed to accept them without reservations.

Felicity had arranged a very elegant tea in the sunroom, and amid the fresh smell of growing things they talked of inconsequential matters. Then, somehow, the conversation got round to the Seminole uprising in Florida.

In the autumn, shortly after General Jackson's appearance at the party in Savannah, the Indians had erected a war pole, and the chief had warned Colonel Meigs, who was in command at Fort Scott, not to cross the Flint River. The Americans, in return, had burned a village and killed a number of the Indians. The retaliation of the Seminoles had been swift and terrible. On the day after Christmas, General Jackson had again assumed command of the American forces.

"Jacques, did you hear that Jackson is rebuilding Negro Fort, on Amelia Island?" Edouard said.

Jacques nodded. "Yes. I also heard they are naming the new fort Fort Gadsden. I suppose that soon the general will be turning his attention to the Seminoles again."

Edouard nodded gravely. "It is rumored that Francis and Peter McQueen are enticing the Seminoles to acts of hostility. It is also said that Woodbine, Arbuthnot and other foreigners are with them."

Rebecca looked questioningly at Edouard. "Who are these McQueens?"

"Creek leaders who fled to sanctuary in Florida after their defeat during the war."

"Does this mean, then, that there will be war with the Seminoles?"

Edouard smiled condescendingly. "Of course, my dear, and it may perhaps not be so bad a thing."

She stared. "Not a bad thing?"

"War with the Seminoles would give Jackson a chance to continue in Florida again and carry out his original plan. You yourself overheard him say that the only solution to the many problems that confront us in that area is to seize Florida from the Spaniards. This, it seems to me, would give us a legitimate reason for doing so."

Rebecca fell silent, thinking of the fighting in India and her parents. Men, it seemed to her, spoke very lightly of war, as if those killed and maimed were little more than pawns in a game of chess. Daughter of a soldier, she had seen some of the results of battle, and she did not understand how they could treat disfigurement and death so cavalierly. And, thinking of Jacques, she knew firsthand what damage war could inflict upon a man.

Edouard was speaking again. "Do you think you will be rejoining Old Hickory, son, if it comes to a fight?"

Rebecca saw Jacques's face pale, and for a moment pity outweighed her anger at what he had done to her.

"No, Father," he said stiffly. "I have had enough of fighting. I have performed my duty. And besides, I have Rebecca to think of now."

He smiled at her tenderly, and Rebecca felt the compassion washed away by renewed anger. How she wished that he *would* go! If he were gone, she could more easily play the dutiful wife. Then she would not have to keep up this constant facade, this pretense that she and Jacques were an ordinary, happy couple!

LATER, WHEN REBECCA looked back over this period in her life, she was to think that the misery of her wedding night was in some way a catalyst that triggered a series of violent and tragic events.

She and Jacques were barely settled in again at Maison de Rêverie when a letter arrived from India with terrible news.

In November, near the time of the beginning of the Seminole uprising in Florida, Appa Sahib, the raja of

Nagpur, made common cause with Baji Rao, the leader of the defeated Mahrattas, and brought up his forces and attacked the British Residency at Nagpur. The resulting battle was one of the most fierce in the history of the British occupation of India. The British troops were terribly outnumbered, and although they won out against the Indians in the end, they lost a quarter of their number. One of those killed was Margaret's father.

Margaret was, of course, inconsolable and took to her bed. Rebecca, who had been very fond of her uncle, tended Margaret personally, not only because of her love for her cousin, but also because in tending Margaret her own suffering was diminished.

Margaret's anguish was such that she developed a fever, which left her disoriented and weak. As Rebecca bathed her pale forehead with a cold cloth, she would toss and cry out that she was to blame for her father's death. She had had a premonition that something evil was going to happen, and she should have warned him. At these times, Rebecca would hold her and comfort her, telling her that she was blameless, but Margaret would not listen.

However, there was one benefit to be gained from Margaret's illness. Rebecca could, with good conscience, spend a great deal of time with her, which meant that she had a good excuse to spend less time with Jacques and his parents. She had moved out of Jacques's rooms, which, since their return, she had naturally been expected to share, and into Margaret's room, where a small cot had been set up for her.

On a night near the end of Margaret's convalescence, Rebecca had finally gotten the other girl to sleep, with the aid of a liberal dose of laudanum. Tired and depressed, she settled onto the narrow, uncomfortable cot and fell almost immediately into a deep, dream-haunted sleep.

Gradually she became aware that her sleep was being disturbed; a faint, wind-sigh of string music was plucking at the edge of her consciousness, dragging her out of her dream and into a half-awake state. The dream, which she could not quite bring to the forefront of her mind, nevertheless lured her back toward sleep, but the music seemed to grow louder, bringing with it a memory that suddenly filled her mind, startling her into full consciousness.

She lay rigid and wide awake, thinking of that night last summer, when someone had come into her room. Her heart was hammering as she strained to hear any unusual sound. At first, all she could hear was the music, soft and insidious, and then her flesh began to crawl, for she heard a soft footfall, as if someone was walking, catfooted, across the rug.

She shivered—there seemed to be a sudden breeze in the room—and then she saw the deeper blackness looming over her and knew that someone was bending over the bed.

She tried to open her mouth to cry out, but her throat was clenched shut by a cold panic that cut off her voice as surely as a gripping hand.

Now she could hear breathing, and she could smell something... What? Tobacco, liquor and something else... Something sweetish and rather sickening.

And then a hand touched her. A man's hand, she knew without doubt. Gently and lasciviously, it pressed upon her upper chest and then stroked down over her breast, pushing the blanket aside, moving over her abdomen, then farther down . . .

All of a sudden her paralysis was shattered, and she jerked upright into a sitting position, at the same time striking out blindly with her fist.

She heard a quick, hissing sound of expelled breath as her fist struck a human midsection and then heard a shuffling sound, followed by the faint noise of a closing door.

Trembling with outrage, Rebecca fumbled in the dark and managed to light the candle. Holding it aloft, she saw that the room was empty, except for Margaret and herself. Had Margaret been aroused?

Getting to her feet took a few seconds, for her legs were weak and unsteady. At the other bed, she determined that Margaret had not moved since falling asleep. She was breathing slowly and regularly. Rebecca silently thanked God that she hadn't called out and awakened her. All Margaret needed at this point was another shock.

She returned to her cot, placing the candle on the bedside table. She knew that she did not dare sleep for the remainder of the night. This was simply not to be endured! She should have told Edouard and Felicity the first time this had occurred, instead of attempting to be diplomatic. Well, in her present frame of mind, she certainly would not make that mistake again. Tomorrow she would confront them both with it.

"You SAY SOMEONE CAME into your room? In the middle of the night?" Felicity exclaimed in distress. "Are you certain, my dear? You have, after all, just had a considerable shock, with the death of your uncle. Isn't it possible that you were dreaming?"

Rebecca set her lips, thinking that she had recently received more of a shock than Felicity knew, and now the anger that had been building in her since her wedding night threatened to spill out in a violent tirade. She managed to keep her voice civil and only mildly sarcastic. "I told you, Felicity, that this is not the first such occurrence. It has happened twice before, once to me and once to Margaret!"

Beside Felicity, Edouard stared at Rebecca narrowly. "But why did you not tell us at the time? Why did you wait until now?"

"We didn't tell you at the time, because we thought it might cause some embarrassment to some family member," she said flatly, far past the point where she cared if she hurt her in-laws' feelings or not. "I'm telling you now, because the same thing has occurred again, and I feel that the situation cannot continue."

"And Margaret slept through this...this visitation?" Edouard said skeptically.

"Margaret was given a dose of laudanum before retiring," she snapped. "And the incident last night was relatively quiet, except for the music."

"That's another thing," Edouard said. "You say you heard the sound of a string instrument plucked, like a harp. I simply don't understand that, not at all. The only instruments in the house that could make such music are the antique Chinese instruments, and as we have told you, no one in the family knows how to play them. I find this all very odd indeed!"

"Not nearly as odd as I do," Rebecca said sharply. "I can see that you do not believe me."

"Now, I did not say that, my dear," Edouard said soothingly. "But you have been rather distraught, since the letter from India."

"Have you told Jacques?" Felicity insisted.

Rebecca hesitated, realizing belatedly that she had erred. Ordinarily, the first thing a dutiful wife would have done would have been to tell her husband.

"No, I came to you first, since it is your home. I hoped that you might offer some explanation."

Felicity flushed. "You think that we would know of something like this and allow it to continue?"

"I honestly don't know *what* to think," Rebecca said. "I only know that it must stop. I will be happy to show you the secret doorway that Margaret and I found, and of course there must be others."

"I shall summon Jacques," Edouard said, "and we will investigate at once."

"THIS IS HOW you open it," Rebecca said, touching the leaf that concealed the hidden spring.

Slowly the wooden panel slid open, revealing the black maw of the passageway.

Jacques bent over and stepped into the darkness. "I see no trace of light at all."

He backed into the sitting room and took Rebecca's arm. "Rebecca, I am so sorry. I wish you had spoken to me of this before, when it first happened. I will investigate the passage and see where it leads."

He frowned at the opening. "I cannot imagine who could be using it." He glanced at his father. "Grandfather never told you there were secret passageways in the house?"

Edouard shook his head. "No, my boy, I am as mystified as you are. Of course, your grandfather was a strange man, with many secrets. This evidently was one of them. But we should not waste time talking. I will have Dhupta bring a lantern, and he and I shall investigate this.''

''By all means, have Dhupta fetch a lantern, but I shall do the investigating,'' Jacques said firmly.

For a moment Rebecca felt a surge of affection for Jacques, for his kindness and consideration. She also sensed that it was most important to him that he be allowed to find this mysterious night visitor; it was something that he *could* do for her.

She also noticed that Edouard's face had taken on a sour look. Moving closer to her husband, she said, ''Speaking of Dhupta, have you considered that *he* might be the prowler? You claim that no one in the family knows how to play the Oriental instruments, but isn't it possible that Dhupta is familiar with them? He is Indian, after all, and the music I heard is somewhat similar to Indian music.''

Edouard gave her a disdainful look. ''Nonsense, my dear. It could not possibly be Dhupta. The man is totally devoted to me, for he owes me his life. In addition, he is, as you have probably surmised, a man of excellent background and family. He was not raised to serve others, you know.''

''That seems quite apparent,'' Rebecca said dryly. ''His manner sometimes verges on insolence. However, he is, as I have said, from India, and Margaret and I are British. Is it not possible that, because of the recent troubles between his people and ours, he bears us some ill will?''

''She is right, Father,'' Jacques said. ''It is not so improbable.''

Edouard shook his head. ''If you knew Dhupta as I do, you would realize that it is impossible. But enough talk. I will have him fetch a lantern, and the three of us—you, and Dhupta and I—will explore the passageway.''

WHEN THE THREE MEN had disappeared into the passageway, Rebecca sought out Felicity in the parlor. "Felicity, what do you know about Dhupta? I have wanted to ask about him since we arrived here. From what I have seen of your country, it strikes me that it is most unusual for a family to have an Indian servant. In all the other homes I have visited, I have seen nothing but black slaves."

Felicity smoothed the front of her gown. She appeared flustered by the question. "I don't know much about Dhupta, my dear; only that Edouard found him in Charleston, where Dhupta had made his way after coming to this country, for reasons to which I am not privy. He had no money, and being dark-skinned, he was in dire straits. Edouard was impressed by his intelligence and background and more or less rescued him by offering him a position here as factotum. The man was most grateful. Since he has been with us, which has been some five years, he has run the house with quiet efficiency, and I have found no reason to complain of him."

Rebecca sighed. "It would make things most convenient if it *was* him."

"Why, whatever do you mean, child?"

"Well, if it is *not* him, then who is it?"

Felicity's hand fluttered to her throat. "I think I had best see to tea. The men will want something after their search."

Quickly she hurried off, leaving Rebecca staring after her curiously. What an extremely odd reaction, she thought.

SINCE TEA WAS SERVED as soon as the men returned from exploring the passageway and since Margaret joined the family that afternoon for the first time in days, there was nothing said about the passageway until they were finished with their tea.

Margaret seemed much improved. There was more color in her face, and she exhibited greater energy than she had shown in the past few days. Rebecca smiled at her often and plied her with rich cakes, since she was looking dreadfully thin.

After tea Margaret excused herself, and Rebecca immediately took Jacques aside. She wanted to talk to him privately, for she felt a vague but growing suspicion of both Edouard and Felicity. Despite what Jacques had done to her, he *was* her husband, he did love her and she believed that she could trust him.

"Well," she said eagerly, "what did you find?"

Jacques gave her one of his endearing, sweet smiles. "It was amazing, Rebecca. Can you believe that the whole house is honeycombed with these passageways? I just wish that I had known about them as a boy. It would have been very exciting exploring them."

"But did you find out where that particular passage goes?"

He shook his head. "I told you, it is a veritable warren. That particular passageway connects with dozens of others, and there are exits in almost every room in the house, including all of the bedrooms."

Rebecca gave a gasp of dismay. "You mean that the prowler didn't necessarily have to come in through the doorway that Margaret and I found? He could have come directly into our rooms through other panels?"

"That's right, he could have."

"Then there is no real way of stopping him, except to close off all the hidden panels."

Jacques shrugged. "If it would be possible to locate all of them, and I doubt that we can do that."

"You seem surprisingly unconcerned."

"Oh, I'm not, darling. I'm just so dumbfounded at finding all those passageways, that I—" He broke off reaching for her hand.

She evaded his hand and sat down in the nearest chair. "What does your father say?"

"He said that he is equally astounded, but he promised that he will get to the bottom of the matter. In the meantime I believe that you should return to our chambers at night, where I can protect you, and we'll have one of the housemaids sit with Margaret during the night."

"And Dhupta, how did he react? Did you notice any signs of guilt about him? Did he act strangely? Or indicate in any way that he was familiar with the passageways?"

Jacques said thoughtfully, "Not that I could see. He behaved in a normal manner. If your night visitor is Dhupta, he is certainly an accomplished actor."

"But have you thought," Rebecca said, "that it is possible that he is *just* that?"

Chapter Eleven

THAT NIGHT, as Jacques had suggested, Rebecca retired to their chambers and was happy to do so. The day's events had brought about a slight change in her attitude toward her husband. Although his confession on their wedding night had been the beginning of her feeling of disorientation, the added problems of her uncle's death, Margaret's illness and the bizarre occurrence last night had brought this feeling to such a peak that she felt a strong need for someone or something stable to hang on to.

Rebecca was a strong woman and prided herself upon being able to cope with any contingency that might arise, but she actually had never faced much in the way of adversity. Things had always come to her easily, and in the event of any small disturbance in the tenor of her life, there had always been someone there for her to turn to: her parents, Margaret or a friend. Now, separated from her parents, with Margaret ill and feeling a strong distrust of Edouard and Felicity, Jacques was the only person to whom she could look for help.

As she lay beside him in the large canopied bed, she was surprised to find that she was weeping.

In the flickering candlelight, Jacques turned on his side and looked down at her, then gently wiped the tears from her face with his fingers. "Rebecca, darling Rebecca,'' he said softly, and took her into his arms.

Gratefully Rebecca burrowed her head against his shoulder, taking comfort from the solidity and warmth of him. When morning came she found herself still in the same position.

The next day, no one reported hearing anything unusual during the night, and the family enjoyed a relatively pleasant breakfast. Margaret seemed even more improved, and Rebecca felt her own normally good spirits and optimism begin to revive. Surely, with everyone now aware of the situation, they would soon find out who was making these nocturnal visits, and the problem would be solved. Perhaps, Rebecca thought hopefully, it *was* one of the servants.

Breakfast was disturbed by the sound of heavy footsteps in the hallway, and Armand strode into the room, bringing with him a feeling of violence and urgency. "I must speak with you, Father," he said without preamble.

Armand carried with him into the room the coolness of the outdoors and the smell of woodsmoke and, for Rebecca, a feeling of shame and embarrassment, as well.

It was unthinkable that he should know of the situation between her and Jacques. Thoughts of that day on the hill pushed their way into her mind. He had known then, of course. That was why he had said what he had about his brother. Why hadn't he told her the truth, instead of giving her only vague hints—hints that could not possibly have made any sense to her at the time? Was his promise to his brother more important than her ruined life?

"Well, you might at least say good morning, Armand," Edouard said crossly. "What is so important that you find it necessary to barge in here like a savage, forgetting your manners?"

Armand stood before his seated family stiffly, almost as if at military attention, his face ruddied by his trip and the cool air. "I need to speak to you privately, Father."

"All in good time. First you will greet your mother like a gentleman, and then you will sit down and join us while we finish our meal. *Then*, you and I shall repair to my study."

Edouard's voice was inflexible and sarcastic, and Armand's face flushed even more as he ungraciously took the chair that one of the house servants pulled out for him.

The exchange between father and son had given Rebecca enough time to pull her own feelings together. She had decided that her only means of dealing with Armand's knowledge of her situation was to pretend that no problem existed. It was a solution that had worked for her before on other awkward occasions.

She glanced up and found Armand's gaze upon her, piercing and intent, but she managed to keep her composure without flinching or looking away.

Armand accepted a cup of tea, a slice of ham, a large serving of hominy and a chunk of corn bread with lashings of butter and preserves. Without speaking again, he began to eat rapidly.

Rebecca, watching him, felt herself growing angry and shot a quick glance at Felicity. She must be very hurt that her son showed her so little courtesy. However, she was surprised to find Felicity's expression completely neutral. Rebecca had noticed that the older woman was moving gingerly again this morning, as if she was bothered by rheumatics or some similar affliction. Rebecca frowned to herself, wondering again just what it was that ailed her mother-in-law. And why did it seem to only affect her here, on the island?

After breakfast Edouard accompanied the impatient Armand to his study, and Jacques retired to the library to peruse the latest Savannah newspaper.

Rebecca, Felicity and Margaret went into the sun-room to sit in the warmth collected behind the glass from the pale winter sun and to work on their embroidery.

The way to the sun-room led past Edouard's study, and as the women passed the door, they could hear the sound of voices raised in contention from inside. Felicity hurried past the door with her face averted.

The sun had managed to burn off most of the morning fog, and the sun-room was pleasant and redolent with the scent of green plants. Each woman took her favorite chair and began to work on her individual project. Rebecca did not usually care a great deal for doing such handwork, but the piece of petit point she was working on—it was to be a footstool cover— was very attractive, a pattern of pink roses on white, and she found the work oddly comforting.

Felicity was very quiet this morning, and Margaret was *always* quiet, and so for a bit Rebecca was content to just sit and work in a companionable silence. She wanted to discuss further with Felicity the matter of the passageway, but she decided that was unwise with Margaret present.

Then the memory of that day at Les Chênes intruded, and she remembered the story that Jacques had told them about the owners of the ruined plantation manor house. She also remembered that Jacques had cut the story short when she had inquired as to what had happened to the unfortunate daughter of the couple who had been burned to death in the fire that had destroyed the mansion. Perhaps her mother-in-law knew what had become of the girl.

"Felicity, I have a question," she said. "When we were at Les Chênes, Jacques told us the story of how the original house there was destroyed."

Felicity looked up, her expression suddenly guarded. "Yes, it was terrible, a very sad affair."

"Jacques said that the man who owned the plantation and his wife were killed in the fire, but he also told us that there was a child, a daughter, who survived, and that she and her nursemaid were brought here to live at Maison de Rêverie. I understand that the girl was raised as a sister to Edouard."

"Yes, that is true."

Felicity was beginning to look apprehensive, and Rebecca wondered why. Was what happened to the girl all that unpleasant?

"Well, we were diverted just then," Rebecca continued, sailing past the small lie. "And Jacques never got to finish the story. Just now I thought of it, and I found myself wondering whatever became of the girl. Did you know her?"

Felicity slowly lowered her embroidery frame to her lap, and Rebecca could see that her hands were trembling ever so slightly. When she spoke her voice was calm, but strangely expressionless. "Why, yes, I knew her. She was still living here when Edouard and I were married. As you say, she was raised as Edouard's sister, and he always thought of her as such."

"What was she like? Was she attractive?"

Felicity's full lips thinned. "I believe she was considered so, yes."

Margaret, who had little interest in the affair, had dropped her own work into her lap and appeared to be dozing.

Feeling that she was onto something interesting, Rebecca leaned forward. "Was she a pleasant person? You found her easy to get along with?"

Felicity picked up her embroidery and began again to ply her needle, staring down at the frame. "I suppose you could call her pleasant, and we got along well enough for the time that we were together."

"What became of her? Did she marry and leave?"

Felicity looked at her strangely. "No. Didn't Jacques tell you? The girl is dead. She died three years after Edouard and I were married."

"Oh!" Rebecca felt a wave of sorrow for this girl she had never known. "How dreadful! Of an illness?"

"Yes. The doctors were never quite certain what it was that took her off."

"Was her nursemaid still alive then? It must have been very sad for her."

"Yes, Bess was still alive. She married here, you know, and had a daughter of her own, Lutie. Perhaps you met her at Les Chênes. She is the housekeeper there."

Rebecca felt a quick jolt of surprise. So *that* was who the beautiful, light-skinned black woman was! It seemed to her that the more she found out about the affairs of the Huntoons, the more complicated they became. She had a strong feeling that there was more yet to learn, something dark and forbidden.

Once again she found herself wondering if Lutie was Armand's mistress. A picture of them coupling, their naked bodies intertwined in passion, filled her mind, igniting a rush of desire that caused her to move uncomfortably. And then the scene in her mind changed to show herself and Armand, and although she had never lain naked in a man's arms, it seemed to her that she knew just how it would feel. She felt her face and body grow uncommonly warm.

Attempting to control her rioting emotions, she stabbed her needle fiercely through the cloth. She would not be having these feelings if her marriage had been consummated! It was like a hunger, she thought, a hunger that gnawed at one just as fiercely as the hunger for food, and she was doomed to go hungry for the rest of her life. It was unfair!

Restless and uncomfortable, angry at herself, Rebecca put down her sewing and got to her feet. "I think I shall go and check to see if Edouard has finished his talk with Armand. I want to speak to him about..." She glanced over to where Margaret was apparently dozing and lowered her voice to a whisper. "About the passageways."

"Oh, yes, my dear. Perhaps you should do that." Felicity seemed inordinately pleased that Rebecca had changed the subject, a fact that was not lost on Rebecca. Why was it that her mother-in-law appeared so ill at ease with the subject of the Huntoon family? And why had Jacques acted so strangely when he had told her the story of the fire? Yes, there was something involved here, some sort of secret, and it would be interesting to ferret out what it was.

When she reached the hall opposite Edouard's study, it was immediately clear that Edouard and Armand had not finished their conversation. Their voices were quite loud, and they both sounded very angry.

Glancing quickly around to see if any of the household staff was about, Rebecca saw that she was unobserved and so she stepped close to the door so that she could hear what was being said.

"Why don't you ever listen to me?" Armand was saying. "You know how much money the cotton crop brings in, in comparison to the indigo and the rice. And now, with the new gins, I will be able to process it more quickly and more profitably. You gave me the responsibility of running Les Chênes, but you won't allow me to put my own ideas into operation. My record speaks for itself. Why won't you take that into account?"

"I can stand here and argue with you all day, Armand, but what it comes down to is that I do not have to explain myself to you. I am still the master of Maison de Rêverie, and of all the Molyneux holdings. Until I say otherwise, you will do as you are told. Now, I wish to hear no more of it!"

There was the hard sound of approaching footsteps on the other side of the door. Quickly Rebecca stepped back and hastened to conceal herself behind a large potted palm. A few seconds later the study door crashed open, and Armand strode out like an attacking soldier, his face dark with anger.

Rebecca watched until he had stalked out of sight around a corner of the corridor. Perhaps this was not the best time to speak to Edouard, right after an angry confrontation with his son, yet she must know if anything new had been discovered concerning the secret passageways.

Rather hesitantly, she rapped on the door with her knuckles. There was a moment's silence before she heard Edouard's harsh voice: "Come in!"

Opening the door, she found Edouard facing a window, hands clasped behind his back, rocking on his heels.

"Cousin Edouard? I beg your pardon for bothering you, but I wondered if you have discovered anything further about the passageways?"

Again, a silence ensued, which seemed much longer than it actually was. At last Edouard turned toward her, and she could see that his face was still mottled with anger.

However, he greeted her with a tight smile. "Ah, our lovely Rebecca. Do come in and sit down."

She didn't really want to sit, but neither did she wish to irritate him further. She took the seat he had indicated, on a settee, the smallness of which she regretted at once when Edouard sat down beside her.

In this close proximity, she could see that his eyes were red-veined and that his face looked puffy and dissipated. His smile became less forced as his gaze studied her face. And then, as he spoke, he lowered his glance to make a quick and furtive survey of her body. "You are looking well, my dear, as blooming as ever. I hope that Margaret will soon be feeling fit, also. Her father's death was such a tragedy."

Rebecca bowed her head in acknowledgment of his words. "Yes. A terrible thing, and it is made even worse by her worry over her mother and my own parents, for we have no idea how matters are with them at present."

"Well, no matter how they stand, you may be certain that your parents are much relieved that you are with us, safely out of danger. Your father said as much in his last communication to me.''

"I know. And Margaret and I are both very grateful for your hospitality to us.''

"It is nothing, my dear. Besides, now you are members of our immediate family.'' He patted her hand, leaning toward her, and she could see the glitter of something in his eyes, which made her long to draw back from him, and she had to will herself not to do so.

"You know, my son is a very fortunate young man. It is a rare occurrence indeed when a man finds a bride as beautiful and charming as yourself. I quite envy him, I do indeed.''

"Why, thank you, Edouard.''

He was so close now that Rebecca could smell his breath, which was somewhat unpleasant, and then she felt his hand close around hers. His skin burned against hers, and for a long moment she felt at a loss. Accustomed as she was to fending off unwelcome advances from men, this was not the usual situation. Yesterday, in anger, she had been overly outspoken because of her concern over the night visitor. On the other hand, she had no real wish to antagonize her father-in-law; it could make living under his roof very unpleasant.

Still smiling, she gently attempted to remove her hand from under his, but he clasped it more firmly and then drew it to his chest, placing it over his heart.

Rebecca now experienced a surge of near panic. What on earth was she to do? It was clear now that if she didn't stop him, Edouard was going to carry his affectionate gestures to the point where they were going to constitute a serious intrusion upon her person and an affront to her character.

"Rebecca!" Edouard said hoarsely, pressing her hand tightly against the fabric of his vest. "Can you feel my heart beating? It has been beating for you since you first came into my house, but you were a maiden then, and I restrained myself. Now you are wed and have tasted the delights of connubial bliss."

Delights of connubial bliss! It was all Rebecca could do to keep from laughing in his face.

He said with heated breath, "Surely, you must now be able to recognize the passion I feel for you!"

Without warning he reached for her and pulled her close against him. The suddenness of his action caught her completely unaware; and before she could really take in what was happening, his lips were upon hers and his hand was fondling her breast.

Shock and revulsion filled her at the feeling of his lips, hot and moist, and at the sickish sweet smell of his breath. Instinctively she drew back from him, crying out, "No, Edouard! Please!"

But Edouard was fully aroused now and ignored her entreaty. With a strength that terrified her, he pulled her to him again, muttering in her ear as he rubbed her breast and probed for her nipple beneath the material of her garment.

"How I've wanted you, my pale Rebecca. How I have imagined your body, rounded and glowing with passion under my hands. I know how to pleasure a woman in many ways that you have not imagined. Jacques is but a boy in the light of my experience. I will make your body explode with pleasure."

She tried again to free herself, summoning all of her strength, and in that moment the heavy double doors of the study creaked as they began to open.

Instantly Edouard let her go, and with one quick and practiced gesture, smoothed back his hair with one hand while crossing his legs to hide his very obvious state of arousal.

Rebecca, confused and very angry, could only draw back against the arm of the sofa as Jacques entered the room.

"Ah, my son!" Edouard said cheerfully. "We were just talking about you. I was just telling Rebecca that certainly we will be able to discover where our night wanderer is entering the passageways and just who it is."

Rebecca, rattled as she was, had to admire Edouard's quickness of thought. She looked back over her shoulder at Jacques, but his expression was almost unnaturally bland. Had he seen what was going on, or had Edouard released her in time, before the door was fully open? Should she say anything? No, that would create an impossible situation. The whole incident was too bizarre and embarrassing.

"That was the reason I wanted to speak to you, Father. I thought that together we might make another effort to locate all of the hidden doors and nail closed all those we find. It may not tell us who the prowler is, but at least it will make a start at preventing anyone from using the passageways."

He looked at Rebecca. "You look quite flushed, Rebecca. Perhaps you should lie down for a bit. We don't want you sick, as well as Margaret."

Rebecca rose at once, grateful for the excuse to escape. "I do feel a bit feverish. I think I will take your advice, Jacques."

Walking to his side, she raised her face and gave him a light kiss on the cheek, both in gratitude for his fortuitous appearance and as a message of sorts to Edouard.

As she left the study Rebecca could hear the two men talking behind her and a renewed feeling of outrage almost made her turn back and confront Edouard. How could a man attempt such a betrayal of his own son and then go on to speak to him normally, as if nothing untoward had occurred? What kind of man was he? It would require a nature of extreme dissolution to behave in such a manner. To do such a thing a man would have to be without character and without morals. And what was she going to do? If the incident was repeated, how could she defend herself against Edouard without letting his family know of it? Oh, why was everything in her life suddenly going awry! Would there be no end to the problems and pain being inflicted upon her?

In her chambers, Rebecca bathed her face with cool water and lay down on the bed. She did feel unwell, but it was probably due to her emotional state. The scene just played out in the study kept repeating itself in her mind, and each time she felt the same shock and outrage. It was ironic, was it not, that both her brother-in-law and father-in-law should have attempted to make love to her and that her own husband could not? What was going to become of her?

Chapter Twelve

FOR THE NEXT FEW DAYS Rebecca managed to avoid being alone. It took considerable planning and caused her a good deal of inconvenience, but the possibility that Edouard might force himself upon her again made the effort worthwhile.

During this time Jacques was even more polite and considerate than ever, and without them even discussing it, he seemed to sense that she did not want to be left alone and went out of his way to see that she was not. Rebecca could not help wondering just how much he *had* seen when he opened the door to Edouard's study.

She longed to ask him, to have the matter out in the open between them, but, of course, she could not. There was always the possibility that he had seen nothing, and bold as Rebecca knew herself to be, there was simply no graceful way for a woman to tell her husband that his father had attempted to take liberties with her!

Margaret continued to improve and appeared to be almost her old self. She was taking an interest in things again, so Rebecca spent quite a bit of time with her, playing at cards, doing needlework or reading.

Since her illness Margaret was taking a greater interest in religion, and her choice of reading matter was most often the Bible. Rebecca had no quarrel with this, since she read the Bible herself on occasion; yet it did bother her a bit to be reading a Jane Austen novel when Margaret was absorbed in the Good Book. It seemed to Rebecca that preoccupation with her religion was tending to make Margaret more serious than ever, and in Rebecca's estimation, the other girl had always been too serious by half and certainly did not need to become more so.

During those times when the members of the family were together, at meals or in the salon after dinner, Edouard acted as if nothing at all had happened between them. His manner toward Rebecca was exactly as it had always been, a situation that annoyed her immensely.

Nothing new had been discovered about the night prowler, but Jacques had investigated the passageways as well as he could and had arranged to have all the secret panels that he could find nailed shut.

By the third night after Edouard had tried to force his attentions upon her, Rebecca was feeling the nervous strain of being constantly on her guard, and to add to her highly emotional state, Armand had ridden in that afternoon for another talk with his father.

Dinner that night was eaten in an atmosphere of awkwardness. As they dined Rebecca kept her eyes cast down so that she would not have to meet the eyes of Edouard or Armand, and after dinner, the family—including Felicity, who had spent most of the day in her room—went into the music room.

Tonight Margaret played her Chopin études, which she did passably well, Rebecca sang a few Irish tunes, accompanied by Jacques, and then Edouard sang several German *Lieder*, and caused Rebecca to seethe with anger when he had the audacity to look at her lecherously as he sang.

Quickly she turned her face away so that the others would not observe her reaction. When she turned she saw Edouard at the sideboard, pouring some kind of spirits from a heavy, cut-glass decanter into cut-glass goblets.

"Here you go," he said cheerfully, motioning to the glasses. "I have just poured some port from my latest shipment, and I would like you all to sample it."

He handed a glass to Felicity, who gave him a nervous nod, and then a glass to Jacques. When he offered one to his younger son, Armand shook his head. "No, Father. You know very well that I do not care for port."

Edouard continued to smile, but his eyes were cold and hard. He said evenly, "Surely you could take some just this once. I should like your opinion on it."

Showing his usual ill temper, Armand turned on his heel to cross the room, from where he glowered at his father. "I said that I don't care for any, and I should like to know when you will be able to discuss business with me."

"Business, always business!" Brusquely Edouard waved his free hand. "Do not press me about business tonight. We will speak tomorrow. Here, Rebecca, you really must try this port. I was promised that it is of the best."

Carefully avoiding his gaze, she reached out for the gleaming goblet and its contents of deep-red wine. She had little taste for port and certainly did not want to drink anything from Edouard's hand, but after Armand's refusal she felt that it would be easier, and attract less notice, if she accepted the wine. Even

Margaret took a glass, although, as Rebecca well knew, her cousin did not care at all for wine.

When all save Armand were in possession of a glass of the port, Edouard proposed a toast: "To all of us, to our health and happiness, and to the realization of our secret desires!"

Rebecca touched the glass to her lips and took just a sip. The wording of Edouard's toast added fuel to the considerable amount of anger she was holding in check. She now knew what at least one of Edouard's desires was, and his brazenness was unbelievable. What was even more unbelievable was his apparent conviction that she had not objected in the least to the liberties he had taken with her. If he had any idea of how nauseating she had found his attentions, he certainly would not continue to smile at her and offer toasts with hidden meanings. It was all she could do to remain silent. She wanted to fling the contents of her glass into his face and reveal him for what he was before his wife and sons!

When they had drunk the toasts, Edouard asked their opinion of the wine and everyone murmured that it was excellent, although Rebecca noticed that Jacques was the only one to drain his glass and ask for another.

After the wine there was some desultory conversation. Shortly Felicity pleaded fatigue and asked to be excused, to go to her rooms. Rebecca immediately took advantage of the opportunity to also excuse herself, and Margaret accompanied her.

Rebecca saw Margaret to her door and then, gratefully, sought the quiet of her and Jacques's large, well-appointed bedchamber. She kept the door bolted while she made her toilet and while she read a chapter of

Pride and Prejudice, which she was finding most enjoyable.

She did not like to unbolt the door before Jacques came to bed, but she was growing drowsy, and the alternative was to leave the door bolted and be awakened when he came in.

Finally she decided to leave the door locked. Better to have to get up and unbar it than to risk another visit from the prowler. She blew out the candle and got into bed.

She was sleeping quite soundly when she heard Jacques's knock, and she slid out of the warm bed and went to open the door without coming fully awake.

She mumbled something to Jacques, hurried across the cold floor and dived back under the comforters, drifting again into pleasant slumber. She stirred, muttering again when she felt the bed sag under Jacques's weight and, then, feeling secure in the knowledge that he was beside her, let herself slide into deep, dreamless sleep.

She awoke with shocking suddenness, aware of two things: she was cold—the comforters had been drawn back—and there were hands stroking her body.

Despite the shock of the abrupt awakening, she knew at once that the hands belonged to Edouard, for she heard his voice, insinuating, crooning, as his hands pressed and rubbed against her breasts: "Rebecca, Rebecca! The moon is full tonight. Look how she lights your body, which is whiter than her own. Rebecca! My pale Rebecca!"

Horrified, Rebecca saw his figure in the moonlight, clad in a dressing gown, leaning over her.

My God! Where was Jacques?

Groping with her left hand, Rebecca felt Jacques's shoulder beneath her palm. Why was he just lying there? It was not possible that he could still be asleep!

She fought against the groping hands of her assailant, crying out, "Jacques! Jacques, help me!"

In spite of her struggles Edouard's hands continued to stroke her body. She heard his soft chuckle and smelled the sweet noxiousness of his breath as he lowered his face close to hers.

"It will do you no good to call him, my pet," he said in that eerie, crooning voice. "He will not wake until morning. I have seen to that, so that we might be alone. All alone, so that I may do to you the things I have long imagined doing. Open for me, my Rebecca."

Clamping her legs tightly together, she endeavored to reach up to claw at his face, but he caught her hands easily and held them captive with one hand.

"You want me, my Rebecca. You know you do. Yet if you enjoy the fight, who am I to thwart you? The peach is sweeter when you must fight to taste it."

Again Rebecca called Jacques's name, refusing to believe that he couldn't hear her, and then, suddenly the memory of the wine, the port, and Edouard's insistence that they all drink it, flashed into her consciousness, and she knew that Jacques was not going to be able to help her. He was drugged! With this realization, full panic struck her, and she threw back her head and screamed, once, then again.

For a moment her screams gave Edouard pause, but then, as if excited by the sound, he laughed again. Even in her panic and despair, she could discern an edge of madness in the laughter.

"That's it, my beauty. Scream in passion, for I shall soon pierce you, soon probe deep inside you!"

The fingers of his free hand fastened in the neck of her nightgown, and as he ripped the garment from breast to hem, she was raised forcibly from the bed, and the back of her neck hurt from the pull of the fabric against it.

The sound of the material tearing was loud in the room. Flailing and kicking, she screamed again. Surely, *someone* would hear her.

Edouard came down on the bed and then was astraddle her thighs, the weight of him as frightening as death itself.

His dressing gown fell open, and he was panting now, a dreadful, animal sound. Again a scream tore its painful way out of her throat, but this time there was an answer. Outside in the hallway she could hear the sound of running feet, and the sound gave her added courage and strength.

Jerking her hands free of Edouard's grasp, she clawed again at his face. This time her nails raked skin.

Edouard cursed and drew back from her.

Someone was pounding on the door now and shouting her name: "Rebecca! Rebecca!"

It was Armand's voice. Thank God!

There was a rattle as he tried the door, and then the pounding again. Dear God! The door was bolted!

Seeming not to hear the sound of his son's voice or the pounding on the door, Edouard again gave that strange, eerie laugh and once more seized her hands.

Rebecca raised her head. "Armand! Armand, help me!"

Edouard, his hands gripping both of Rebecca's wrists, was now trying to force her thighs apart. Her muscles were trembling with strain and fatigue, and she did not know how much longer she could hold out against him.

"Armand!" She screamed it at the top of her voice.

Edouard was muttering now. "No! No! No!"

There was the sound of voices outside the door and then the noise of something striking it heavily—once, twice and yet again. The sound of wood rending, a great crash. Now there was bright light, and other people in the room, around the bed. Someone had hold of Edouard, pulling him away from her. Her body was free, cold and exposed in the night air; voices were shouting and cursing. People were struggling, and there was the sound of furniture being overturned. She felt as if she might become hysterical. One paramount thought—she must cover herself. They must not see her like this.

And then someone was tugging the covers up over her bruised body. Margaret? Was it Margaret?

There was the sound of a fist striking flesh, and the struggling mercifully ended. In the ensuing silence, Rebecca heard someone murmuring to her, someone crying.

And then the light came closer to her face, and she shut her eyes against the glare and pulled the comforter over her face, burrowing beneath it, like a fox going to earth.

Now Margaret talking, loudly, in a tone that Rebecca had never heard before, a sound of fury and outrage. And then men's voices, Armand's and Dhupta's. Dhupta?

Jarring footsteps and a dragging sound that faded away down the hallway, and then Margaret's voice again, only now gentle, full of tears.

"Rebecca...it's all right now. They've taken him away. Oh, do talk to me. Did he hurt you? Did he...? Please, Rebecca. You are safe now."

And then the sound of weeping.

Slowly, feeling her heartbeat return to normal and her thoughts to some kind of coherence, Rebecca felt her tense muscles gradually relax. Carefully, inch by inch, she uncoiled her body and, then, finally, pulled the comforter slowly down to expose her face.

Margaret was leaning over her, her face pale and streaked with tears, her eyes wide with shock. "Rebecca! Is something wrong with Jacques? He lies so still!"

Rebecca's throat felt restricted and painful, but she managed to shake her head. "He was given a sleeping potion. The wine," she whispered.

Margaret's eyes widened even further as understanding came to her. "What if we all had drunk it?" Her face grew paler still. "What if Armand had drunk it?"

Sinking down upon the bed, she took Rebecca into her arms, and at her cousin's comforting touch, Rebecca felt the tears of her anger and anguish finally begin to flow.

For long minutes the two young women wept together, and then at last, when her tears were exhausted, Rebecca lay back with a deep, hiccuping sigh. Her eyes and nasal passages felt swollen, but some of the horror of her experience had been washed away by her tears.

A sound came from the ruined doorway, and her heart began to hammer again. Turning her head, she saw that it was Armand, carrying a small, wooden chest.

Hastily she turned her face away. She did not want him to see her like this, and she had no wish to endure his pity. Despite the fact that it was Armand who had saved her, the circumstances were too embarrassing for her to be at ease in his presence.

She heard him cross the room and stop at the side of the bed where Jacques lay, snoring slightly. When Armand crossed around the bed to stand beside Margaret, Rebecca turned her face again, this time toward Jacques, who slept on, unaware.

There was the sound of wood on wood as Armand put the chest down upon the bedside table. His voice, when he spoke, was low. "Jacques seems to be all right. At least, he is breathing normally. He appears to be drugged."

"Rebecca told me." Margaret's voice was still thick with tears. "Cousin Edouard put a sleeping potion in the port."

Armand muttered a profanity under his breath. "Thank God that some of us didn't drink it. Margaret, is Rebecca all right? He didn't...he didn't actually *harm* her, did he?"

"I don't think so. She is bruised, of course, and scratched, from fighting him."

"That is why I brought this. It is the family medicine chest. There are unguents, strips of white linen, if they are needed, and a bottle of laudanum. I think it would be a good idea for her to take some so that she can rest more easily."

"Yes, I shall give her some. Oh, Armand! It is all so terrible, so frightening! Why did he do it? He was always so kind to us."

Armand's low voice was tight with emotion. "I feel somehow responsible. I know what my father can be like. However, I assumed that he would have the dignity and good sense to restrain himself in the case of relatives. I realize now that my judgment was in error."

Rebecca felt a rise of anger, overriding her embarrassment. She turned to face Armand. "What do you mean by that? Has he done something like this before, to others?"

Armand said slowly, "Not precisely. He..."

"Why didn't you tell us?" she said furiously. "You must have known who was prowling the house at night, using the secret passageways!"

Armand stared at her in astonishment. "What are you saying? No one told me of any such occurrence. Do you mean to say that this is not the first time something like this has happened?"

"Not quite what happened tonight, no, but someone came into both Margaret's room and mine in the night and frightened us badly."

Armand shook his head, and his scowl was forbidding. "Evidently I wasn't here when any of these things occurred, and no one told me of it. If I had known, I should have done something about it, even if he is my own father."

"Did you know of the passageways?"

Armand hesitated, then nodded. "Yes, that I knew. At Les Chênes you heard Jacques tell of my father's adopted sister, Elissa. Her nursemaid, Bess, was like a second mother to me. Bess told me of the passageways before she died."

"I don't understand," Margaret said. "If *you* knew of their existence, why didn't the rest of the family know of them?"

Armand shook his head once more. "Well, obviously my father did."

Margaret's voice was a whisper. "What have they done with him? Cousin Edouard, that is. When you and Dhupta subdued him, he was like a madman."

"He is tied to his bed, and Dhupta is guarding him. You may both rest easy now."

Rebecca said scornfully, "I doubt that I shall rest easy for some time." She was beginning to feel feverish, and as she moved, seeking a more comfortable place, a sharp pain in her shoulder caused her to gasp aloud.

"I am damned sorry about what happened, Rebecca," Armand said. He turned to Margaret. "You had best give her the laudanum and tend her injuries. I will return the first thing in the morning to see how she is."

As he turned away to leave, Margaret reached out and caught his sleeve. "Armand...what about Cousin Felicity? Is she all right?"

"She drank some of the wine, as you saw. Not as much as Jacques, but enough to make her sleep heavily. I dread to think of how she will react when she is told of what happened here tonight. But the important thing now is to see to Rebecca. You will stay with her?"

"Of course."

With a last, lingering look at Rebecca, Armand left the room.

Exhausted, Rebecca sank back upon the pillow, moving only to take the laudanum that Margaret offered her and to allow her cousin to slip a clean nightgown over head after she had ministered to her hurts.

Chapter Thirteen

As ARMAND MADE HIS WAY down the hall toward his own room, he felt as if the entire weight of this great house lay across his shoulders. He knew that he would remember to the end of his days the images that now burned in his mind as if etched in fire: Rebecca, her struggling body pale and fragile in the candlelight; his father astraddle her, like some ravening beast, clawing at her body.

Guilt and anger battered at him. If only he had known of the earlier prowlings, he would certainly have guessed that the night walker was Edouard. The things that Armand had learned from Bess, so long ago, had not changed his feelings toward his father but had only succeeded in intensifying the feelings he had had toward the man since childhood. There was a streak of something evil in Edouard, something strange and twisted. A legacy from *his* father, Jean Molyneux, if Bess's story was to be believed, and Armand had no doubt that it was.

Jacques, beloved favorite son, knew little or nothing of his father's true nature, and Armand had never told him what he had learned from the old black woman. It would have accomplished no purpose, and it would only have hurt Jacques.

Armand smiled wryly to himself. Oh, yes, he was very good at keeping secrets. A noble trait, except because of it a young woman was now trapped in a sham of a marriage and, in addition, had almost been raped by a man whom she had considered her friend and protector.

And what of Felicity, who had suffered perhaps the most at the hands of her husband? She knew first-hand of the cruelty Edouard was capable of. Surely she must have guessed who walked the passageways at night, who invaded the girls' rooms. Why had *she* not stopped him? Armand knew, of course, that she feared his father, and yet how could she let such—yes, selfish—fears keep her from speaking up when the welfare of two young women was at stake?

Entering his room, he set down his lamp and threw himself across the bed, the image of Rebecca's pale, nude limbs and body burning across the back of his eyes. He felt a deep shame as his body responded to that image. Didn't he want the same thing Edouard had wanted? Was he really any better than his father?

MARGARET, SEATED IN A CHAIR close to Rebecca's bed, watched over her cousin's restless sleep. Despite the fact that she had had little sleep herself, Margaret did not feel in the least fatigued; rather, she was filled with a strength that came from resolution and purpose.

Rebecca tossed and moaned in her dreams, and Margaret felt the threat of tears behind her eyes. How could this have happened? Cousin Edouard, who had been so kind, so considerate of their comfort and welfare? It was difficult to relate that well-dressed, well-mannered gentleman to the creature she had seen torn forcibly from Rebecca's body.

Margaret's face burned. When they had pulled Edouard away, she had seen it! That threatening, red protuberance that projected from between the flaps of his dressing gown... But she must not think of that ugly *thing* threatening Rebecca. Rebecca was safe now. And surely, soon, news would come from her mother telling them that the conflict was over and that the rest of their family was safe. Only then would the nightmare be over. Life would go back to the way it had been when they had first arrived here. It had all been so beautiful, so wonderful then. How could the world suddenly have gone so wrong?

On the day they had arrived, Rebecca had said that the island seemed to be enchanted, and perhaps it was, but there were dark enchantments in the world, also. Margaret knew that now. She had always, theoretically, known that there was evil in the world, but she had never before met it face-to-face. In a few nightmarish moments that had changed, but she was grimly determined that it would not defeat her. It would not claim her, and it would not claim Jacques nor Rebecca.

Rising from her chair, she walked around the bed and gazed down at Rebecca's sleeping husband. He was curled up on his side like a child, and his face looked young and vulnerable in sleep. Poor Jacques! He, too, was caught up in this wickedness, and he, like herself and Rebecca, was an innocent bystander.

After a last lingering look at his sleeping face, she returned to sit beside her cousin. Strange, she had always looked upon Rebecca as the strong one, the one who took charge of things. And now their positions were reversed. She smiled smugly to herself. Now she, Margaret, was the strong one, and with the help of

Almighty God, she would be equal to the task of taking care of herself and the ones she loved.

FOR THE FIRST FEW SECONDS after Rebecca wakened, it seemed like an ordinary morning. Eyes still closed, she stretched, and her body complained with sharp pains in several places, bringing the incidents of last night into stark focus.

"Rebecca? Are you all right, my dear?"

It was Jacques's voice, and she opened her eyes to see him sitting beside the bed, in the chair that Margaret had occupied during her vigil last night. His face was pale, and there were dark rings beneath his eyes. "Are you all right?"

Rebecca's throat was raw and sore, and when she spoke her voice was hoarse. "Yes. Could I have some water, please?"

Quickly he filled a glass from the pitcher on the chest of drawers and brought it to her, lifting her tenderly so that she might drink.

After he had returned the pitcher and the glass to their places, he sat down again, this time on the edge of the bed, and softly brushed the hair back from her forehead.

She suffered his touch but took no comfort from it. Looking at the mellow gold of the bar of sunlight that stole from a crack between the draperies on one window, she said, "What time is it?"

"Nearly three in the afternoon. I sent Margaret to bed this morning, when I finally woke up, and I have been here with you since."

Tenderly, with some hesitation, he touched her face. "Rebecca, I hardly know what to say to you. There simply aren't words to tell you how I feel. To say that

I'm sorry is simply not enough, I know. To think of such a thing happening! My own father!"

Two red spots of anger burned in the pallor of his cheeks. "How could he have done this thing? How could it have happened? And to think that I wasn't even able to help you. I feel so useless, such a fool!"

Rebecca saw his pain registered in his face, but somehow it did not really touch her. She knew very well that it was not his fault that he had been drugged, and yet some perverse part of her could not help blaming him for not coming to her rescue when she needed him and now would not let her offer him the comfort of telling him that she understood.

Instead she said, "What have they done with him?"

"He is locked in his room, and Dhupta watches him. Father is apparently over his period of mania, and he claims to remember nothing of last night's events."

Rebecca raised her head too quickly, causing her neck a certain degree of discomfort. Ignoring the pain, she said, "And you believe him?"

Jacques's expression darkened. "I am not certain. It is difficult to believe that my own father would *knowingly* do something so terrible."

Rebecca scooted up in the bed until she was upright against the headboard. She was so annoyed with him that she had difficulty in speaking at all reasonably. "Jacques . . . You are an intelligent man. Surely you know by now that your father put a sleeping potion in the wine, and at that time he was in complete control of his wits, for he drugged the wine with forethought. Surely that shows that he knew very well what he was doing. In fact, that he planned it all with some care!"

Jacques flushed deeply. "You're right, of course, Rebecca. But I am not entirely useless. As I sat here watching you sleep, I have been thinking, planning what we should do. I have decided that we must return to the house in Savannah. We cannot possibly stay under the same roof with my father after what has happened. I thought we would leave in a few days, when you feel able to travel."

Rebecca considered the proposal. It was the obvious solution, of course, and the idea made her feel better at once. How strange it was that only a few days ago she had been impatient to leave Savannah so that she would not have to be alone with Jacques. Now Savannah looked like a refuge from things even more unsettling than her unconsummated marriage!

"If we go we must take Margaret with us. We can't leave her here."

Jacques nodded. "Of course."

"And what of your mother?"

"I have not discussed it with her yet," he said with a shrug. "She has not come out of her room all day and will not let anyone in to speak with her, except her personal maid. The news of what happened shocked her badly. She is, has always been, devoted to my father. You can imagine how she must be feeling."

Slowly Rebecca nodded. Indeed she could. It must be a stunning blow to have your husband attack another woman under your own roof, particularly when that woman was your son's wife.

"I must speak to her," she said. "She must know that I do not hold her in any way responsible."

Jacques looked doubtful. "Do you feel well enough?"

Carefully Rebecca stretched her limbs. Her body ached, and she still felt a weariness that she suspected was partly a result of her state of mind, but she felt quite capable of getting out of bed and moving about.

"I will be fine," she assured him. "And I do think I should speak to your mother. If you will please hand me my dressing gown? It's there on the chest at the foot of the bed."

Jacques rose and reached for her dressing gown. As he did so, Rebecca pulled the fabric of her nightdress away from her body and looked at herself. The ugly colors of deep bruises were developing upon her breasts and stomach, and a linen bandage obscured a portion of her abdomen.

When Jacques turned toward her with the dressing gown, she hastily let her nightdress fall back into place. Seeing the bruises and the bandage had made her feel sick inside, for they were the physical marks, the proof, of her violation. Although Edouard had been prevented from performing the ultimate vandalization of her body, she knew that he had taken something from her that she would never find again, and in that moment she wished him dead. Dead and gone; never to bother them again!

AT FIRST, Felicity did not want to admit Rebecca to her chambers. It took a bit of persuasion, by both Jacques and Rebecca, before Felicity's personal maid, a slender brown-skinned young woman was finally told to admit Rebecca, who went in alone.

Rebecca found the older woman lying in her bed, her hair disheveled, her body slack and her face red and distorted from weeping.

In spite of her own pain and anguish, Rebecca felt compassion for her mother-in-law, whom she saw as a simple, uncomplicated woman, with generous instincts and a kind heart.

Moving a bit stiffly, Rebecca sat down on the edge of Felicity's bed and took the other woman's limp hand in hers. Felicity flinched away at her touch and closed her eyes.

"Felicity," Rebecca said gently, "I had to speak to you. I wanted to assure you that I am fine and that I hold you in no way responsible. Edouard did not...he did not hurt me badly. And I had to let you know how sorry I am that you had to be hurt, as well. I think I can understand how you must be feeling."

Tears flooded Felicity's eyes and ran down her cheeks. She opened her eyes, which held a silent plea. "I'm so ashamed," she whispered. "I should have stopped him, but I was so afraid."

Rebecca patted the other woman's hand. "But it was not your fault. The guilt is not yours. Why, you have been so good to us, looked after us like a mother."

Felicity's tears began to flow more heavily, and a thick sob caught in her throat. "But I knew, you see. At least, I guessed."

A dreadful certainty began to creep into Rebecca's mind. "Guessed what?"

"That it was Edouard who was sneaking into your rooms at night. But I...I didn't *want* to believe it was true, you see. I was afraid to face the truth. And now it has come to this...this atrocity! God is punishing me for my cowardice."

Rebecca still held Felicity's hand, but she was sitting very still now, drawn in upon herself. Gazing down at her mother-in-law, she could see that the woman's gown had fallen open, and upon the white skin of Felicity's shoulder, there was a large, dark, painful-looking bruise.

Suddenly it all came together in Rebecca's mind: Felicity's strange "illness," the way she sometimes walked and moved, as if she were in pain; the days that she stayed secluded in her room; the abrupt changes in her personality; the obvious apprehension when she was in the presence of her husband.

"He beats you, doesn't he?" Rebecca said. "That is the reason you are afraid of him."

Felicity pulled her hand from Rebecca's grip and quickly gathered her gown closed. "Yes," she said in a whisper. "I am not complaining. Perhaps I have deserved his discipline. It is a wife's duty to be loyal to her husband, you see. And he is a good husband, in many ways. But I realize that I should have protected you and Margaret. That is also my duty, and I have failed you..."

Reaching out, she gripped Rebecca's shoulders. Her fingers dug in fiercely. "You must not tell him that you know about this...." She removed one hand and gestured to the spot where Rebecca had noticed the bruise. "Despite the fact that I failed you horribly, will you please do me that courtesy?"

Feeling sick inside, Rebecca nodded. She could not understand how any woman could endure a man's abuse. But she said, "I shall not tell him. As a matter of fact, I doubt that I shall ever be able to bring myself to even speak to Edouard again. But I simply cannot understand why you insist on defending him! How can you feel loyalty to a man who mistreats you so, who beats you and causes you to live in constant fear?"

Felicity sank back upon her pillows and closed her eyes. "It is not entirely his fault, you see. There are things that you do not understand, my dear. Things that his parents did to him. But more to the point, what else *can* I do? I have no other life than Edouard and this house."

"But you could have gone to your sons about his cruelties to you, asked their protection."

Felicity shook her head. "Oh, no. That would have torn our family apart. I did not want them to know. It is a thing between Edouard and I alone."

"You could have had your sons take you away from here."

Felicity smiled sadly. "And how would we have lived? Everything we have comes from Edouard. He is sole owner of the Molyneux estates and fortune. If Jacques had quarreled with Edouard over me, his father might have disowned him and Jacques's inheritance would have been lost."

"And Armand's, also."

"Oh, yes, of course," Felicity said quickly. "I mentioned Jacques first because he is the elder. Rebecca, you must promise me that you will say nothing of this to either Jacques or Armand. If you should tell them, you will be undoing all that I have labored so hard to protect."

Reluctantly Rebecca agreed. "I promise, of course, if that is your wish. But don't you have other family to whom you could go?"

Felicity gave Rebecca a strange, sad smile. "My parents are dead. There is a brother, but do you really think that he would approve of my leaving my lawful husband and attaching myself to him and his family, to be dependent upon his charity? You are young, Rebecca, and still full of energy and spirit. I do not mean to be unkind when I say that you have yet to experience some of life's realities.''

Rebecca set her lips stubbornly. She was, of course, young, but young or old, she could not see herself submitting to the kind of treatment that Felicity had evidently been subjected to throughout her married life. The idea was simply not acceptable. Still, she managed to hold back her instinctive response, returning instead to one of the subjects she had come to discuss. ''Felicity, Jacques and I are leaving. We are going to return to Savannah. You must understand that, under the circumstances, it is impossible for us to stay here.''

Felicity was nodding. ''Yes, of course. It would, no doubt, be for the best.''

''Margaret will come with us, and we would like you to come with us, also.''

Felicity raised a thin hand, as if in protest. ''My dear child, you have evidently not understood me. I will never leave Edouard, no matter what he does or how he behaves. I do not condone what he did, but I am his wife and my place is at his side. I believe it is certainly wise that you and Margaret leave, and, of course, Jacques must go with you but I shall remain.''

Rebecca sighed. Felicity is right, she thought. I certainly do not understand.

She said, ''Then I can do nothing but pray that he will cease to abuse you. We will be leaving in a day or so, as soon as we have packed our things.''

Felicity took Rebecca's hand. "I shall miss you, dear. You and Margaret have brought me so much pleasure. I have enjoyed so much pretending that you were the daughters I never had."

Touched, Rebecca threw her arms around the woman. "If you change your mind, promise me that you will come to us in Savannah."

"I shall never change my mind. But I will keep in touch. I will send letters on the packet. Also, you must take with you whatever servants you will need."

"Thank you, Felicity. Now I must go and tell Margaret that we will be leaving, and instruct the maid to start packing."

TWO DAYS LATER Rebecca and Margaret stood at the window of the large sitting room and gazed out at the grounds of Maison de Rêverie. All of their belongings had been packed and were being loaded into the large wagon to be transported to the dock. The landau stood in front of the main entrance, waiting to take them.

"It's odd," Rebecca said musingly, "but in spite of all that has happened, I shall miss the island. It is so beautiful."

Margaret was frowning. She looked pallid and nervy today, and Rebecca was glad for her sake, as well as her own, that they were leaving.

"I suppose I shall miss it, too," Margaret said. "But you speak as if you will never return here. After all, Jacques will inherit one day, and it will be his and yours."

"Yes, I suppose you're right. Yet at this very moment, I feel a sense of finality. Odd, isn't it? But that is neither here nor there. In a few moments we will be leaving, at least for the present, and I must admit that I am most anxious to get away."

As Rebecca began to turn away, she gave one last glance out the window and saw the figure of a man approaching the house at a stumbling run.

"Margaret," she exclaimed. "Look! Who is that?"

Margaret, who was almost at the door, turned back and joined Rebecca at the window. The man was close enough now for them to see his face. Rebecca recognized him as one of the grounds workers. His eyes and mouth were flared wide with obvious fear. Then he ran around the house, out of their sight.

The two women shared a look of puzzlement as a loud banging commenced in the direction of the back door to the house, and together they hurried from the room, with Rebecca in the lead.

In the hall they encountered Jacques, looking harried and pale. "Good! You are ready—" he broke off, turning his head as the sound of raised voices from the rear of the house distracted him. "What the devil is all the racket about?"

Rebecca took his arm. "Margaret and I saw a slave running toward the house, looking frightened. Something must have happened. Perhaps we should see what it is before we go."

For a moment they all fell silent, listening as the voices grew louder, and someone, a young woman by the sound of it, began to wail.

Without further word Jacques and the two women hurried toward the sound of the commotion.

At the rear of the house was a medium-sized room used as a holding place for food brought in from the cookhouse. It was here that Jacques and the women found a gaggle of servants surrounding Dhupta, who was talking to the grounds worker Rebecca and Margaret had seen from the window. Twisting his ragged hat in his hands, the man seemed to be in the grip of some dreadful horror.

Jacques forced his way into the center of the group, addressing Dhupta. "Just what is going on here? What is the matter with this man?"

Dhupta, his usually impassive face drawn and anguished, made a slight bow. "I regret to have to tell you sir. This man, if he is telling the truth, says that your father is dead. He says that he was working near one of the small pavilions, the one near the pond, and found the master's body there."

Armand's voice said behind them, "What in the holy hell is going on here?"

Jacques turned a blind gaze on him. In a choked voice, he said, "This man says that Father is dead."

Chapter Fourteen

FROM THE SAME WINDOW from which she and Margaret had watched the hurrying grounds worker earlier, Rebecca now watched as the body of Edouard was carried toward the house.

Armand and Dhupta were carrying the body—a formless bundle wrapped in canvas—while Jacques walked beside them, head bowed and shoulders slumped. It was a tableau that caused Rebecca's stomach to cramp with a dull pain, and slowly she turned away from the window.

She hated Edouard for what he had done to her. There had been times over the past two days when she had wished him dead, but now that her wish was fulfilled she felt only horror and guilt, as if her wishing had made it so. The actuality of death, she realized, was a cold and painful thing, in no way akin to the fury that often caused one to wish it.

Feeling weak and drained, she moved to the fireplace chair where Margaret was slumped. Margaret had fainted when she had learned of Edouard's death, but now she looked composed, though pale.

"They are bringing him into the house," Rebecca said in a low voice, seating herself in the chair next to Margaret. "It would appear that what the worker said is true. Edouard . . . The body is wrapped in canvas."

She swallowed to force down the bile that was rising in her throat.

"We won't have to leave Maison de Rêverie now," Margaret said.

The matter-of-fact statement caught Rebecca completely by surprise. "What?"

"I said, we won't have to leave here now. If Edouard is dead, then it is safe to stay here."

Rebecca stared at her cousin in astonishment. What she said was true, of course, and yet it would not have occurred to Rebecca to voice such a thought. It struck her as somewhat inappropriate to be speaking of benefits gained from Edouard's death. But perhaps it was just the shock. Shock often made people react oddly.

"No, I don't suppose we will have to leave now," she said slowly. "But, Margaret, I feel so guilty! I thought that I wanted him dead! But now...!"

Margaret got up, and bending down, she smoothed Rebecca's hair and touched her face. "Don't be silly, Rebecca," she said almost playfully. "You know what you say isn't true. If wishing people dead would make them so, half of the population of the world would die. You are in no way to blame, and you must not torture yourself so. Besides, Edouard was an evil man. You, of all people, should know that. His death is no doubt God's way of taking vengeance upon him."

Rebecca stared at her, frowning slightly. Although Margaret had always been prim and proper, and much given to platitudes, this remark, this judgment, seemed unduly harsh. There was something in Margaret now, Rebecca thought, that had not been there a few weeks ago—a kind of hardness and a certain strength. Rebecca was not certain that she liked it.

At that moment her thoughts were interrupted as Jacques came into the room. There was mud on his boots and breeches, and his face sagged with grief.

He stood looking at them in heavy silence before he finally spoke. "Father was in the pavilion, just as Thomas said, lying there on the floor."

Getting up, Rebecca crossed to him and took his hand. "Jacques, I am so sorry. I really am. No matter what he did, this should not have happened. How did he die? Was it apoplexy?"

Jacques stared at her but did not appear to really see her. "No, he was stabbed in the heart. His own hand was upon the knife."

Rebecca gasped, feeling the blood drain from her head. She clutched at his arm for support. "Do you mean that he killed himself?"

Jacques shook his head. "I don't know. Nobody knows. I suppose it is possible."

Clutching his head between his hands, he dropped into a chair. "How am I going to tell Mother?" He lowered his hands and stared up at Rebecca, this time seeing her and letting her see the despair in his eyes. "I didn't really believe it, you know. Not until I saw him there with the knife in his chest. I've seen dead men, in battle, but this is different. No matter what he did, he was my father!"

"I know, Jacques, I know," she murmured. She pulled his face against her, comforting him.

IT WAS RAINING the day of Edouard's funeral, a fine mist under low, gray clouds, a condition that only added to the gloom of the occasion.

Felicity, thickly veiled to hide her tear-ravaged face, leaned heavily on Jacques's arm. She moved very slowly, like an invalid.

Armand, his face set and stern, walked with Rebecca and Margaret, as they approached the Molyneux mausoleum, where Edouard would lie next to his father and mother. Behind them came Dhupta, and then the house staff and the grounds workers. Everyone on the island was there.

There was no minister in attendance. Felicity had wanted to send for one, but Armand had convinced her that, under the circumstances it would not only be undesirable, but hypocritical. Edouard had professed to believe in no god and, as far as Armand knew, had never been inside a church, except when he and Felicity were married. Instead Jacques said a few halting words over his father's mortal remains, and the family returned to the house.

The only outsider present at the brief ceremony was Edouard's solicitor, Harold Franks, a tall, dour man who wore what seemed to be a permanent expression of disapproval.

He was there to read Edouard's will. The reading took place in Edouard's study, with the entire family, and Dhupta, present.

Rebecca had felt numbed and strange ever since she had arisen that morning, as if she were cocooned in cotton batting or as if only a portion of her spirit was inhabiting her body. Seated next to Jacques, she listened to the dry, droning voice of Harold Franks, with only a part of her mind.

It seemed to take him an interminable time to read the will, which contained no surprises. Outside of a generous bequest to Dhupta, for serving as a "good and faithful servant," everything went to Jacques, as the elder son.

Rebecca, being English, was familiar with the custom of primogeniture. In England all property automatically went to the eldest son, so she was not particularly surprised at the bequest. She sneaked a glance over at Armand, who was sitting on her right. He was scowling darkly.

When the reading of the will was disposed of, Jacques rose and approached his brother. "I'm sorry, Armand. I had no idea that Father would leave everything to me. I had assumed that Les Chênes, at least, would be left to you."

Armand said stonily, "It's not your fault. It is his. I should have known that he would leave me nothing. I was wrong to ever think anything else."

"I can do one thing," Jacques said thoughtfully. "I can let you run Les Chênes as you see fit, make the changes that you have always wished to make."

Armand stared at him in disbelief. "You would do that?"

"Of course. It is your right." Jacques shrugged.

"That is generous of you." Armand stood and clapped his brother on the shoulder. "Thank you, Jacques."

Harold Franks moved out from behind Edouard's desk. "Well, I must take my leave. My condolences to you all."

As Jacques escorted the solicitor out and returned, Dhupta stepped up to stand in the center of the room. Bowing from the waist, with his hands together, palm to palm, he then straightened and said, "Sirs and madams, I humbly request your attention."

All conversation stopped, and Jacques nodded to his father's servant. "Of course, Dhupta. Speak out."

Dhupta bowed again. "Thank you, sir. I wish first to say that soon, thanks to your father's bequest, I will be able to return to my native country. But before I go there are things I feel that I should tell you, things that I could not speak of while the master lived. I owed him my life, you see, and so could not betray his confidence."

Mystery upon mystery, Rebecca thought wryly, secret piled on top of secret. And this time involving the mysterious Dhupta! How many secrets did this house contain? How many things had been kept hidden because men made promises to one another? And how many had been, and would be, hurt by these promises?

She exchanged glances with Margaret and then noticed that Felicity had gotten up from her seat.

Dhupta bowed again. "I do not wish to offend the *madame*, but I believe she would also be interested in what I have to say. I think it important that you all know these things. The two young ladies—" he nodded toward Rebecca and Margaret "—have suffered fright and much unpleasantness, and they no doubt feel anger toward the master. I think it only just that they should know the truth."

Felicity now stood fully erect; she raised her hands as if to fend off Dhupta's words. "Does what you have to say concern my husband?"

"Yes, *madame*. Your husband and my poor self."

Felicity shook her head firmly. "Then I do not wish to hear it. Whatever it is, I do not wish to know it. There has been too much. Simply too much. How can it help me to know more? Tell the others, if you feel you must. I shall retire to my room."

"Mother!" Jacques said, moving toward her.

Felicity waved him away. "No, Jacques. I am quite determined about this. You listen to what he has to say, since he seems to think it important. I shall be all right. I just need to rest."

After his mother had left the study, Jacques looked doubtfully at Rebecca and Margaret. "Are you certain that you wish to hear what Dhupta has to say?"

"Yes," Rebecca said with a quick nod. "I would feel much better having things out in the open. If there are things that should be explained, let us, by all means, hear them. How do you feel about it, Margaret?"

Margaret, her hands clasped tightly together in her lap, hesitated briefly, fearing that whatever Dhupta's disclosure might be, it would only make an unpleasant situation worse, yet not able to bring herself to object. "All right, if you all think it wise."

"Thank you," said Dhupta. "Now, shall I begin? It is rather a complicated story, you see, and not an easy one to relate."

He looked directly at Rebecca and Margaret. "First, I wish to make my apologies to the young ladies, who have, I fear, formed an unfavorable impression of me. I would like to make it known at this time that I am indeed sorry for this. Although you are British and I am Indian, I bear no animosity toward you. Despite what your countrymen have done to my homeland, I have no right to accuse you, for I have done worse. If I have seemed cold and unfriendly toward you, it was only because the master demanded all of my time and energy. As long as he lived I was bound to think first and always of his welfare, for those were the terms of our agreement.''

"Agreement?" Armand demanded harshly. "Just what was this agreement?''

"As I said, your father saved my life. I will not lengthen this story with an account of all the details of my life, but I was, as the young ladies have no doubt surmised, born a Brahman, the only son of an important family, in Kashi, or Varanasi, the city you British call Banaras.

"It will suffice to say that a time came when I did a very foolish thing. It is not necessary that you know just what, but it was an offense to Lord Siva and a great stain upon the honor of my family. The name I use, it is not my own. Shamed and panic-stricken, I fled India, making my way through many countries around the world, until I at last washed up on this distant shore, my funds expended.

"It was a cruel time for me. I, one of the *raiees*, an aristocrat in my own country, was treated like a pariah here, because of the color of my skin.

"It was at that time, at the lowest ebb of my life, that Edouard Molyneux found me. A man of culture, he recognized me for what I was and struck a bargain with me. He exacted a promise from me, a promise to be absolutely loyal to him and to him only. In exchange he would give me shelter and employment in his home. I would be a servant, but not a common servant and not treated as a slave. And that is how I came to this island and this house.''

He paused, and Armand said, ''But surely that is not all you have to tell us!''

"No, sir.'' Dhupta sighed. "It is not all.

"Your father confided many things to me, things that he had never spoken of to another. He knew, you see, that I would keep his secrets, and every man has a need to unburden himself, particularly when he carries as heavy a burden as the one Edouard Molyneux bore.

"He spoke often of his childhood, which, as he related it to me, had been...unusual. He had suffered in some way at the hands of his parents. He was not too specific about the details. These fears of his childhood still preyed upon him and haunted his dreams. Because of this he developed a dependence upon hashish; that and other drugs that could bring him forgetfulness.

"When he smoked hashish, it would quiet and soothe him, but the other things he took made him wild and restless, sometimes driving him to the brink of madness. When he was under the influence of these drugs, that was when he wandered in the passageways, the dark labyrinths of his childhood. No one else in the family knew of them, he said."

"So you knew it was him," Rebecca said accusingly. "And you didn't stop him or warn us."

Dhupta, his brown face still serene, nodded. "That is true. I cannot deny it. But, as I have tried to explain, I was helpless to interfere. My loyalty was to him, to Edouard Molyneux, and it was my destiny to follow it. I am sorry that you suffered because of it, but there was nothing that I could do."

Rebecca retorted, "Ridiculous! All this prattling of promises and honor! And all the while Margaret and I were victims. What if Edouard had managed to accomplish his purpose that dreadful night? If he had succeeded, would you still think a simple apology now sufficient?''

During her tirade Dhupta stood with his head bowed. Now she felt Jacques's restraining hand upon her arm, and realizing that her anger, at this point, would accomplish nothing, she subsided.

Dhupta raised his head and continued as if she had not spoken. ''At these times, when he could not sleep, he liked to hear the old instruments, the ones his father had brought from China. Being versed in music, and finding the instruments not too dissimilar from the sitar of my native country, I would play for him.''

''That was the music we heard!'' Margaret exclaimed. ''It was you then!''

''Yes, my lady.''

''But why the secrecy?'' Armand asked. ''Why did it matter to Father if we knew that you could play the instruments?''

Dhupta shrugged. ''His mind was a complicated thing, sir. I believe that this, too, had something to do with his childhood, perhaps the fact that his father played the instruments. He enjoyed games, your father. Like a child.''

''Games!'' Rebecca said scornfully.

Dhupta gave her a level glance. ''He was not an evil man. Despite the things he may have done, not an evil man. A weak man, perhaps, bent from childhood in an unhealthy way. A troubled soul, surely. My responsibility was to look after him in the dark times when his soul wandered, but he did not tell all of his secrets, not even to me. Sometimes he would elude me, and other times he would go to what he always called his 'secret place.' Even I was not allowed to go there.''

"A 'secret place'?" Jacques said in a puzzled voice. "What kind of a secret place?"

"That I do not know, sir. I believe that it is somewhere in the passageways, a hidden room perhaps. I only know that when he went there, he went alone, and when he returned he would need many pipes of hashish to soothe his spirit. I asked him, many times, why he would choose to go to a place that caused so much pain to his soul, but he would only brush my questions aside. My own opinion is that something in his nature compelled him, something dark and driven. We are all driven by our destiny!"

There was a long silence as Dhupta waited stoically, as if for their judgment.

Finally Jacques spoke. "I thank you, Dhupta, both for being a true friend to my father and for telling us what you have. It at least makes my father's behavior more understandable."

Dhupta smiled. "To understand all is to forgive all, as my people say."

"You say you wish to return to your own country. Is the problem from which you fled now resolved?"

Dhupta smiled again, a slight curving of his lips that did not reveal his teeth. "Alas, no sir. However *I* have changed, and I realize now that it is my fate to return and atone for what I have done. No matter what happens upon my return, Kashi, the City of Light, will be my salvation."

"Your salvation?" Jacques asked.

"Yes. You see, we Hindus believe that if a man dies in Varanasi, he attains *moksha*, or liberation, an end to the cycle of reincarnation through unity with the eternal. To die in Varanasi means the attainment of perfect peace. I shall return to make my *puja*, my religious observance, and immerse myself in the water of *Ganga Ma*, the Mother Ganges, the holy river. Then I shall face whatever fate Siva has in store for me. *Rama mama satya hai*. The name of God is truth."

"Will you stay with us long enough for us to find someone else to run the house?" Jacques asked. "I fear Mother will not be well for some time, and we need someone with a knowledge of the house and a firm hand."

Dhupta bowed with his hands together. "Assuredly, sir, I shall stay for as long as need be. Mother India is very patient."

Chapter Fifteen

AS THE WEEKS WENT BY, life at Maison de Rêverie began to return to some semblance of order. No one had forgotten the horror of Edouard's death, but the details of everyday life, in their very ordinariness, created an illusion of normality behind which each member of the family might deal with his own feelings.

Felicity, after the first few days, began to come out of her rooms for meals and started to show signs of becoming again the warm, talkative woman whom Rebecca and Margaret had met on their first day at Pirate's Bank.

Jacques was busy assimilating the details of his father's business affairs and was grateful for the comfort of this activity, for it kept him from thinking too much of his father.

Still suffering from the effects of Edouard's attack and the subsequent shock of his death, Rebecca felt fragile, rather like an invalid recovering from a severe illness. She had, for the moment, at least, come to terms with her marriage. Although it was not a complete marriage and never could be, it still offered her something of value. In her present state of mind, Jacques's quiet consideration and love offered her a shield of sorts that she could hide behind, and she was grateful for that.

There were times, of course, when her anger surfaced. Lying beside Jacques at night in their bed, feeling his warmth against her, she would suddenly be overcome by the painful ache of desire.

Sometimes, if Jacques was sleeping deeply, she would touch herself—her breasts, her body—and imagine that it was Jacques doing so. And often, to her shame, the image of Jacques would change slowly, unaccountably, to that of Armand.

Sometimes, in this way, she could bring herself a measure of relief, but it was like eating bread made of sawdust. She needed, wanted, the substance of love, a man to hold her, to make love to her. And yet there were times when she felt almost content. She tried not to think about what would happen when she was fully recovered, when her energy returned.

Armand still remained at Maison de Rêverie. Other than his brief outburst at the reading of his father's will, his behavior and disposition seemed to have changed for the better. Perhaps, Rebecca thought, it was because his father was not there to antagonize him with his cutting remarks.

One reason Armand was still on the island was because he was helping his brother with the business details of their father's estate. The two brothers seemed closer than Rebecca could remember them being in the time that she had known them.

Armand had told her that he would return to Les Chênes soon, but from what she had heard of the conversations between him and Jacques, he intended, whenever possible, to spend more time on Pirate's Bank. Rebecca found herself thinking of this, often, with a combination of apprehension and pleasure. She knew that it would be dangerous for her to see too much of Armand. When she was near him she often thought of that day on the hill, or worse, her own imaginings in the dark of the night. It was unsettling to have him near and yet exciting.

Surprisingly Margaret was blooming. She expressed no sorrow for Edouard's death. She told Rebecca that she viewed his death as a just punishment for his behavior.

Margaret's grief for her father's death had lessened somewhat, and even her apprehension for her mother and for Rebecca's parents had faded. She now had the feeling that they were well, that they had not been harmed in the uprisings. She also felt a new purpose, for she had found a strength in herself that she had never known she possessed. Rebecca was still shaken by her experiences, and Margaret knew her cousin needed her. It was, she found, quite nice to be the strong one for a change. No wonder Rebecca had always been so sure of herself, so energetic!

Felicity also had need of her, for she was only now beginning to throw off her depression over her husband's death, and she often looked to Margaret for company and advice concerning household matters, even though Dhupta was still supervising the running of the great house.

It seemed to Margaret, when she thought about it at all, that Edouard had been a devil who had poisoned all of their lives and now that he was gone, they could begin to live again in a sane and healthy way.

"DO YOU REALLY THINK she would do?" Felicity's tone was dubious. "I know she has been looking after Les Chênes for many years, but that is a very small house, nothing like Maison de Rêverie."

"I think she would do nicely, *madame*," Dhupta replied. "Master Jacques informs me that she spent her girlhood here, so she already knows the house. And you yourself have said that her mother was a clever and industrious woman."

"I don't know. I just never considered her. Jacques, what do you think?"

The family was gathered in the small salon, and the matter under discussion was that of letting Lutie, Armand's housekeeper, take over as housekeeper at Maison de Rêverie.

"Why I think that is an excellent suggestion, Mother," Jacques said. "Lutie is extremely capable, and it would certainly be more convenient for us to have someone who is already familiar with the house and the staff than a stranger. Of course, it would mean that Armand would have to find someone else for Les Chênes." Jacques looked questioningly at his brother.

Armand shrugged indifferently. "I should miss Lutie, naturally. She's been with me since I took over the responsibility for the plantation, but this would be a fine opportunity for her. I certainly wouldn't begrudge her the chance to better herself. Also, I know that Dhupta is growing anxious to return to his own country, and I think we owe him an early solution to the problem of his replacement."

"I agree with you," Jacques said. "Dhupta, you may begin to make preparations for your trip. And, Armand, will you arrange for Lutie to come?"

Armand nodded. "I'll send one of the house servants to summon her this afternoon."

Rebecca, sitting quietly, kept her gaze upon the cup of tea in her hand. Lutie, here? The beautiful, light-skinned black woman had remained like a small thorn in Rebecca's thoughts from the day she had met her at Les Chênes. The suspicion that she was Armand's mistress was difficult to dismiss, and the thought of them together filled her with an illogical jealousy.

But, she told herself now, Armand had shown no reluctance to have Lutie leave his house. Surely that must mean that they were not intimate. On the other hand, it could still mean that they *were* intimate, but that he really cared for her and wished to see her improve her station in life. To be housekeeper for a grand house like this one was a great responsibility and a great honor. Also, Armand was spending considerable time here now. He would still get to see her, and—

She broke off her thoughts, scolding herself. Why in heaven's name was she *having* such thoughts? She had no right to feel jealousy over Armand.

"Well, Rebecca, it would appear that our problem is solved."

Startled out of her musings, Rebecca glanced up. "What? I'm sorry, Jacques, I must have been daydreaming."

Jacques smiled softly. "Well, we have just settled the matter of someone to replace Dhupta. We are going to bring Lutie here, and Dhupta can return home. It is the perfect solution."

TWO DAYS LATER Lutie arrived, looking as regal as an African queen, despite the fact that she was riding in a wooden wagon, surrounded by boxes and trunks.

Since it was a warm day, Rebecca, Margaret and Felicity were sitting on the veranda, working on their needlework, when Lutie arrived.

Rebecca eyed the items that Lutie had brought with her. It seemed to her that the woman had a great many possessions for a slave. Of course, if she was Armand's mistress, that would explain it. As Lutie got down from the wagon and mounted the steps to the veranda, Rebecca grudgingly admitted to herself that the woman walked with a grace and poise that royalty might well envy.

Leaning toward Felicity, she said sweetly, "My, she seems to have brought a great many things with her. Somehow I had the impression that slaves don't usually have many possessions." Even as she spoke Rebecca realized how catty she sounded and wished she could recall the words.

Felicity was smiling. "You are right, my dear, to an extent, particularly if you are referring to field hands. But household slaves have a few more privileges, and someone like Lutie, who has been with the family all her life, has more still. She is almost *like* family, in a way."

Rebecca did not have time to respond, for the woman was upon them now, stopping before Felicity to make a slight curtsy.

"It is good to see you, Mistress Molyneux. It has been a long time."

Her voice, Rebecca was *not* delighted to note, was pleasant and rather deep. Seen up close, her face was even more striking than Rebecca remembered. Her nose was slightly aquiline and her lips rather thin, but well molded. Her black hair was hidden beneath a bright, patterned turban.

Felicity stood and put her hands lightly upon Lutie's shoulders. "And it is good to see you, Lutie. I've missed you, you know, since you went to Les Chênes."

"I heard about the master. I am sorry for your loss."

Rebecca noted with some interest that she did not say that she was sorry the master was dead.

Felicity's face, for a moment, lost its animation. "Thank you, Lutie. It was God's will."

"Well, I shall look after you now. I will try to make things easier for you."

"You have met our two young cousins from India, I believe, at Les Chênes. Margaret Downing and Rebecca Trenton Molyneux, Jacques's new wife."

Rebecca found herself staring into Lutie's intelligent, dark eyes. Was there a hint of amusement lurking in their depths? There was certainly curiosity. Used to analyzing people herself, Rebecca now found herself on the receiving end of a thoughtful perusal, and for a moment she felt uncomfortable, wondering just how the other woman saw her.

"Good afternoon, ladies. Congratulations on your marriage, Madame Molyneux. I had received word of it and was glad for Master Jacques."

Rebecca's eyes narrowed. I'll just wager you were, she thought, since that means I'll be not threat to you where Armand is concerned!

Felicity said, "And, of course, you know Dhupta."

Dhupta had come out of the house and now bowed to the new arrival. "Welcome, Miss Lutie. I have your room prepared for you." He motioned to the young house servant who was busy unloading Lutie's belongings. "Take them to the room that has been mine." He turned to Lutie. "I have moved my possessions out, so that you might occupy the housekeeper's room. For the time being I have moved into one of the smaller rooms."

Lutie shook her head. "There was no need for you to do that."

Dhupta smiled suddenly, a white flash of teeth, and Rebecca noted it with angry amusement. Lutie was indeed formidable if she could charm even the inscrutable Dhupta! Dhupta *never* smiled. But perhaps she was being unfair. It might simply be that Dhupta was happy that he would soon be able to start his journey home.

"I wished to do so," he said. "I shall be departing soon, and there is no need in your having to settle in twice."

"Well, that does make me feel better," Felicity said as Dhupta escorted Lutie into the house. "I have been dreading Dhupta's leaving us and wondering who we could get to take his place. Now I will no longer have to worry. I have come to believe that Lutie will do very well."

"She looks very capable," Margaret commented. "And from what I have seen of the black people here in Georgia, she seems to be quite unusual. I think she is very beautiful."

"Yes, she is that," Felicity said. "Her mother, Bess, was an unusual woman, also. Very intelligent." She paused for a moment, and a thoughtful expression crossed her face. "I cannot say that I really cared for her mother, though. She often forgot her place. But I have always been fond of Lutie. Yes, I am delighted that Dhupta suggested her. I think that now things will go along quite smoothly."

Listening to her mother-in-law's words, Rebecca was swept by a feeling of depression. Things might go more smoothly as far as life at Maison de Rêverie was concerned, but would they go more smoothly for *her*? She thought not. She found the idea of Lutie being here, supervising the household, very unsettling. And yet, why should it really concern her? It was nothing to her if Armand and Lutie were lovers. At least, it shouldn't be.

Abruptly she put down her needlework and got to her feet. She needed to be by herself for a while. "I think I shall take a bit of a stroll. I will be back before too long."

Margaret glanced up from her own work, scrutinizing Rebecca's face closely. "Would you like me to come along? I can put this aside until later."

Rebecca managed what she hoped was a reasonably successful smile. "No, no. You go ahead with your work. I would just as soon walk alone. I am committing some verse to memory, and it will give me a chance to go over it as I stroll."

Margaret looked doubtful. "If you're sure..."

"I'm sure." Rebecca forced a cheerful note into her voice. "I will see you both later."

"Be certain to take your parasol," Felicity said. "You don't want to spoil that lovely complexion."

Rebecca nodded dutifully and went inside to where a large elephant's foot stand held a supply of parasols and umbrellas. Picking out one that matched the blue of her dress, she returned to the veranda, smiled again at the two women and then descended the steps briskly, to give the illusion of purpose.

She continued her brisk pace until she was in the shade of the right-hand *stoa*, which led away from the house to the edge of the immediate grounds and into one of the winding pathways.

Once in the shade of the walkway, she was out of their sight, and she slowed her pace. The green, filtered light, soft and restful, and the smell of the vines and flowers usually eased her feeling of restlessness. She was fond of the arbored walkways and, often, when she wished to be alone, came to sit on one of the stone benches that were placed at intervals along them. Today, however, she felt an urge to walk, to get away from the house and into the semiwild tangle of the pathways.

At the end of the covered walkway, she put up her parasol and stepped into the warm spring sunlight. The warmth felt good. Perhaps if she walked far enough, the sun's heat would penetrate into the depths of her, where she always seemed to feel cold nowadays.

ARMAND STEPPED OUT onto the veranda just in time to see Rebecca walk away in the direction of the walkway. Standing there for a moment, he watched her small figure until it disappeared into the green opening.

He wanted very much to ask where she was going, but it would hardly do to ask straight out, so he said idly, "I see that Lutie has safely arrived and that Dhupta is familiarizing her with the household routines."

"Yes," Felicity responded. "I was just telling the girls how relieved I am. Having Lutie here will take a great load off my mind."

"And how are you feeling today, Margaret?"

Margaret gave him a look of surprise. "Why, very well, actually, Armand. It is kind of you to inquire. I feel quite strong now."

"Good. Excellent." Armand rocked slightly upon the balls of his feet and spoke in the same conversational tone, "Was that Rebecca I just saw going into the walkway?"

Felicity said, "Yes. She felt the need for a bit of exercise."

"Yes. Well, I had best get back to work. I am going over some figures for Jacques while he is in Beaufort, and I want to get them finished before he returns this afternoon. See you both at teatime."

As he went back inside the house Armand uttered a harsh laugh under his breath. Lord, what a dissembler he was getting to be! Sneaking about with sly questions so that he might learn where Rebecca was going. Telling an out-and-out falsehood so that he might sneak after her. What was he coming to?

However, deriding himself in no way slowed him as he hastened through the house and out the rear door, then cut through the kitchen garden toward the outside of the walkway. He had to get at least a glimpse of Rebecca before she chose one of the paths. If he did not it would be impossible to know which path she had chosen.

Evidently she had slowed down once within the walkway, for he caught a glimpse of her bobbing blue parasol entering the center path, just as he came around the end of the walkway.

Feeling a quite disproportionate sense of relief, he slowed his pace so that he could follow her and yet remain unseen.

Watching the parasol bob up and down, he attempted to keep his thoughts from his reasons for what he was doing. However, a part of his mind knew his purpose very well, and this part kept him involved in a nagging dialogue with himself:

Jacques is your brother, and Rebecca is Jacques's wife.

Yes, but his wife in name only!

That doesn't matter. Legally she is his wife, and he loves her. I know what you want. And if you were to get it, you could hurt him terribly.

I don't want to hurt him! I think we are closer now since Father's death than we have ever been. I know that if I betray him now, it would bring him a double hurt. But Rebecca is unhappy. Anyone can see that.

That is not your affair.

But it is. She feels something for me. I know it. I can see it in her eyes. I can feel it between us, like a current, like the pull of the tide.

Tide or no tide, it would be wrong. You've always prided yourself on being an honest man. Is this an honest thing to do, following your brother's wife through the woods like a common thief?

I've tried to stay away from her. You know how hard I've tried, but I can't help myself, dammit!

Striking his thigh with his fist, hoping that the pain would shut out the nagging voice, Armand lost sight of Rebecca for a moment. And then a flash of blue shone briefly amid the green of the trees, and he saw that she had turned off at one of the old, almost hidden pavilions, the one that was so surrounded by vines and plants gone wild that it was completely invisible from the path. He could feel his heart begin to pound with an almost intolerable excitement at the thought that in a moment he would be alone with her, alone for the first time since that day on the mainland, at the site of the ruined plantation house.

Chapter Sixteen

INSIDE THE FRAGILE PAVILION, Rebecca leaned back against one of the corner posts.

This particular pavilion had not been kept in good repair, and there were spots where the wood was dangerously rotted; but it was secluded and Rebecca thought, very beautiful.

The white paint that had once covered it had long ago been worn away by rain and sun. The wood of which the building was constructed had weathered to a soft gray, which blended into the surrounding trees and plants, making the pavilion appear a part of nature, as if it had grown there.

Sitting inside, surrounded by trees, shrubs and plants, was almost like being inside a green cave. Above and around her, the thick canopy of leaves and the delicate latticework filtered the sun so that the interior of the pavilion was dappled with spots of pale light.

Closing her eyes, Rebecca willed herself to relax, listening to the sounds around her: the rustle of the breeze among the leaves; the chattering of squirrels. And the birds...they sounded as if they had abandoned themselves to the spring, such an outpouring of melody. One could hardly imagine that such small bodies could utter such a volume of sound. Somehow their song only served to deepen her depression. Yes, it was spring, and all of nature was coming alive, but she might as well be an old woman, in the autumn of her life.

Slowly tears began to seep from beneath her closed eyelids, and she gave herself up to the luxury of melancholy.

A sharp crack, the sound of wood breaking and a slight movement of the floor of the pavilion caused her to open her eyes. There before her stood Armand. He made no move to come closer but simply stood staring at her, his glance locked with hers.

His eyes . . . there was something in his intense eyes so intimate, so meaningful, she could not tear her gaze from his. Wild bubbles of excitement seemed to be fizzing through her veins. She could not get enough air, no matter that she was breathing rapidly.

"Rebecca?" he said, taking a single step toward her.

The word was both a plea and a command, and Rebecca knew that she would not stop him. He would come closer. He would touch her. He would . . .

His gaze still fixed upon hers, Armand took another step, and then another. He was standing over her now, looking down into her eyes, and still she had not spoken, could not speak, could only stare, knowing that if he kissed her she was lost, and wanting to be. Nothing mattered now, not Jacques, not Margaret or Felicity or her parents. At this moment there was no right or wrong, there was only overwhelming desire and need.

Slowly he bent toward her, and as mindless as a sunflower turning its face up to the sun, she tilted her face up to his.

His lips, when they touched hers, sent a scalding torrent of pleasure rushing through her body.

Not taking his mouth from hers, Armand put his arms around her and lifted her so that she was pressed against the length of his body. His grip was fierce, almost painful. His hands, one low and one high upon her back, pressed her to him, until she felt that her body was blending with his.

And then his hands were in her hair and upon her breasts as his tongue opened her lips and touched hers, and she jumped, for it was as if his tongue had touched her sex, flooding her with an almost unbearable need. It was too much, too intense.

Pulling her lips from his, she took a sobbing breath, as he pressed the side of his face against hers.

Against her lower body she could feel the hard pressure of him, and she felt his body tremble with need. Everything about him spoke of his passion, and the knowledge of how much he wanted her fueled her own excitement.

He tilted her face up with a finger under her chin, seeking her mouth again with his; and now his hands were working at the buttons of her dress, but the tiny buttons refused to yield to fingers made clumsy by emotion.

With a groan of frustration he released her for a moment, bent down and raised her skirt. Then his hands, those exciting, seeking hands, were at the waistband of her drawers, pulling them down, and without even thinking she stepped out of them and kicked them aside, as his hands caressed her buttocks and thighs.

And then he was drawing her down upon the leaf-covered floor of the pavilion, his fingers, firm yet gentle, exploring her body, his mouth and tongue possessing her.

Aroused beyond control, Rebecca reached out boldly to touch him, knowing that she wanted completion, satisfaction.

At her touch, Armand made some adjustments in his clothing and then rose on his knees above her. She lay beneath him, her breath coming quickly, until she felt the hot touch of him against her, and then, without hesitation, she opened to him.

Such was her state of arousal that she scarcely noticed the brief pain that accompanied his first thrust. And as he began a steady series of movements she instinctively matched her motions to his, as she was filled with a mighty tide of love and closeness for this man whose body was now a part of her own.

REBECCA HAD NO IDEA how much time had passed. She knew that she had slept, and that some sound outside the pavilion had awakened her. Frightened for a moment, she stared around her. If someone should come upon them like this . . .

But there was no one in sight, and no sound now, save the natural ones.

Armand lay beside her, his left arm across her body protectively, his right shoulder and arm beneath her head. He was breathing steadily, and she thought he was asleep, but when she looked into his face, she saw that his gaze was fixed upon her. His face—which she was accustomed to seeing so grave—wore a slight smile. He looked, she thought suddenly, much younger, almost boyish.

"Rebecca," he said tenderly. "My beautiful, beautiful Rebecca."

She smiled at him. Oh, how good she felt! Tired and sated, and used, used as a woman should be. Fulfilled.

"I cannot say I'm sorry," he said slowly. "It would be a lie. I could never be sorry for what happened. But I do want you to know that I didn't plan it. I didn't set out to seduce you. I just couldn't control myself."

Rebecca's smile turned wry. "I do believe the same can be said of me."

He pulled her close in a sudden embrace. "Oh, Rebecca! I've wanted you so badly, for so long. God knows I've tried to stay away from you, but only a saint could have borne what I felt and not tried to be with you . . . Rebecca?"

Touched by his words and the passion in them, she kissed him lightly on the lips. "Yes, Armand?"

"Come away with me. Leave Jacques, and we will go away together. We will find a place where we are not known. This is a big country."

Rebecca turned her head and hid her face against his chest, the breath driven from her by his proposal. She had not thought of this! The possibility had not even entered her mind. In fact, she realized that all thought had fled the moment he appeared in the pavilion. Although she now realized how much she had wanted Armand, what had happened had occurred without thought, without plan. Leave Jacques? Could she? There would be a terrible scandal.

"Rebecca?" Pulling back, he looked down into her eyes.

She shook her head. "Armand, Please! I can't think just now."

He stared at her intently, studying her face as if to memorize it. "Will you at least consider it? I mean what I say."

Relieved to be granted a reprieve, she nodded quickly. "Oh, yes! I'll think on it. I promise."

He smiled broadly, his eyes crinkling at the edges. He looked so boyish, so handsome, that she felt something swell inside her, and she kissed him upon the mouth. Ah, he tasted so sweet, and she felt such pleasure and happiness in his arms. How could she ever have thought him a boor?

He pulled her tightly to him, until she feared that her ribs would be crushed, and found her mouth with a fierce, demanding pressure. She did not mind the discomfort but kissed him back and made no objection when he took her again, this time with a touch of roughness that was an expression of his desperate need, an echo of her own feelings. Now that she had found him, had experienced his love, how could she give him up?

REBECCA AND ARMAND returned to the house at different times and by different paths. Rebecca crept into the house, careful not to be seen. Her dress was soiled with dust from the floor of the pavilion, and without a mirror or a comb, she had been unable to put her hair to rights.

Feeling at once guilty and aglow with pleasure, she entered the house through the rear entrance and stealthily made her way to her room, where she quickly stripped off the soiled dress and placed it with the clothing to be laundered by the maid.

Looking at herself in the glass above the washstand, she could not help smiling at her image. She felt more alive than she had in weeks. Even the guilt she felt only added to her sense of excitement. Quickly she began to wash away the signs of her sin. It would not do for Jacques to come in and see her like this. It seemed to her that word of what she had just experienced was written across her forehead in letters large enough for anyone to see.

She had finished washing herself and had put on clean underthings and gotten her hair in order, when a knock upon the door made her jump guiltily. She whirled around, her pulse racing. But it could not be Jacques. He would simply have entered the room. Besides, it was too early for him to have returned from Beaufort.

"Who is it?" she called out, and was surprised to hear that her voice sounded perfectly normal.

"It's Margaret. May I come in?"

Rebecca hesitated. Although she knew that Margaret was easy to fool—she had certainly done it enough times—but as much as she loved her cousin, she found herself inexplicably reluctant to face the other girl. Oh, how she wished that Margaret was the type of person to whom one could tell such a secret! But Margaret was so good, so innocent and pure; her very presence would be like a reprimand. Still, it was impossible to turn her away, for that would not be consistent with their relationship.

"Of course, Margaret. Come in," she said, trying to sound as welcoming as possible.

The door opened, and Margaret entered the room, looking, Rebecca thought, very serious and thoughtful. Seating herself on the chest at the foot of the bed, she said, "Did you have a nice stroll?"

Rebecca, pretending to be arranging her hair, turned and gave her cousin a sunny smile. "Oh, yes. Quite pleasant. There were a million birds, it seemed. I feel quite revived."

"Well, we didn't see you come into the house," Margaret said, "and Felicity sent me out looking for you. It's time for tea."

Rebecca felt herself relaxing somewhat. After all, it was only Margaret. She said brightly, "I came in the back way. There was a spot of mud in the pathway, and while watching the birds, I stepped in it. I didn't want to track it into the parlor. What's for tea?"

Margaret was staring at her intently. "Fresh bread and butter, sweet potato biscuits, jam tart and some early berries with cream."

Rebecca sighed. "Sounds heavenly. I feel like I could eat it all. My walk gave me quite an appetite."

She reached for a pink dress of fine lawn that she had placed upon the bed before beginning her toilet. Slipping it on, she thought of the touch of Armand's hands upon her body, and the flood of resulting memory caused her to feel again the heat of desire. As she pulled the dress over her head, she turned away so that Margaret could not see her face. Oh, what a wanton feeling! She should be experiencing shame but could not. However, she must make an effort to control herself.

Turning to Margaret, she showed a calm face. "There! Ready at last. Now, shall we go down and attack tea?"

WHEN REBECCA first joined the family for tea, she had been very uncomfortable, not knowing how she would feel or react upon having to face Armand in the family gathering. However, Armand had been distant and polite, and the rest of them so ordinary and natural, that she soon felt relatively at ease.

Jacques was back, having returned a bit early from his trip. "I was talking to Joshua Sterling in Beaufort today," he said now.

"That fool," Armand said with a grunt, not meeting his brother's gaze. "I suppose he had something to talk about, as usual."

Jacques grinned. "Of course. Whenever did he not? But this time, at least, it was news of substance, and it was verified by others with whom I spoke in the village."

He turned to Felicity. "Might I have another cup of tea, Mother? It appears that General Jackson has finished building Ford Gadsden and is about to proceed on into the interior of Florida. It would also appear that what Father said was right. Jackson does intend to use the Seminoles as an excuse to push the Spanish out of Florida."

"More fighting!" Felicity said with a sigh as she carefully poured Jacques's tea.

"There will never be peace as long as the Spanish hold Florida, Mother. General Jackson has said so himself. They are too close to our own borders. If we take Florida it will give us a measure of safety and stability. No one really wants war, but sometimes it *is* necessary."

Felicity grimaced and glanced at Rebecca and Margaret. "That is what you men always tell us. But I often wonder if it is really so. I am as patriotic as the next woman, yet I have no wish to sacrifice my sons on the battlefields. I believe most women feel the same."

"It is a matter of honor, Mother," Jacques said lightly.

Rebecca, looking at Armand from under downcast eyelashes, saw him frown and look away. He, too, is feeling guilty, she thought. And there was that word again, "honor." Men seemed to bandy it about so freely, and yet she was not quite certain what they really meant by it. Armand, for instance, had kept an honorable silence concerning his brother's condition, bringing unhappiness to her and, as it turned out, to himself, as well. Now Jacques spoke of honor, and yet in marrying her, he had certainly not behaved in what she would consider an honorable manner. The word would seem to mean what men wanted it to mean at the time they spoke it. Normally she would have voiced her thoughts, but at the moment she deemed it prudent to remain silent.

"Well, I certainly hope that you are not considering joining General Jackson, Jacques," Felicity said. "You have Rebecca to think of now and Maison de Rêverie, as well."

Jacques looked quickly at Rebecca and then away. "Have no fear, Mother. I have no intention of marching off to war again. I believe that I have given quite enough to my country."

REBECCA DREAMED of Armand at night and during the day, her thoughts returning again and again to what had happened between them in the pavilion. Each time she mentally relived the incident, she would be overcome by desire, and yet, despite this, she knew that such a thing must not occur again. What they had done was wrong, but it had been done without intent. If it happened again it would be deliberate, done with forethought. And it was dangerous. The island was small, there were many servants, and servants gossiped. Although she longed for Armand, her passion had not completely clouded her good sense and practicality.

At first, when she thought of what Armand had proposed, Rebecca sometimes thought that it might be possible, but the longer she considered it, the more she knew that it was not. Despite her willfulness and audacity, she was still a woman of her time. The thought of the scandal and what it would do to the family was frightening. If she and Armand fled together, they would have to forever cut themselves off from all the others whom they loved. Her parents, Felicity, Margaret—she would never be able to see them again.

And Jacques! Whatever harm he had done to her, he had done because he loved her. If she ran away with Armand, his shame might well be unbearable, the final indignity.

When thinking about it, her thoughts would inevitably turn to the conversation with Felicity and her reasons for not leaving Edouard. Rebecca remembered very well what Felicity had said about the fact that she had no money other than that provided by her husband. As far as Rebecca knew, Armand had no money of his own, and if he took her away he would lose any claim he might have upon the Molyneux fortune. And if she left her husband to run away with another man, she could certainly never ask her parents for money. She and Armand would be outcasts. Could she live in such a fashion? Great as her love and desire were for Armand, she did not think so. It was impossible, and, she had to admit, she was afraid.

Two days passed in which she existed in a fog, wavering between desire and apprehension. She wanted Armand to come to her, and she did not. She wanted him to make love to her again and yet knew it was impossible. She felt like a wire walker at fair time, attempting to keep herself balanced upon a frail thread.

When Armand did finally approach her, he caught her unaware. It had been a glorious day, clear and bright, but not yet too warm. The sky, an unusually deep, bright blue, was tufted with clouds so white and perfect that they looked like the product of a painter's brush. There seemed to be a special glow to the air, and the colors of the new spring flowers seemed almost unreal. Looking at the sky reminded Rebecca that she had done no painting for a long time. She had once been quite fond of doing watercolors, but it had been over a year since she had touched a brush. She really should take it up again, now that the weather was nice and she had free time on her hands.

It was evening now, and she was standing on the veranda, watching the wild wash of color staining the sky. It was so beautiful that it made her throat ache, and she felt that tears would soon flood her eyes. Oh, how she wished that she was watching this sky with Armand beside her, wished that she was free to do so without guilt or shame.

"Rebecca?"

She whirled with a start of surprise and saw Armand standing behind her, the last light of the setting sun gilding his face and hair. For a moment she felt that her heart had stopped.

She glanced around quickly, but no one else was in sight. "Armand," she whispered, and then stopped, unable to go on.

"The others are all inside," he said quietly. "Felicity and Margaret are still dressing for dinner, and Jacques is in the study, working on the books. We have a moment to ourselves."

Looking into his eyes, Rebecca felt her will weakening. Perhaps they *could* manage to meet alone and keep it a secret. Was that what he had come to ask her?

"Rebecca." He moved a bit closer to her but did not touch her. "This is the first time I have managed to find you alone. Have you been thinking about what I asked you?"

Rebecca felt as if a band was tightening about her throat.

"Have you?"

She nodded quickly. "I've done nothing else but think of it, until I feared it would drive me mad."

His voice was suddenly eager. "Well, will you come away with me? If you say you will, I will make preparations."

What could she answer? How *could* she answer? She wished with all her heart and being that she could say yes, and yet she knew she could not.

"Rebecca?" Reaching out, he touched her cheek with his finger and looked deep into her eyes. "What is your answer?"

Slowly she shook her head. "Oh, how I wish I could, Armand! It sounds so simple, so lovely. But I could not do that to Jacques. And can you imagine how your mother would feel? And Margaret? Besides, there's my own family. It would disgrace them all. Jacques has already been..." Her voice died away as pain darkened his eyes.

"Yes!" he said roughly. "I know about Jacques. I know that he has been hurt, and unmanned, and I also know that he can never be a real husband to you. It was unfair and cruel of him to marry you, knowing that. Can't you see that? How can you go on, living such a lie? It can only grow worse as time passes. Some day, you will want children. What then?"

Rebecca ached to touch him, to have him put his arms around her and hold her, but she did not dare. At any moment one of the others might come out of the house.

"He has wronged me, yes, and yet he *is* my legal husband. He has been very kind to me in every way he can. And if we did this mad thing, where would we go? How would we live? I am not used to a rough life. I...I love you, Armand. Perhaps it's selfish of me, but I simply cannot do what you ask. Not now!"

Armand's lips tightened, and Rebecca knew that she had hurt him. "Yes," he said thinly. "It's true that I have no money of my own, or at least not a great deal. Life would be hard for us, but I am prepared to face that, for you." His voice was accusing. "I am able-bodied and intelligent. I could find work to support us."

Rebecca felt tears burn her eyes. Oh, why could he not have spared both of them this pain?

Gazing at him pleadingly, she shook her head violently. "I am sorry, Armand. I am so sorry!"

At that moment the ornate front door swung open, and, framed in the light from the inside, Jacques stood looking out into the near darkness of the veranda.

"Oh, there you are, my dear. I've been looking everywhere for you."

Rebecca forced a smile and hurried to his side. "I was just admiring the sunset. It was very grand. You should have been out here viewing it, instead of being locked up in that gloomy study with your accounts." She knew that she was talking too much, but she could not seem to stop herself. "Armand missed it, too, for he just joined me. Really, you two have simply grown too spoiled by the beauty here. You just ignore it."

Jacques smiled down at her, adoringly, indulgently, as if she were a pretty child, and took her arm. "Perhaps you are right. Brother, we shall have to change our ways."

Armand stepped into the pool of light from the doorway. "I think, perhaps, that I already have. There is something I wish to talk to you about. Ever since you passed on the news of General Jackson's latest venture, I have been thinking of joining him...."

"You, Armand?" Jacques said in astonishment. "I never once thought you would go off to do battle!"

"Well, he needs men, and this particular fight is important to us, and to Georgia. With Florida under the American flag, we will be able to relax and go about our business. The way the situation is now, we never know what the Spanish or the Seminoles will do next. Of course, it will mean that you must handle both Les Chênes and Middlemarsh until I return. But I have a good overseer who should be able to handle affairs at Les Chênes with a minimum of supervision."

Rebecca clung tightly to Jacques's arm to keep from falling; Armand's words had struck her like a blow. They were supposed to, she realized. Otherwise he would not have spoken them at this time but waited until he and Jacques were alone.

Armand going to war! She could not bear to even think about it.

Jacques shook his head dazedly. "You've never spoken of this before, Armand. I confess that I'm a bit taken aback. You know how much I rely on you." He sighed heavily. "Let me think about this, and we'll talk again, after dinner."

"We can talk, yes, but it won't change my mind," Armand said stolidly. "I am determined on this. I leave at first light in the morning." Without looking at Rebecca he marched into the house.

"Well!" Jacques expelled his breath and stared after his brother. "I must say that this comes as a great surprise to me. Don't you think this is very sudden, my dear?"

Rebecca felt dead inside, but she managed to keep her voice steady as she replied, "Yes. Very sudden indeed."

Chapter Seventeen

REBECCA, FROM HER SEAT on the high stool, looked down the length of the long wooden table, where Darcy, the Molyneux cook, was rolling out dough, supervised by Lutie.

Rebecca was there under the pretense of learning how to prepare a certain recipe that she admired—stewed squirrel with vegetables and gravy, in a rich crust—but in actual fact, she was studying Lutie. Since Armand's departure, her curiosity concerning the other woman had grown until it was almost an obsession.

Armand's going off to war had left Rebecca feeling depressed and abandoned, a feeling that was intensified by the fact that everyone else at Maison de Rêverie seemed quite content.

Of course, Jacques missed his brother, but he was so involved in the running of the two plantations and other business matters that he had little time left for anything else.

Margaret, who had never cared for Armand anyway, seemed just as pleased to have him gone; she appeared quite content with her Bible reading, her needlework and an occasional walk or ride about the grounds.

And Felicity...well, Rebecca found it very odd that her mother-in-law did not seem really concerned about the fact that her younger son was by now fighting Seminoles, running the risk of being maimed or killed. Released from a life of strain and repression by Edouard's death, Felicity was now blooming like a late spring flower. If it were not for the concerns of decency—the fact that a sufficient time had not passed since Edouard's demise—she would, Rebecca felt sure, have been arranging a garden party. She had said only last night that it was really too bad they could not yet entertain on a large scale.

Amid all this cheerful domesticity Rebecca felt out of place and terribly bored. She was very worried about Armand, but there was no one to whom she could confide her feelings. Desperately, to keep herself sane, she cast about for things to keep her busy. She took up her watercolors again, and she rode often, pounding down the pathways as she had once seen Armand ride, as if one could manage to race away from one's personal demons.

And there was always Lutie. Dhupta had departed for his beloved Banaras, and Lutie had assumed full responsibility for running the huge house. Her presence was felt everywhere, supervising, managing, making the wheels run smoothly. Rebecca could not avoid seeing her, and whenever she saw her, she wondered about the woman and Armand. But it was more than that, more than mere jealousy of a woman who may have been Armand's lover. There was something inherently fascinating about the beautiful black woman. Partially, Rebecca supposed, it was because of Lutie's past; the fact that her history was intertwined with Maison de Rêverie and the Molyneuxs. She was the daughter of the slave, Bess, who had been nursemaid to the mysterious Elissa Huntoon,

Edouard's foster sister. Since Lutie was older than Jacques, she must have seen and known Elissa when Elissa was a young woman. From that first day at Les Chênes, when Jacques had told her about Elissa and the tragic death of her parents, Rebecca had been intrigued by Elissa's story, and by the fact that no one seemed to know or at least did not care to tell what had become of her.

Rebecca longed to talk to Lutie, to question her, but somehow she could not nerve herself to the point of doing so. It was not that she was afraid of the other woman; it was just that she was unable to read her easily, as she was able to read most people she met, and this made her wary of the woman. Also, Lutie was the first person, male or female, to view her, Rebecca, with quite such an air of amused understanding, an attitude that angered and annoyed Rebecca exceedingly.

Now, pretending more interest than she felt, Rebecca leaned forward, giving Darcy a practiced smile, as the woman placed the circle of dough, which had been scored in an attractive design, over the contents of a deep, cast-iron pie pan and began crimping the edges.

The woman smiled, her teeth white in her dark, wrinkled face. "And that's it, missy. Then you put it in the wall oven in the fireplace, so that it gets a steady heat, so the crust gets nice and brown. Remember, you got to keep the fire burning real even. Not too hot or the crust will burn afore the fillin' is done."

Rebecca nodded. "I'll remember, Darcy. And thank you, Lutie, for letting me watch."

Lutie's dark eyes held their expression of amusement. "You are welcome, Madame Molyneux. It is nice to see you taking an interest in our local recipes."

Rebecca, piqued by the woman's manner, took pains not to show it. "Why, I'm interested in everything about your beautiful Georgia, Lutie. After all, it's my home now as well."

Lutie said gravely, "Well, I should think that is Georgia's pleasure, *madame*."

Caught off balance by the compliment, Rebecca gave the older woman a sharp look. Was she being sarcastic? But no, Lutie's dark eyes met hers squarely, and for once she did not appear to be secretly laughing. For the first time, Rebecca realized that she and this woman could very possibly become friends.

Following that cooking lesson, Rebecca made it a habit to seek Lutie out and to talk with her whenever possible. Lutie was always busy—Maison de Rêverie had a great many responsibilities—and at first the conversations were little more than an exchange of pleasantries. But as time went on she found the woman willing to talk to her for longer periods of time and on many different subjects. Rebecca was surprised to find Lutie knowledgeable in areas she would not have expected a slave to be familiar with. She began to think that Lutie looked forward to their talks, and also she started to realize that Lutie, too, was lonely. After all, she seemed to be much better educated than the other slaves on the island, and her position as housekeeper set her somewhat apart, leaving her neither fish nor fowl, not one of the common slaves but then again not really one of the family. It must be a difficult position, Rebecca concluded.

And as Rebecca forged an acquaintanceship of sorts with the housekeeper, she began to realize that she and

Margaret were communicating less and less nowadays. Oh, there was no lessening of their affection for one another, and Margaret still, as of old, put her own wishes second to those of her cousin. However, it seemed to Rebecca that Margaret was growing more, well, "closed in" was the only way to describe it. She had never been a great talker or what one might consider a lively person, but now she seemed to keep almost everything closed up inside. She appeared quite content, had put on weight, in fact, which was not unbecoming, but she apparently felt little need for conversation. She seemed happiest when reading her Bible or working on her embroidery.

In the evenings, when the family gathered, Margaret would listen silently to the others, particularly Jacques—on whose every word she appeared to dote—with evident pleasure, yet she seldom offered any comments of her own.

Rebecca had long felt that Margaret had a special feeling for Jacques, at least as much of a feeling as her nature would permit, and Rebecca found this rather touching and sad. In a moment of insight she realized that Jacques should have married Margaret. They would have been perfect for one another. He could not perform the sexual act, and Margaret had no desire to experience it, while she, Rebecca...

But thinking along those lines brought only sorrow and the ache of longing for Armand.

Rebecca found that she missed her cousin in the role of confidant, even though there had always been certain things that she could not tell her, and so it was that she and Lutie began to develop their friendship, a friendship that Rebecca began to enjoy and that she hoped would soon ripen to the stage where she might ask Lutie the questions to which she longed to know the answers.

Another occupation that helped Rebecca pass the time was her search for Edouard's hidden room. When she had begun to look for things to keep her mind busy, she had remembered what Dhupta had told them concerning the secret place to which Edouard frequently repaired and from which he returned in great mental distress.

Rebecca had always liked puzzles and enjoyed solving them. Maison de Rêverie, it seemed to her, was itself a giant puzzle, made up of different parts: the mystery of Edouard's bizarre behavior; the mystery of why no one seemed to want to talk about or remember Elissa Huntoon; the question of what *really* went on at Maison de Rêverie in the days when it was occupied by Jean and Mignon Molyneux; and the mystery surrounding their deaths. There might very well be something in Edouard's secret room that would help to explain these things. At any rate, searching for the room gave her something to do, something that would distract her from thoughts of Armand and her unhappiness.

When the idea of searching for the room first occurred to her, she had talked to Margaret about it. Experience had taught her that she would probably have to do considerable persuading to get Margaret to help her, but it also told her that Margaret would eventually accede to her wishes. However, when she broached the subject with Margaret one afternoon as they were strolling in the gardens, she was not prepared for Margaret's flat and very definite refusal.

"Rebecca, how can you even suggest such a thing? Sometimes I really can't understand you! After all the terrible things that have happened, you, of all people, should be glad that all of that is behind us! Why on earth would you want to rake it all up again?''

Startled by Margaret's vehemence, Rebecca was momentarily at a loss for words. This was not her cousin's usual, halfhearted demurral—the token protest that Margaret herself realized would soon be demolished by Rebecca's persuasive powers. Margaret's eyes were dark with disapproval, and she spoke with no hesitation whatsoever.

Rebecca found herself in the unaccustomed position of having to defend her actions to her cousin. ''I'm not trying to rake anything up,'' she said in what she hoped was a reasonable tone. ''I just want to find the answers to some questions that have been troubling me. What is so wrong in that?''

Margaret's lips were a thin line. ''What is wrong with it is that these matters are none of your affair. Edouard is dead. What does it matter what he had in that room, if there even *is* a room? How can it change anything? How can it help?''

Rebecca shrugged. In the face of Margaret's attitude, she had no ready answer. How could she adequately explain a burning curiosity to someone who possessed no curiosity at all? It was clear that Margaret, this time, was not going to be bullied or persuaded, and so she let the matter drop.

She could not, of course, mention the subject to either Jacques or Felicity. Felicity did not want to be reminded of anything unpleasant concerning Edouard, and Jacques, Rebecca felt certain, would also prefer to forget the past.

She could have begun her search alóne, but the passageways were dark and labyrinthian, and she had no wish to lose her way or hurt herself, so she needed *someone*.

She finally settled on the young black boy who helped take care of the horses, young Jeremy. He was a lively, intelligent lad, twelve or thirteen years old, small for his age, but strong and wiry.

The stablemaster, an easygoing man named Sampson, probably thought it odd that the young *madame* requested the presence of the young stablehand so often at the main house; yet such requests were not without precedent. Often, when there was heavy work to be done in the big house, men would be summoned from other tasks. Rebecca explained the frequency of her requests by saying that she was testing Jeremy for a possible house post, and indeed it was her intention to see that he would eventually be assigned to household duties. She had become quite fond of the lad, and it seemed to her that a child so bright and willing deserved something better to look forward to in life than a future of mucking out stalls.

"WE BE OVER THIS PART before, Miss Rebecca." Jeremy's high young voice echoed eerily in the wooden passageway.

It was very warm and close in the passageway. Rebecca slowed her step and peered ahead. The yellow glow of the whale-oil lantern showed beams, joists, spiderwebs and dust.

"Are you certain?"

The boy, his face heavily shadowed by the flickering light, nodded quickly. "Sure as can be. See, there's the mark you put."

Rebecca sighed. It was true. They were back in the area off the library. She could see the notation she had written on the wall beside the door. The system she had conceived, of leaving trail marks, so to speak, in areas through which they had already passed and of also marking letters on the walls to let them know in which part of the house they were at any given time was working well enough. Still, it seemed to do little good in aiding them to find their way into new areas, for the passageways had been cleverly constructed in the form of a maze, in which it was only too easy to get lost. The diagram, which she was trying to make as they explored, seemed to offer little help.

She sighed. "Well, make another mark, to show that we passed this way again. You know, Jeremy, it strikes me that there must be another doorway here somewhere that my husband didn't find. If my diagram is correct, there is a whole section of the house that we have not been through as yet. And since there are passageways all through the rest of the house, it stands to reason that there must be a passageway there, as well. Are you tired, or shall we go on for a bit longer?"

Jeremy's white grin lit up the darkness. "I ain't tired, Miss Rebecca. I never get tired. Momma says I'm strong as a horse."

Rebecca had to laugh. "Well, I'd hardly think you're *that* strong, but we'll go on for a while longer, and then when we get back, I'll see that you have some nice cakes and fruit to take home to your mother, as well as a bit of chocolate I've been saving."

Jeremy's grin widened. "You awful good to me, Miss Rebecca. My momma says that you are a kind lady, and I should be happy you took a likin' to me."

Rebecca reached out and touched his small, round head in affection. "Well, now, treasure hunters should get *some* reward, don't you think?"

He looked up at her, his eyes wide. "Is that what we lookin' for, Miss Rebecca? A real treasure, like what the people say them old pirates hid on the island?"

Rebecca laughed again. "Well, not really, except in a general sense." Then, realizing that the boy could not possibly understand her, she added, "But anything you search for can be called a treasure, don't you think?"

Jeremy cocked his head quizzically. "I suppose so, Miss Rebecca. That is, if you say so."

Well, thought Rebecca, that's about all any commander can ask, isn't it?

Despite the heat and the dirt, one of the few times that she came close to forgetting her problems was while searching the dark passageways. Although the search was tedious, it was also quite exciting. Each time she discovered a hidden door, it was like another mystery exposed, and each time it was possible that this door would be the one heretofore undiscovered—the one that would lead to Edouard's "sanctuary," or whatever one might call his hidden retreat.

Most of the doors were not difficult to discover from inside the passageways, because of peepholes. These holes were concealed amid ornamentations or carving on the other side, making them almost invisible from the rooms into which they offered a view. In the dark passageways they acted as tiny beams of light, showing the locations of the sliding panels.

Rebecca's procedure was to look through the holes to identify the room. Peering through the holes, she thought that she could almost understand why someone might resort to such an action. To be the hidden observer, to watch others who were unaware of your presence—to some people, it might impart a sense of power.

As they came to each new room she would write the name of the room on the inner wall of the passage-way, along with the mark that indicated that they had passed this way. Finally she would make notes on her diagram.

They moved on now, Jeremy ahead of her, holding the lantern as high as he could, so that she might see her way. As Rebecca stepped over a rather large timber on the floor, she became aware that Jeremy had suddenly stopped and was holding the lantern up close to the wall on the right.

"What is it, Jeremy? Have you found something?"

Jeremy said excitedly, "I'm not sure, Miss Rebecca. I think so, could be!"

Stepping up beside him, Rebecca studied the section of wall that was illuminated by the lantern. There seemed to be a long crack on the wall at that point, a crack that extended in a straight line from ceiling to floor.

"Move the lantern to the left, Jeremy," she said, feeling excitement growing in her.

The lad did so, and about three feet to the left of the first crack, she saw a second. "Jeremy, I think we may have found something! Here, I'll take the lantern; you push on the wall there."

Jeremy handed her the lantern and pushed where she had indicated. A bit of plaster dust sifted down, and the wall creaked and groaned but nothing else happened.

"Now try the other side," Rebecca said, raising the lantern higher.

Jeremy tried again, at a point near the second crack, and this time was rewarded by a louder creaking sound as the wall shifted slightly under his hands.

Rebecca set the lantern on the floor and lent her strength to that of Jeremy. With both of them shoving the section of the wall between the two cracks began to pivot, at first slowly and then more quickly, until another dark passageway was exposed.

Rebecca bent and picked up the lantern, holding it high. The yellow light only penetrated a short distance into the passageway. It appeared identical to the one in which they stood, but she was certain that it was one which they had not explored.

Jeremy glanced up at her, grinning widely. "I think this be a new one, Miss Rebecca. Don't think we been down this one before."

Peering intently into the area exposed by the light, she nodded. "I think you're right, Jeremy."

"We goin' in?"

Rebecca hesitated. She was anxious to investigate this new tunnel, but the oil in the lantern was getting low, and they had already been exploring for quite some time. If they were gone too long, questions would be raised as to where she had been gone so long, and in consideration of Jacques and Felicity, Rebecca was attempting to keep her explorations as secret as possible.

"I think we'll wait," she said slowly. "The lantern is getting low on oil, and I'm sure you are hungry, Jeremy. We'll mark this doorway and leave it open slightly for good measure, so we can find it easily the next time."

THE NEXT DAY, Jeremy's services were required in the stables, and Rebecca did not dare request his help at the house.

She and Jacques went for a horseback ride in the morning, and then in the afternoon, when Jacques was busy in his study, she sought out Lutie, finally finding her in the kitchen garden, in back of the house.

Lutie and the head gardener were deep in conversation, so Rebecca moved off to stroll through the flower gardens, where the cut flowers for the house were grown. The scent of the flowers was heavy on the humid air, and the hum of bees, added to the afternoon warmth, made her feel a bit drowsy.

There was a lovely, small willow tree on one side of the garden, with a stone bench beneath it. Seating herself, Rebecca leaned back against the trunk of the tree. Looking out through the veil of green leaves made her think of the pavilion in the woods and that soft, green afternoon with Armand.

Despite herself, tears began to well in her eyes. Where was Armand now? Tidings came very slowly here, even from an area as close as Florida. Was he all right? Had he been hurt? The thought of what had happened to Jacques in New Orleans intruded into her mind, and she shuddered. Did Armand ever think of her and that afternoon in the pavilion? Dear God, how she missed him, wanted him! Was it possible that he missed her, as well?

"Miss Rebecca?"

With a start, Rebecca opened her eyes to see Lutie standing before her.

"Having a nice rest in the shade?"

Hastily blinking the tears out of her eyes, Rebecca smiled. "Actually, I was waiting for you, Lutie."

"Why, now nice! I think, in that case, that I'll just sit down myself for a bit. It has been a very busy day. Madame Molyneux has invited company for dinner. It is just a small gathering, but it will be the first social engagement she has held since Master Edouard died."

Rebecca looked over at the other woman in some surprise. "I didn't know of her plans. I didn't see her this morning at breakfast. But I think it will be nice to see some different faces for a change."

Lutie nodded. "I expect it will. I suppose it gets lonely here for you at times. Now, you said you were waiting for me. Is there something special you want?"

"Well, yes, there is. I don't want to be presumptuous, Lutie. I mean, I don't wish to intrude upon your privacy or anything like that, but there are some questions I would very much like to ask you."

Lutie was smiling, a touch of that secretive amusement in her eyes. "I thought there might be. And the answer is no."

"No?" Rebecca was startled and taken aback. She had not expected a flat refusal.

Lutie's smile widened, and her dark eyes glinted. "I don't mean that I won't answer your question, Miss Rebecca. I mean that the answer to your question is no, I have never been Master Armand's mistress. That *is* what you wanted to ask, isn't it?"

Disconcerted, Rebecca could only stare, her mouth agape. Never had she been so surprised by another person's response, and then she saw that Lutie was quietly laughing.

"Oh, you should see your face, Miss Rebecca! I'm sorry if I have offended you, but that *was* what you wanted to know, wasn't it?"

Rebecca, pulling her wits together, was not quite certain how to respond. That kind of remark was something that she, herself, might have said to non-plus someone, and now here she was, startled and at a loss for words, discomfited.

Suddenly she joined Lutie's laughter. Both because she was delighted to find that her suspicions were wrong and because Lutie was really amazing. And, of course, Lutie was right. That may not have been the question she was going to ask immediately, but it was most certainly in her mind, and Lutie had recognized it.

Shaking her head ruefully, she said, "Lutie, you are an unusual person. How long have you known?"

Lutie's expression became serious. "Since that first day when you visited Les Chênes. I could see the question in your eyes, plain as anything."

"Well, I've always been a curious person, and you must admit that it was a question that might very well have occurred to anyone. I mean, you are a very beautiful woman, Lutie. You must realize that!"

Lutie lowered her head. "I expect so, but being beautiful, when you are a slave, is not always such a good thing."

"What do you mean? I would think that any woman would wish to be beautiful."

Lutie shrugged slightly. "To a black woman, being beautiful usually means that you become a white man's plaything. I have been fortunate. My momma protected me when I was young, and after she died Mr. Armand took me to work at Les Chênes, so that Master Edouard . . . well, I suppose there is no harm in telling you, since you know well how he was. The reason Mr. Armand took me with him was because of his father. He knew that I would have killed that man if he had laid a hand on me again."

Rebecca felt a deep sense of shock at this further revelation into the dark nature of Edouard Molyneux. At the same time, she experienced a stirring of excitement, for this was part of the history of Maison de Rêverie, part of the secret she wished to know.

Lutie had hesitated; now she placed her hand over Rebecca's. Her hand was long and slender, with strong fingers. Rebecca felt no displeasure at her touch. "I am a good ten years older than Mr. Armand, Miss Rebecca, and yet he has looked out for me and treated me like a close friend all these years. My momma, Bess, was like a mother to him, and I suppose you could say that I was like an older sister. Without Mr. Armand to look after me, I don't know what might have happened. I might have ended up like...well, no matter. Master Edouard is dead now, and some things are best forgotten, if they can be."

Rebecca wondered what Lutie had been about to say but felt that now was not the time to press the matter. She had another reason for seeking out Lutie today.

Lutie started to get to her feet. "Well, I must get back to my duties—"

Rebecca said quickly, "Lutie, did you know about the passageways in the big house? Before, I mean?"

Lutie took on a guarded look. "I didn't know of them when I was a child but my momma did. She was sick quite a while before she died, and during that time she rambled on a lot about the old days. She mentioned the passageways, but I never dared enter them myself.''

''Did your mother ever mention a secret room, a place where Edouard used to go?''

Lutie's expression altered subtly, and she looked away. ''Why, I don't think so. No, I don't recall that she did. Why? Is there such a room?''

Rebecca closely studied Lutie's face. She had the feeling that the other woman was being evasive for some reason, but she could not be certain. ''Dhupta spoke of a room, a 'secret place' where Edouard went from time to time. I was just curious about it.''

''Well, I wouldn't worry about it, Miss Rebecca,'' Lutie said briskly. ''It's time to be looking ahead, not into the past. I don't suppose there is anything in that room, if there is such a room, that it would please you to find.''

Almost Margaret's exact words, Rebecca thought. But Lutie knew something, and Margaret did not. The fact that Lutie did not want to talk about it made it all the more intriguing. Well, Lutie had told her quite a bit today. Perhaps another time she would reveal more.

This time Lutie did get to her feet. ''Well, I'd best get into the kitchen and see how Darcy is doing and then make sure that everything is prepared for tonight. If you will excuse me, Miss Rebecca?''

Rebecca nodded and watched the other woman walk gracefully away. The knowledge that Lutie and Armand had not been lovers after all was like a heavy weight removed from her mind. She wondered if Lutie suspected her feeling for Armand and decided that, as astute as Lutie was, it was likely that she did. However, she was confident that the woman would keep this knowledge to herself.

IN A BETTER MOOD than she had been in for some days, Rebecca entered the house with the intention of going to her room and sorting through her clothing for something suitable to wear for dinner. Because the family was still officially in mourning, it would have to be something dark, but it seemed a long time since she had dressed for company and she wanted to look especially nice.

As she neared the bottom of the staircase, she saw Margaret standing there as motionless as if she had been posed for a tableau. There was an odd expression upon her face.

As Rebecca approached closer, Margaret still did not move, and Rebecca began to feel some alarm. What on earth was the matter?

"Margaret?" she said, putting a hand on her cousin's arm. It felt rigid to her touch. "Margaret? Is something amiss?"

Margaret gave a start. Blinking her eyes and turning her head stiffly, she seemed surprised to see Rebecca standing by her side. "Rebecca?"

"Of course, it's Rebecca! You're looking right at me, for heaven's sake! What ails you, Margaret? You're standing there like one of those statues in the garden, stiff as a plank. Aren't you feeling well?"

Margaret appeared puzzled. "Was I really acting like that? How strange. I was just about to go upstairs, you see, and then...well, it has never taken me like this before."

Rebecca studied her cousin thoughtfully. "*What* has never taken you like this before?"

"You know. The things I feel. My premonitions."

Rebecca felt a chill go through her. "You just had a premonition?"

Margaret nodded, and her voice was dreamy. "Yes. Usually they are just feelings, I just *know* that something is wrong or that something has happened. But this time it was almost as if I was there! I could see it in my mind, like a dream. More than a dream, like it was happening before my very eyes."

"Margaret, what was it? What did you see?"

Margaret's expression was still dreamy, her voice almost a whisper. "I saw men fighting. Red Indians and soldiers!"

The cold was spreading through Rebecca now. She said urgently, "Yes? Go on!"

"I saw Armand falling, falling a great distance. Falling to his death!"

Chapter Eighteen

ARMAND WAS in a wild and angry mood as he rode south out of Savannah.

His decision to join Andrew Jackson had been made in the instant that Rebecca had refused to go away with him. It had been born of frustration and anger, as well as the need to get away from the source of his pain.

Before that day in the pavilion, seeing Rebecca with Jacques, being near her and yet unable to touch her, had been an agony. Now that he had held her and made love to her, now that he knew she wanted him as he wanted her, his longing was unbearable. She was all he could think about. Even when he was working, the image of her white body tortured him. The image of her face, relaxed in abandon, seemed to float before his eyes, blotting out all else. Staying near her under these circumstances was clearly impossible.

Joining Andrew Jackson's march into Florida gave him an acceptable alternative, one that Felicity and Jacques would accept without question and one that would hurt Rebecca. He was honest enough to admit to himself that he had wanted that—to cause her to feel some of the pain that he was feeling, perhaps not a commendable reaction but an honest one.

Of course, things would have been difficult for them if she had agreed to go away with him. All of the arguments she had voiced were valid, and yet he felt angry at her for posing them. If she really cared for him, nothing else should matter. It was incomprehensible to him how a woman like her, with such passion and fire, a woman made for physical love, could stay with a man who would never be able to be more to her than a loving brother. Yet she had made her decision to stay, and so he, Armand, must go. The way he felt now, even the thought of possible death did not dismay him. Perhaps it might even be the best solution all around. He felt tense and angry, and uncaring as to his own fate. Perhaps a war was what he needed. Here was a situation where he could put his anger and frustration to good use.

Spurring his horse to greater speed, he rode on.

Armand reached old Negro Fort, on the Apalachicola River, the last week of March. General Jackson had been there since mid-March, with almost two thousand men under his command. He had rebuilt the old fort and renamed it Fort Gadsden.

It had been a wet spring, and the rivers Armand had been forced to cross were running high and much of the land was little more than swamp.

Jackson received Armand in his tent, greeting him heartily. "So, I am to have another Molyneux in my command, am I? Well, if you fight as well as your brother, Armand, you will do yourself and your father great honor."

"My father is dead," Armand said stiffly.

Jackson drew back in surprise. "My condolences, Armand. Your father was an interesting fellow. I never understood him, but then..."

Who did understand Edouard Molyneux, Armand thought.

The general was going on, "... afraid I cannot offer you a commission, sir, as I did your brother. Circumstances are somewhat different now. By the eternal, I sometimes think I have more officers than soldiers!"

"That's all right, sir. I ask only to be able to serve."

"That you may, and I am honored to have you. You may draw a pistol, rifle and ammunition from the quartermaster. I am afraid that rations are in short supply, but when haven't they been? We are on half rations at present. But we shall march shortly. The Seminoles are being agitated by the McQueens, who fled to Florida after I defeated them when your brother was with me."

Jackson stepped to the open tent flap and stared out, hands laced together behind his back. "There are other agitators. The British officer, Woodbine. The Scotsman, Arbuthnot. Villains all, but by the Almighty, we shall win out!" The general faced around, smacking a fist in his palm.

Except for the McQueens, the names were not familiar to Armand, but he said respectfully, "I am confident that we shall, General."

"With lads like yourself in my command," Jackson said with a rare grin, "how can we fail?"

THE DAY AFTER Armand arrived at Fort Gadsden, General Jackson received word that the Seminoles had asked arms of the Spanish commander at St. Marks. The conclusion was that the Indians were probably in control of the town. The general marched his forces at once, also dispatching several gunboats with orders to blockade the west coast of Florida to prevent anyone from escaping by water.

The troops met only small resistance at St. Marks, and Armand did not fire a shot. The Spanish flag was lowered at the stone fort as most of the Seminoles fled south down the Florida peninsula.

One important captive was found in the Spanish commandant's quarters—the Scottish merchant, Alexander Arbuthnot. Armand was surprised to see that the man who supposedly was the strongest agitator of the Seminoles was an old man of seventy, with flowing white hair and a courtly manner.

Armand was present when General Jackson greeted Arbuthnot. "Well, sir! At least I treed one coon. Do you know what the Baltimore *Register* stated should be your fate? They said that your fate should be that of a sheep-killing dog!"

Arbuthnot drew himself up. In a gentle voice he said, "My only friends in this world, sir, are the Indians. They have been ill-treated by the English, as well as the Spanish and robbed by the Americans."

"I will not debate the matter with you, sir. But the bald fact is that the Seminoles are our enemies. You will be held for trial, brought before a court martial on charges of inciting the Red Sticks to war, spying and giving aid to the enemy. By God, sir, I shall see you executed!"

THE NEXT MORNING, April second, Jackson led his troops out of St. Marks. It was his hope to surprise the Indians at the village of Chief Boleck—or Billy Bowlegs, as he was more popularly known. The village was situated on the Suwannee River, 170 miles distant.

Armand had never experienced such a cruel time. A fellow trooper, a rawboned Tennessean by the name of Rath Carpenter, noticed his discomfort with a grin.

"Ain't no white army ever marched over this ground before. Old Hickory, he goes where nobody else has been."

Armand could well believe it. There was no trail as such, only jungle and swamp. Alligators slithered along with the marching soldiers. Insects swarmed in clouds, chief among them giant mosquitoes, making sleep almost impossible at night.

Armand concluded that he would have gotten little sleep in any event; General Jackson drove himself and his men hard. They covered the distance in eight days. They were engaged by bands of Indians twice, and Armand fired his first shots in battle. The brief skirmishes slowed the forward thrust of the troops scarcely at all.

When they reached the Indian village, they were in for another disappointment—the reed huts were vacant. Billy Bowlegs and his followers had fled into the swamps. But that night two Englishmen stumbled into the camp of the Americans and were captured. One was an adventurer, Lieutenant Robert Ambrister of the Royal Colonial Marines and the second was a man by the name of Peter Cook.

Among Cook's possessions was found a letter from Alexander Arbuthnot to his friend, Billy Bowlegs, warning the chief that he would be risking his followers by engaging such superior forces as those commanded by General Jackson.

The general was infuriated when he read the letter. He knew now why he had marched all that distance to find the Indians gone. Enraged, he made his way back to St. Marks, this time making the long journey in five days. He was grimly determined that Arbuthnot and Ambrister should pay the extreme penalty.

This was made clear to Armand on the second day of the long march. As he slogged wearily through ankle-deep mud, battling at mosquitoes, he grumbled to the man by his side, "I cannot understand why Jackson is in such a hurry. The Indians are the other way; we're not marching to engage them."

Rath Carpenter said, "The general is anxious to see to it that them two prisoners we took back there and that Scottish bastard back at St. Marks have their necks stretched." The Tennessean threw back his head and gave vent to a bray of laughter that reminded Armand of the honking of a donkey.

"I really cannot see any reason for hanging Lieutenant Ambrister. The man is just a soldier."

Carpenter snorted. "A soldier, is it? First place, the fellow's an enemy—"

"But he's a soldier, like we are," Armand argued. "Would it be right to hang us, should we be captured?"

"The fellow fights for money, not for his country. I heard the stories about him. He fought at Waterloo against Napoleon, they say, but then he went to the Orient and was suspended from his command. Coming here, he fell in with Captain Woodbine. To my way of thinking, the general's, too, Captain Woodbine is the cause of all this ruckus. He got his hands on a grant of land down here in Florida, but he can only enjoy it so long as the province remains out of American hands. 'Tis in his own interests, then, that he keeps the Red Sticks all stirred up, hoping they will keep us out of Florida. This Ambrister fellow is aiding him in that."

"But this man Arbuthnot, he's not even a soldier—he's a merchant and an old man to boot."

"But he's a spy and an agitator, and there's nothing the general hates more. Don't worry, Old Hickory will see they stretch a rope." Again, the bray of laughter.

Armand said, "There has to be a court martial first and a verdict. Perhaps they won't be found guilty."

"Perhaps they won't be found guilty?" Carpenter peered at him out of eyes suddenly sly with suspicion. "Sounds to me like you might be an enemy sympathizer. Better not let the general hear you speaking such. That's a French name you've got, ain't it? Molyneux. Mayhap you should be fighting on the other side."

Armand fell silent, dropping back a few steps, plodding on through the mud and entangling jungle. Why was he even debating with Carpenter, anyway? He did not care much for the man. He was a good fighting man, but he was crude and unlettered. It was fine to be stubbornly loyal to one's commander, but even great men—and Armand was prepared to grant that Andrew Jackson was such a one—had their flaws.

On their return to St. Marks, General Jackson brought Ambrister and Arbuthnot before a court martial, composed of thirteen of Jackson's officers sitting in judgment.

The evidence against Arbuthnot was strong, consisting of a number of witnesses, including Peter Cook, Ambrister's companion, who was granted amnesty in exchange for his testimony. There was also strong documentary evidence; letters in the Scotsman's own handwriting—appeals to the British governor of Nassau for troops and arms from Chief Bowlegs, letters to the British minister in Washington and the governor of Havana pleading the cause of the Indians and various similar communications.

Naturally, Armand, being only a foot soldier, was not present at the proceedings in the old stone fort, but word was passed on, and information concerning the proceedings was common knowledge.

Arbuthnot made a dignified plea but was able to refute most of the charges against him, and in the end he could only say that he hoped that his judges would "Lean on the side of mercy." He was found guilty and sentenced to hang.

An hour later Robert Ambrister faced his accusers. Ambrister was a personable man, a knowledgeable soldier and a glib talker. Even in the short time he had been a prisoner, he had won many friends among Jackson's officers. Before the court martial he made a frank petition for mercy, which was denied.

A court martial verdict required a two-thirds vote of the panel. The first court poll found exactly two-thirds voting guilty and Ambrister was sentenced to be shot, but then one member of the panel asked to change his vote and the sentence was changed to fifty lashes and imprisonment for one year.

When the verdicts were made known to Andrew Jackson, he affirmed the sentence of Arbuthnot but disapproved the reconsideration of Ambrister's sentence of death. He ordered that Ambrister be shot.

The executions took place on the morning of April twenty-ninth while the troops were being assembled to march to Fort Gadsden.

Armand flinched when he heard the volley of musket fire that signaled the death of Robert Ambrister.

Then he heard that annoying honk of laughter and whirled about to see Rath Carpenter grinning at him.

"What's the trouble, Frenchie?" the Tennessean said in a jeering voice. "Didn't I tell you the general would see to it that the spies got their just deserts? Too much for that weak stomach of yours? If you ain't got the stomach for it, if you let the execution of those two unman you, you shouldn't be here."

It was all too much—the frustrations over the loss of Rebecca, the dreary marches, the killings, the execution of the two men. But what triggered his fury, he concluded later, was the word, "unman." It reminded him too vividly of Jacques.

He threw down his musket and took two steps toward his tormentor. "Damn you, Carpenter!" he said thickly. "I've had enough of you!"

"Have you, now?" Carpenter said in a taunting voice. "What do you figure doing about it, Frenchie?"

Armand advanced, hands clenched at his sides. Just before he came within reach of the other man, Carpenter's eyes flared wide and he swung his musket at Armand like a club. Armand twisted slightly sideways, both hands coming up to catch the musket barrel. The impact stung his palms, but he retained his grip and with a mighty twist tore it from the Tennessean's hands.

Still half-turned, he tossed it aside, just as Carpenter dealt him a hammer blow alongside the head. Armand staggered back, head ringing, and almost lost his balance but managed to recover in time to meet the other man's rush. Carpenter was taller by several inches and he had a longer reach, but Armand was quicker, more agile. He blocked several blows, took two stiff jolts to the body, then managed to maneuver himself into a position to deliver a telling punch of his own. His fist struck the Tennessean on the cheek and sent him reeling back.

Armand noticed that no one was interfering with the fight. Instead the men had gathered around in a circle, cheering the combatants on. Most of the cheers were for Carpenter, which was understandable enough, since Armand was a stranger to most of them.

His opponent was charging again, eyes wild, fists windmilling. Armand hunched his shoulders and ducked. Coming in low, he pummeled the man's mid-section, driving him back.

Then Carpenter brought his clenched hands across the back of Armand's neck. The blow was enough to stun an ox. It drove Armand to his knees. He scrambled out of the way on his hands and knees and got to his feet just in time to meet Carpenter's rush. Again he warded off a rain of blows; he realized now that Carpenter's arms were too long for him to reach his face effectively. He set himself and went down low again. This time he did not try for body blows but kept driving until he was close enough to wrap his arms around the other man's waist. With all his strength he twisted, and they fell together to the hard-packed earth of the parade ground, rolling over and over.

Carpenter pounded on Armand's head and shoulders, but Armand kept his head down, holding on grimly, so the blows were, in the main, ineffectual. Then Carpenter reached a hand around, his powerful fingers searching for Armand's eyes.

Armand rolled the other man over one last time and came out on top, astraddle Carpenter's chest. He held the man pinned to the ground with his thighs. He had the advantage now. Given the Tennessean's position, he could not get any real force behind his punches. He rained blows on Armand's head and shoulders, but most of them were harmless.

Armand began to pound the other man's face, short blows first with his left and then his right. He put most of his remaining strength into the blows, and Carpenter's face began to bleed. He grunted, straining to throw Armand off, but he was not successful. Then he was reduced to trying to protect his face, throwing his head from side to side, trying to cover it with his hands.

Armand bored in, venting his anger and frustration in a savage volley of blows.

Suddenly a great voice thundered above them: "What is this? My own men, fighting among themselves? By the Almighty, I will not have it!"

Strong hands seized Armand under the arms and hauled him upright. He did not offer any resistance. On his feet, panting heavily, he stared down at the man on the ground. All the fight had gone out of Carpenter. He was curled up in the fetal position, hands over his battered face.

"Wasn't the battle with the Red Sticks enough fighting for you?" Jackson's voice roared in his ear.

Armand turned to look into the general's angry face.

Jackson blinked in surprise. "Molyneux! I would have thought better of you, fighting in the dirt like dogs!"

Armand remained silent.

"Come, Armand." Jackson took his arm and led him aside, out of hearing of the others. "Now, sir, tell me what the quarrel was about."

For a moment Armand was reluctant to speak. If the general learned the reason behind the fight, he would likely become even more incensed.

Then Armand decided to the devil with it and plunged recklessly ahead. "We disagreed about the verdict and the executions, sir."

"Did you, now?" General Jackson's bushy eyebrows rose. "Since I recognize your opponent as one of my Tennessee volunteers, I believe it safe to assume that you disagreed with the executions?"

Armand swallowed, bracing himself for the general's wrath. "Yes, sir, I did."

"And for what reason, may I inquire?" Jackson's mild reaction surprised Armand.

"Well, Ambrister was a soldier, like us. Should we expect to be executed, should we be captured?"

"Lieutenant Ambrister was an adventurer," Jackson said harshly. "He conspired with George Woodbine to stir up the Red Sticks against us. Was that the act of a soldier?"

"But Arbuthnot was nothing more than a merchant, a businessman."

"The fellow was a spy, an agitator, sir!" Jackson sighed, running a long-fingered hand through his hair. "Armand, this is your first taste of battle, is it not?"

Armand nodded. "Yes, General."

"If I may be pardoned for saying so, you are rather naive. We are at war, sir! In a war, examples must be made, and that is the reason I brought these two villains up on charges, the reason I overruled the court on the sentencing of Ambrister. The honor and pride of the United States is involved here!"

Strangely, Armand's thoughts jumped back to Maison de Rêverie and the day Jacques had returned from Beaufort with the news of this man's military campaign into Florida. He recalled Jacques's words about honor and the look of disdain that had flashed across Rebecca's face at the word. Although she did not voice it, Armand had read the contempt in her eyes. He had known that she was thinking of Jacques being unmanned in the Battle of New Orleans in defense of that honor.

General Jackson was going on, "War is often cruel, Armand. Nobody knows that better than a soldier, certainly nobody better than a man in the position to decide life and death. By the Almighty, you think I *liked* ordering those men executed? But consider this well. What if I had let them go free down there in Florida? What if they had stirred up the Seminoles again? In that event, it is more than likely that more of our brave lads would die."

He put an arm around Armand's shoulders. "Soon this will be all over. Soon I shall march in and take Pensacola, and that will be an end to it. Then you may put all this behind you and return to your home, happy with the knowledge that you have done your duty. Now, it is time to begin our journey back to Fort Gadsdcn."

Watching the tall general stride away, Armand had a sudden inclination to just walk away. He had joined up of his own volition—what reason was there to keep him from just leaving?

On the other hand, he drew away from the thought of returning home right now. The problem that he was trying to escape from still existed. Back home he would have to see Rebecca and Jacques together, knowing that he could not touch her, knowing that she was lost to him.

Besides, he had come down here to do his duty for Georgia and for his country. What kind of a man would he be if he left before that duty was performed?

The march to Fort Gadsden took four days. Armand was determined to avoid Rath Carpenter. He was ashamed of himself for, as the general had put it, "fighting like dogs in the dirt."

Fortunately Carpenter stayed out of his way as much as possible. Whenever Armand did find himself in Carpenter's company, he would catch the man's eyes glaring at him balefully from out of his bruised face.

True to his word, General Jackson marched his troops west a few days later, on May seventh. It was the most arduous march yet. The ground was little more than a marsh, and they walked in water and mud all the way to Pensacola. The officers' horses stumbled and fell repeatedly, and one by one, they had to be destroyed, until even the officers were forced to walk. Boots rotted, and half the men were barefoot by the time they reached their destination.

On the twenty-fifth they attacked Pensacola. Resistance was not heavy, but they encountered spots of fierce fighting as they advanced into the city.

On the second day Armand was fired upon by a man hiding in the deep recesses of a doorway. He caught a glimpse of him just as he poked the barrel of his musket out of the doorway, and the instant before he fired, Armand threw himself to the ground, rolling. There was an overturned cart in the street, and Armand rolled behind it.

Musket ready, he peered cautiously over the barricade. Evidently thinking he had scored a hit, the man stepped out of the doorway. From the look of the uniform, the man was a Spanish soldier. Armand took careful aim and fired. The musket ball went true, striking the soldier in the chest and sending him reeling back against the building. He crumpled to the ground and lay still.

Armand dropped to reload just as another musket ball thudded into the cart where his head had been. It took him a moment to realize that the ball was fired from *behind* him!

He scrambled sideways and looked back over his shoulder. About thirty yards behind him stood a man in the fringed uniform of a Tennessee volunteer. Armand had no more than a fleeting glimpse before the man ducked around a corner and out of sight.

Armand gathered himself to give chase, then relaxed. Whoever he was, the man had too much of a lead to be caught. Two questions crossed Armand's mind. Had the man fired at him, or had a shot gone astray? Had the man been Rath Carpenter?

Should he confront Carpenter, accuse him? But in the midst of a battle was hardly the time to settle personal grudges. He would just have to remain on his guard.

During the rest of that day and the next, Armand was too busy fighting in the streets and across the rooftops to be concerned with Carpenter. In any event, he did not come across the Tennessean again.

And on the twenty-eighth it was all over—Pensacola surrendered. On the following day Jackson seized the royal archives, appointed one of his officers as military and civil governor of the state of Florida and issued a proclamation declaring that the revenue laws of the United States were in force.

On May thirtieth, leaving a part of his command occupying Pensacola, Andrew Jackson departed, in triumph, leaving for his home in Tennessee and a reunion with his wife, Rachel.

Armand knew he could go home now, but he was still reluctant to do so. To stave off thinking about it, he climbed onto the roof of one of the tallest buildings in Pensacola, from which vantage point he could observe General Jackson riding out of the city at the head of his troops.

He had come around to understanding that, as much as he might have disagreed with the ethics of the two executions, it had been a military decision, and that Jackson had done what he considered right.

Absorbed in watching the general's departure, he was late in realizing that there were sounds behind him on the roof—the shuffling of footsteps. Not really alarmed, he started to turn. Before he could turn completely about, hands seized him roughly, propelling him toward the edge of the roof. Caught off balance, he could not set his feet to resist the pressure.

And then he was falling toward the cobblestones below, and the last thing he heard was that familiar honk of laughter.

Chapter Nineteen

"MY DEAR FELICITY, I cannot tell you how delighted I am to be a part of this group tonight," Joshua Sterling said. "Everyone in Beaufort was dreadfully upset by Edouard's untimely demise, and many of them asked to be remembered to you, when I told them I was invited here this evening. I know that it has been a terrible time for you, but I am so pleased that you now feel recovered enough to see your friends."

Felicity nodded, smiling. "Thank you, sir. It has been a trying time, but it is in the past now."

Sterling, smiling fatuously at Felicity, looked, Rebecca thought, more like an elderly horse than ever. In his evident delight at being one of the few guests invited for tonight's dinner, she expected him, at any moment, to part his large yellowed teeth and whinny!

Felicity had seated Sterling on her right, and to Rebecca's chagrin, she had been seated on the other side of him. The other guests—there were eight in all— were also from Beaufort or other islands in the Port Royal area, and although Rebecca did not know all of them well, she had met them at one time or another. They were, Rebecca noticed, a pleasant but rather dull group, more Felicity's friends than Edouard's, she suspected. But then, that was as it should be. Edouard's rather flamboyant and more frivolous friends might have been out of place on this occasion of Felicity's first reentry into social life.

Now Sterling turned toward Rebecca, giving her the benefit of his horse-toothed smile. "Ah, Rebecca! Lovely as ever, I see. Marriage must agree with you!" He rolled his eyes and fixed his gaze, as was his wont, upon an area just below the neckline of her gown. She found this habit of his extremely annoying, for it made her feel that he was not addressing her but her bosom, and in her present mood, she felt an almost irresistible urge to simply let him sit there until *it* answered him.

Although she had been looking forward to this dinner to break the tedium of late, her conversation with Margaret earlier had quickly destroyed her blossoming feeling of pleasure and spoiled any possible chance of really enjoying the evening. It was an agony simply to have to make pleasant conversation when her mind was filled with images of Armand, wounded, dying or dead!

For once she heartily wished that Margaret had kept her visions, or whatever they might be, to herself. She glanced down at the other end of the table to where Margaret was seated and saw that her cousin was talking to the gentleman seated upon her left, with every appearance of enjoyment.

Rebecca felt a stab of resentment pierce her pain. It bothered her that Margaret—who usually became quite upset when she experienced her presentiments—did not seem particularly perturbed by this one. Rebecca knew that her cousin did not care a great deal for Armand, and yet certainly she could not have any reason to feel any real animosity toward him. Her attitude struck Rebecca as rather odd.

All evening Rebecca had been attempting to comfort herself with the thought that Margaret's predictions did not always come to pass, but that thought brought small comfort, once the seed of fear had been planted. The only thing she could do was to act as normally as possible, so that Felicity and Jacques should not wonder why she was so depressed. It would never do for them to learn what Margaret had said. Coming on top of the other recent tragedies, it could only have the very worst effect upon them. No, she must keep her pain and worry to herself and get through this evening somehow.

Joshua Sterling, Rebecca noticed with relief, had turned to Felicity and seemed to be exerting considerable effort toward entertaining her. The thought crossed Rebecca's mind that the old roué was, in not too subtle a fashion, wooing her mother-in-law. What a dreadful thought! It would be just like Sterling, now that Edouard was dead, to put himself forward as a suitor to the widow. Felicity, after all, was still an attractive woman, and although Jacques was his father's heir, it was his duty to see that his mother was always well taken care of. What more charming sinecure could an elderly gentleman with only a modest income hope for? If he should—God forbid!—marry Felicity, he would have a beautiful home to live in, have all of his wants taken care of and he would never have to lift a finger for himself.

Rebecca did not know whether to laugh or groan. Although she found Sterling fatuous, pompous and often offensive, she had to admit that she rather admired his ability to make the most of any offered opportunity. However, surely Felicity could do better for herself. Surely, she would not be taken in by the attentions of this aging faun! She must be able to see something of Edouard's concupiscence in him.

Determinedly turning away from Sterling and Felicity, Rebecca looked around the table, studying the faces there—pleasant, rather empty faces, showing no great intelligence or talent. Nice, dull people—the kind of people with which she would probably have to spend the rest of her life.

Oh, Armand, she thought, perhaps I should have done as you asked, gone away with you. At least we would be together, and I would not be wondering if you are lying somewhere dead or wounded!

The next morning Rebecca awoke from a restless sleep, feeling both tense and depressed. She knew that she must do something to keep herself occupied and to keep her thoughts away from Armand. The first thing after breakfast she sent one of the housemaids down to the stables to request Jeremy's presence at the big house.

A short time later, Jeremy, all smiles, arrived at her rooms. Rebecca knew that he truly enjoyed their explorations and that his enjoyment was not simply because he was temporarily relieved from shoveling manure in the stables.

"We goin' huntin' again, Miss Rebecca? We goin' down the new passageway today?"

"We certainly are, Jeremy."

He ducked his head with a wide grin. "My momma says to thank you for the fruit and cakes."

"She's very welcome, I'm sure. Now, today I think we will take two lanterns. One doesn't give enough light. We'll go right to the library entrance and then down that new passageway and see what we discover."

Jeremy's grin broadened. "Maybe today we find that treasure."

His high spirits were infectious, and although nothing except Armand's safe return could have lightened Rebecca's mood entirely, the boy's cheerful presence did make her feel a bit better.

She patted his dark head. "Perhaps. But first I want to speak to my husband. Here, I had Darcy send up some milk and cookies for you. I'll return in a few minutes."

As Jeremy, with a small boy's constant hunger, attacked the cookies and milk, Rebecca went down the hall to the study, where Jacques was already working. She had not told him that she was exploring the passageways, for she thought it better for his peace of mind that he did not know. Before she set out on one of her expeditions, she usually checked to see that he was occupied and was likely to remain so for some time.

Now, as she entered the study, she saw that he was sitting at the desk, his head cradled in his hands. He glanced up at the sound of her footsteps.

"Rebecca. How are you going to occupy yourself this morning?"

"Oh, I don't know," she said lightly. "Perhaps a bit of sewing. Or I may do some painting. You look worried, Jacques. Is anything the matter?"

He smiled palely. "Not really. At least not anything serious. It's just that with Armand gone...well, I never realized how much he did at Les Chênes or how much I was relying on his help in handling the rest of Father's affairs. Armand seems to have a flair for such matters, and I must confess that I do not. Still, I shall cope well enough, I suppose. It is just that it's taking a great deal of my time."

Rebecca bent down and kissed him upon the forehead, and he smiled at her gratefully. "You are a great comfort to me, Rebecca. I hope you realize that."

She nodded. "Yes, my dear. I know. Well, I will leave you to your work. I'll see you at noon."

She left the room as he turned to his papers, feeling like a small girl who had just outwitted a parent. Jacques would be in his study all of the morning, and she and Jeremy would be free to roam the passageways without fear that he would come looking for her.

"WELL, HERE IT IS, Jeremy. Let's go in." Holding her lantern high, Rebecca squinted into the new section of passageway.

"Looks like all the rest," said Jeremy cheerfully as he entered the doorway before her. Since he was young, agile and unhampered by skirts, it was their practice for him to lead the way.

They moved slowly, for they had learned that these old hidden corridors often were littered with boards and other debris, which it was all too easy to trip over in the dim light. Also, as they moved, they watched for the tiny shafts of light that showed the locations of the hidden doorways.

When they had traveled for only a short distance, Jeremy gave a soft cry. "Look here, Miss Rebecca! We come up on some stairs."

Rebecca, peering over the boy's shoulder, could see that this was indeed true. Ahead of them, the passageway stopped abruptly at the foot of an extremely narrow flight of steps.

"It ain't goin' to be easy climbin' these stairs in the dark," Jeremy said dubiously. "They awful narrow, and not very deep."

Rebecca touched his shoulder lightly. "You're right; it won't be easy, but together we can do it. We can't stop now, can we?"

"All right, Miss Rebecca. I'm real good at climbin', but you best be careful."

The steps did prove difficult, for there was no banister, and Rebecca was forced to keep her balance by bracing one hand against the wall as they ascended.

The steps seemed to go up forever, but at last they reached the top and the continuation of the passageway.

At this point Rebecca began to feel a slight shiver of fear, for she had not the least idea where they were or where the next exit might be located. And who knew what they might encounter?

However, after they had traveled only a short way, they came across a door. Opening it, they found themselves in a bedroom, which Rebecca at first did not recognize. It was only after opening the clothes cupboard and recognizing Edouard's clothes that she realized that they were in Edouard's room.

Quickly she made her usual markings and returned to the passageway; being in Edouard's room had filled her with a feeling very akin to horror.

Within the next half hour they discovered doorways to several other bedrooms, including Margaret's and the room that had been Rebecca's before she married Jacques and an entrance opening into the sitting room situated between these two bedrooms.

Shortly afterward, as they were making their way down the passageway again, Jeremy, who had been moving slowly ahead, paused suddenly.

"I think it be another doorway, Miss Rebecca, but different, like the one belowstairs."

Feeling a leap of excitement, Rebecca moved quickly to his side and inspected the section of the wall in the light of her lantern. It did appear that this was another revolving panel, like the one that they had discovered down below. Her heartbeat quickened; she had the feeling that her search was at an end.

She set her lantern on the floor, and Jeremy did likewise. When they pushed upon the panel, it gave way immediately, without the slightest sound, turning on its pivot easily.

"This must have been used regularly," Rebecca said. "Now let's see where it leads us."

Jeremy stepped through the panel first and then skidded to such a sudden stop that Rebecca almost fell over him.

"Jeremy!" she exclaimed. "What is it?"

Jeremy turned a wide-eyed gaze on her. "Just look, Miss Rebecca. It's different here. All fancy like!"

Rebecca looked ahead to where the lantern light illuminated the passageway. As she did so she drew in her breath sharply. Jeremy was right—this section was drastically different than any which they had found before. Instead of bare boards, plaster, dust and spiders, this area had been completely finished and had been kept clean.

The walls and ceiling were covered with a rich, red velvet, banded with gold braid, and beneath their feet, a long, narrow runner—Persian, she was sure—extended before them until it stopped at the foot of a deep-red velvet curtain, which blocked their passage.

Six sconces, three to a side, covered with gold leaf, hung upon the walls. As Rebecca raised the lantern, she could see that they held candles, protected by ruby red, cut-glass chimneys.

Also upon the walls, between the sconces, were six paintings, small, about a foot and a half square in ornate gilt-and-ormolu frames.

Lifting the lantern even higher, she examined the painting nearest her and sucked in her breath with a gasp. The painting was like nothing she had ever seen before. In the center, against a black background, was a golden circle containing a five-pointed star. Inside the star was the figure of a naked man, his sex rampant, arms and legs outstretched so that his head and limbs fitted within the five points of the star. The man's face stared directly at her, and his eyes had been painted in red, so that they seemed to glow like flames in the lantern light.

Hastily Rebecca lowered the lantern, hoping that Jeremy had not seen the picture, but when she looked around for the boy, she found him studying another picture, his small face upturned, his mouth forming an O of surprise.

This painting, which, like the first, she now realized was done in the style of Polydoro, depicted a large black goat standing upon his hind feet, like a man. With one sharp hoof, he appeared to hold a twisted staff, around which wound a huge green snake. In the other was a human skull. Again, as in the figure of the man, the sexual organ was fully delineated—indeed, exaggerated—so that it dominated the picture.

Experiencing a wave of revulsion, she hurried to Jeremy and hustled him away. She knew without doubt now that this section of the passage led to Edouard's hidden room, and it had to be behind the velvet curtain. Thinking of the pictures, she felt her face and body grow hot. They were disgusting, yet possessed the fascination of the forbidden and the shocking. What could they mean, and why had Edouard chosen such subjects to be depicted? A deep sense of foreboding, mixed with a sharpened curiosity, filled her. If the passage leading to Edouard's secret retreat was decorated like this, what would the room itself be like? She must not let Jeremy see it, that much was certain.

"Do you think that's another door, Miss Rebecca?" He was pointing at the curtain.

His voice sounded subdued, and Rebecca could tell that he was badly frightened. She had learned that the slaves tended to be superstitious, and seeing that picture must have been a great shock to the child. Should she take him into the house, send him to the stables and return here later, alone?

She hesitated, knowing that she also felt some of what Jeremy was experiencing. No, she did not want to come here alone, and there was certainly no one else she could get to accompany her.

She leaned down to the boy, placing her hand gently on his shoulder. "Jeremy, don't be afraid. It is only a picture, even though it is an ugly one. We just won't look at it, or at any of the others, all right?

"Now, I think that you are right. I'm sure there is a door behind that curtain, and I am going to look. But I want you to stay here, just outside. I want you to be very brave, Jeremy, because I am counting on you. I won't be very long, just a few minutes, I promise. And I want you to promise *me* something in return. Don't look at the pictures, just look at the rug or at the curtain. Do you think you can do that? Can you be a brave boy?''

Jeremy nodded, but his eyes looking at her showed his apprehension and fear.

Acting on a sudden inspiration, Rebecca removed the necklace she was wearing, a silver pendant in the form of a heart, and hung it around the boy's neck. "There! That will protect you. If you become frightened, just touch it, and you will feel brave again.

Jeremy immediately clutched the pendant to him and then heaved a great sigh. "It works, Miss Rebecca. It works, I can feel it!''

She patted his shoulder. "Good. Now, I won't be more than a few minutes.''

Standing up, she held the lantern high with her right hand and started to push the curtain aside with the left. As soon as she did she saw yet another painting behind the curtain. Hastily she dropped the cloth and turned back to Jeremy, whose gaze was fixed upon her face.

"Jeremy, just one more thing. Will you close your eyes for just a moment? Just close your eyes and count to twenty aloud and very slowly. Can you count to twenty?''

Jeremy nodded and closed his eyes tightly. To the sound of his counting voice, Rebecca pushed back the curtain and exposed an ornate painted and inlaid door. This door painting, being approximately five feet in height and three feet wide and being immediately in front of her, had even more of a horrific impact on her than the small paintings on the walls of the passage.

She was confronted again by the goat figure, again upright, and this time holding the hand of a pale, naked woman, with long, black hair and rosy-tipped breasts. The goat man's eyes were inset with rubies, which glittered eerily in the light and his male member was carved from some dark wood, like ebony, tipped with another ruby. The organ, she noticed, stood out from the door, and she understood, with distaste, that it was meant to be a door handle.

Bright coral tipped the woman's breasts, and her eyes—cold blue sapphires—seemed to stare at Rebecca with knowing cruelty.

The figures had been placed against the background of a painted forest, and between the main figures and the trees, there seemed to be a procession, a long line of faint, barely visible figures, both hideous and coldly beautiful. Above, in the dark sky, was a horned moon by whose pale light the figures were faintly illuminated.

Despite her concern that Jeremy might catch a glimpse of the painting, for a moment, Rebecca could not take her eyes from it. Dear God, she thought fearfully, what was she going to find behind that door?

Reaching out gingerly, she grasped the obscene handle and pushed inward.

She found herself standing in a room that was quite large. The ceiling and walls were covered with the same red velvet that lined the passageway, and there appeared to be no doorway other than the one through which she had entered.

Rebecca's first impression was of things, many things: statues, paintings, gold goblets, candelabra, something that looked to be some kind of an altar and behind it another painting of the horned goat man.

Her heart was hammering, and she was conscious of the heavy, sickly sweet smell of incense.

Fighting against a feeling of dizziness, she opened her lantern and from it, lighted one of the candles and used that to light the rest of those in the candelabra on the altar. The light thus provided made the painting behind the altar appear to move, and for a moment Rebecca went rigid with panic.

After a moment she regained control of herself and studied the painting. It depicted the goat man seated upon the throne, his right hand raised, his left holding a blazing torch. Behind his hairy shoulders were spread two huge batwings, and upon his forehead rested the symbol of the encircled, five-pointed star. At the foot of the throne stood two horned human figures, one male and one female.

She had found Edouard's secret place, and it was no wonder that he came away from it sorely disturbed. Questions sped through her mind. Why had this room been built? What was its purpose? What did it mean?

She could not stay here long enough to examine it today, she knew. She had promised Jeremy that she would only be a few moments, and in addition, she was beginning to feel dizzied and faint by what she had already seen.

Looking around quickly, she searched for something that might help explain this place. To the right of the candelabra she had just lit, she saw two books, both quite large, bound in black leather. On the cover of each was that sign again—the encircled star. Could she carry both books? She decided that she could manage, if Jeremy carried both lanterns.

Picking up the top book, she carried it and the lantern into the hall and set the book down beside Jeremy. He was sitting with his back against the wall, huddled within himself, as if against attack. His face lit up with gladness at the sight of her.

Quickly he scrambled to his feet. "We goin' now, Miss Rebecca?"

"Yes. Just one minute more. There's another book I want to take with me. Now mind you don't open that one, Jeremy. I'll be right back."

She hurried into the room, picked up the other book, blew out the candles and returned to the passageway, closing the door behind her, careful that the curtain concealed it from the boy.

"Now we can go," she said, handing her lantern to Jeremy. "You will need to tote both lanterns so that I may carry these books. We'll leave the passageway through the entrance to the small sitting room, all right? No use going back the way we came."

Jeremy bobbed his head. "Yes, Miss Rebecca!"

At a trot, Jeremy led the way down the passage, and Rebecca felt guilty, knowing that the boy had been badly frightened but was being very brave about it. She would have to let him keep the pendant, she thought. It was the very least she could do to compensate him for the fear she had caused him to suffer.

Chapter Twenty

ALTHOUGH REBECCA WAS EAGER to attain her own quarters, where she could study the books in privacy, she was careful to take her usual precautions against being seen coming out of the woodwork, so to speak.

Before opening the door to the sitting room, between what used to be her and Margaret's bedrooms, she peered through the peephole to be certain that no one was in the room, and before they left the sitting room, she went into the hallway to check whether or not it was also empty.

It did not matter a great deal if a servant saw them, for they would never question the activities of the members of the family; however, if they were to meet Jacques, Margaret or Felicity, Rebecca had no wish to be forced to explain the lanterns and the books. She knew they must never learn anything of what she had found in the secret room. The only one she might have been able to tell was Armand, for she had always felt that he knew a good deal more of the family history than the others. But Armand was not here....

But she must not think of him. She must concentrate on getting to her rooms without being seen.

"I guess you found what you was lookin' for, Miss Rebecca?" Jeremy said hopefully as he stored the two lanterns in the hall cupboard as Rebecca directed. "I guess we won't go lookin' no more?"

She did not miss the implications of his question and again she felt a stab of guilt. "Yes, Jeremy. I found what I was looking for, although it wasn't quite what I expected. I'm sorry that it turned out to be so... well, so frightening."

Jeremy said stoutly, "Oh, I wasn't afeared, Miss Rebecca. It's just that old Sampson, he need me down at the stables."

Rebecca smiled down at him. The poor child! He was not going to admit in front of her that he had been terrified.

"Look, Jeremy. I told you that I was going to see if we could find a place for you in the big house. I've talked to Lutie, and she agrees that she could use a bright lad like you."

He looked at her doubtfully.

"You won't have to go into the passageways again. My promise on that. You can just forget all about them."

Unconsciously he reached for and clutched the little silver heart.

"And you may keep that, the little charm, to protect against all bad things. What do you say to that?"

Jeremy's face broke into a broad smile. "If you want me in the house, Miss Rebecca, then I stay. My momma be real happy 'bout that. She say I can make somethin' of myself if I do that."

Rebecca squeezed his shoulder. "You already *are* something, Jeremy, something very nice, and I really appreciate how you have helped me. Now, go on down to the kitchen and tell Darcy to give you the package I had her make up for you. And then, tomorrow, you report to Lutie."

After Jeremy left, Rebecca hurried to her and Jacques's chambers and hid the books in her clothes cupboard. Then she threw herself down on the bed and stretched. Her back ached from carrying the heavy books, but she was not in the least tired. On the contrary, she was filled with an unhealthy kind of excitement. She felt nervous as a cat and as curious as one, too, wanting to see what was in the books and yet afraid to look.

She closed her eyes for a moment and, against the darkness of her eyelids, saw again the goat man and his consort. What *was* that room? What had it been used for? She thought of the altar. Was the room some kind of an unholy chapel? A chapel built to the worship of a horned god? Had Edouard worshipped the devil?

Rebecca, because of her upbringing, had little familiarity with the concept of devil worship. She knew a bit about witchcraft and magic, for the British in India considered the Indian religions a form of superstition, and in India, it was difficult *not* to believe in magic. Also, she had heard the usual bits of gossip, the talk of curses, the evil eye and so on. However, this strange room, with its awful images and atmosphere of evil, was completely outside of her experience. She did not want to think of those paintings, and yet they burned in her mind with a feverish fascination. In one sense, she had found what she had sought—Edouard's secret room—but in finding it she had only uncovered yet another puzzle. But she had the books. Perhaps they could provide answers to some of her questions.

Rising from the bed, she realized that her face felt hot and that her gown was filthy from the dust of the passageways.

Looking down at the ormolu clock on the mantel-piece, she saw that it was almost time for the midday meal, and she had promised Felicity and Margaret a game of cards in the afternoon. There would be no time today when she could be certain of being undisturbed, and she could not risk perusing the books at night, for fear that Jacques might come upon her. There was nothing for it; she would have to wait until tomorrow to examine them.

Walking into her dressing room, she poured water from the large pitcher into the bowl on the wash-stand. As she did so, she examined her flushed face in the mirror. How was it possible for a person to feel anticipation and relief at the same time?

SHE FOUND THE NEEDED TIME midmorning of the next day. Jacques was in his study, Felicity was in the garden and Margaret was in the sun-room, working on her needlepoint. Rebecca knew that she could count on at least an hour or two of privacy.

Telling Margaret that she needed to work on her wardrobe, she hurried to her room, closed the door and removed the books from her clothes cupboard.

She carried them to the small table where the light was good and laid them down; plain, heavy, black leather books, with that strange sign engraved in gold upon their covers. If she had not seen that room, she would think them ordinary enough, the design even attractive. But knowing where they came from, having seen that sign in context, the sight of the books filled her with a sense of fascination mixed with revulsion.

Tracing the outline of the star with the tip of one finger, she felt a shiver of fear. She thought that there was a certain curiosity that was based on something dark in human nature. There were things at which one did not want to look and yet one looked. She had seen an accident once, in London, when a coach had run over an old woman. She remembered how the people had gathered around, and how she herself could not bear to see the old woman sprawled and bleeding on the cobblestones. And yet she *had* looked. For just one moment she had looked and then been sorry that she had.

In India there were many things that it was really best not to see—a noseless leper; a crippled woman; a child dying of starvation. Some people avoided seeing them or at least managed to pretend they did not exist, but Rebecca always saw them, and the sight of them always saddened her.

These books were the same. After seeing Edouard's room she knew that what the books contained could not be pleasant, and yet she simply had to know what was in them.

Settling herself in the comfortable wicker chair, she pulled the first book toward her. It was a bit wider than the other, and the heavier of the two. Gingerly she turned back the cover.

On the title page of thick, rich vellum was a name inscribed in red, the letters intertwined with vines, flowers and small horned creatures with evil faces and gaping mouths—a mixture of the horrid and the beautiful. The name was that of Polydoro.

She turned the next page and was confronted not by words but by a picture similar to the ones she had seen in the passageway outside the secret room and in the room itself.

The colors were vivid, and the images seemed to jump from the page to the eye, like living things: a man and woman, both seated upon thrones, behind them, against a dark background, again the sign of the five-pointed star and the circle. The man clad in a deep-red cloak, wearing a horned crown of gold leaves upon his head, the woman in a similar cape, wearing a crown that held the curve of the new moon above the wearer's brow. Around the seated figures a gathering—men and women, garbed in the same red cloaks, and in front of them, their small naked bodies glowing with a somehow unpleasant luminescence, two small children, a boy and a girl.

Rebecca pulled the book nearer and leaned forward to study the faces, then reared back in surprise. She was certain that the man and the woman on the thrones were Jean and Mignon Molyneux, for the faces were the same as those depicted in the portraits on the landing of the great staircase.

She bent forward again, closely studying the faces of the children. The boy had a slender, olive-skinned face rather similar to the face of the woman. Rebecca drew in her breath with a hiss. The child had to be Edouard, for it looked just like him.

Now she studied the girl child—slender, small-boned, with an aureole of fluffy, golden hair.

As Rebecca examined the pictures she became aware of the expressions on the faces staring back at her. They had a look of similarity, a look of amused, secretive knowledge, coupled with a kind of dark satisfaction. Rebecca felt herself shudder. Even the boy's face bore the look, which made it even more noticeable that the little girl's did not. Alone in the group, the girl's small face showed a sorrow too deep for a child that small to bear and a glowing innocence. This contrast made the painting very powerful, and Rebecca stared at if for a long time. She assumed that the painting depicted Jean and Mignon and their friends, during one of their "games," which she now felt certain was a good deal darker and more sinister than the type of activity that that word generally described. What really horrified her was the presence of the children. Were the children usually present at these activities or had Polydoro simply posed them in this picture as a conceit, a bit of artistic contrast?

She turned to the next page and found her question answered, to a degree.

The second painting consisted of the depiction of twelve faces, arranged around the perimeter of a circle, like the hours on the face of a clock. In fact, she now realized it *was* the depiction of an obscene clock face, with the hands of the clock shown as male organs, pointing to the hour of twelve. The center of the clock face was heavily ornamented with the same sort of embellishments that adorned Polydoro's name on the flyleaf—demons, strange, too-lush flowers and vines, snakes and toads.

At the top, in the place of the figure twelve, was Jean Molyneux's face, and opposite it, at the place usually occupied by the hour of six, was Mignon's.

Three o'clock and nine o'clock were marked by the children's faces. The other faces were unfamiliar to Rebecca, but she noticed that next to Jean's face, at one o'clock was the face of a very beautiful woman.

She had a rather sweet face or perhaps she once had, thought Rebecca, for now there was something in the eyes, something about the mouth. The woman had the same golden hair and blue eyes as the little girl, and Rebecca wondered if she was the child's mother.

Rebecca made a moue of distaste. If the woman was the mother, how could she have countenanced having her own child a part of this depravity? It was difficult to even conceive of a woman capable of such a thing.

Opposite the blond woman was the likeness of a dark man with a rather mean mouth and angry eyes. Rebecca wondered if, since these two were depicted flanking Jean, they had some special place in the hierarchy of the group.

Shaking her head, she began to turn the next page with a feeling of relief. These pictures were disturbing, but not nearly so much as the ones in the passageway and the hidden room, and they *were* informative. After looking at all of them, she might very well have a good idea of what had taken place in that room.

Gazing down at the third picture, she felt her stomach spasm, and she looked quickly away. Then, despite herself, she looked back. The painting was beautifully and lovingly detailed, the bodies clear and glowing against the dark background. Upon a red velvet lounge, richly piled with bright pillows, lay a man and a child, bodies entwined in the act of love. The man was obviously Jean Molyneux, and the child, the small golden-haired girl. Polydoro had captured their expressions clearly. Jean's dark delight and satisfaction, the child's shame and unhappiness were shown all too plainly.

Rebecca had to swallow, for she felt that she might be sick. Slowly she turned the next page and the next. Each painting showed people coupling—Jean and the blond woman, the dark man and Mignon, the others, two by two, three by three and then all twelve together.

Rebecca's mind was numb with shock, but she knew that she had to see them all. She had reached a point where she thought she could see nothing worse, when she came upon the picture of the two children; two children who should have been fresh with innocence and who were instead debauched and degraded in this facsimile of adult behavior.

Thank God there was only one page more! She turned it and saw that it expressed the very essence of this dreadful book and, doubtless, the essence of Jean and Mignon's unholy practices.

There, on the same red velvet couch, was Mignon with her lover. In this painting, Edouard's small face proclaimed what had caused his madness; a wild division of terror and an awful, shameful knowledge.

Rebecca slammed the book shut and pushed it away from her. Margaret and Lutie had been right. She had not learned anything from the discovery of that dreadful room that she really wanted to know.

Feeling ill, she leaned back in the chair and closed her eyes. Immediately, against darkness, she saw that terrible picture again. That poor, twisted child! What kind of a chance had he been given? With such a background it would have been impossible for him to have grown up normally. And the little girl. Who was she? Who had she become?

"Rebecca? Are you ill?"

Rebecca jumped. Jacques! Oh, my God! He must not see the books.

Standing quickly, she saw Jacques coming toward her. She turned so as to place herself in front of the table, hoping that he would not notice the books.

"What were you doing, my dear? Margaret said that you came upstairs to sort out your dresses or something. You look quite pale."

Rebecca gave him a nervous smile. "I was arranging my wardrobe. That is, I intended to, but I felt a bit tired and just sat down for a few minutes. I feel fine now. What are you doing away from your accounts?"

"Oh, I've had enough for one day. I felt in need of a change. I thought we might take a ride along the beach and have a picnic. I mentioned it to Margaret, and she thought it was an excellent idea."

"Well, yes, it does sound nice. I'll just change my clothes. It will only take a minute."

He watched her, faintly puzzled, for she had made no move to leave her spot in front of the table.

Slowly he walked toward her, and her heart began to hammer painfully. He was going to see the books, and there was nothing she could do!

When he reached her, he glanced over her shoulder at the table. "These are very odd-looking books, Rebecca. I don't believe I've ever seen them. Did you get them from the library?"

Rebecca, at a loss for words, hesitated, then said hurriedly, "Why, yes. They're just some old books I found stuck back in a dark corner. Nothing interesting, really."

"I see. Well, you had better get changed. That dress really won't do for a picnic on the dunes."

"Yes, Jacques, of course." She could not stand there any longer. It would only make him more curious than ever.

She walked toward her clothes cupboard, looking over her shoulder at him. With dismay she saw him reach out for one of the books and then was relieved to see that it was the other book, the one she had not yet opened. If God was kind, hopefully this book would contain nothing awful, nothing shocking.

Reaching blindly into the cupboard, she kept her gaze on Jacques as he opened the book, watching his face crease into a frown.

"Rebecca, do you read Latin?"

"Well, yes, although not very well."

"Do you know what this book is?"

"Not really," she said truthfully, frantically wondering what was in the book.

Jacques's voice held a note of shock. He held the book in his hands, reading aloud, "'*Liber spirituum.* Book of words, book of deeds, blessed be, thou book of art!' Rebecca, this is a book of shadows. A witches' bible! You say you got it out of *our* library!"

He turned to stare at her, his expression incredulous.

Rebecca, completely nonplussed now, did not know how to respond. "I...I found it. I was curious. The cover was so odd, and yet I was just going to look at it. I hadn't even opened it yet. If I had known what it was..."

Jacques shook his head in exasperation and, placing the book on the table, picked up the other one.

Rebecca had often heard the phrase, "her heart fell," and for the first time she fully grasped its meaning, for she felt as if her heart had fallen straight down into her stomach, a terrible sinking feeling that made her feel weak.

Jacques had opened the book of Polydoro's paintings and was looking at the first picture. The blood drained from his face, and his mouth worked but he uttered not a word, nor did he look at her. She stood, cold and trembling, as he turned from page to page, his face growing still whiter as the pages turned, until, at last, he saw the awful, final picture of his father and grandmother. He stared at it for a long time and then slowly placed the book upon the table. He staggered slightly, catching at the table for support. When he finally turned toward Rebecca, she could not look at him.

"Where did you find this filth, Rebecca? It was not in the library, that I know. I am familiar with every book on the shelves, and I have never seen these. Tell me where you got them!"

Rebecca wanted to swallow, but there was no moisture in her throat. Still, she refused to look at him.

"Tell me!" he said in a terrible whisper. "I demand that you tell me!"

She finally found her voice. "I found Edouard's secret room, the one Dhupta told us about. I discovered the books there. I took them because I thought they might help explain...oh, I am so sorry, Jacques! I know that he was your father and that you loved him. It must be awful to know..."

Still in that terrible voice: "Take me there."

Rebecca finally looked at him. "Oh, no, Jacques! You don't want to go there. It's...well, it's like those pictures, a diseased, awful place."

"Yet you went there."

She raised her hands and looked at him pleadingly. "Yes, I did. But I had no idea of what I would find. I don't know what I expected, really. Searching for that room was just something to do, to pass the time. Now I wish that I had minded my own affairs. I would give *anything* not to have found it, not to have seen…those pictures."

Jacques's face had become that of a stranger, his voice cold now, and harsh. "Take me to the room, Rebecca."

"But Margaret is waiting for us to take her on the picnic…"

"I will go downstairs and tell her that you are not feeling well and that I am gong to sit with you, so we must postpone the picnic. Be ready when I return."

He turned and left the room, closing the door quietly after him. Rebecca stood in the middle of the room without moving. What had she brought about? She felt like Pandora, of Greek legend; she had loosed a host of evils upon her world, by virtue of her curiosity. But her actions could not be undone. She had no choice but to do as Jacques asked.

THE TRIP through the dark passageways, this time, generated no excitement in Rebecca. She had to watch the pain and disillusionment on Jacques's face as he examined the ornate entryway, the inlaid door and the interior of the room. He made his examinations methodically, as if it were an unpleasant duty he had to get through. It was as if he had to see everything so that he might know every detail of his father's and his grandfather's degradation and shame.

At last he signified with a nod of his head that he was ready to leave. He had not spoken since they had left their quarters.

When at last they were in their own rooms, Rebecca turned to him. "Jacques, please speak to me! I know you are sorely hurt and that in a sense I am the cause of it. But believe me, I did not intend to hurt you. I had no idea what I would find."

Her pleading glance was rebuffed by his stony stare. "I don't wish to talk about it, Rebecca. I never want to discuss it again, do you understand? You must tell no one what you have found, particularly Mother. I think it would kill her."

Rebecca's hand flew to her throat. Despite the situation between herself and Jacques, she did care for him, and it hurt her to have him employ this cold tone to her. After all, it was not she who had done these terrible things, but his father. All she had done was bring them to light!

"Jacques, how can you possibly think I would tell anyone? What kind of a person do you think I am?"

His dark look told her that at the moment he was not at all certain, and she remembered something which she had once read. In ancient times kings and generals had often killed the person who brought them bad tidings. Hardly a fair way to vent one's anger, but perhaps, in a strange way, understandable. Jacques was angry now, angry and hurt, but later, after he had recovered from his shock, surely he would be more reasonable.

"I suggest that you remain here until I return," he said in that same cold voice.

She said nothing but merely watched as he turned to the table, picked up the books—as if they were something poisonous, which indeed they were—and left the room.

Feeling emotionally spent and bruised, Rebecca threw herself across the bed, tears of anger and frustration burning her eyes. A wave of longing for Armand turned the tears into wracking sobs of loneliness, not untinged with self-pity.

She dozed, with thoughts of Armand floating like ghosts in her light dreams.

Chapter Twenty-one

THE AFTERNOON WAS WARM, and quite humid, as Rebecca sat down on the stone bench under the willow tree in the back garden, hoping to catch Lutie when she came out to inspect the vegetables in the garden.

She was in a thunderous mood and was aware that she was. Indeed, she found some amusement in her own gloomy musings.

Several days had passed since the morning that Jacques had found her with Edouard's books, but Rebecca's hopes that her husband would be able to forget what he had seen, that he would return to his usual good nature, had proved ill-founded. As the days had gone by Jacques's mood had only grown darker. He had begun to spend more and more time in his study, and Rebecca suspected that it was not simply because he was attending to business.

More than once she had noticed the smell of liquor on his breath when he came to meals, and during the meals, and other times when the family was together, he was uncommunicative and sullen.

Margaret seemed to have caught his mood. Often Rebecca found her cousin staring at her reproachfully when Jacques was particularly subdued, as if to blame her for his condition. Rebecca found this particularly annoying. Even if it had been her fault, what business was that of Margaret's? She wondered what Margaret would say if she found out what Jacques had done to her, Rebecca?

But then, that was fairly predictable, wasn't it? Margaret would not necessarily think that Jacques had done Rebecca any real harm. She would probably consider their marriage ideal; a marriage of the spirit, without any of those awkward physical yearnings to sully it.

Over the past few days Rebecca had been doing a great deal of thinking. When Jacques had come into the room to tell her about the planned picnic on the dunes, he had already spoken to Margaret about it; had asked her first if she cared to go. And there had been other things, as well, little things; the way Margaret hung on his every word, for instance. As a practiced coquette, Rebecca well knew how men could be flattered by a good listener. Margaret, in her own bloodless way, was wooing Jacques, and Jacques—perhaps even more vulnerable under the circumstances than the ordinary man—was responding.

This realization had caused Rebecca some startled moments. Margaret her rival? What a very odd thing. And how strange that, even though Rebecca no longer wanted Jacques in the way a woman wants a man, she should feel injured. After all, she had been unfaithful to him. Whatever had or what might go on between Jacques and Margaret, it certainly would not be physical, and yet Rebecca still felt a sense of betrayal. How odd we human creatures are, she mused with a rather bitter smile, how odd and contradictory!

The only one who seemed to be constantly in a sunny mood nowadays was Felicity. There had been another one of the small, private dinner parties, and although the majority of the guests were different than the ones who had attended the first, Joshua Sterling was present. This was obviously Felicity's doing, since she had made up the guest list. Rebecca was pleased that Felicity seemed to have put her unhappiness behind her. However, Rebecca was still worried over the credentials of her suitor. But perhaps she should simply be happy for Felicity. At least someone in the house was enjoying herself, and if anyone deserved it, it was Felicity.

There had been no news from Florida. Whenever a packet arrived, Rebecca was at the dock to meet it, seeking the latest information, and there were never any letters from Armand, not even to his mother. Sometimes Rebecca thought her heart would truly break from the need of him.

And then, on top of all this, Margaret, only yesterday, had delivered another lecture.

They had been in the garden, which was fresh and fragrant in the morning air, picking flowers for the house. Margaret, who up until then had been very quiet, suddenly turned to Rebecca.

"Rebecca, I know that you are going to be angry with me, but I simply must say this."

Caught unaware, Rebecca carefully put the rose she had just cut into her basket and gave Margaret a frown. "Really, Margaret, if this is going to be another one of your lectures, please spare me. I don't wish to hear it. I'm simply not in the mood for it. It will likely only serve to depress me."

Margaret's mouth thinned down to a narrow line. "There are other things more important than happiness, Rebecca. Things like duty and honor!"

Rebecca did not attempt to stifle her groan. Honor, again!

Before she could frame a retort, Margaret plunged on. "Haven't you noticed how unhappy poor Jacques is? Don't you care that he is having a difficult time handling his business affairs?"

Rebecca stared at her in astonishment. "Trouble with his business affairs? What on earth are you talking about? As far as I know, his business affairs are fine. He certainly never told me otherwise."

Margaret sniffed with disapproval. "Perhaps that is because he wishes to spare you any distress. Perhaps if you took more of an interest..."

Rebecca was in no mood to listen to her cousin give her advice on how she should be treating her husband. "It seems to me," she said cuttingly, "that you have a great deal of nerve lecturing me on how a wife should behave. After all, you have never been one!"

Margaret flushed, and she set her mouth stubbornly. "That's as may be, but I still know what I see, and I see that Jacques is terribly unhappy!"

"Jacques! Jacques!" Rebecca said rather wildly. "Is that all that you can talk about? Haven't you, for instance noticed that *I* am unhappy, also? Why is it only Jacques's unhappiness that matters?"

"Why should *you* be unhappy?" Margaret responded. "Edouard was prevented from doing you any real harm, and now that he is dead, what have you to fear? You are married to the man you wanted to marry, a wonderful man. You are mistress of a beautiful home and other estates, the last news from India was good and your parents are well. What could you possibly be unhappy about? You should get down on your knees and thank the Lord for your good fortune."

This statement was delivered with such a righteous air that it was all Rebecca could do to hold her tongue. But she was helpless to fight back. She could not possibly tell Margaret the truth about Jacques, or about Armand. To do so would be a disaster for all of them. And so there was absolutely nothing she could say. For once Margaret had bested her.

She sighed. "Margaret, let's not quarrel. We have always been so close. Lately I feel that we have somehow been growing apart. Come, let's make up. I will even promise to see what I can do to lift Jacques's spirits, if that will make you happy."

"It is not my happiness in question." Margaret's mouth lost some of its tenseness, but she did not smile. "I'm sorry if you are not happy, Rebecca, but if you are not, then perhaps it is of your own doing. And of course I am still your friend. I shall always be. That is why I must speak out when I see you behaving in a manner that is not in your best interest. Surely you can understand that?"

"I am not certain that I do," Rebecca said. A suspicion crossed her mind. Could Margaret possibly suspect about her and Armand? But no, her cousin was not the kind of person to catch nuances in relationships. Still, what could she have been referring to when she had said that if Rebecca was unhappy, she might have brought it upon herself? Surely she did not know anything about Edouard's room? Jacques would never speak of it, and *she* certainly had not . . .

Rebecca's thoughts were abruptly interrupted by the sound of the back door slamming shut. She glanced up to see Lutie coming down the steps, evidently headed toward the garden, having passed Margaret who had gone to her room.

Quickly she called Lutie's name and waved.

Looking into the sun, the black woman shaded her eyes with her hand. "Rebecca, is that you?"

"Yes, Lutie. Can you spare a few minutes to talk?"

Lutie began to walk toward her, and again Rebecca was struck by her sinuous grace and proud carriage.

"I suppose I can spare a few minutes for the mistress of the house," Lutie said, smiling.

She was in the shade of the tree now. With a sigh, she sat down beside Rebecca on the stone bench. "What did you wish to talk about?"

For a moment Rebecca did not answer, thinking over what she was about to do. She firmly believed in promises, believed that they should be kept, yet she felt that she simply *had* to talk to someone. She tried to convince herself that talking to Lutie would not be an actual breach of faith, for she knew that she could trust the other woman absolutely.

"Lutie, when I talked to you before, when I mentioned the passageways in the house, I sensed, somehow, that you knew more about them than you were willing to tell me at the time."

Lutie's eyes narrowed, but she made no reply.

Rebecca went on quickly. "I also mentioned the fact that Dhupta spoke of a 'secret place' where Edouard used to go. I am speaking of it again, because I have to talk to someone, and you are the only one I can confide in."

Lutie put a slender, brown had on Rebecca's arm. "Are you certain you want to talk about this?"

"Yes. I have to have some advice, another opinion than my own. Will you listen?"

Lutie sighed. "I have a strong feeling that you have been very foolish, Rebecca, but I will do whatever I can to help you. You should know that."

Rebecca gave her a tremulous smile. "Thank you, Lutie. You see, I found that room, that secret place, and it was awful. You can't imagine!"

"I have some idea, I think," Lutie said slowly. "As I told you, when my momma was sick, just before she died, she told me a number of terrible things. Some of what she told me, she told me because she thought that the truth should be known and some of it was fever-talk. But putting the two together, I think I have a pretty good picture of what old Jean Molyneux was up to."

Rebecca let her breath out in relief. "Good! Because I don't know if I could have described to you what I saw, except to say that it was horrible, and sick, and frightening, and after I saw it, I could understand why Edouard was the way he was. His parents made him that way, Lutie. They made him do things . . . well, you say that you have some idea. They must have been some kind of monsters to do that to a child. And he wasn't the only child, either. There was a little girl, a delicate, little blond girl. Her face haunts me. I think it may well haunt me for the rest of my life. I keep wondering who she was and what became of her."

Lutie folded her hands in her lap. "That little girl was Elissa Huntoon. Her parents were close friends of Master Jean and Mignon Molyneux, and they spent a great deal of time here. Momma, when she was in the fever, called them 'the devil's left and right hands.'"

"Yes, yes," Rebecca said excitedly. "There is a painting that shows them on the right and left side of

Jean Molyneux. That must be what your mother meant.''

"Rebecca, as long as you know what you do, you might as well know the rest about the Huntoons. Evidently, Master Jean Molyneux had a powerful passion for Elizabeth Huntoon, Elissa's mother. It seems that it was his practice to have physical knowledge of all the women in that intimate group of his he called his coven. But it was Elizabeth that he most favored, even above his own wife, Mignon.

"Evidently, after being a part of Jean Molyneux's group for two or three years, Elizabeth Huntoon suddenly sickened of the kind of life she and her husband and daughter were leading. My momma said that Madame Huntoon got religion and began to fear for her soul.

"Momma had known that something funny was going on here at Maison de Rêverie. She had heard some gossip from the Molyneux servants, and she had seen how distraught little Elissa was every time her parents brought her home from a visit with the Molyneuxs and how the girl wept and carried on when her parents wanted to take her back there.

"Momma knew that something wicked was happening to that child, whom she loved like her own. Momma was on pretty friendly terms with Madame Huntoon, who relied on her, and she encouraged the woman to mend her ways, at least as much as she could, without overstepping her bounds.

"Finally Madame Huntoon just flatly told Jean Molyneux that she wasn't going to be a part of his 'games' any longer and neither was her daughter. I don't know how Master Huntoon reacted; Momma didn't tell me.

"But Jean Molyneux was furious. He was rich and spoiled and so used to getting his own way that he just couldn't abide it when someone said no to him. Momma told me that no one liked to talk about it, because Master Jean was such a rich and powerful man, but she said it was common knowledge on the islands, and even in Savannah, that he was mad. He evidently acted sane enough most of the time, but there were other times when he flew into mighty rages and did terrible things. Momma knew of at least two slaves that Master Jean beat to death himself. It wasn't like they tried to escape or anything like that. It was just because of some little thing they did that he didn't like.

"She said he was a cruel, evil man and that she knew for a fact that it was he who burned down the manor house at Les Chênes and caused the deaths of Elizabeth and Richard Huntoon. Momma claimed that she saw him, through the window, running away from the house just before the fire took hold. If she hadn't been awake that night, because little Elissa was fretful, she and Elissa would have died too."

Rebecca said, "That first day at Les Chênes, Armand said that Jean and Mignon died that very same night!"

Lutie nodded somberly. "That is true. Momma got the story from some of the Molyneux servants. They were awakened some time after midnight by their mistress's screams. One woman said that the screams were so awful that she had to put her pillow over her head to drown out the sounds."

"Then why didn't they investigate, go see what was the matter?"

Lutie shook her head. "They had heard screams of that nature before, and they knew enough to stay in their rooms and mind their own business. I still don't believe you understand how it is for slaves, Rebecca. We don't have any rights, and a master can do just what he wants with us. We are property, you see, like his cattle and his horses. If any of them had tried to interfere that night, they would no doubt have suffered sorely for it.

"Anyway, soon the screaming stopped, and the servants all went back to sleep. It was young Edouard who found them the next morning. First his mother, in the tower room, all laid out with flowers on her breast and her hair spread out around her, like a picture in a book. And then his father in the trophy room, hanging by the neck from a long, black leather strap.

"The servants said that Mignon Molyneux's face was all contorted in fear or pain, and she hadn't died easy. Momma said that the talk among the servants was that it looked like she had been poisoned, but the doctors never admitted to that. Because the Molyneuxs had been so rich and powerful, the whole affair was hushed up as much as it could be under the circumstances."

"Then what you are saying is that Elizabeth Huntoon told Jean Molyneux that she was no longer going to have anything to do with him and that in a fit of madness, he set fire to the Huntoon manor house, then returned to Maison de Rêverie, killed his wife and then himself?"

"That's what my momma thought, and she knew as much about what was going on as anybody at that time."

Despite the heat, Rebecca gave a slight shudder, and for a moment felt very cold. "What a sad, horrible story! And yet it fits in with all the rest I have learned. You know, sometimes it is difficult for me to believe all this really happened. It is worse than that frightening novel of Horace Walpole's, *The Castle of Otranto*." She flushed. "I have never told anyone that I read that. My parents would have apoplexy, I'm sure. But what I mean to say is that this whole thing is unbelievable! I feel like it is all some kind of nightmare, from which I will eventually awaken."

"It is no nightmare, I'm afraid," Lutie said with a sigh. "I am not familiar with the book you speak of, but I do know that anything that one man can imagine, another man can do or do even worse. With all respect, I think that you have not seen much of the wickedness of the world, Rebecca."

Rebecca smiled wanly. "That may be true, Lutie, but it would seem that I am making up for it now."

Both women sat in silence for a bit, each engrossed in her own thoughts, and then Rebecca said, "You know, little Elissa was very fortunate to have had your mother to look after her. She and Elissa must have been very close."

"They were. My momma was the only person Elissa trusted. Her own parents had failed her, done terrible things to her. Bess was the only one she could count on."

"And then your mother and Elissa went to live at Maison de Rêverie. Didn't that seem odd to your mother? And didn't it upset Elissa to go and live where those bad things had happened to her?"

Lutie shrugged. "It wasn't a matter of choice. There was no other course open to them. It was arranged for the Molyneux estate to buy the Huntoon plantation, with the money to be held in trust for Elissa until she attained her majority. The purchase naturally included the Huntoon slaves, including Momma. As far as Elissa was concerned, the Huntoons were dead, and there were no close relatives to take Elissa in. She had no place else to go.''

''But how did Edouard's aunt and uncle come to take Elissa in?''

''It was Edouard's idea, I understand. He and Elissa had been friends since babyhood, and even though he was still only a boy, he would one day be master of the house, and his aunt and uncle acceded to his wishes. They evidently thought that the presence of another child in the house would help Edouard to recover more easily from the shock of his parents' deaths.''

Rebecca shuddered again, thinking back to the painting of the two children together in the book, and Lutie took note of her expression.

''I know now what the relationship between Edouard and Elissa eventually became, but Momma didn't know what had really gone on during Jean Molyneux's games. Like I said, she had *some* idea but only hints and whispers. It wasn't until later that she saw what Edouard was becoming and realized the influence he had on Elissa. By that time it was too late, of course, and all she could do was protect the girl as much as possible. I don't think Momma ever really knew the full extent of Master Edouard's depravity. Or perhaps, like Mistress Felicity, she didn't really want to know.''

''What finally happened to Elissa? No one will really talk about it. Someone, I think it was Felicity, said that she died young, but that is all she would tell me."

Lutie looked down at her hands in her lap. "I am sorry, Rebecca, but I've told you all I can. I won't lie to you and say that I don't know more, but what I have told you is most of the story. You had best be content with that, for that is all I can tell you. Other people are involved."

Rebecca looked at her intently for a moment and then touched her hand. "I thank you for what you have told me. My curiosity has led me into some dark places. But at least now I have a good idea of the reasons behind Edouard's behavior, and his death. What you have told me, unpleasant though it is, will make my mind easier."

"I am glad of that. But you did say you wanted my opinion and my advice."

"Yes, I did. You see, I have tried to keep what I found a secret from Jacques and Felicity, knowing it would upset them. Unfortunately, Jacques saw a book of paintings that I found in Edouard's hidden room, and then he made me take him to the room . . ."

"And there he saw, for the first time, what his father had really been?"

Rebecca nodded sadly. "And he has been acting very strangely since. I am afraid that learning about his father has affected him more strongly than I had been dreading it would. He spends almost all of his time in the study now, and I am certain that he is drinking heavily."

"It is a bad thing that he saw that room and its contents," Lutie said somberly. "But there is nothing that can be done about that now. Has he gone there again?"

Rebecca glanced at her with a start. The idea that Jacques might have returned to the room had not occurred to her. "I don't really know. Truthfully, I haven't thought of that possibility. He appeared so upset about the room and the books. He warned me not to speak of either, to him or to anyone else. I assumed that he had it boarded up. I certainly didn't think he would return there. For what earthly reason would he?"

"Rebecca, I do not say this lightly, but as I told you, his father was, by all accounts, mad."

Rebecca recoiled in horror. "And they say that madness runs in families. Oh, no! I can't believe Jacques . . . !"

Lutie looked at her steadily. "I think you should watch him closely and try to keep him calm. If you could convince him to see a doctor, mayhap the doctor could give him something to calm him. And if I were you, I would try to find out if he *is* visiting that room. That room, I believe, is the heart of all the evil that began with Master Jean and passed down to his son. It should be destroyed. If Master Jacques is going there, it can only cause him harm."

Chapter Twenty-two

WHEN REBECCA RETURNED to the house after her conversation with Lutie, she was determined to talk with Jacques, to force him to communicate, if necessary. Matters simply could not continue this way!

Lutie's thought that Jacques might be returning to the hidden room was probably valid, Rebecca concluded. Despite his disgust upon seeing the book of paintings and the room itself, despite his refusal to discuss the subject or to allow Rebecca to talk about it, something dark in him—the strain of madness that marred his grandfather and father—might compel him to go there.

Another appalling thought occurred to Rebecca. What of Armand? If Jacques had inherited the fatal flaw from his grandfather and father, might not Armand have inherited it, as well? It might account for his brooding nature and dark moods. Were they caused by his circumstances or by the family weakness? How could she bear it if Armand, too, were to go mad?

For a moment she wished that she might swallow her pride and take the next boat sailing for India. She knew that her parents would probably be pleased to have her back, but she would be returning as a failure, a woman who had found it necessary to flee to escape a bad marriage. True, other women before her had done so, but not women like her, women who had been offered their pick of husbands, women who were renowned for their beauty, pride and intelligence. Oh, how the friends of her parents would gossip and how her own friends would laugh to themselves to see her brought down. No! She refused to return to face such humiliation. Better to face the problems here, insurmountable as they might seem, than to return to India in defeat and shame.

Also, she could not leave without seeing Armand again. She knew now that if he returned and if he still wanted her, she would go away with him. She had begun to realize that life was much too short to spend with someone you did not love and who could not truly love you. If she and Armand would have to be poor to be together, then so be it. Poverty would not be pleasant, but she did not believe it could possibly cause her more anguish than she was feeling now.

Before Jacques's study, she stood with her ear to the door, listening for sounds from within. When she heard nothing she slowly opened the door and peered in. The room was empty.

Wondering where he could be, she began to search for him throughout the house.

She found Margaret in the music room, practicing at the pianoforte, and Felicity reading a book in the small parlor, but neither had seen Jacques since breakfast or knew where he might be.

Perhaps, Rebecca thought, he was in their rooms. But a search of the upstairs yielded no trace of him, and she began to feel the weight of discouragement. She hoped very strongly that he was somewhere outside the house. Perhaps he had decided to go riding or to take a walk.

Finally she faced the truth, for in her heart she knew where he was. Should she go to the hidden room and see if he was there? That was the only way she would know for certain. Yet it would be difficult to approach the room without him hearing or seeing her, and despite her resolution to confront him, she didn't feel that she could endure a direct confrontation in that room. If they were to converse rationally, it had to be somewhere else.

Feeling restless and miserable, she paced the bedroom. *Should* she go looking for him? Or should she simply wait and confront him later with her suspicions?

Like a caged tigress, she prowled, stopping to look at herself in the ornately framed mirror over the large carved chest where Jacques kept some of his things. Her face looked paler than ever, and her eyes had dark shadows, like bruises, beneath them. This place, the strain of all that had happened, was sapping her strength and vitality. She must take better care of herself. If and when Armand returned, she did not want him to find her pale and drawn.

Her glance moved from the mirror down to the chest, and she was struck by a sudden impulse to raise the lid. To her great surprise, the chest was locked. She had never found Jacques to be secretive, and as far as she knew, he did not make a habit of locking their cupboards, desks or cabinets. So why had he locked this chest?

Her next thought was to wonder where he had put the key. Had he carried it with him? That was unlikely, since she knew it was a large, heavy key, much too cumbersome to carry around. It was usually left in the keyhole in the chest.

She crossed the room to bolt the door and then began a quick search of the room, looking in all the little, secret places where she and Jacques put things—the small drawers in the desk and tables. She even shook the vases on the mantelpieces but heard no answering rattle.

As a last resort, she went to his clothes cupboard and began going through the pockets of his coats and breeches. It was there she finally found the key, secreted in the deep pocket of a heavy coat.

Fearful that Jacques would come knocking at the door any moment, she hastened to the chest and inserted the key. It turned stiffly—the lock was quite heavy and old-fashioned—and then finally clicked open.

Eagerly she raised the lid and peered inside. To her great disappointment, she saw only folded clothing, but then, of course, if Jacques was hiding something, he would not be likely to leave it in plain sight. She removed the clothing, garment by garment, and finally found what she was looking for, buried about halfway down the chest. It was another book, smaller than the two she had found in Edouard's sanctuary, but again bound in black leather and bearing upon its cover the now-familiar sigil.

With trembling hands she took it out, thinking that this was definite proof that Jacques had revisited the hidden room. He could have found the book nowhere else. But why had he brought it up here to hide away?

Checking again to see that the door to the bedchamber was bolted, she took the book to the chair by the window and opened it, fearful of what she would see.

The book was written in French, which she read and understood well. On the flyleaf, in a bold, clear hand, was inscribed: "Jean Vincent Molyneux, His Journal." First she leafed through the book rapidly, noting that the entries were not consistent. Jean had not written in his journal every day, but only when the fancy took him, it seemed. Then, going back to the first page, she began to read:

"Tuesday, May 2, 1764, Charleston, the Carolinas:
On this day I have decided to start a new journal, in honor of the beginning of my new life in the Colonies.

This is a beautiful country; very large and rich in natural resources. This portion of it to which I have come, the Carolinas, offers good lands for the taking, and a man who has been forced to flee his native country could do worse than settle here. It is still a primitive land, and yet it has attracted many men of culture to its shores. Here, in Charleston, a fair-sized city on the coast of the Carolinas, I have managed to find congenial company; and now I shall begin seeking a good plot of land for my own, where I may begin to build an estate. As long as I am banished here, I intend to make the best of the situation.

I have become acquainted with Novelo Polydoro, the well-known Italian painter, who is living now in Charleston, and he tells me that there are many large islands off the coast that are very beautiful. He has suggested that we gather together a group of our friends and make a search for what he refers to as a 'magic island,' an island of enchantment, where I might build my own house of dreams. It is a pleasant conceit and one which intrigues me.

Others have told me that there is good farmland to be had, both in the Carolinas and in Georgia, suitable for the growing of indigo and rice. They say that the settlers of Savannah, Georgia, are attempting to cultivate silkworms, with a view to becoming a great silk center. When we make our search for my private island, I shall insist that we visit Savannah, also, for I hear that the Englishman, Oglethorpe, who founded the city and his Trustees have an experimental garden there, which it might be interesting to observe.

I seldom think of my old life in Paris now. I have received no word from my father and have sent him none. Considering our feeling for one another, it is well that we have an ocean between us. He will never be capable of understanding me, and I suppose that I should be grateful that he did not send me packing with empty pockets, instead of settling a goodly sum upon me when I left Paris, upon my assurances that I would leave France forever.

I am certain that he felt assured that I would quickly spend it all upon women, gambling and drink, but despite his bad opinion of me, I am not an entire fool and have no wish to live in penury. Land is cheap here in this new world, and I fully intend to advantage myself of it. A man with money to invest can build himself an empire. I intend to do so."

Rebecca glanced up from the book for a moment with a relieved sigh. Well, she thought, this isn't so bad. There was nothing shocking so far, nothing to upset Jacques. This seemed the narrative of a normal enough, though slightly whimsical young man. Perhaps rather effete in his tastes, with a touch of vanity and caprice, but not a monster.

She resumed reading:

"Monday, June 18, 1764, Charleston, the Carolinas:

Today, I bought a kingdom, and it will be all my own. I will be the supreme ruler and high potentate, and my word shall be law there.

Polydoro tells me that I have delusions of grandeur, but he laughs when he says it, and I tell him that he is simply recognizing a kindred spirit.

The island is called 'Pirate's Bank,' a name derived from the legend that it has, in the past, been a haven for sea-going scoundrels, and I am informed that there is said to be pirate treasure buried there, an intriguing idea to be sure. My island is located off the southern coast of the Carolinas, seaward from the large island of Port Royal, on which is situated the town of Beaufort.

Thomas Hilliard, a young poet who has recently joined our little social group, has suggested that we must have a treasure hunt, and Polydoro, of course, encouraged him. It might offer an interesting diversion, at that, and it would give me an opportunity to invite the beautiful young woman whom I met just last week in Charleston.

Her name is Mignon Dubois, and she is newly arrived in the Colonies. Her father is very wealthy but quite formidable, and I could tell that he did not take a particular liking to me—no doubt because of his daughter's obvious interest. These jealous fathers are all the same, I have discovered. In the dark part of their being, they long to sleep with their daughters themselves, and they hate any younger man whom they fear may pluck their nubile treasure from the parental bough!

Partaking of this particular fruit would certainly be a pleasure, for she is a genuine beauty, young and juicy, and as ready for plucking as a ripe plum. I have resolved to seduce her at the soonest possible opportunity, and a journey to Pirate's Bank, in company with a goodly crowd so that her father shall not become anxious, would be a lovely opportunity.

Wednesday, July 9, 1764, Pirate's Bank:

Eureka! What a wonderful day, for I have discovered two treasures! While the others were digging up the shores of my island, under the theory that since treasure chests are heavy, they would most likely have been buried hear the shore, I lured Mademoiselle Dubois to a secluded spot, well hidden by trees and underbrush, and there robbed her of what her dear papa has been so fiercely protecting. In general, I harbor mixed feelings concerning the benefits of seducing virgins, for to experience a good, full-blooded lovemaking, one needs an experienced and preferably uninhibited partner, yet virgins do offer certain unique pleasures. Among them, of course, the pleasure of being the first, of taking from them that which they consider so sacred, that small membrane of flesh that makes them a virtuous young woman. Usually they are wont to be tearful afterward, but Mademoiselle Dubois remained in good enough spirits after her deflowering, and I cannot but think that she was eager for the experience. If I continue to find her pleasing, I may even wed the girl, for it is past time for me to settle down and do my duty to keep my branch of the Molyneux line extant. My father, bless his pontifical soul, warned me before I left France that I should not sire any children.

Since he never bothered to explain that particular request, I can only assume that he considers my behavior so heinous that he does not wish my blood to be carried forward. However, I, like any other man, wish to leave something behind me, a memorial, so to speak. Call it male vanity, if you will.

But now to the other treasure. Two of my young friends, while digging near a large oak tree near the sandy beach on the seaside of the island, unearthed a wooden chest, which contained a large quantity of gold coins, as well as jewels of considerable value. They also discovered the bones of at least two men, buried in the same pit.

Since the bones were atop the chest, one can only suppose that the men were killed and buried there by the order of their leader, so that no one except himself would know the whereabouts of the treasure.

Despite the bones, my entourage was delighted, and in gratitude for their efforts on my behalf, I rewarded them each with several gold coins. The rest, as rightful owner of the island, I intend to use to build a palatial residence, which I shall call Maison de Rêverie. My mind is already busy with plans and ideas. I see the whole island as a playground, a paradise where I and my companions may do as we like, without the stares and whispers of stuffy townspeople. It will be the grandest house in the Carolinas, I vow, in the Colonies, for that fact. I can hardly wait to draw up the plans and to order the materials.''

Rebecca, taking note of the time, skipped through the next few entries, which went into considerable and boring detail concerning the construction of the house and jumped to a later, more interesting entry:

"Monday, September 16, 1766; Maison de Rêverie:

At last! Maison de Rêverie is completed, and Pirate's Bank is indeed now an enchanted island!

Despite provincial workmen and the many setbacks and difficulties of construction, the house now stands, a monument to—if I may say so—my imagination.

The locals are all agog, for they have never seen a house built in the Oriental style, and I must admit that the furor is all that I could have hoped for.

Surrounded by parks, pathways and hidden pavilions, the house sits gracefully, looking out over it all.

Despite its unusual architecture—unusual, at least, for this place and time—the house is very comfortable, with many large rooms, and, of course, my hidden passageways and the secret room.

When the workmen were constructing the passageways and the room, I could not help but think of the bones buried with the treasure chest we found that day on the island. It is a pity that I dare not follow the example of that ancient pirate or the custom of the Egyptian pharaohs and have the workers interred in the passageways, so that no one would know of them but myself and my confidants. But then, that is the price one pays for living in modern society. In any event, they will soon be moving along to other tasks, dispersed like chaff on the winds of the future, and I seriously doubt whether any of them have the imagination to guess what use I intend to make of my toys.

I and a few of my close friends will decorate the room ourselves. I have my chest, brought over from

Paris, which contains most of the tools of my interest. It is a pity that some were left behind, particularly some of the books. I presume that it will be impossible to locate a copy of *Malleus Maleficarum* or *The Key of Solomon* in this new world. If only I had not been forced to leave in such unseemly haste. Well, there is no good in complaining. I shall have to manage with what I could bring with me.

I have been broaching the subject of my interest to some of my friends whom I believe might be the most sympathetic to such games, and most of them have responded favorably. Even Mignon, whom I have thought, given her youth and innocence, might find my ideas repugnant, seems fascinated. I flatter myself that this is my influence at work. She is a really delightful and amenable girl, and I am happy that I decided to marry her. She was most eager to accept. Even her father has come round to a certain extent, a fact that is proven by his wedding gift, a lovely house in Savannah, for which I showed myself duly grateful. Savannah is much closer to Pirate's Bank than Charleston, and it has been much easier to oversee the work on the island.

I have also recently acquired a plantation of goodly size, near the Georgia coast. Some of the land is suitable for growing rice, and some I intend to plant in indigo. Everything has been going so well for me, I sometimes wish my father could see how well his errant son is doing for himself, for it would do my heart good to see the old bastard forced to admit that he was wrong!''

Rebecca, looking again at the clock on the mantel, closed the journal. So, Jean Molyneux's interest in the evil arts had been of long-standing, something he had brought with him from his native France.

She thought back to his statement that his father had warned him not to have children. Did that mean that evidence of Jean's madness had already shown itself? Was that one of the reasons his father had sent him away? Evidently Jean had done something terrible enough to warrant his banishment from his own country—what it was did not really matter now. What mattered was that he had brought some kind of evil with him, to this place, and then had gone on to cultivate it.

Rebecca decided that she didn't dare risk reading further in the journal now. It was close to teatime, and Jacques might return to their rooms at any moment. Hurriedly she replaced the book in the chest, and the key in the pocket of the topcoat, and then changed her dress for tea.

She and Margaret and Felicity were already seated around the table when Jacques joined them. He looked haunted, Rebecca thought. There were dark circles under his eyes, and his eyes were blank, inward focused. Rebecca felt a throb of compassion for him.

As he sat down between Margaret and Rebecca, Felicity began to chatter, and Margaret gave Rebecca a disapproving glare.

Rebecca felt an immediate flare of anger. Just who did Margaret think she was? Did she think that she had been appointed Jacques's guardian? It was really ridiculous! Jacques was a grown man, and certainly responsible for his own actions.

"Here, dear, I've already poured your tea," Felicity said. "And have one of these lovely little tarts.

Darcy baked them just this morning with berries from our own garden. My, you do look a bit peaked, my dear. Have you been working too hard again? Rebecca, don't you think he looks a bit pale?"

Jacques gave his mother a mechanical smile. "Just a trifle tired, Mother. It's nothing you need worry about."

Margaret continued to glower at Rebecca, and Rebecca felt herself growing tense. Didn't she have enough on her mind without Margaret making things more difficult?

"You do look somewhat pale, Jacques," she said for Felicity's benefit. "Perhaps you should not work quite so hard. Take a little time to rest."

"The work must be done," he said stiffly, without meeting her gaze.

"But you must take care of yourself, Cousin Jacques," Margaret said earnestly, leaning forward so that he was forced to look at her.

He gave her what appeared to be a genuine, though rather weary smile. "Thank you for your concern, Margaret. I shall bear your advice in mind."

Although Felicity continued to chatter on, speaking of the garden and the last dinner party—Rebecca noticed that the name of Joshua Sterling came up with alarming frequency—the others scarcely said another word. Rebecca felt cross and uncomfortable. She just *knew* that after tea, Margaret was going to corner her and deliver another lecture, and Rebecca feared that this time she was going to lose her temper.

Chapter Twenty-three

REBECCA AND MARGARET were still in the parlor, drinking a last cup of tea.

Felicity had gone to her room, and Jacques, he said, was returning to his study.

Rebecca, too, had risen to leave, hoping to make her escape before Margaret had a chance to scold her again, but Margaret had reached out and taken her arm. "I have something to discuss with you, Rebecca."

Wearily Rebecca watched her husband and mother-in-law leave the room. "All right, Margaret. I presume you intend to lecture me again concerning Jacques. I thought I had made my feelings clear about that. Are these lectures of yours going to occur on a daily basis?"

Margaret, with a determined set to her mouth, brushed aside her cousin's comments with a wave of her hand. "Did you see how he looked? You simply must do something, Rebecca. You're his wife! You married him for better or worse, in sickness and health. The Bible says—"

Rebecca gestured angrily, cutting the other girl off. She felt as if she were a violin whose strings had been tightened too far. "You might do well to remember that I *am* his wife, not you! For heaven's sake, Margaret, can't you mind your own business? Do you suppose that I don't know he is not well?"

A dark flush splotched Margaret's cheeks and throat. "Then why aren't you doing something for him?"

Rebecca sighed in exasperation. "Margaret, there is nothing I *can* do. Jacques's illness, if you wish to call it that, has nothing to do with me, and will not be eased or cured by any action that I can take! You simply have no idea of what is going on."

Margaret said defiantly, "Well, then tell me what is going on. Perhaps it will help me to understand a wife who cares so little for her husband's welfare!"

Rebecca set down her cup and saucer with such force that it almost shattered the fragile china. For a moment she was sorely tempted to blurt out the truth. "I cannot tell you that, Margaret. I can tell you, truthfully, that you could not bear to know all the details of what has gone on in this house. However, I will tell you this much.... There is a very good chance that Jacques is suffering from the same kind of mental illness from which his father suffered, and his father before him!"

Margaret gasped and stared at her with narrowed eyes. "Mental illness? Are you saying that Jacques is *mad*?"

Rebecca glanced away. "Perhaps not yet, but he is definitely in an unhealthy mental state, the cause of which I cannot explain to you, except to say that it would be best for him to get away from this house! I am going to try to persuade him to return with me to Savannah, and to see the doctor there."

"This house?" Margaret said in disbelief. "How could his problem have anything to do with this house? Why, he loves it. You know he does."

Rebecca felt like striking her cousin. How could she be so obtuse, so wrongheaded, unwilling, or unable, to see anything that might contradict her opinions? "Yes, I know he loves this house, but there is something here that only makes his condition worse. It had the same effect on his father."

Margaret was frowning. "Jacques is not in the least like Edouard. How can you say that? His father was . . . he was evil! Jacques is good!"

"Yes, Jacques is good, in his way. But he also has something of his father in him. Believe me, there is every evidence that Jean Molyneux was mad, and Edouard was certainly mad, also. If I don't get Jacques away from this place, he may very well follow in their footsteps." She got to her feet abruptly. "Now, that is all I am going to say on the subject!"

Turning away, Rebecca hurried from the room. Her head was splitting, and she was resolved to speak to Jacques as soon as possible about moving into the house in Savannah. The idea had only come to her as she was talking to Margaret, yet she knew that it was sensible, a possible solution. She must get Jacques away from the influence of that room, away from the memories and images it evoked.

She went looking for Jacques and found him in his study, as he had said he would be.

Smiling, she approached him and leaned over to kiss him upon the forehead. He pulled away from her proffered caress with a frown.

She pretended not to notice and said brightly, "Jacques, I have a suggestion to make. Your mother is right in saying that you look overtired, and you have been spending far too much time working. Let's go to the Savannah house for a few weeks. I know it's not the custom to go this time of the year, but I think it would be good for you to get away for a bit. There are too many memories here—"

She stopped, for the expression on his face was growing darker by the second. "You know I can't leave here now," he said roughly. "I told you that I am having problems with the business matters that Father left. Why do you even suggest such a thing?"

Rebecca attempted to keep her voice calm. "Because your health is more important than your business affairs, and because I do not want to see you become ill."

With dismay she noted that his fingers were drumming on the table, as if a great nervousness or impatience was consuming him. Jacques had always been so calm, she thought bleakly, so in control of himself and his emotions. This man who sat here now was like a stranger.

"What makes you think I am ill?" he demanded.

"Well, just look at yourself. Take a good look in the mirror for a start and then think about how you have been these past few days. You're simply not yourself! If we go to Savannah, you can rest, consult with a doctor..."

He gave her a lopsided grin, almost a sneer, that made her draw back, for it was nothing like his usual, faintly melancholy smile.

"Perhaps this *is* me. The real me."

Fighting against a rising apprehension, she placed a hand upon his shoulder and felt his muscles tense under her touch. "No, Jacques. The real you is a gentle, kind man, and all of us who care for you would like to see you become that man again."

That awful smile again. "So you three ladies have been discussing me, have you?"

"It's not that way at all, Jacques, and if you were yourself, you would realize that. It's clear to all of us that something is wrong, and all we want to do is to help."

His eyes had a sly glitter. "And you really think you can?"

"Yes. At least, I hope so, and I believe that the first step should be for you to get far away from that room and what is in it. It's no use denying it, Jacques. I know that you have been going back there, and I can see what it is doing to you."

He pushed himself away from the desk and stood up. The look in his eyes caused her to involuntarily flinch away from him. "Can you indeed!"

In what she interpreted as a threatening move, he leaned toward her. Now his eyes had the look of fever—bright and a bit wild. "I have told you, Rebecca, that you are to forget about that room. If you mention it again...if you *ever* mention it again, I shall not be responsible for the consequences. Do you understand?"

There was a great deal more on Rebecca's mind, but her instincts warned her to be silent. For the first time she felt afraid of Jacques, afraid of what he might do.

"Now, if you will be so kind as to leave me alone, I would appreciate it. I have much work to do." He turned his back on her.

Without another word Rebecca hurried from the room. Outside in the garden, she walked off her agitation in the sunlight, attempting to drive out the cold that, despite the heat of the day, seemed to have driven deep into her bones and flesh.

Some time later, after she had her emotions under control, she went into the house and down the hall to the study. She gently tried the door. It was locked, and she could hear no sound from within. She felt certain that he had gone to Edouard's room again.

She went upstairs to their chambers and to Jacques's clothes cupboard. She retrieved the key to the chest. Within a few moments, she had Jean Molyneux's journal in her hands and was seated near the window. Not knowing how much time she would have, she turned to a page near the end of the book and began to read:

"Friday, September 25, 1772, Maison de Rêverie:

Have just met our new mainland neighbors, Richard and Elizabeth Huntoon, who have now settled in the recently completed manor house on the plantation that Madame Huntoon, a Frenchwoman, has named Les Chênes, for the many oak trees on the property.

The house is pleasant enough but offers no competition to Maison de Rêverie. Elizabeth Huntoon is exquisite and puts even my own fair Mignon to shame. Richard Huntoon is a rather typical Englishman, stolid, bullish in physique, somewhat lacking in polish. They are, coincidentally, the parents of a five-year-old girl child, Elissa, born only two months after my own son, Edouard.

I am already working on plans to acquire them for our little group. Since the Almsways have left the Carolinas, we are short two people of our desired twelve, and in my estimation, Elizabeth would certainly be a most welcome addition. Her husband is obviously a ruttish sort of fellow, and I am certain I will be able to reach him through an appeal to his baser appetites. As for Elizabeth, once her husband is persuaded, I am hoping that like all good spouses, she will bow to his desires and wishes. Also, I sense in her a certain pliability and curiosity that indicates that she might not find our little games all that distasteful, once she has enjoyed them. Altogether a delightful prospect!''

Rebecca tore her gaze from the flowing script on the page before her. So this was the beginning of the relationship between the Huntoons and the Molyneuxs! She looked down once more and leafed ahead, searching for other references to the Huntoons, but there were only a few more entries in the journal and none of them made further mention of the Huntoons or the secret ceremonies.

She closed the book and put it down. There must be other journals. Surely, Jean had not stopped keeping them. She went through Jacques's chest thoroughly, being careful to keep the clothing folded and to put everything back in its original place, but she found no other books.

They must still be in the secret room then. For a moment she considered going in search of them, and then, disgusted with herself, she tried to get her thoughts in order. Why did she feel this compulsion to learn more? She knew all that it was necessary to know. What she must do now was think seriously about her problem, about what she was going to do.

After her conversation with Jacques, she knew that she was not going to get him to willingly leave Maison de Rêverie. Whatever strain of madness ran through the Molyneux family, seeing that room and learning the real history of his father and grandfather had brought it to life in Jacques. Now the room and the past that it represented exerted a hold upon him that Rebecca realized she could not break.

What were her alternatives? She had already eliminated the possibility of returning to India and her parents. What was left?

Oh, if only Armand were here! If he would only return. Margaret had said no more concerning her premonition, but the memory of her cousin's words hung in Rebecca's mind like a dark cloud, always present, always cold and threatening. But if Armand *was* dead, wouldn't his family have received word? She must stay in the vicinity until some kind of information was received, and yet she felt that she could not bear to remain in this house a day longer.

Picking up the journal, she got up to return it to the chest and then stopped short, her breath catching in her chest. The hidden panel beside the fireplace was sliding slowly open.

Rebecca clenched her fingers so tightly around the book that they started to hurt. A superstitious fear began to fill her like icy water; and she almost expected

Edouard to step through the panel, leering and pale in his grave clothes.

But it was Jacques who stepped through the opening; a dark-faced Jacques, almost as frightening as the monster she had imagined.

He was staring at the journal clutched against her breasts, and she knew that he had been watching her through the peephole. How long had he been there?

Slowly he walked toward her, and she gave way before him, until her back was against the wall. She uttered a low cry as he reached out and snatched the book from her grasp.

"You simply cannot leave things alone, can you?" he said in a cruel voice. "I have told you repeatedly. Forget the room, forget what you saw and what you learned. But you insist on looking further. Now you have violated my personal things!"

He shook the book in her face. "This was not meant for your eyes. This was meant only for my father and for myself, the rightful heirs of Jean Molyneux. How dare you open it! How dare you read it!"

Jacques was shouting now, and Rebecca pressed herself as close as she could against the wall. "I only wanted to know, to understand!"

Without warning he struck her on the side of the face. He had not used all of his strength, but still Rebecca felt her head rock with the blow, and a stinging sensation began to spread across her cheek.

"Understand! How could you possibly understand?" he said savagely. "You are only a woman and not a true Molyneux at that. How could you ever understand the power that my grandfather and my father possessed? The dark glory of it? You want to keep me from having it, don't you? You still resent the fact that I am unable to consummate a fleshly union. You think me less than a whole man. You despise me for it and so wish to keep me from the full power that my grandfather and father knew. Well, I am well aware of your intent, woman, and you shall not thwart me. By the dark gods, you shall not!''

Rebecca, rigid with fear, stared at him, unable to believe that this raving man was the Jacques she had known. It was frighteningly clear to her that he lacked even a vestige of control and that she was in grave danger.

As he reached out for her she feinted to the right, then lunged left, ducking under his flailing hand. Her fear and anger spurred her on, and she gained the door, shot back the bolt and was in the hall before he could catch her.

She flew down the hall. She could hear him coming after her, his footsteps heavy on the wooden floor, and she ran to the top of the stairs and started down, not even feeling the steps beneath her feet.

She was not certain at what point Jacques ceased to pursue her, but he was not behind her when she burst into the kitchen where she knew there would be people. She stopped short, panting as Darcy and the kitchen staff stood staring at her, dumbfounded.

"BUT HE *is* dangerous, Margaret. I am telling you the God's truth! I tried to get him to go with me to Savannah, and he refused. I asked him to see a doctor, and he refused. Now he has threatened me! I have made up my mind. I am going to Savannah, and I want you to come with me.''

Rebecca and her cousin were in the small sitting room off Margaret's bedroom. Rebecca was pacing in her agitation, and Margaret stood at the window, looking out at the gardens.

She answered Rebecca without turning. "You simply misunderstood, Rebecca. You know that Jacques is not a violent man. If he lost his temper and threatened you, it must be because of something you said."

For a moment Rebecca feared she was losing her own sanity. She grasped the other girl's shoulder and spun her about so that they were face-to-face. "Listen to me! Jacques is no longer the man we thought we knew. Look at the mark on my face. He struck me!"

Margaret's lips thinned out in an expression that Rebecca had come to dread. "Then you must have goaded him, provoked him. You know that you can be very difficult, and men do not care to put up with such behavior."

Goaded beyond endurance, Rebecca shook her cousin roughly. Words jarred out of her: "Margaret! I believe you are as mad as he. Are you completely blind? It is dangerous for us to stay here. He is growing worse daily. There is no telling what he will do next."

With surprising strength Margaret grasped Rebecca's wrists and pried her hands loose. Pushing away, she straightened her dress, quite calmly, as Rebecca stared helplessly at her.

"Felicity is Jacques's mother, and she does not seem worried about his mental stability, only his physical well-being. You react too strongly, Rebecca. You always have. It is your wifely duty to stay here and look after him, and I am certain that you will come to realize that is the best thing for you to do."

Maddened by her cousin's obstinate placidity, Rebecca lost all patience. "His wife in name only, Margaret. He has never been a real husband to me."

"I don't want to hear..."

Unheeding, Rebecca rushed on, "He is incapable of being a real husband to anyone, Margaret. He was wounded in the war. So, you see, we really aren't man and wife!"

Margaret turned away. "I refuse to listen to such filth! You were married in the church. You are married in the eyes of God!"

"Even God would not consider what we have a real marriage, and I am leaving Jacques. What do you propose to do? Stay here and look after him yourself? Oh, you needn't think that I haven't noticed you mooning over him! Is the reason you keep saying I am his wife over and over because you want to remind yourself of that fact? Well, if it is, you no longer need to torture yourself, because I give him to you freely. He should make an ideal husband for you!"

Margaret threw her head back, her expression exalted. "I will not deny that I love Jacques, but it is a love that you could never understand. It is a love of the spirit, of the soul."

Abruptly Rebecca's anger died, to be replaced by a weary resignation. Margaret, in her own way, was as daft as Jacques.

"Margaret," she said softly, "there is nothing wrong, nothing shameful, about physical love between a man and a woman. God created it. He meant for us to share one another's bodies, as well as our lives. He meant for us to have children. Spiritual love is all very well, but people need both. Can't you see that? I didn't intend to disparage Jacques. His condition is not his fault. And it is not wrong for you to love him. You can't control whom you love, but you should not worship him, like some sort of deity! Please come with me to Savannah. I fear for our welfare if you stay here."

Margaret stared at her coldly. "Nevertheless, I shall remain. Jacques needs me, and Felicity has come to rely on me. You do what you choose. You always do, don't you?"

THAT NIGHT, Rebecca slept in her old bedroom, the one adjoining the small parlor.

Dinner had been a miserable affair. Jacques was not present for the meal. He had sent word that he was working and would have dinner in his study. Margaret maintained an injured and sullen silence.

Only Felicity chattered on, apparently oblivious to the emotional undercurrents between Rebecca and Margaret.

Rebecca had never felt less like eating, and she toyed with her food as she pondered just how to tell Felicity that she wished to go to Savannah. It was going to be very awkward, there was no getting around that. She could not possibly tell her mother-in-law her real reason. First of all, she was sure that Felicity would express the same disbelief as had Margaret. The two women shared at least that one trait—the ability to ignore that which they did not wish to recognize.

Rebecca felt a twinge of guilt as she looked across the table at Felicity. Would she and Margaret be in danger if they were left alone with Jacques? She did not think so. It was only she, Rebecca, who seemed to ignite Jacques's rage. She knew about the room, and she knew about his deteriorating mental condition. Somehow these two facts had turned his mind and his feelings against her. She reminded herself that even Edouard, although he had mistreated his wife, had not seriously harmed her. No, Margaret and Felicity were safe from Jacques, but she was not and since her presence appeared to make him worse, it would be better for him as well if she was elsewhere. She simply must think of a logical way to explain herself to Felicity, so that it did not seem too strange, too unusual.

Perhaps she could explain her wish to go to Savannah with the excuse of shopping and a need for some diversion. As for Jacques remaining behind, that could be explained by his own words—he had too much work to do here. The fact that Margaret was not accompanying her, that was the sticking point. But then, she thought suddenly, why not ask Felicity to go with her? Felicity had not been off the island since Edouard's death and might be persuaded that a short visit to Savannah could be a welcome diversion.

Smiling at her mother-in-law, she said brightly, "Felicity, I have been thinking. We haven't been off the island in ages, and I really need to do some shopping. I would very much like to go to Savannah for a stay. Would it be too inconvenient if I opened the house there for a bit? We wouldn't need to take much staff, perhaps just Jeremy, Hector and Molly." Hector and Molly were a married couple who worked well together, and Molly was an excellent cook.

Felicity looked surprised and then thoughtful. "Well, I suppose it would be all right. Have you talked it over with Jacques? Will he want to leave the island at this time?"

Rebecca shook her head. "Oh, Jacques won't be going. He says he's much too busy right now, but he told me to go ahead and enjoy himself. He's been so busy lately, he hasn't had much time to spend with me anyway."

The lie came easily to her tongue, and she ignored Margaret's sharp glance of disapproval. She purposely had not mentioned that Margaret, also, would not be going. Let her cousin make her own excuses for not wanting to go. It would probably work better that way.

Felicity said dubiously, "Well, I suppose we three women *could* go. I must confess that I should like to visit the shops. I need a number of things, and I know that it must get boring for you young women here." She glanced at Margaret questioningly.

"I am not in the least bored, Cousin Felicity," Margaret said stiffly. "Actually, I would prefer to stay here."

Felicity's glance moved again to Rebecca, and then she smiled brilliantly. "All right then, Rebecca! It is just you and I. I would never have thought of going to Savannah just now, but since you have mentioned it, I believe that I do look forward to it."

She turned to Margaret. "Are you certain you won't be lonely, dear? Of course, Lutie will take care of the house and look after you, but you will lack for company."

Margaret flushed darkly. "I shall have all the company I need, Cousin Felicity. You needn't worry about me."

"Well then, I shan't," Felicity said with a sparkling smile.

Rebecca thought to herself that there was something to be said for the person with an uncomplicated nature. A more analytical person than Felicity would probably have asked a great many embarrassing questions. Rebecca felt a swift surge of affection for her mother-in-law and was cheered immensely by the thought that she would have company in Savannah, for she had not really relished the thought of occupying the Savannah house alone. Her own thoughts were much too dismal to make good company.

Chapter Twenty-four

"WELL, THAT WAS really nice." Felicity, removing the pins from her hat, smiled benignly at Rebecca.

Rebecca smiled, happy that her mother-in-law was enjoying herself. The two women had just returned from having afternoon tea with Elvina Trevor, an old friend of Felicity's, a pleasant, talkative woman who had regaled them with slightly naughty stories and local gossip.

Since arriving in Savannah, time seemed to have picked up its flow. The days, which had dragged badly on the island, now passed pleasantly and quickly. Felicity, pleased as a prisoner just released from long confinement, had been dragging Rebecca hither and thither; to shops, concerts, renewing acquaintance with family friends. So that Rebecca had been able to forget, at least occasionally, her worries and fears.

In Savannah they had finally received news about General Jackson's campaign in Florida. The latest reports said that Jackson had routed the Seminole and that he had executed two British traitors, who had been helping the enemy. Also they had learned that he had occupied Pensacola, had taken Fort Barrancas and now Florida was under the military control of the United States.

Some of the men from Savannah who had served under Jackson had already returned home, telling stories of marching through fever-ridden swamps, short rations and other hardships.

There was still no word of Armand, and Rebecca, thinking of Margaret's premonition, had almost given up hope that he was still alive. However, she never discussed the subject with Felicity. One thing Rebecca still found difficult to understand was her mother-in-law's apparent unconcern about the fact that nothing had been heard from Armand since he had ridden off to join General Jackson. It seemed unnatural for a mother not to worry about her son under such circumstances. Perhaps it was again that trait of her nature that caused her to simply ignore anything that might be unpleasant or upsetting.

As for herself, Rebecca had been doing a great deal of thinking and, despite the pleasant diversions of the town, considerable worrying. She was convinced that she had done the right thing in coming to Savannah, but she could not stop wondering from time to time what was happening back at Maison de Rêverie. Was Jacques growing better or worse? Had her leaving helped him regain his mental balance? And Margaret, how was she faring? And Lutie? She missed her chats with Lutie.

Before leaving the island Rebecca had had a long talk with the black woman, telling her why she was going and asking her to do her best to look after Jacques and Margaret. Lutie, to Rebecca, seemed the only stable influence in this whole peculiar, convoluted situation.

"You know, I really must get that recipe for cream cake from Elvina," Felicity was saying as she straightened her hair in the mirror over the mantel-piece in the sitting room. "It was simply delicious. And wasn't it a pleasant surprise to see Mr. Sterling there?"

She looked at Rebecca in the glass, and Rebecca thought she saw a look of entreaty in the older woman's eyes.

Rebecca had not been particularly pleased to find that Joshua Sterling was in Savannah, nor to have him show up at the tea, but in the face of Felicity's appealing look, she said, "Why, yes, Felicity, it was indeed a surprise."

Felicity flushed slightly, her gaze still questioning, and Rebecca suddenly realized that Sterling's unexpected appearance in Savannah was doubtless not a coincidence. After agreeing to the trip to Savannah, Felicity must have managed to get word to him.

Rebecca found herself smiling. Why, the slyboots! Who would have thought that Felicity possessed such initiative or such audacity?

Not entirely sure how she should respond, Rebecca sent out a tentative feeler: "If I may be so bold, Felicity, it does seem to me that Mr. Sterling is quite taken with you."

Felicity's blush deepened, and she straightened a ringlet that she had just arranged a moment ago. "Oh, do you really think so? Well, that is flattering, I suppose. I mean, at my age, one does not really expect male admirers."

Rebecca relaxed, for she could see that Felicity was anxious, even eager, to talk about her suitor. The other woman also no doubt needed someone to share her thoughts with, and the subject of Joshua Sterling was probably something she did not feel she could share with either Jacques or Margaret. Perhaps she simply needed *someone's* approval.

"Nonsense, Felicity," she said briskly. "You are a very handsome woman and good and kind, as well. I am only surprised that you aren't literally besieged with admirers!"

Felicity giggled, a girlish sound that touched Rebecca with its innocent pleasure. "Oh, Rebecca, you are the limit! Of course, I don't suppose I should be seeing so much of Joshua, since officially I'm still in mourning, but I must confess that he makes me laugh. He can be very entertaining, you know."

She paused, staring down at her hands. "I shouldn't tell you this, at least not yet, but Joshua has done me the honor of requesting my hand in marriage." She faced around, her eyes bright. "Naturally, we will have to wait until my period of mourning is over, but I have told him yes! Oh, Rebecca, do you think I am a dreadful woman? I know I should not have even *listened* to his proposal at this time, but he put it so nicely and so delicately..."

Rebecca studied the other woman with affection and tenderness. She needs my approval, she thought, and then...well, why not? Just because I find the man boring and a bit obnoxious doesn't mean that she does, and I suppose he does have his good points. At least I don't think he will ever beat her. And it would be nice if someone received some happiness out of this.

She stepped to Felicity and took her hands. "I don't see any harm in it, Felicity. After all that you have been through, you deserve whatever happiness you can get. And if Joshua Sterling can bring you that, there is no need to feel ashamed or to worry about convention. After all, no one knows but you and him, and me of course, that his proposal was perhaps a bit hasty, and I shan't tell. My congratulations to you both."

Felicity beamed. "I am so glad you feel that way! By the way, Joshua asked permission to call on us tomorrow and has offered to take us for a drive."

"Why, that sounds very nice," Rebecca said, thinking that tomorrow, when it was time to depart for the outing, she would plead a headache and stay home, allowing the two lovebirds some time alone. Felicity might protest, for propriety's sake, but if the carriage was there and everything arranged, she was convinced that Felicity would not be able to resist going.

REBECCA STOOD at an upstairs window and watched Felicity and Joshua Sterling wheel away in the open carriage. Felicity had been as pleased and fluttery as a young girl at the arrival of her suitor, and Sterling, Rebecca had to admit, treated Felicity with proper gallantry. Observing them together, Rebecca had decided that the old roué seemed genuinely fond of Felicity, and his obvious interest certainly acted like a tonic upon her.

Neither of them had protested too much when Rebecca had announced that she had a dreadful headache and that she would be unable to accompany them.

Now that she was alone in the house, except for the servants, she did not know what to do with herself. The soft, humid breeze that fluttered the curtains caressed her face like a lover's breath, and her thoughts jumped to Armand and that day in the pavilion. That had been her first experience with physical love, and the memory of it continued to haunt her, giving her both pain and intense pleasure. Causing her to burn during the long, lonely nights and yet giving her solace with the thought that, at least once, she had known real love.

The sky outside was that sharp, bright blue that seemed indigenous to this area, and she knew that later in the day the heat would be uncomfortable. But just now the breeze was soft, and the scent of flowers was rich in the air.

Overcome with lassitude and yearning, Rebecca moved a chair by the window and sat down, where she could gaze out onto the street and the people.

All of those people, moving to and fro, where were they going? What were their lives like? They all looked so normal, so intent upon their own affairs. Did any of them harbor secrets such as hers? It was likely that they did. You could never really know what lurked under the surface of another human being. The most average-seeming men or women might have experienced a terrible tragedy or some shameful secret in their past.

Then her eye was caught by a glimpse of a tall figure in a black dress and yellow head wrap coming down the street. It looked amazingly like Lutie, and suddenly alert, Rebecca sat forward.

It *was* Lutie! There was no mistaking that magnificent carriage. Alarm rang in Rebecca like a bell, and she quickly got up from the chair and hurried downstairs. What on earth was Lutie doing in Savannah? There could only be one answer—something had happened at Maison de Rêverie, and it could not be anything good.

She flew down the stairs and reached the front door just as Lutie's knock reverberated through the house. "I've got the door, Jeremy," she called as Jeremy's small figure, attired in his new uniform, appeared in the archway to the parlor. "You go on back and help Molly in the kitchen."

Jeremy's curiosity was evident on his lively face, but he nodded obediently and turned away.

Rebecca had the door open and was looking anxiously into Lutie's face. "Lutie! What are you doing here? What has happened?"

Lutie leaned against the door, and belatedly Rebecca realized that the woman was very tired. She immediately motioned Lutie inside. "I'm sorry, Lutie, come in. Sit down. You look exhausted. I'll call Jeremy to bring us some tea."

Lutie nodded and gratefully entered the cool interior of the house. "I am. Been traveling most of the night. Where's Mistress Felicity?"

"She's gone out for a drive with Joshua Sterling. They won't be back for some time."

Lutie closed her eyes briefly. "Good! I'm not sure it would be the right thing for her to hear what I have to tell you."

Rebecca ushered her into the parlor and tugged at the bellpull. When Jeremy, round-eyed with curiosity, came in, she told him to fetch tea and sandwiches and a bottle of brandy.

Lutie sank down on the parlor divan with a sigh of relief, and Rebecca sat beside her. "Something has happened, hasn't it? Is Margaret all right? Jacques hasn't harmed her, has he?"

"Not so far as I know. At least not yet."

"Then what has happened?"

Lutie gazed down at her hands, clasped together in her lap. "I'm sorry, Rebecca, to be bringing you bad news, but it can't be helped."

"What is it, Lutie?" Rebecca said quietly, bracing herself for the worst.

"Well, after you and Mistress Felicity left, things went along well enough for a day or so. I tried to keep an eye on Master Jacques and Miss Margaret, as you asked me to, and as far as I could tell, Master Jacques was acting calm enough. He came down to meals, and he talked to Miss Margaret.

"And then, three days ago, he began acting very strangely. I could hear him at night, walking though the passageways and talking to himself in a loud voice. When you shout in one of those passageways, you know, you can hear it in the other rooms. The house servants started to talk about spirits in the walls. They were absolutely terrified and fled the house. They are all staying in the slave quarters now, and the rumors have spread to the others and their families. They would all leave the island if they dared."

At that moment Jeremy appeared pushing a tea cart, which he delivered to Rebecca, and then, with evident reluctance, he left the room, looking over his shoulder.

Rebecca poured a cup of tea, and after dosing it liberally with brandy and sugar, handed it to Lutie. Lutie took a grateful swallow and relaxed against the back of the divan.

"So, what happened next? What about Margaret?"

"Miss Margaret was very strange. I am willing to admit that I was badly frightened by the way Master Jacques was acting, but she stayed as calm as a rock. Last night she told me that she was going to help him, that the Lord had told her it was her duty. I warned her that, in his present state, Master Jacques might be dangerous, but she only smiled at me. It was the strangest smile. She acted as if she had not heard a word I said. 'I will make him well again. It is God's will,' she said, just like that.

"And then, while we were talking, Master Jacques came into the room, and it was easy to see that he was not himself. He looked feverish and terribly excited, and I could see that he had not bathed or changed his clothes for some time.

"He stared at us both and then went to Miss Margaret and looked deep into her eyes."

Lutie paused. "Do you suppose I could have another cup of tea?"

Rebecca nodded and quickly poured the tea, again adding brandy.

Lutie continued, "And then he said something that probably meant something entirely different to Miss Margaret than it did to me. It was something about her going with him and being his queen. And about starting again, beginning a new 'coven,' I think he said. I'm certain that he was talking about the practices that his grandfather followed, but of course Miss Margaret had no way of knowing that.''

Rebecca felt a sudden chill. ''And then what happened?''

''I whispered in her ear, 'Don't go, Miss Margaret,' but she only gave me that queer smile and said, 'I told you, Lutie, I am going to help him!'

''I even took hold of her arm and whispered again, 'There are things you don't know, Miss Margaret. Please trust me and don't go with him!'

''But she jerked her arm away and offered it to Master Jacques. I knew then that I had to come and get you. I don't know what is in Master Jacques's head, but whatever it is, I just know that there is going to be bad trouble. I didn't know what else to do but come to fetch you.''

''You did the right thing, Lutie.'' Rebecca patted the woman's arm.

She closed her eyes. What on earth was she going to do? Of course, she would have to hasten to Pirate's Bank at once. But should she take someone with her? A doctor? The authorities?

If she brought someone, news of Jacques's affliction would soon be all over the island and the mainland, as well, and she didn't want to cause any embarrassment to the family, especially Felicity. Also, there was the possibility that Jacques may have calmed down by this time. But if he *was* violent, how could she and Lutie handle him by themselves?

She finally decided there was only one course of action. She and Lutie would return alone, and then, if the situation warranted, it, she would send one of the servants for help. The most important consider-

ation at the moment was to see that Margaret did not
come to any harm. If necessary, if Margaret was still
determined to stay close to Jacques, she and Lutie
should be able to handle her physically and take her
off the island by force.

She opened her eyes. "Lutie, you stay here and rest
for a bit, while I go and pack a few things and write a
note to Felicity. I hate to ask you to make the return
trip so soon, but if what you say is true, I think we
must get back there as quickly as possible."

"I can manage, Rebecca," Lutie said with a weary
smile. "I can rest some on the boat. What are you
going to tell Mistress Felicity?"

"I'll think of something. Certainly not the truth."
Rebecca shivered suddenly from head to foot. She
managed a weak smile. In a trembling voice, she said,
"It seems that someone just walked over my grave."

Lutie leaned across to put her arms around her.
"Don't worry, Rebecca. It won't do any good to fret
about what we may find back on Pirate's Bank, because there is nothing we can do about it until we get
there. One thing I've learned from life, and from all
the books that Master Armand let me read: it is always best to think strong, to look on the best side of
things." She nodded rapidly. "Even if things turn out
worse than you imagined them, it's easier to cope with
them if you think strong!"

For a long moment Rebecca clung to the other
woman, blinking back the tears, drawing strength
from her. "I'll try, Lutie, but it is awfully hard not to
imagine all sorts of possibilities, and all of them are
very unpleasant!"

Chapter Twenty-five

IN THE LATE AFTERNOON, the wind had sprung up, and as the small boat approached the lee side of Pirate's Bank, the dark clouds that had been banking in the east began to spread across the sky.

There was a great deal of chop, and the small vessel creaked and groaned as her sails bellied tautly in the freshening wind.

Rebecca, facing into the wind, felt the sting of salt spray upon her face.

"I told you there was a storm brewing!" the captain bellowed from his position at the tiller. "Does this island of yours have a safe, sheltered harbor? I may have to lay up there till this blows over."

The boat was listing sharply, making it difficult for Rebecca to move to his side so that she would not have to shout to be heard. "Yes, there is. It's well protected by an outer island. We keep our own boats there."

The captain's expression showed relief. At the waterfront in Savannah, Rebecca and Lutie had found that there were no boats scheduled to depart for the north that afternoon, and so Rebecca had been forced to look for a boat whose owner was willing to make the run. The only one who would agree to set out so late in the day was the owner of this small sloop, and she had to offer him an outrageous sum to get him to take them to Pirate's Bank.

Lutie, huddled in her cloak, seemed to be sleeping, despite the wind and spray and the choppy movement of the boat. Rebecca realized how tired the other woman must be and felt a surge of gratitude for Lutie's strength and wisdom. Lutie was, she realized, the first *true* friend she had ever had, the first woman with whom she had experienced an equal give and take.

Margaret and she were like sisters, women raised together, familiar with one another's ways and yet not necessarily having anything in common except the bond of family relationship and proximity.

As close, in their way, as she and Margaret had been, they had never really shared any meeting of the mind or spirit. Their tastes, their ways of looking at life, their hopes were, and had always been, miles apart.

Despite the differences in their positions and up-bringing, Rebecca and Lutie, even on such short acquaintance, had shared thoughts and feelings that she and Margaret would never be able to share.

Poor Margaret! If only they could have seen ahead. But who would have guessed that their journey to the Americas would turn out the way it had?

Strangely enough, Rebecca did not feel sorry for herself. It was Margaret for whom she felt a tragic foreboding.

In spite of all the things that had happened to her, Rebecca knew that she would survive and did not regret coming to the United States. She felt that other things would happen to her in her lifetime—good things, exciting things. It was just something that she *knew*.

With Margaret, it was different somehow. It was difficult to express, even in her own mind, but it was as if Margaret's life had been stunted in some way by the things that had happened in Pirate's Bank, as if her life and growth had stopped. Even if her cousin lived to be an old woman, Rebecca could not see her life changing. She could only visualize Margaret growing older, stiffer and more closed in. Rebecca wondered if that had always been her destiny or if the influence of Maison de Rêverie and the terrible events that had occurred there had changed her. Before the trip to America, even when they had first arrived, there had been some openness in Margaret, some willingness to experience life. Now all that was changed. If only she is all right, Rebecca thought, I'll find some way to *make* her leave the island.

Docking was difficult, and by the time Rebecca and Lutie got ashore, they were both soaked to the skin.

Since their arrival was unannounced, naturally there was no one to meet them at the dock. After paying off the owner of the sloop and telling him that he might use the shelter of the boat shed until the storm had passed, the two women set out on foot for the house, hurrying in the hope that they might reach their destination before the black-bottomed clouds boiling above them dumped their watery cargo.

The wind tugged at their clothes and hair, making walking difficult, but Rebecca, filled with urgency and apprehension, hardly noticed it. They walked quickly and silently as the wind tossed and rattled the branches of the trees and blew road dust into their faces.

They reached the big house just as the first rain-drops began to patter onto the crushed rock of the circular drive.

Rebecca gazed up and saw the swooping Oriental roof of the great house limned against the storm-darkened sky. Thinking back to the first day she had seen it, Rebecca recalled how beautiful and inviting she had thought it. Now, strangely, it looked foreign and eerie. There were, she noticed, no lamps lit. The windows were dark and empty looking. Why were the lamps not lit? It would be dark inside the house. Ex-changing a worried look with Lutie, she quickened her steps until she was almost running.

The front door was unlatched, and Lutie pushed it open. The large entryway, illuminated only by the big window at the top of the stairwell, was dim and shad-owed.

"I'll find a lamp," Lutie said in a hushed voice, stripping off her damp cape.

Rebecca nodded and removed her own bonnet. By the time she had also removed her cloak, Lutie was back, carrying one of the smaller lamps from the par-lor.

The light cast large, wavering shadows, and despite the fact that it was not cold, Rebecca found herself shivering. Although the wind and rain drummed noisily against the house, inside, there was only the chilling, eerie stillness of emptiness.

Always before, there had been sound: the soft sounds of sweeping and polishing, footsteps echoing on the polished floors, voices. Now there was none of that. It was as if the house itself had died.

Rebecca wrapped her arms around her upper body and stared at Lutie. "I don't hear a thing, do you? Where can they be?"

Lutie shook her head. In the lantern glow her strong, handsome face looked as if it had been cast in bronze. "Let's start at the top of the house and work down. I think it best that we stay together, don't you?"

Rebecca laughed nervously. "Very definitely." She glanced around the entry room. "Should we take something, some kind of weapon? If Jacques..."

Holding the lamp with her left hand, Lutie put her right arm around Rebecca's shoulders. "You don't need to feel bad about suggesting it. I was thinking of it, too. I'm afraid that it is all too possible that Jacques may be dangerous. Something to protect ourselves would not be amiss."

"But what? What can we use?"

"I think a poker from the fireplace would do as well as anything."

Rebecca nodded quickly. "Yes! I'll get one from the parlor. A few minutes later they were mounting the stairs, the light from the lamp moving before them, its yellow light flickering over the stairs as the wind shrieked and moaned around the house. Periodically the house would tremble, as if from a blow.

They began on the top floor and went through every room, including the servants' quarters. Rebecca had never before been quite so conscious of the size of the great house. The rooms seemed endless, and as they went from one to another, all empty, her feelings of fear and tension began to mount.

Her and Jacques's quarters, she noticed, looked messy and uncared for; the bed not made, the floor not swept. It looked as if no one had used it for several days.

Margaret's room, on the contrary, was clean and rigidly neat, however, it too had an unused feeling about it.

As they left the last of the empty rooms on the second floor, Rebecca shook her head dolefully. "Oh, Lutie, I dread finding the downstairs empty, too. If we don't find them there..."

Lutie nodded, her expression tense. "I know. The hidden room."

Rebecca sighed, a soft sound like a moan. "The thing is, Margaret would never go to such a place, at least not willingly, not if she knew what it was. If she has seen that room, those paintings, well, I just don't know what state of mind she might be in by now, I really don't. If Jacques forced her to go there, it could be disastrous for her."

"Well, maybe we'll find them downstairs. It's possible."

But her expression told Rebecca that Lutie thought this highly improbable. Nevertheless, there was nothing to do but continue with their search.

As they reached the landing between the first and second floors, a tremendous flash of lightning cracked the sky, illuminating the stairwell for a moment with a blaze of brilliant light.

The roll of thunder came almost at once; it seemed to be directly overhead. Rebecca could not keep herself from trembling as the huge chandelier on the landing began to sway dangerously. The icy tinkle of the crystal pendants echoed coldly, piercing her mind like frozen splinters of fear.

And then, just as the sound of thunder died away, she heard another sound, a sound that at first seemed so unlikely that she did not realize just what it was, thinking that it must be another roll of thunder.

She stopped, frozen in place, and saw that Lutie had paused, also, and appeared to be as shaken as she.

The sound was that of a piano. Someone was playing huge, crashing chords, a wild thunder of music fit to challenge the storm.

The women exchanged glances. "The music room," whispered Rebecca. "It must be Jacques, but I have never heard him play like that!"

Grasping the iron poker tightly and taking small comfort from it, Rebecca stayed close to Lutie as they made their way down the stairs and toward the sound of the music.

The doors to the music room were closed, but there was a faint ribbon of light showing beneath them. This close to the source, the music indeed seemed as loud as the thunder—a wild, primitive sound that shook Rebecca to the very soul.

Holding the lamp near the door, Lutie tried the door handle. "It's not locked," she whispered. "Shall I open it?"

Although fear had her by the throat, Rebecca nodded. There was no use in waiting. They must go in, must face Jacques, whatever his mood. Was Margaret in there with him? Was she unharmed?

Motioning to Lutie to open the door, Rebecca raised the poker as the other woman put her hand upon the metal of the carved door handle. It turned easily and noiselessly, and the door swung slowly inward.

The music was coming from the larger of the two pianos, the one near the window.

The only light in the room came from a candelabra upon the piano, which held the stubs of three candles. The draft from the opening door and the air currents in the room caused them to flicker and nearly go out.

In the erratic light Rebecca could see a man seated at the piano. His gaze was fixed upon the keyboard and his head was bent forward so that she could not see his face, but even in the bad light she knew that it was not Jacques.

A strange mixture of feelings began to fill her—disappointment, hope, fear, apprehension.

Tightly gripping Lutie's free arm, she led her into the room far enough so that the light might illuminate the figure seated at the piano.

Engrossed in the music, still he did not look up. It was not until the light from the lamp struck his face, causing her to cry out his name, that he realized they were in the room.

"Armand!" Rebecca cried, her clear voice cutting through the sounds of the storm and the music. "Dear God! Armand!"

IT HAD BEEN A LONG, hard trip back to Pirate's Bank, and during that journey, Armand had been looking forward to his return with mixed feelings.

In his present condition, with his leg still not completely healed, he needed a place to rest and recuperate. But the real reason for his return was very simple and could be expressed in one word—Rebecca!

After Rath Carpenter had pushed him from the roof in Pensacola there had been a dark hole in time, filled with pain and a jumble of images, partly real, partly imagined, but as incomprehensible as a bad dream.

When the fever and delirium finally faded, he found himself in a narrow, hard-mattressed bed in a small bedroom, with a tall, bewhiskered man with narrow eyes and a thin wedge of a nose frowning down at him.

"Well!" the man said gruffly. He spoke with a marked British accent. "So you have finally decided to come around. I wasn't certain you would make it."

Armand, conscious of a dull pain in his right leg, glanced down and saw that it was encased in heavy splints.

"A bad break," the man said. "Punctured the flesh. Thought I might have to take it off. You're a fortunate young man."

Armand looked at him warily. "Who are you, sir? And where am I, and how long have I been here?"

"Why, you're still in Pensacola, and you've been here over a week. As for who I am, I'm Dr. Henry Beller, and this is my home. I was a doctor with the British forces, but when they left I stayed behind."

"General Jackson?"

"He's back home in Tennessee by now, I expect. The general and his troops were gone when you were brought to me. You were in no condition to be jostled about the country in a medical wagon, with no real doctor in attendance. As I said, you're a fortunate young man. If I do say so myself, there is nobody better than I am at mending a break."

"I didn't just fall, you know." Armand tried to push himself up from the bed. Pain lanced through his legs, and he fell back. "I was pushed."

"Oh, I know. Someone saw the man commit the deed, and he will be facing a court martial. Bloody bastard! Fighting in battle wasn't enough for him. He had to try and kill one of his own. Bloody odd lot, you Americans."

Armand could only nod wearily. He felt extraordinarily weak and tired.

Doctor Beller squinted down at him. "You'd best rest now. Your first day back among us, so to speak. My wife, Sarah, will bring you some broth and custard. We need to put some weight back on you."

With a curt nod, Doctor Beller left the room, and Armand gratefully closed his eyes. So this was how his military career was going to end!

He touched his splinted leg. He had forgotten to ask if it was healing well and whether he could expect to regain the full use of it when it was completely healed. The doctor had seemed quite sanguine about it, so the prognosis must be good. Still, he might just be pleased because it had not been necessary to amputate. Well, whatever the outcome, he still had his leg, thank God, and he wouldn't have to go looking for Rath Carpenter.

In the middle of that thought he dozed off and awoke an hour or so later when the doctor's plump and pretty wife bustled in with a tray of broth, freshly baked bread and custard, which smelled wonderful. Armand thought he was quite hungry, yet he was able to eat only a small portion.

During the next few weeks he grew very fond of the crotchety doctor and his cheerful wife. The couple were probably in their fifties, and they treated Armand like the son they never had. Mrs. Beller fussed over him and cooked delicacies to tempt his appetite, and Doctor Beller played chess with him in the evenings and offered various pieces of advice about life and the manner in which it should be lived.

In an odd way, despite the discomfort and pain of his leg, Armand was almost happy there. Nothing was demanded of him, nothing was expected; he only had to eat, sleep and mend.

But finally, when the leg began to feel better and he had regained most of his strength, he grew restive. It was time to go. He couldn't impose on the Bellers forever. He must be on his way.

They refused to take any money from him. Armand resolved that when he returned to Savannah he would buy something nice for their home and have it shipped to them.

Savannah! Les Chênes, Maison de Rêverie, Rebecca! All thoughts seemed to lead, in the end, to Rebecca.

He had tried, without marked success, not to think of her, but her image had remained with him despite everything he could do. She had been with him on the harsh marches, with him in his blanket on the hard ground during the mosquito-infested nights, even with him in battle. No manner of thinking, no power of reasoning, would exorcise her from his thoughts. He had to see her again. His brush with death had made him aware that, no matter now difficult he might think his life was, no matter what dark things had happened in the past and might happen in the future, he valued his life and wanted to live it in as constructive and happy a manner as possible. And to attain that happiness, he knew that he must make one more try to convince Rebecca that her future lay with him, that anything was possible for them if they were together. He was certain that she would never find happiness at Maison de Rêverie.

Perhaps, he thought, it was impossible for *anyone* to really live happily there. He wondered if it was possible for evil to sink into a house—into the very timbers, the paint and plaster—changing it subtly in some way not visible to the naked eye. Leaving it lovely and graceful on the outside, but making it inimical to the men and women who lived there. If so, that was what had happened to Maison de Rêverie. But he must return there, at least this one last time.

Since his leg was still stiff and painful, Dr. Beller strongly advised against attempting to travel on horseback, and there were no roads suitable for a vehicle. The doctor managed to book passage for Armand on a coastal packet headed for Charleston. And so, loaded down with a large basket of food, several bottles of homemade wine and the good wishes of the Bellers, Armand set out for home, wondering what he would find there. It would be a long trip around the southern tip of Florida and then north up the coast.

THE MORNING of the day he reached home had started out clear, not a cloud in sight, but by afternoon, when Pirate's Bank heaved into sight, clouds had begun to pile up on the horizon, and it was obvious that a storm was brewing.

The island itself looked the same—green and jewel-like—and despite himself, Armand had to admire its beauty, but his thoughts were concerned with Rebecca. How was she faring? How would she react when she saw that he had returned?

When he disembarked from the packet, he was surprised to find the dock deserted. Since the arrival of a packet was looked forward to eagerly, and since any ship approaching the island was clearly visible, normally there was someone on the dock to meet it, to pick up any mail or supplies or just to receive the latest news.

But this afternoon there wasn't a soul in sight, and Armand realized with dismay that he would have to walk up to the house. The distance was not great, but he knew that on his bad leg it would be an ordeal. Still, there was no help for it.

By the time he had reached the house, he was limping badly. He had still seen no one. Usually the place would be swarming with workers—men tending the extensive grounds, repairing the roads and driveways. Apprehension struck at his heart—something was amiss. And it was so still; as if the island had suddenly been emptied of all life.

Hurrying now despite the game leg, he climbed the steps to the house and paused before the huge carved doors. Standing there, he felt peculiar, as if all this, which was so familiar, was suddenly strange.

So out of place did he feel that he lifted one of the heavy brass knockers and let it fall against the rich wood, as if he was indeed a stranger to this place. The sound seemed to reverberate oddly, but then he realized that a peal of thunder had coincided with his knocking. The storm was building rapidly now.

He waited, resting his bad leg for several moments, but there was no answer to his knock. He gave the door handle a turn and pushed one side of the great door open.

The entryway smelled musty. As he walked farther into the room something crunched beneath his feet— leaves.

He stopped again and looked around in disbelief. There was dust upon the floor, and leaves had evidently blown in at some time when the door was open. But that was impossible! The house was always kept spotless. Neither Felicity nor Lutie would allow such laxness in the household staff. What was going on here?

"Hello!" he called loudly, and then again: "Hello?"

Except for the sound of his own voice, the house was as quiet as a tomb. My God, where was everybody? Even if the family was gone somewhere for the day, there still should be numerous servants in the house.

His leg was throbbing, and he longed to sit down but knew that he could not rest until he had found out why the house was empty.

Limping badly now, he walked through one room after another, finding nothing. At last, when he was sure that there was not a living soul in the house, he sank down into the chair at Jacques's desk in the study.

His mind a beehive of questions, Armand stared at the account books before him on the desk. It was plain that the house was not only empty but that it had been untended for some days. Had everyone left the island? If so, why? What had happened? And where was Rebecca?

Idly, he looked down at the open account book before him and pulled it toward him. What in hell's name was this? It made no sense. The figures were all ajumble, and there were odd, sometimes incomprehensible words written among them.

Pulling the book closer, he examined it more thoroughly, starting with the present, peculiar entries and going backward. A few minutes later he shoved the book away, feeling sick and stunned; the entries clearly delineated a man's mental deterioration.

At the point where Jacques had first begun to keep the accounts, the entries were clear enough, but as the entries progressed, they became more and more confused, until they were indecipherable, the notations of a madman. Dear God! What had happened to Jacques? Had it been necessary for them to send him away? But if even that was true, it still would not explain the absence of the entire household.

Pushing away from the desk, Armand went through the lower floors again, calling Rebecca's name, until he was hoarse, coming at last to the music room, where he stretched out on the large settee and put his leg up.

He lay with his hand over his eyes, and as the wind gained in force and the afternoon darkened a terrible fear and pressure began building in him.

At last he arose stiffly and limped over to the piano. He had always been able to find solace in music, and the piano had often served as a means for him to vent his feelings, although he had never cared to play for an audience, only for himself.

Lifting the cover, he touched the pale ivory of the keys, thinking of Rebecca's flesh as he did so. Where was she? Was he too late? Had she gone back to India?

The storm was upon the island in full force now, and the room had grown quite dark. Standing, he reached for the candelabra on the piano and lit the three candle stubs that it held.

In the fitful light he raised his hands and sent them crashing down upon the keys as a deep roll of thunder rumbled over the house, causing the windows to rattle.

Absorbed in the music, in the release of his violent feelings, he was oblivious to the sounds of the storm. It was only when the light struck his face and he heard his name called that he glanced up, blinking, not really believing what he was hearing. And then again he heard his name spoken by a beloved voice.

Still unbelieving, he stood, looking at the small figure running toward him from a circle of light.

"Rebecca?" he said in awe, and then she was in his arms, soft and warm, and smelling of the scent she wore, her lips upon his cheek, his chin and at last upon his mouth, and a great joy surged through him. It was no dream. It was Rebecca, alive and warm and real!

Chapter Twenty-six

As REBECCA CLUNG to Armand, hugging him with all of her strength, feeling his face against hers—slightly rough from a day's growth of beard—everything fell away, and she was filled with a wild happiness. He was alive, he was well and he still cared for her! For the moment that was enough.

Finally he held her away and looked down into her face as if to memorize her features. "Thank God! Where have you been? I was afraid you had gone away or that something terrible had happened to you. And where is everyone else? The place looks deserted!"

The memory of why they were here suddenly returned to her. "Oh, Armand! I'm afraid something terrible has happened. Come, let us sit down. There is so much to tell you, and none of it is pleasant. It is a godsend that you are here!"

"Lutie," Armand said, gazing over Rebecca's shoulder. "I'm sorry not to have greeted you sooner, but I didn't see you."

Lutie's smile was warm in the lamplight. "I understand, Master Armand. No offense taken. You and Rebecca have your talk. It's important that you know what has been going on if you are to help us. I will go into the kitchen and prepare us something to eat. I'm sure we could all do with food and something to drink, and a bit of rest before . . . well, Rebecca will tell you about it. I won't be long.''

Lutie vanished in the growing darkness, and Rebecca took Armand's hand and led him toward the settee. As he moved she noticed that he was limping badly.

"Oh, my darling! You were wounded?"

"Shh," he said. "It's all over now, and in time, I will be as good as new. A very good doctor has assured me of that. I will tell you about it later."

The moment they were seated, he pulled her into his arms again and kissed her deeply, so that she felt everything inside her melt, and all she wanted was that he should never stop; but at last she pushed him away gently.

"Armand . . . I want it to go on forever, but I must talk to you first. It is very important."

He sighed and touched her cheek. "I know. It's obvious that something is very wrong here, but I've missed you so much. When I arrived and found the house deserted, I was stunned. You can't know . . ."

She gripped his hand in both of hers and pressed it to her cheek. "Oh, yes, I can. I can imagine very well, for I feel the same. Before I tell you all that has happened, I must say just one thing. I was wrong. I should have gone away with you. And if you still want me when this is over, I will gladly go with you."

Armand took her into his arms again. "Rebecca. Rebecca, my proud, spirited girl." She has changed, he thought; whatever has happened has wrought a change in her. "I know what it must have cost you to say that, to be the first to speak. Do you know how happy that makes me? Whatever else happens, whatever else *has* happened, I can bear it, now that I know you love me as I love you. Now, tell me what you have to say, for I know there is an urgency here."

As quickly and succinctly as possible, Rebecca told him what had occurred since he had left. As she spoke she felt tension draining out of her, as if in the telling of the awful series of incidents, some of the pain and anguish they had caused was being abated.

"And that is why you found the house deserted and in the condition it is in," she finished.

Lutie came back in time to overhear her last remark; she was wheeling a large, heavily laden serving cart.

She wheeled the cart up to them. "Most of the slaves, including the house staff, are down in the slave quarters. We haven't been down there yet."

Armand took a thick sandwich and ate it hungrily. "Thank you, Lutie. I hadn't realized it, but I am starving. Let me have some of that tea, with lots of milk and sugar."

Lutie began to pour the steaming tea as Armand swallowed a bite and said, "Do you think any of the house staff knows anything helpful? Perhaps they saw Jacques and Margaret go off somewhere."

Lutie gave him a cup of tea and shook her head. "We're afraid they didn't go off."

Armand looked at Rebecca and then back to Lutie. "What do you mean?"

Rebecca said, "She means that we think there is a good chance that Jacques and Margaret are still in the house. It would probably be better if they *had* gone."

Armand's eyes darkened. "You mean they may be in that secret room you spoke of? You think he may have taken her there?"

Rebecca nodded and accepted a cup of tea and a sandwich from Lutie. "Yes. And if he took Margaret there...well, I told you how she is. If she has seen what is in that room...I just don't know how it would affect her. Ever since the night when your father...well, that night had a very bad effect upon her. She was always easily upset, and she had such rigid ideas of what was right or wrong, but after that night she appeared to grow worse. She has always thought that Jacques was a saint. If he has taken her into that room, it will be all the worse for the fact that he knows about it, don't you see?"

"Yes, I do," Armand said with a nod. "My God!" He passed a hand over his eyes. "I don't know whether to hope we find them there or not!"

"I know. It is going to be dreadful either way, isn't it?" She took his hand.

Armand returned the pressure of her hands and then looked up at Lutie. She returned his glance with a nod that seemed to be answering an unvoiced question.

Rebecca, puzzled, glanced from one to the other. "What is it? Is there something else, something I don't know?"

Lutie smiled at her, a gentle smile with something of sadness in it, but it was Armand who answered. "I'm afraid there is, Rebecca. Something that I should have told you long before, when I originally asked you to go away with me. It is something you have a right to know if you are going to be my wife."

Rebecca flung up her hands. "I don't want to know. I love you and you love me, and that's all that matters. If there is something awful in your past, I don't *want* to know!"

Lutie began to laugh, and after a moment Rebecca joined her, laughing until tears came into her eyes. Armand stared at them, clearly wondering if they had suddenly gone daft.

Finally Rebecca managed to get her laughter under control. "I'm sorry, darling. This whole think is certainly no laughing matter, but I just realized how ridiculous that sounded coming from me, someone who has been as cat-curious as I am. Lutie has seen more of that side of me than you have, and when she looked at me just now, I realized how it must sound to her. But seriously, you don't have to tell me. If it is about some other woman..."

"No, Rebecca, it is nothing like that," Armand said, flushing darkly.

"And it is nothing he must be ashamed of," Lutie said, "but it is something that you should know. If you like, I can tell her," she said to Armand.

He nodded. "It might be best. After all, it was you who first told me."

Lutie sat down, pulling the chair close to the settee and Rebecca. "You see, Rebecca, Armand is not Edouard and Felicity's son—not their natural son, that is. Only five people knew that, and two of them are dead. Even Armand himself didn't know until I told him."

Rebecca felt her mouth fall open with astonishment as several things became immediately clear to her. "So that is why Felicity didn't seem to care as much for him as she did Jacques! That is why Edouard was so cold to him! But how did you know this, Lutie?''

"I said that five people knew the truth. One of them was my momma, Bess. She could see the way things were going, and before she died she told me the whole story and made me promise that if things ever got bad for Master Armand, I was to tell him the truth, and I did.''

"You said only five people knew the truth. Who was the fifth?''

"Do you remember that afternoon in the garden, Rebecca, when I told you that I couldn't tell you any more about Elissa Huntoon, because her story involved others? Well, now that Master Armand wants you to know the truth, I can tell you the rest.''

Rebecca looked at Armand in question, and he nodded. "Elissa Huntoon was my mother, Rebecca, although I never knew her. She died bearing me.''

"She didn't just die, Armand," Lutie said harshly, "she was killed!''

"Killed? In childbirth? I don't understand," Rebecca said.

"Tell her, Lutie," Armand said.

Lutie leaned forward and stared into Rebecca's eyes. "You know what went on during Master Jean's games, and that the children took part. Well Edouard had the same kind of feeling for Elissa that his father had had for her. He considered her his property, and perhaps he even loved her, in his twisted way.

"Everyone says that she was raised as his sister, and in a way, that was true. But their relationship was not that of a normal brother and sister, if you understand my meaning?''

Rebecca nodded, thinking of the pictures.

''Momma tried to keep him away from Elissa, but since she was only a slave, there wasn't much she could do. Elissa was fascinated by Edouard. You see, she had been accustomed to the way things were between them for so long that she didn't know anything else.

''But in the end, Edouard didn't marry Elissa. Instead, he married Felicity Hemsworth, whose father could offer a large dowry. You see, Edouard already *had* Elissa, and by marrying Felicity he acquired yet another pretty young woman and a sizable amount of money, as well.''

''Elissa just accepted this?''

''Yes. Just as she accepted everything from Edouard. Of course, it wasn't long after the wedding that Felicity discovered the truth about Edouard's real relationship with his supposed sister, and as you can well imagine, it crushed her.

''Momma liked the new Mistress Molyneux and felt very sorry for her, but there was really nothing she could do, except to try and be her friend. She told me that Felicity survived by ignoring the situation, by pretending that it didn't exist.

''Well, Mistress Felicity had a baby, Jacques. I remember when he was born, I was six years old. And that seemed to trigger something in Elissa. Momma said that Elissa wanted a baby, too. She loved children, and she offered to help care for Jacques, but Felicity would not let her near him.

''Momma told me that she felt so sorry for them both, Mistress Felicity jealously guarding her child, the one thing that was really hers, and Miss Elissa yearning for a baby of her own.

"Elissa confided in Momma, for Momma was the only mother she had. I can remember them talking, Miss Elissa so slender and pale and my mother so strong and dark. Elissa said that Edouard did not want her to have a child, that he did not want to share her with anyone.

"Well, Elissa began to pine which made Edouard furious. And then, two years later, it began to become clear that she was carrying a child of her own. When Momma learned about it, she was happy for Elissa, despite the fact that she assumed it would be Edouard's child. And then Elissa told her that it was *not* Edouard's. Elissa had been seeing another man in secret, a young German who ran a chemist's shop in Beaufort.

"They had first met when she went to town on a shopping trip, and then they had become lovers. The young man wanted to marry her, and Elissa was more than agreeable, for she had finally realized that there was another kind of life than that which Edouard offered her.

"When Momma heard this, she became terrified for Elissa. Momma knew what Edouard was capable of, and she knew that he would never let Elissa go. She advised Elissa to run away with her young man, far away to some place where Edouard could never find them. Elissa said that her young man couldn't give up his shop and his business, and that Edouard must understand.

"Well, of course he didn't. When Elissa told him that she wanted to marry the German, Edouard flew into an insane rage. He struck her and stormed out of the house. He was gone for three days, and when he returned he was as cheerful and pleasant as you could wish. He even brought Elissa a present, a new dress, and acted as if nothing at all had happened.

"This caused Elissa to believe that Edouard had decided to let her go. But that wasn't the way of it, and soon she knew it, for her young man had vanished, just up and disappeared. When Elissa tried to find out what had happened to her lover, nobody seemed to know. He simply had not come into his shop one morning, and all of his clothes and things were still in the small house he owned in town. Momma said that Miss Elissa cried for a week and then seemed to resign herself.

"When Edouard realized that she was with child, he beat her badly, causing her to give birth prematurely. Despite the fact that the baby was born early, he survived. But Elissa did not. Maybe if she had not lost the will to live, she might have survived, even after the beating, but Momma said that she just gave up. It was like she *wanted* to die."

"And that baby was Armand?"

"Yes, Rebecca. I am sure that Edouard wanted to kill him, too, but even he didn't have quite the courage to kill an innocent baby. Momma took over his care, finding a wet nurse for him in the slave quarters."

Rebecca was frowning. "But if Edouard hated him so, why did he raise him as his son?"

Armand gave a harsh laugh. "For appearance' sake! Despite his peculiar ways, Edouard endeavored to keep his reputation as spotless as any other man's.

And telling everyone that I was his son, Jacques's younger brother, solved that problem.''

Armand's tone became bitter. "And finally, after a few years had gone by, it seemed that even Edouard and Felicity had forgotten that it wasn't true. But underneath, they always knew. When I was small I used to wonder why my parents did not love me. Children feel things more sharply than adults realize.''

"At that time you didn't know?''

"Not until Lutie told me, long after I was grown.''

Rebecca threw her arms around him. "Oh, my poor darling! But I shall make it up to you. I will love you so much that you will forget all the unhappiness you have suffered!''

They heard the sound of the clock chimes, and Lutie stood abruptly. "It is growing late. If we are going to the hidden room, we had best be about it. We may have waited too long as it is.''

INSIDE THE PASSAGEWAYS, the sound of the storm was muted, but the house creaked and groaned around them, and Rebecca felt her body draw in upon itself, as if shrinking away from the task at hand.

Because she was the only one who knew where the secret room was located, she was in the lead, carrying one of the lanterns. Armand, carrying a stout, knobbed stick and a length of rope, followed so close behind her that she could feel his breath upon her neck. Behind him came Lutie, bearing another lantern.

After a bit Rebecca paused. "This is it. This panel pivots and gives access to another short passage, at the end of which is the room.''

Stepping back so that Armand could get to the panel, she watched as it pivoted smoothly beneath his strong hand. She looked around at Lutie.

The other woman whispered reassuringly. "No matter what we find, Rebecca, we have to face it."

Rebecca reached for her friend's hand. "I know. It's just that there has been so much . . ."

The panel was open now, and Armand took the lantern from Rebecca and held it through the opening so that it illuminated the passage on the other side.

Rebecca heard him draw in his breath and then let it out with a gasp. "Good God, I had no idea! Who would ever have guessed that this was hidden away here?"

"This is not the worst of it," Rebecca said softly. "There is a door behind that drapery at the end, and inside the room . . . well, you will have to see for yourself."

Armand stepped through the opening, Rebecca and Lutie right behind him. As they did so, a faint sound could be heard, clear and yet soft—someone was singing.

Armand stopped short. "What is that?"

They all froze, scarcely breathing, and the sound grew clearer. Rebecca recognized it as Margaret's voice. She was singing an old hymn that they had sung as children, and the juxtaposition of that pure, sweet sound and the atmosphere of the entryway caused a chill to course down her spine.

"It's Margaret!" she said in an urgent whisper. "She's in the room!" She breathed a sigh of relief. Whatever else they might find, Margaret was alive!

"If Jacques is in there with her, it would be best if we took them by surprise," Armand said in a low voice. "And I think it would be best if you two waited out here."

"No!" Rebecca whispered tensely. "I'm going with you. Margaret's in there. She may need me."

"I'm not being left behind, either," Lutie said firmly.

"All right then," Armand said, "but stay behind me. Pull back the curtain, will you, Lutie?"

Lutie drew aside the curtain, and the painting on the door was disclosed. Armand stared at it in shock.

Rebecca indicated the door handle, and an expression of disgust crossed his face. Gingerly he grasped the obscene object, and it turned easily.

Putting a finger to his lips, he slowly and quietly opened the door. As he did so, Margaret stopped singing. The light from Armand's lantern was the only illumination in the room, and it took a few moments for all of their eyes to register the details of what they were seeing.

Looking past Armand, Rebecca saw that all of the paintings had been turned to the wall. There appeared to be something—clothes or a pile of rugs—on the floor in front of the altar.

As Armand moved farther into the room, his lantern throwing more light, Rebecca let out a gasp, her hand going to her mouth. What she had thought was a pile of rugs was Margaret crouched on the floor, wrapped in a red velvet cape. She was cradling something in her arms, and as the light struck her, she turned toward them, showing a white face and eyes as clear and vacant as a dreaming child's.

Staring into the light, she began to sing again, her voice soft and clear.

Armand moved toward her, and the light from his lantern illuminated Margaret's frail figure and the object she held so tenderly in her arms. It was covered with the same red velvet as her cape.

Warily, Armand leaned over her, reaching down for the cloth.

"No!" she shouted fiercely, huddling over her bundle protectively.

Armand glanced around at Rebecca in appeal, and she lowered herself to her knees beside her cousin. "It's all right, Margaret. Really it is. Let us see what you're holding. We won't take it away from you, I promise."

"Rebecca?" Margaret said in a blurred voice. "Rebecca?"

Feeling her throat thicken with tears, Rebecca gripped her cousin's thin shoulder. She had lost a great deal of weight. "Yes, dear. It's Rebecca. Now let us see what you have there. That's a good girl."

Sighing, Margaret relaxed her grip and allowed Rebecca to pull back the heavy cloth, smiling serenely at Rebecca's stricken cry.

There, framed by the blood red of the velvet, was the marble-white face of Jacques.

"I helped him," Margaret said in that unnatural voice. "He is with God now."

Slowly, as Rebecca watched in horror, Armand reached down and drew back the rest of the fabric to expose Jacques's body, which lay on its side, curled around the gold and jeweled knife protruding from his chest.

"Dear God in heaven!" Armand exclaimed.

"Margaret . . . what happened?" Rebecca asked, unable to take her gaze from the knife handle and the stain of blood around Jacques's heart.

Margaret smiled sweetly. "See how peaceful his face is? I helped him go to God," she said conversationally. "I wanted to make him happy again; I told you that. Poor Jacques was in such pain. But it was so hard. He felt so bad, and nothing I did seemed to ease him. And then he brought me here, to this ungodly place. I had to stop that. I had to save him from the evil that had taken his father and his brother. They are all gone to God now, and God will judge them. He will forgive them their sins."

Rebecca felt herself begin to tremble uncontrollably, and Armand dropped to his knees beside her and put his arm around her shoulders.

"Margaret," he said softly, "what do you mean, 'they are *all* gone to God?'"

"Why, Edouard and Armand and Jacques, of course."

"But I am Armand."

Her smile turned sly. "Oh, no. You are not Armand. I didn't help Armand, as I did Edouard and Jacques. I would have, but he went away and was killed in the war. I saw it in a vision."

She turned her smile on Rebecca. "They are all gone. Now we can be happy again, Rebecca. They won't put their wicked hands on you again. I have seen to that!"

Rebecca managed to find her voice. "Margaret, you . . . You say you 'helped' Edouard. What do you mean?"

Margaret scowled at her as if she were a recalcitrant child. "It is not like you to be slow, Rebecca. I am surprised at you. It was very simple, really. After what Edouard did to you, I knew it was he who had come into our rooms before." She made a moue of distaste. "He was a wicked man, a nasty, evil man!"

"But how did you . . . ?"

"I told you, it was simple," Margaret said in exasperation. "I asked Edouard to meet me in the pavilion after dinner. He came, because he wanted to do bad things to me—I know that—but God's will made my hand strong."

"And Armand? Why did you want to . . ." Rebecca cleared her throat. "Why did you want to help Armand?"

Margaret frowned. "Because he was evil, too, and nasty in the same way. I watched him with you in the pavilion. I saw what he did to you."

Rebecca began to weep softly. "Oh, Margaret! What have you done?"

Margaret stroked Rebecca's hair tenderly. "It will be fine now, Rebecca. You'll see. You mustn't cry."

"Margaret," Armand said, "you must let go of Jacques now. Rebecca will take you to your room, where you can rest. I will take care of Jacques."

Margaret's expression turned crafty. "Oh, no! You can't take Jacques away. He is good again now. All the evil is gone. And I cannot leave here yet. First, I must destroy this room. This room is the devil's den. His picture is right there on the wall!" She flung out one hand to indicate the reversed painting hanging over the altar.

"We will take care of the room, Margaret," Armand said gently. "We will clear all of this out and burn it. I promise you. You go along with Rebecca."

Stubbornly Margaret shook her head. "No! I must do it myself. It is God's will."

Armand took her by the arms to lift her, but she pulled away with surprising strength, coming to her feet. "No! Let me alone!"

Before any of the others could move, Margaret picked up the lantern that Lutie had set down upon the altar and raised it high over her head. "It must be cleansed!" she intoned. "Cleansed in fire!"

She flung the lantern to the floor, where it exploded in a shower of flaming oil, quickly igniting the draperies and rugs.

"Rebecca, Lutie, get out of here!" Armand shouted. "Hurry! I'll bring Margaret. Lutie, you take the other lantern."

Already in motion, holding his left arm so that it shielded his face, he reached for Margaret and threw his arm around her. Seeing that he had Margaret, Rebecca turned and followed Lutie through the door and into the outer chamber. There she stopped and turned to look for Armand.

To her relief, she saw him pulling Margaret, now docile, through the doorway. Behind them, the entire room seemed to be ablaze.

Rebecca went through the panel opening after Lutie, who was shouting at her to hurry, but once through the door, she looked back again, just in time to see Margaret, with a shriek of triumph, break free of Armand's grasp and plunge back into the room, which was now an inferno.

"Oh, no! Margaret!" Rebecca cried in a harsh scream that tore at her throat.

She started to run after her cousin, but Armand seized her, pulling her against him. "No, Rebecca, you'll only die with her. It's no use. The only thing we can do now is to save ourselves!"

As they fled down the passageways and then out of the house, Rebecca felt that they were, indeed, fleeing hell. The flames spread with greedy rapidity, following, it seemed, their footsteps, reaching out for them.

The house filled with clouds of thick smoke, and the interior was hot as a furnace. they finally burst through the front door, breathless and shaken. Armand hustled them across to the far side of the drive, where they all three clung together.

Rebecca noticed that the storm had passed. The only sounds were those of crackling flames and falling timbers. Against the dark sky the flames twisted and danced, enveloping the house in great sweeps of yellow and orange. Dimly she became aware that the Molyneux slaves had gathered around them staring at the leaping flames with solemn faces.

"Poor, deranged Margaret," she whispered.

Armand drew her into the shelter of his arms. "She would have had to have been put away, darling, and a madhouse is a dreadful place."

Rebecca became aware that tears were coursing down her cheeks; she had not realized that she was crying. "At least she is with Jacques now. She loved him, you know, in her own way."

Freeing herself partially from Armand's arms, she reached out for Lutie and drew her in close, so that the

three of them stood with their arms around one another.

They waited there quietly, wrapped in their own
thoughts, while the fire destroyed Maison de Rêverie,
obliterating the past and making the earth clean and
pure for the new life that lay before them.

Dear Friends and Readers:

I have just finished my second book for Worldwide Library, and as usual when I finish a book, I am caught up with excitement about it, an excitement I hope you will share.

The new book is entitled *Thursday and the Lady*, and it is the story of Jemina Benedict, a young woman just becoming aware of her own strengths in the Boston of 1848.

Jemina is a woman with ideas of her own, and Boston, her staid banker father and conventional mother are not big enough, or strong enough, to contain Jemina's ambitions.

Despite objections from her parents, Jemina goes to Philadelphia, where she meets the noted editor of the famous *Godey's Lady's Book*, Sarah Hale, and is hired as a contributing editor for the magazine.

Here Jemina also meets the alternately fascinating and aggravating Owens Thursday, who wears a black eye patch that hints at a mysterious past, and has a rather notorious present as a well known reporter for the *Philadelphia Ledger*.

She also becomes involved with the attractive and gentle Warren Barricone, a married man with an invalid wife, who works for the *Lady's Book* and who, Jemina soon becomes aware, is very much attracted to her.

Jemina's story is that of a strong woman, intent upon fulfilling her ambitions and desiring to integrate these ambitions with her personal happiness—not so different from those of many young women today. But Jemina lives in the world of the mid 1800s, when society had its own ideas about what women should and should not do, and her strong-minded opinions and determination to do what she thinks is right lead her into trouble, and finally into great danger at the hands of the conscienceless sweatshop owner Lester Gilroy.

Thursday and the Lady will be out in November of 1987. I hope you will look for it, and that you will enjoy reading it as much as I have enjoyed writing it.

Love,

Patricia Matthews

All men wanted her,
but only one man would have her.

Desert Storm

Nan Ryan

Her cruel father had intended
Angie to marry a sinister cattle baron twice her age.
No one expected that she would fall in love with his
handsome, pleasure-loving cowboy son.

Theirs was a love no desert storm would quench.

JULIE ELLIS

author of the bestselling
Rich Is Best **rivals the likes of**
Judith Krantz and Belva Plain with

THE ONLY SIN

It sweeps through the glamorous cities of Paris, London, New York and Hollywood. It captures life at the turn of the century and moves to the present day. *The Only Sin* is the triumphant story of Lilli Landau's rise to power, wealth and international fame in the sensational fast-paced world of cosmetics.
